Praise for the Novels
of Lauren Willig

The Masque of the Black Tulip

"Delightful."

—*Kirkus Reviews*

"Willig picks up where she left readers breathlessly hanging. . . . Many more will delight in this easy-to-read romp and line up for the next installment."

—*Publishers Weekly*

"What's most delicious about Willig's novels is that the damsels of 1803 bravely put it all on the line for love and country."

—*The Detroit Free Press*

"Studded with clever literary and historical nuggets . . . a charming historical/contemporary romance [that] moves back and forth in time."

—*USA Today*

"This is a genre-bending soup of mystery, romance, and espionage, laced with wit."

—*Taconic Press*

"Willig has great fun with the conventions of the genre, throwing obstacles between her lovers at every opportunity."   —*The Boston Globe*

"Enchanting."

—*Midwest Book Review*

The Secret History of the Pink Carnation

"A deftly hilarious, sexy novel."

—Eloisa James, author of *Taming of the Duke*

continued . . .

THE MASQUE OF THE

Black Tulip

Lauren Willig

 NEW AMERICAN LIBRARY

New American Library
Published by New American Library, a division of
Penguin Group (USA) Inc., 375 Hudson Street, New York, New York 10014, USA
Penguin Group (Canada), 90 Eglinton Avenue East, Suite 700, Toronto,
Ontario M4P 2Y3, Canada (a division of Pearson Penguin Canada Inc.)
Penguin Books Ltd., 80 Strand, London WC2R 0RL, England
Penguin Ireland, 25 St. Stephen's Green, Dublin 2, Ireland (a division of Penguin Books Ltd.)
Penguin Group (Australia), 250 Camberwell Road, Camberwell, Victoria 3124,
Australia (a division of Pearson Australia Group Pty. Ltd.)
Penguin Books India Pvt. Ltd., 11 Community Centre, Panchsheel Park,
New Delhi - 110 017, India
Penguin Group (NZ), cnr Airborne and Rosedale Roads, Albany,
Auckland 1310, New Zealand (a division of Pearson New Zealand Ltd.)
Penguin Books (South Africa) (Pty.) Ltd., 24 Sturdee Avenue,
Rosebank, Johannesburg 2196, South Africa

Penguin Books Ltd., Registered Offices:
80 Strand, London WC2R 0RL, England

Published by New American Library, a division of Penguin Group (USA) Inc. Previously
published in a Dutton edition.

First New American Library Printing, November 2006
10 9 8 7 6 5 4 3 2

REGISTERED TRADEMARK — MARCA REGISTRADA

New American Library Trade Paperback ISBN: 0-451-22004-8

The Library of Congress has cataloged the hardcover edition of this title as follows:

Willig, Lauren.
The masque of the black tulip / Lauren Willig.
p.   cm.
ISBN 0-525-94920-8
1. Napoleonic Wars, 1800–1815—Fiction. 2. London (England)—Fiction. 3. Women
spies—Fiction. I. Title.
PS3623.I575M37 2006
813'.6—dc22   2005020748

Printed in the United States of America

To Brooke,
paragon among little sisters,
between whom and Henrietta
any resemblance is more than coincidental

THE MASQUE OF THE

Black Tulip

Chapter One

———— ❦ ————

London, England, 2003

I bit my lip on an "Are we there yet?"

    If ever silence was the better part of valor, now was the time. Palpable waves of annoyance emerged from the man beside me, thick enough to constitute an extra presence in the car.

Under the guise of inspecting my fingernails, I snuck another glance sideways at my car mate. From that level, all I could see was a pair of hands tense on the steering wheel. They were tanned and callused against the brown corduroy cuffs of his jacket, with a fine dusting of blond hairs outlined by the late-afternoon sun, and the white scar of an old cut showing against the darker skin on his left hand. Large hands. Capable hands. Right now he was probably imagining them clasped around my neck.

And I don't mean in an amorous embrace.

I had not been part of Mr. Colin Selwick's weekend plans. I was the fly in his ointment, the rain on his parade. The fact that it was a very attractive parade and that I was very single at the moment was entirely beside the point.

If you're wondering what I was doing in a car bound for parts unknown with a relative stranger who would have liked nothing better than to drop me in a ditch—well, I'd like to say, so was I. But I knew exactly what I was doing. It all came down to, in a word, archives.

Admittedly, archives aren't usually a thing to set one's blood pounding, but they do when you're a fifth-year graduate student in pursuit of a dissertation, and your advisor has begun making ominous noises about conferences and job talks and the nasty things that happen to attenuated graduate students who haven't produced a pile of paper by their tenth year. From what I understand, they're quietly shuffled out of the Harvard history department by dead of night and fed to a relentless horde of academic-eating crocodiles. Or they wind up at law school. Either way, the point was clear. I had to rack up some primary sources, and I had to do it soon, before the crocodiles started getting restless.

There was a teensy little added incentive involved. The incentive had dark hair and brown eyes, and occupied an assistant professorship in the Gov department. His name was Grant.

I have, I realize, left out his most notable characteristic. He was a cheating slime. I say that entirely dispassionately. Anyone would agree that smooching a first-year grad student—during my department's Christmas party, which he attended at *my* invitation—is indisputable evidence of cheating slimedom.

All in all, there had never been a better time to conduct research abroad.

I didn't include the bit about Grant in my grant application. There is a certain amount of irony in that, isn't there? Grant . . . grant. . . . The fact that I found that grimly amusing just goes to show the pathetic state to which I had been reduced.

But if modern manhood had let me down, at least the past boasted brighter specimens. To wit, the Scarlet Pimpernel, the Purple Gentian, and the Pink Carnation, that dashing trio of spies who kept Napoleon in a froth of rage and the feminine population of England in another sort of froth entirely.

Of course, when I presented my grant proposal to my advisor, I left out any references to evil exes and the aesthetic properties of knee breeches. Instead, I spoke seriously about the impact of England's aristocratic agents on the conduct of the war with France, their influence on parliamentary politics, and the deeper cultural implications of espionage as a gendered construct.

But my real mission had little to do with Parliament or even the Pimpernel. I was after the Pink Carnation, the one spy who had never been unmasked. The Scarlet Pimpernel, immortalized by the Baroness Orczy, was known the world over as Sir Percy Blakeney, Baronet, possessor of a wide array of quizzing glasses and the most impeccably tied cravat in London. His less-known successor, the Purple Gentian, had carried on quite successfully for a number of years until he, too, had been undone by love, and blazoned before the international press as Lord Richard Selwick, dashing rake about town. The Pink Carnation remained a mystery, to the French and scholars alike.

But not to me.

I wish I could boast that I had cracked a code, or deciphered an ancient text, or tracked an incomprehensible map to a hidden cache of papers. In fact, it was pure serendipity, disguised in the form of an elderly descendant of the Purple Gentian. Mrs. Selwick-Alderly had made me free of both her home and a vast collection of family papers. She didn't even ask for my firstborn child in return, which I understand is frequently the case with fairy godmothers in these sorts of situations.

The only drawback to this felicitous arrangement was Mrs. Selwick-Alderly's nephew, current owner of Selwick Hall, and self-appointed guardian of the family heritage. His name? Mr. Colin Selwick.

Yes, *that* Colin Selwick.

To say that Colin had been less than pleased at seeing me going through his aunt's papers would have been rather like saying that Henry VIII didn't have much luck with matrimony. If decapitations were still considered a valid way of settling domestic problems, my head would have been the first on his block.

Under the influence of either my charming personality or a stern talking-to from his aunt (I suspected the latter), Colin had begun to thaw to nearly human behavior. I must say, it was an impressive process. When he wasn't snapping insults at me, he had the sort of crinkly-eyed smile that made movie theaters full of women heave a collective sigh. If you liked the big, blond, sporting type. Personally, I went more for tall, dark, and intellectual myself.

Not that it was an issue. Any rapport we might have developed had rapidly disintegrated when Mrs. Selwick-Alderly suggested that Colin give me access to the family archives at Selwick Hall for the weekend. *Suggested* is putting it a bit mildly. *Railroaded* would be more to the point. The traffic gods hadn't done anything to help the situation. I had given up trying to make small talk somewhere along the A-23, where there'had been an epic traffic jam involving a stalled-out car, an overturned lorry, and a tow truck that reached the scene of the crime and promptly broke down out of sympathy.

I cast another surreptitious glance in Colin's direction.

"Would you stop looking at me like you're Red Riding Hood and I'm the wolf?"

Maybe it hadn't been all that surreptitious.

"Why, Grandmother, what big archives you have?" As an attempt at humor, it lacked something, but given that it was the first time my vocal cords had had any exercise over the past two hours, I was reasonably pleased with the result.

"Do you ever think about anything else?" asked Colin. It was the sort of question that from anyone else I would have construed as an invitation to flirtation. From Colin, it just sounded exasperated.

"Not with a dissertation deadline looming."

"We," he pronounced ominously, "still have to discuss what exactly is going to go into your dissertation."

"Mmmph," I said enigmatically. He had already made his feelings on that clear, and I saw no point in giving him the opportunity to reiterate them. Less discussed, more easily ignored. It was time to change the subject. "Wine gum?"

Colin emitted a choked noise that might have been a laugh if allowed to grow up. His eyes met mine in the rearview mirror in an expression that might have been, "I like your nerve," or might have been

"Oh, God, who let this lunatic loose in my car and where can I dump her?"

All he actually said was "Thanks," and held out one large hand, palm up.

In the spirit of entente, I passed over the orange and flipped a red one into his palm. Popping the despised orange into my own mouth, I sucked it meditatively, trying to think of a conversational gambit that wouldn't touch on forbidden topics.

Colin did it for me. "If you look to your left," he said, "you should be able to see the house."

I caught a brief, tantalizing glimpse of crenellated battlements looming above the trees like a lost set from a Frankenstein movie before the car swung around a curve, bringing us into full view of the house. Built of a creamy-colored stone, the house was what the papers might call "a stately pile," a square central section with the usual classical adornments, with a smaller wing sticking out on either side of the central block. It was a perfectly normal eighteenth-century gentleman's residence, and exactly what one would expect the Purple Gentian to have lived in. There were no battlements.

The car scraped to a halt in the circle of gravel that fronted the entrance. Not waiting to see if he was going to open the door for me, I grabbed the oversized tote in which I had crammed two days' worth of weekend wear, and scrambled out of the door of the car before Colin could reach it, determined to be as obliging as possible.

My heels crunched on the gravel as I followed Colin to the house, the little pebbles doing nasty things to the leather of my stacked loafers. One would have expected assorted staff to be lining the halls, but instead the front hall was decidedly empty as Colin stepped aside to allow me in. The door snapped shut with a distinctly ominous clang.

"You can just take me to the library and then forget all about me," I suggested helpfully. "You won't even know I'm here."

"Were you planning to sleep in the library?" he inquired with some amusement, his eyes going to the overnight bag on my arm.

"Um . . . I hadn't really thought about it. I can sleep wherever."

"Indeed."

I could feel my face flaring with light like a high school fire alarm, and rapidly tried to ameliorate the situation. "What I mean is, I'm easy."

Urgh. Worser and worser, as Alice might say. There are times when I shouldn't be allowed out of the house without a muzzle.

"Easy to have as a houseguest, I mean," I specified in a strangled voice, hoisting my bag farther up on my shoulder.

"I think the hospitality of Selwick Hall can stretch to providing you a bed," commented Colin dryly, leading the way up a flight of stairs tucked away to one side of the hall.

"That's nice to know. Very generous of you."

"Too much hassle clearing out the dungeons," explained Colin, twisting open a door not far from the landing, revealing a medium-sized room possessed of a dark four-poster bed. The walls were dark green, patterned with gold-tinted animals that looked like either dragons or gryphons, squatting on their haunches, stylized wings poking into the forequarters of the next beast over. He stepped aside to let me precede him.

Dumping my bag onto the bed, I turned back around to face Colin, who was still propping up the door. I shoved my hair out of my eyes. "Thanks. Really. It's really nice of you to have me here."

Colin didn't mouth any of the usual platitudes about it being no problem, or being delighted to have me. Instead, he tipped his head in the direction of the hall and said, "The loo is two doors down to your left, the hot water tends to cut out after ten minutes, and the flush needs to be jiggled three times before it settles."

"Right," I said. He got points for honesty, at least. "Got it. Loo on the left, two jiggles."

"Three jiggles," Colin corrected.

"Three," I repeated firmly, as though I was actually going to remember. I trailed along after Colin down the hallway.

"Eloise?" A few yards ahead, Colin was holding open a door at the end of the hall.

"Sorry!" I scurried down the length of the hall to catch up, plunging breathlessly through the doorway. Crossing my arms over my chest, I said, a little too heartily, "So this is the library."

There certainly couldn't be any doubt on that score; never had a room so resembled popular preconception. The walls were paneled in rich, dark wood, although the finish had worn off the edges in spots where books had scraped against the wood in passing one too many times. A whimsical iron staircase curved to the balcony, the steps narrowing into pie-shaped wedges that promised a broken neck to the unwary. I tilted my head back, dizzied by the sheer number of books, row upon row, more than the most devoted bibliophile could hope to consume in a lifetime of reading. In one corner, a pile of crumbling paperbacks—James Bond, I noticed, squinting sideways, in splashy seventies covers—struck a slightly incongruous note. I spotted a moldering pile of *Country Life* cheek by jowl with a complete set of Trevelyan's *History of England* in the original Victorian bindings. The air was rich with the smell of decaying paper and old leather bindings.

Downstairs, where I stood with Colin, the shelves made way for four tall windows, two to the east and two to the north, all hung with rich red draperies checked with blue, in the obverse of the red-flecked blue carpet. On the west wall, the bookshelves surrendered pride of place to a massive fireplace, topped with a carved hood to make Ivanhoe proud, and large enough to roast a serf.

In short, the library was a Gothic fantasy.

My face fell.

"It's not original."

"No, you poor innocent," said Colin. "The entire house was gutted not long before the turn of the century. The last century," he added pointedly.

"Gutted?" I bleated.

Oh, fine, I know it's silly, but I had harbored romantic images of walking where the Purple Gentian had walked, sitting at the desk where he had penned those hasty notes upon which the fate of the kingdom rested, viewing the kitchen where his meals had been prepared. . . . I made a disgusted face at myself. At this rate, I was only one step away from going through the Purple Gentian's garbage, hugging his discarded port bottles to my palpitating bosom.

"Gutted," repeated Colin firmly.

"The floor plan?" I asked pathetically.

"Entirely altered."

"Damn."

The laugh lines at the corners of his mouth deepened.

"I mean," I prevaricated, "what a shame for posterity."

Colin raised an eyebrow. "It's considered one of the great examples of the arts and crafts movement. Most of the wallpaper and drapes were designed by William Morris, and the old nursery has fireplace tiles by Burne-Jones."

"The Pre-Raphaelites are distinctly overrated," I said bitterly.

Colin strolled over to the window, hands behind his back. "The gardens haven't been changed. You can always go for a stroll around the grounds if the Victorians begin to overwhelm you."

"That won't be necessary," I said, with as much dignity as I could muster. "All I need is your archives."

"Right," said Colin briskly, turning away from the window. "Let's get you set, then, shall we?"

"Do you have a muniments room?" I asked, tagging along after him.

"Nothing so grand." Colin strode straight towards one of the bookcases, causing me a momentary flutter of alarm. The books on the shelf certainly looked elderly—at least, if the dust on the spines was anything to go by—but they were all books. Printed matter. When Mrs. Selwick-Alderly had said there were records at Selwick Hall, she hadn't specified what kind of records. For all I knew, she might well have meant one of those dreadful Victorian vanity publications compiled from "missing" records, titled "Some Documents Formerly in the Possession of the Selwick Family but Tragically Dropped Down a Privy Last Year." They never cited their sources, and they tended to excerpt only those bits they found interesting, cutting out anything that might not redound to the greater credit of the ancestry.

But Colin bypassed the rows of leather-bound books. Instead, he hunkered down in front of the elaborately carved mahogany wainscoting that ran, knee-high, around the length of the room, in a movement as smooth as it was unexpected.

"Hunh?" I nearly tripped over him, stopping so short that one of my knees banged into his shoulder blades. Grabbing the edge of a bookshelf to steady myself, I stared down in bewilderment as Colin bent over the wooden paneling, his head blocking my view of whatever it was he was doing. All I could see was sun-streaked hair, darker at the roots as the effects of summer faded, and an expanse of bent back, broad and muscled beneath an oxford-cloth shirt. A whiff of shampoo, recently applied, wafted up against the stuffy smells of closed rooms, old books, and decaying leather.

I couldn't see what he was doing, but he must have turned some sort of latch, because the wainscoting opened out, the joint cleverly disguised by the pattern of the wood. Now that I knew what to look for, there was nothing mysterious about it at all. Glancing around the room, I could see that the wainscoting was flush with the edge of the shelves above, leaving a space about two feet deep unaccounted for.

"These are all cupboards," Colin explained briefly, swinging easily to his feet beside me.

"Of course," I said, as if I had known all along, and never harbored alarming images of being forced to read late-Victorian transcriptions.

One thing was sure: I need have no worries about having to entertain myself with back issues of *Punch*. There were piles of heavy folios bound in marbled endpapers, a scattering of flat cardboard envelopes looped shut with thin spools of twine, and whole regiments of the pale gray acid-free boxes used to hold loose documents.

"How could you have kept this to yourself all these years?" I exclaimed, falling to my knees in front of the cupboard.

"Very easily," said Colin dryly.

I flapped a dismissive hand in his general direction, without interrupting my perusal. I scooted forward to see better, tilting my head sideways to try to read the typed labels someone had glued to the spines a long time ago, if their yellowed state and the shape of the letters were anything to go by. The documents seemed to be roughly organized by person and date. The ancient labels said things like LORD RICHARD SEL-WICK (1776–1841), CORRESPONDENCE, MISCELLANEOUS, 1801–1802, or SELWICK HALL, HOUSEHOLD ACCOUNTS, 1800–1806. Bypassing the household accounts, I kept looking. I reached for a folio at random, drawing it carefully out from its place next to a little pocket-sized book bound in worn red leather.

"I'll leave you to it, shall I?" said Colin.

"Mmm-hmm."

The folio was a type I recognized from the British Library, older documents pasted onto the leaves of a large blank book, with annotations around the edges in a much later hand. On the first page, an Edwardian hand had written in slanting script, "Correspondence of Lady Henrietta Selwick, 1801–1803."

"Dinner in an hour?"

"Mmm-hmm."

I flipped deliberately towards the back, scanning salutations and dates. I was looking for references to two things: the Pink Carnation, or the school for spies founded by the Purple Gentian and his wife, after necessity forced them to abandon active duty. Neither the Pink Carnation nor the spy school had been in operation much before May of 1803. Wedging the volume back into place, I jiggled the next one out from underneath, hoping that they had been stacked in some sort of chronological order.

"Arsenic with a side of cyanide?"

"Mmm-hmm."

They had. The next folio down comprised Lady Henrietta's correspondence from March of 1803 to the following November. Perfect.

On the edge of my consciousness, I heard the library door close.

Scooting backwards, I sat down heavily on the floor next to the open cupboard, the folio splayed open in my lap. Nestled in the middle of Henrietta's correspondence was a letter in a different hand. Where Henrietta's script was round, with loopy letters and the occasional flourish, this writing was regular enough to be a computer simulation of script. Without the aid of technological enhancement, the writing spoke of an orderly hand, and an even more orderly mind. More important, I knew that handwriting. I had seen it in Mrs. Selwick-Alderly's collection, between Amy Balcourt's sloppy scrawl and Lord Richard's emphatic hand. I didn't even have to flip to the signature on the following page to know who had penned it, but I did, anyway. "Your affectionate cousin, Jane."

There are any number of Janes in history, most of them as gentle and unassuming as their name. Lady Jane Grey, the ill-fated seven-day queen of England. Jane Austen, the sweet-faced authoress, lionized by English majors and the BBC costume-drama-watching set.

And then there was Miss Jane Wooliston, better known as the Pink Carnation.

I clutched the binding of the folio as though it might scuttle away if I loosened my grip, refraining from making squealing noises of delight. Colin probably already thought I was a madwoman, without my providing him any additional proof. But I was squealing inside. As far as the rest of the historical community was concerned (I indulged in a bit of personal gloating), the only surviving references to the Pink Carnation were mentions in newspapers of the period, not exactly the most reliable report. Indeed, there were even scholars who opined that the Pink Carnation did not in fact exist, that the escapades attributed to the mythical flower figure over a ten-year period—stealing a shipment of gold from under Bonaparte's nose, burning down a French boot factory, spiriting away a convoy of munitions in Portugal during the Peninsular War, to name just a few—had been the work of a number of unrelated actors. The Pink Carnation, they insisted, was something like Robin Hood, a useful myth, perpetuated to keep people's morale up during the grim days of the Napoleonic Wars, when England stood staunchly alone as the rest of Europe tumbled under Napoleon's sway.

Weren't they in for a surprise!

I knew who the Pink Carnation was, thanks to Mrs. Selwick-Alderly. But I needed more. I needed to be able to link Jane Wooliston to the events attributed to the Pink Carnation by the news sheets, to provide concrete proof that the Pink Carnation had not only existed, but had been continuously in operation throughout that period.

The letter in my lap was an excellent start. A reference to the Pink Carnation would have been good. A letter from the Pink Carnation herself was even better.

Greedily, I skimmed the first few lines.

"Dearest Cousin, Paris has been a whirl of gaiety since last I wrote, with scarcely a moment to rest between engagements. . . ."

Chapter Two

———— ✿ ————

Venetian Breakfast: *a midnight excursion of a clandestine kind*

—from the Personal Codebook of the Pink Carnation

"...Y esterday, I attended a Venetian breakfast at the home of a gentleman very closely connected to the Consul. He was all that was amiable."

In the morning room at Uppington House, Lady Henrietta Selwick checked the level of liquid in her teacup, positioned a little red book on the cushion next to her, and curled up against the arm of her favorite settee.

Under her elbow, the fabric was beginning to snag and fray; suspicious tea-colored splotches marred the white-and-yellow-striped silk, and worn patches farther down the settee testified to the fact that the two slippered feet that currently occupied them had been there before. The morning room was usually the province of the lady of the house, but Lady Uppington, who lacked the capacity for sitting in one place longer than it took to deliver a pithy epigram, had long since ceded the sunny room to Henrietta, who used it as her receiving room, her library (the real library having the unfortunate defect of being too dark to actually read in), and her study. Haloed in the late-morning sunlight, it was a pleasant, peaceful room, a room for innocent daydreams and restrained tea parties.

At the moment, it was a hub for international espionage.

On the little yellow-and-white settee rested secrets for which Bonaparte's most talented agents would have given their eyeteeth—or their eyes, for that matter, if that wouldn't have gotten in the way of actually reading the contents of the little red book.

Henrietta spread Jane's latest letter out on her muslin-clad lap. Even if a French operative did happen to be peering through the window, Henrietta knew just what he would see: a serene young lady (Henrietta hastily pushed a stray wisp of hair back into the Grecian-style bun on the top of her head) daydreaming over her correspondence and her diary. It was enough to put a spy to sleep, which was precisely why Henrietta had suggested the plan to Jane in the first place.

For seven long years, Henrietta had been angling to be included in the war effort. It didn't seem quite fair that her brother got to be written up in the illustrated newsletters as "that glamorous figure of shadow, that thorn in the side of France, that silent savior men know only as the Purple Gentian," while Henrietta was stuck being the glamorous shadow's pesky younger sister. As she had pointed out to her mother the year she turned thirteen—the year that Richard joined the League of the Scarlet Pimpernel—she was as smart as Richard, she was as creative as Richard, and she was certainly a great deal stealthier than Richard.

Unfortunately, she was also, as her mother reminded her, a good deal younger than Richard. Seven years younger, to be precise.

"Oh, bleargh," said Henrietta, since there was really nothing she could say in response to that, and Henrietta wasn't the sort who liked being without something to say.

Lady Uppington looked at her sympathetically. "We'll discuss it when you're older."

"Juliet was married when she was thirteen, you know," protested Henrietta.

"Yes, and look what happened to her," replied Lady Uppington.

By the time she was fifteen, Henrietta decided she had waited quite long enough. She put her case to the League of the Scarlet Pimpernel in her best imitation of Portia's courtroom speech. The gentlemen of the League were not moved by her musings on the quality of mercy, nor were they swayed by her arguments that an intrepid young girl could wriggle in where a full-grown man would get stuck in the window frame.

Sir Percy looked sternly at her through his quizzing glass. "We'll discuss it—"

"I know, I know," Henrietta said wearily, "when I'm older."

She didn't have any more success when Sir Percy retired and Richard began cutting a wide swath through French prisons and English news sheets as the Purple Gentian. Richard, being her older brother, was a great deal less diplomatic than Sir Percy had been. He didn't even make the obligatory reference to her age.

"Have you run mad?" he asked, running a black-gloved hand agitatedly through his blond hair. "Do you *know* what Mother would do to me if I so much as let you near a French prison?"

"Ah, but does Mama need to know?" suggested Henrietta cunningly.

Richard gave her another "Have you gone completely and utterly insane?" look.

"If Mother is not told, she will find out. And when she finds out," he gritted out, "she will *dismember* me."

"Surely, it's not as bad as—"

"Into hundreds and hundreds of tiny pieces."

Henrietta had persisted for a bit, but since all she could get out of her brother was incoherent mumbles about his head being stuck up on the gates of Uppington Hall, his hindquarters being fed to the dogs, and his heart and liver being served up on a platter in the dining room, she gave up, and went off to do some muttering of her own about overbearing older brothers who thought they knew everything just because they had a five-page spread on their exploits in the *Kentish Crier*.

Appealing to her parents proved equally ineffectual. After Richard had been inconsiderate enough to go and get himself captured by the Ministry of Police, Lady Uppington had become positively unreasonable on the subject of spying. Henrietta's requests were met with "No. Absolutely not. Out of the question, young lady," and even one memorable "There are still nunneries in England."

Henrietta wasn't entirely certain that her mother was right about that—there had been a Reformation, and a fairly thorough one, at that—but she had no desire to test the point. Besides, she had heard all about the Ministry of Police's torture chamber in lurid detail from her new sister-in-law, Amy, and rather doubted she would enjoy their hospitality any more than Richard had.

But when one has been angling for something for seven years, it is rather hard to let go of the notion just like that. So when Amy's cousin, Jane Wooliston, otherwise known as the Pink Carnation, happened to mention that she was having trouble getting reports back to the War Office because her couriers had an irritating habit of being murdered en route, Henrietta was only too happy to offer her assistance.

It was, Henrietta assured her conscience, a safe enough assignment that even her mother couldn't possibly find fault with it, or start looking about for England's last operational nunnery. It wasn't Henrietta who would be scurrying through the dark alleyways of Paris, or riding hell-for-leather down rutted French roads in a desperate attempt to reach the coast. All she had to do was sit in the morning room at Uppington House, and maintain a perfectly normal-sounding correspondence with Jane about balls, dresses, and other topics guaranteed to bore French agents to tears.

Normal-sounding was the key. While in London for Amy and Richard's wedding, Jane had spent a few days at her writing table, scribbling in a little red book. When she had finally emerged, she had presented Henrietta with a complete lexicon of absolutely everyday terms with far-from-everyday meanings.

Ever since Jane's return to Paris two weeks ago, the plan had proved tremendously effective. Even the most hardened French operative could find nothing to quicken his suspicion in an exchange about the relative merits of flowers as opposed to bows as trimming for an evening gown, and the eyes of the most determined interceptor of English letters were sure to glaze when confronted with a five-page-long description of yesterday's Venetian breakfast at Viscountess of Loring's Paris residence.

Little did they realize that "Venetian breakfast" was code for a late-night raid on the secret files of the Ministry of Police. Breakfast, after all, was supposed to take place early in the morning, and thus made a perfect analogue for "dead of night." As for Venetian . . . well, Delaroche's filing system was as complex and secretive as the workings of the Venetian *Signoria* at the height of their Renaissance decadence.

Which brought Henrietta back to the letter at hand.

Jane had begun it "My very dearest Henrietta," a salutation that signified news of the utmost importance. Henrietta sat up straighter on the settee. Jane had been rooting about in someone's study—the letter didn't specify whose—and he had been all amiability, which meant that whatever papers Jane had meant to find had been easily found, and Jane had been unmolested in her search.

"I have sent word to our great-uncle Archibald in Aberdeen"— that was William Wickham at the War Office—"in care of Cousin Ned." Henrietta reached for the red morocco-covered codebook. "Cousin" she had seen before; it translated quite simply as "courier." Henrietta reached the proper page in the codebook. "See under Ned, Cousin," instructed Jane. Mumbling a bit to herself about people with regrettably organized minds, Henrietta flipped forward to the Ns. "Ned, Cousin: a professional courier in the service of the League."

Henrietta scowled at the little red book. Jane had sent her all the way to the Ns for that?

"Given dear Ned's propensity for falling in with the wrong sort of company," Jane continued, "I deeply fear he shall be so busy carousing and roistering about, he shall neglect to fulfill my little commission."

Having achieved some notion of the way Jane's mind worked, Henrietta flipped straight to the Cs, indulging in a small smirk as she beheld, "Company, wrong sort of," just beneath, "Company, best sort of," "Company, better not sought out," and "Company, convivial." Her smirk faded somewhat at the knowledge that "Company, wrong sort of" signified: "a murderous band of French agents, employed for the primary purpose of eliminating English intelligence officers." Poor Cousin Ned. Likewise, "Carousing," a page back, had nothing to do with bacchanalian excesses, but instead meant "engaged in a life-or-death struggle with Bonaparte's minions," an activity that sounded highly unpleasant.

"But what *is* it?" Henrietta muttered at the unresponsive piece of paper in her hands. Had Jane discovered new plans for the invasion of England? A design for the destruction of the English fleet? It might even, mused Henrietta, be another attempt to assassinate King George. Her brother had foiled two of those, but the French kept on trying. At least, they assumed it was the French, and not the Prince of Wales trying to get back at his father for forcing him to marry Caroline of Brunswick, who bore the dubious distinction of being the smelliest princess in Europe.

"Do tell dear Uncle Archibald," continued Jane tantalizingly, after a long and tedious description of the gowns worn by half the women at the imaginary Venetian breakfast, "that a new horrid novel is even now on its way to Hatchards and should be arrived by the time you receive this epistle!"

Henrietta thumbed through Jane's little book. "Horrid Novel: a master spy of the most devious kind."

There was no entry for Hatchards, but since Hatchards bookshop was in Piccadilly, Henrietta had no doubt that Jane was trying to signify that this master spy was even now somewhere in the vicinity of London.

"I assure you, my dearest Henrietta, this is quite the horridest of horrid novels; I have never encountered one horrider. It is really quite, quite horrid."

Henrietta didn't need the codebook to grasp the import of those lines.

That there were French spies in London wasn't terribly shocking; the city was riddled with them. The papers had trumpeted the capture of a group of French spies masquerading as cravat merchants just the week before last.

Richard, in one of his last acts as the Purple Gentian, had uprooted the better part of Delaroche's personal spy network, a varied group that had comprised scullery maids, pugilists, courtesans, and even someone posing as a minor member of the royal family. (Queen Charlotte and King George had so many children that it was nearly impossible to keep track of who was who.) There were spies reporting to Delaroche, spies answering to Fouché, spies for the exiled Bourbon monarchy, and spies who spied for the sake of spying and would offer their information to whoever offered them the largest pile of coin.

This spy, clearly, was something out of the ordinary.

Sitting there, with the letter crumpled in her lap, Henrietta was struck by an idea, an idea that made the corners of her lips curl up, and put a mischievous sparkle into her hazel eyes. What if . . . No. Henrietta shook her head. She shouldn't.

But what if . . .

The idea poked and prodded at her with the insistence of a hungry ferret. Henrietta gazed raptly into space. The curl at the corners of her lips turned into a full-blown grin.

What if she were to unmask this particularly horrid spy herself?

Henrietta leaned against the side of the settee, propping her chin on her wrist. What harm could it do if there were an extra pair of eyes and ears devoted to the task? It wasn't as though she would do anything foolish, like hide the information from the War Office and set out on the task alone. Henrietta, a great devotee of sensational novels, had always maintained the liveliest contempt for those pea-witted heroines who refused to go to the proper authorities and instead insisted on hiding vital information until the villain had chased them through subterranean passageways to the edge of a storm-racked cliff.

No, Henrietta would do exactly as Jane had requested, and deliver the decoded letter to Wickham at the War Office via her contact in the ribbon shop on Bond Street. The point, after all, was to apprehend whoever it was as quickly as possible, and Henrietta knew that the

War Office's resources were far more extensive than hers, sister to a spy though she might be.

All the same, what a coup it would be if she could find the spy first! Certain people—certain people by the surname of Selwick, to be precise—would have a great big "I told you so" coming to them.

There was one slight shadow marring the shining landscape of her daydream. She didn't have the slightest notion of how to go about catching a spy. Unlike her sister-in-law Amy, Henrietta had spent her youth playing with dolls and reading novels, not tracking the fastest way to Calais in the event that one was to be chased from Paris by French police, or learning how to transform oneself into a gnarled old onion seller.

Now, there was an idea! If anyone would know how to go about tracking down France's deadliest spy with the maximum flair, it would be Amy. Among other things, on their return from France, Amy and Richard had converted Richard's Sussex estate into a clandestine academy for secret agents, laughingly referred to within the family as the Greenhouse.

There was nothing like getting advice from the experts, thought Henrietta airily as she flung letter and codebook aside and skipped across the room to her escritoire. Turning the key, she lowered the lid with an exuberant thump and yanked over a little yellow chair.

"Dearest Amy," she began, dabbing her quill enthusiastically in the inkpot. "You will be delighted to know that I have determined to follow your fine example. . . ."

After all, Henrietta thought, writing busily, she was really doing the War Office a favor, providing them with an extra agent at no additional cost. Goodness only knew whom the War Office might assign to the task if left to themselves.

Chapter Three

———— ❦ ————

Morning Call: *a consultation with an agent of the War Office*

—from the Personal Codebook of the Pink Carnation

"You sent for me?" The Honorable Miles Dorrington, heir to the Viscount of Loring and general rake about town, poked his blond head around the door of William Wickham's office.

"Ah, Dorrington." Wickham didn't look up from the pile of papers he had been perusing as he gestured to a seat on the opposite side of his cluttered desk. "Just the man I wanted to see."

Miles refrained from pointing out that sending a note bearing the words "Come at once" did tend to radically increase the odds of seeing someone. One simply didn't make that sort of comment to England's chief spymaster.

Miles maneuvered his tall frame into the small chair Wickham had indicated, propping his discarded gloves and hat against one knee, and stretching out his long legs as far as the tiny chair would allow. He waited until Wickham had finished, sanded, and folded the message he was writing, before uttering a breezy "Good morning, sir."

Wickham nodded in reply. "One moment, Dorrington." Inserting the end of a wafer of sealing wax into the candle on his desk, he expertly dripped several drops of red wax onto the folded paper, stamping it efficiently with his personal seal. Moving briskly from desk to door, he handed it to a waiting sentry with a few softly spoken words. All Miles caught was "by noon tomorrow."

Returning to his desk, Wickham eased several pieces of paper out of the organized chaos, tilting them towards himself. Miles resisted the urge to crane his head to read what was on the first page.

"I hope I haven't come at a bad time," Miles hedged, with an eye on the paper. Unfortunately, the paper was of good quality; despite the candle guttering nearby, there was no way of reading through the page, even if Miles had ever mastered the art of reading words backwards, which he hadn't.

Wickham cast Miles a mildly sardonic look over the edge of what he was reading. "There hasn't been a good time since the French went mad. And it has been getting steadily worse."

Miles leaned forward like a spaniel scenting a fallen pheasant. "Is there more word on Bonaparte's plans for an invasion?"

Wickham didn't bother to answer. Instead, he continued perusing the paper he held in his hand. "That was good work you did uncovering that ring of spies on Bond Street."

The unexpected praise took Miles off guard. Usually, his meetings with England's spymaster ran more to orders than commendations.

"Thank you, sir. All it took was a careful eye for detail."

And his valet's complaints about the poor quality of cravats the new merchants were selling. Downey noticed things like that. His suspicions piqued, Miles had done some "shopping" of his own in the back room of the establishment, uncovering a half dozen carrier pigeons and a pile of minuscule reports.

Wickham thumbed abstractedly through the sheaf of papers. "And the War Office is not unaware of your role in the Pink Carnation's late successes in France."

"It was a very minor role," Miles said modestly. "All I did was bash in the heads of a few French soldiers and—"

"Nonetheless," Wickham cut him off, "the War Office has taken note. Which is why we have summoned you here today."

Despite himself, Miles sat up straighter in his chair, hands tightening around his discarded gloves. This was it. The summons. The summons he had been waiting for for years.

Seven years, to be precise.

France had been at war with England for eleven years; Miles had been employed by the War Office for seven. Yet, for all his long tenure at the War Office, for all the time he spent going to and from the offices on Crown Street, delivering reports and receiving assignments, Miles could count the number of active missions he'd been assigned on the fingers of one hand.

That was one normal-sized hand with five measly fingers.

Mostly, the War Office had looked to Miles to provide them a link with the Purple Gentian. Given that Miles was Richard's oldest and closest friend, and spent even more time at Uppington House than he did at his club (and he spent far more time at his club than he did at his own uninspiring bachelor lodgings), this was not a surprising choice on the part of the War Office.

During Richard's tenure as the Purple Gentian, the two of them had worked out a system. Richard gleaned intelligence in France, and relayed it back to the War Office via meetings with Miles. Miles, for his part, would then pass along any messages the War Office might have back to Richard. Along the way, Miles picked up the odd assignment or two, but his primary role was as liaison with the Purple Gentian. Nothing more, nothing less. Miles knew it was an important role. He knew that without his participation, it was quite likely that the French would have suspected Richard's dual identity years before Amy's involvement had precipitated the matter. But, at the same time, he couldn't help but feel that his talents might be put to better—and more exciting—use. He and Richard had, after all, apprenticed for this sort of thing together. They had snuck down the same back stairs at Eton, read the same dashing tales of heroism and valor, shared the same archery butts, and made daring escapes from the same overcrowded society ballrooms, pursued by the same matchmaking mamas.

When Richard had discovered that his next-door neighbor, Sir

Percy Blakeney, was running the most daring intelligence effort since Odysseus asked Agamemnon whether he thought the Trojans might like a large wooden horse, Richard and Miles had gone together to beg Percy for admittance into his league. After considerable pleading, Percy had relented in Richard's case, but he still refused Miles. He tried to fob Miles off with "You'll be of more use to me at home." Miles pointed out that the French were, by definition, in France, and if he wanted to rescue French aristocrats from the guillotine, there was really only one place to do it. Percy, with the air of a man facing a tooth extraction, had poured two tumblers of port, passed the larger of the two to Miles, and said, "Sink me if I wouldn't like to have you along, lad, but you're just too demmed conspicuous."

And there was the problem. Miles stood six feet, three inches in his bare feet. Between afternoons boxing at Gentleman Jackson's and fencing at Angelo's, he had acquired the kind of musculature usually seen in Renaissance statuary. As one countess had squealed upon Miles's first appearance on the London scene, "Ooooh! Put him in a lion skin and he'll look just like Hercules!" Miles had declined the lion skin and other more intimate offers from the lady, but there was no escaping it. He had the sort of physique designed to send impressionable women into palpitations and Michelangelo running for his chisel. Miles would have traded it all in a minute to be small, skinny, and inconspicuous.

"What if I hunch over a lot?" he suggested to Percy.

Percy had just sighed and poured him an extra portion of port. The next day, Miles had offered his services to the War Office, in whatever capacity they could find. Until now, that capacity had usually involved a desk and a quill rather than black cloaks and dashing midnight escapades.

"How may I be of service?" Miles asked, trying to sound as though he were called in for important assignments at least once a week.

"We have a problem," began Wickham.

A problem sounded promising, ruminated Miles. Just so long as it wasn't a problem to do with the supply of boots for the army, or carbines for their rifles, or something like that. Miles had fallen for that once before, and had spent long weeks adding even longer sums. At a desk. With a quill.

"A footman was found murdered this morning in Mayfair."

Miles rested one booted leg against the opposite knee, trying not to look disappointed. He had been hoping for something more along the lines of "Bonaparte is poised to invade England, and we need you to stop him!" Ah, well, a man could dream.

"Surely that's a matter for the Bow Street Runners?"

Wickham fished a worn scrap of paper from the debris on his desk. "Do you recognize this?"

Miles peered down at the fragment. On closer inspection, it wasn't even anything so grand as a fragment; it was more of a fleck, a tiny triangle of paper with a jagged end on one side, where it had been torn from something larger.

"No," he said.

"Look again," said Wickham. "We found it snagged on a pin on the inside of the murdered man's coat."

It was no wonder the murderer had overlooked the lost portion; it was scarcely a centimeter long, and no writing remained. At least, no writing that was discernible as such. Along the tear, a thick black stroke swept down and then off to the side. It might be the lower half of an uppercase script I, or a particularly elaborate T.

Miles was just about to admit ignorance for a second time—in the hopes that Wickham wouldn't ask him a third—when recognition struck. Not the lower half of an I, but the stem of a flower. A very particular, stylized flower. A flower Miles hadn't seen in a very long time, and had hoped never to see again.

"The Black Tulip." The name tasted like hemlock on Miles's tongue. He repeated it, testing it for weight after years of disuse. "It can't be the Black Tulip. I don't believe it. It's been too long."

"The Black Tulip," countered Wickham, "is always most deadly after a silence."

Miles couldn't argue with that. The English in France had been most on edge not when the Black Tulip acted, but when he didn't. Like the gray calm before thunder, the Black Tulip's silence generally presaged some new and awful ill. Austrian operatives had been found dead, minor members of the royal family captured, English spies eliminated, all without fuss or fanfare. For the past two years, the Black Tulip had maintained a hermetic silence.

Miles grimaced.

"Precisely," said Wickham. He extricated the scrap of paper from Miles's grasp, returning it to its place on his desk. "The murdered man was one of our operatives. We had inserted him into the household of a gentleman known for his itinerant tendencies."

Miles rocked forward in his chair. "Who found him?"

Wickham dismissed the question with a shake of his head. "A scullery maid from the kitchen of a neighboring house; she had no part in it."

"Had she witnessed anything out of the ordinary?"

"Aside from a dead body?" Wickham smiled grimly. "No. Think of it, Dorrington. Ten houses—at one of which, by the way, a card party was in progress—several dozen servants coming and going, and not one of them heard anything out of the ordinary. What does that suggest to you?"

Miles thought hard. "There can't have been a struggle, or someone in one of the neighboring houses would have noticed. He can't have called out, or someone would have heard. I'd say our man knew his killer." A hideous possibility occurred to Miles. "Could our chap have been a double agent? If the French thought he had outlived his usefulness . . ."

The bags under Wickham's eyes seemed to grow deeper. "That," he said wearily, "is always a possibility. Anyone can turn traitor given the right circumstances—or the right price. Either way, we find ourselves with our old enemy in the heart of London. We need to know more. Which is where you come in, Dorrington."

"At your disposal."

Ah, the time had come. Now Wickham would ask him to find the footman's murderer, and he could make suave assurances about delivering the Black Tulip's head on a platter, and . . .

"Do you know Lord Vaughn?" asked Wickham abruptly.

"Lord Vaughn." Taken off guard, Miles racked his memory. "I don't believe I know the chap."

"There's no reason you should. He only recently returned from the Continent. He is, however, acquainted with your parents."

Wickham's gaze rested piercingly on Miles. Miles shrugged, lounging back in his chair. "My parents have a wide and varied acquaintance."

"Have you spoken to your parents recently?"

"No," Miles replied shortly. Well, he hadn't. That was all there was to it.

"Do you have any knowledge as to their whereabouts at present?"

Miles was quite sure that Wickham's spies had more up-to-date information on his parents' whereabouts than he did.

"The last time I heard from them, they were in Austria. As that was over a year ago, they may have moved on since. I can't tell you more than that."

When was the last time he had seen his parents? Four years ago? Five?

Miles's father had gout. Not a slight dash of gout, the sort that attends overindulgence in roast lamb at Christmas dinner, not periodic gout, but perpetual, all-consuming gout, the sort of gout that required special cushions and exotic diets and frequent changing of doctors. The viscount had his gout, and the viscountess had a taste for Italian operas, or, more properly, Italian opera singers. Both those interests were better served in Europe. For as long as Miles could remember, the Viscount and Viscountess of Loring had roved about Europe from spa to spa, taking enough waters to float a small armada, and playing no small part in supporting the Italian musical establishment.

The thought of either of his parents having anything to do with the Black Tulip, murdered agents, or anything requiring more strenuous activity than a carriage ride to the nearest opera house strained the imagination. Even so, it made Miles distinctly uneasy that they had come to the attention of the War Office.

Miles put both feet firmly on the floor, rested his hands on his knees, and asked bluntly, "Did you have a reason for inquiring after my parents, sir, or was this merely a social amenity?"

Wickham looked at Miles with something akin to amusement. "There's no need to be anxious on their account, Dorrington. We need information on Lord Vaughn. Your parents are among his social set. If you have occasion to write to your parents, you may want to ask them—casually—if they have encountered Lord Vaughn in their travels."

In his relief, Miles refrained from pointing out that his correspondence with his parents, to date, could be folded into a medium-sized snuffbox. "I'll do that."

"Casually," cautioned Wickham.

"Casually," confirmed Miles. "But what has Lord Vaughn to do with the Black Tulip?"

"Lord Vaughn," Wickham said simply, "is the employer of our murdered agent."

"Ah."

"Vaughn," continued Wickham, "is recently returned to London after an extended stay on the Continent. A stay of ten years, to be precise."

Miles engaged in a bit of mental math. "Just about the time the Black Tulip began operations."

Wickham didn't waste time acknowledging the obvious. "You move in the same circles. Watch him. I don't need to tell you how to go about it, Dorrington. I want a full report by this time next week."

Miles looked squarely at Wickham. "You'll have it."

"Good luck, Dorrington." Wickham began shuffling papers, a clear sign that the interview had come to a close. Miles levered himself out of the chair, pulling on his gloves as he strode to the door. "I expect to see you this time next Monday."

"I'll be here." Miles gave his hat an exuberant twirl before clapping it firmly onto his unruly blond hair. Pausing in the doorway, he grinned at his superior. "With flowers."

Chapter Four

—— ✤ ——

"The Black Tulip?"

Colin grinned. "Somewhat unoriginal, I admit. But what can you expect from a crazed French spy?"

"Isn't there a Dumas novel by that name?"

Colin considered. "I don't believe they're related. Besides, Dumas came later."

"I wasn't suggesting that Dumas was the Black Tulip," I protested.

"Dumas's father *was* a Napoleonic soldier," Colin pronounced with an authoritative wag of his finger, but spoiled the effect by adding, "Or perhaps it was his grandfather. One of them, at any rate."

I shook my head regretfully. "It's too good a theory to be true."

I was sitting in the kitchen of Selwick Hall, at a long, scarred wooden table that looked like it had once been victim to beefy-armed cooks bearing cleavers, while Colin poked a spoon into a gooey mass on the stove that he promised was rapidly cooking its way towards being dinner. Despite the well-worn flagstones covering the floor, the kitchen appliances looked as though they had been modernized at some point in the past two decades. They had begun life as that ugly mustard yellow so incomprehensibly beloved of kitchen designers, but had faded with time and use to a subdued beige.

It wasn't a designer's showcase of a kitchen. Aside from one rather dispirited pot of basil perched on the windowsill, there were no hanging plants, no gleaming copper pots, no color-coordinated jars of inedible pasta, no artistically arranged bunches of herbs poised to whack the unwary visitor on the head. Instead, it had the cozy air of a room that someone actually lived in. The walls had been painted a cheery, very un-mustardy yellow. Blue-and-white mugs hung from a rack above the sink; a well-used electric kettle stood next to a battered brown teapot with a frayed blue cozy; and brightly patterned yellow-and-blue drapes framed the room's two windows. The refrigerator made that comfortable humming noise known to refrigerators around the world, as soothing as a cat's purr.

A fall of ivy half-blocked the window over the sink, draping artistically down one side. Through the other, the dim twilight tended to obscure more than it revealed, that misty time of day when one can imagine ghost ships sailing endlessly through the Bermuda Triangle or phantom soldiers refighting long-ago battles on deserted heaths.

Clearly, I had been spending too much time cooped up in the library. Phantom soldiers, indeed!

All the same . . . Twisting to face Colin, I leaned my elbows against the back of my chair and asked, "Does Selwick Hall have any ghosts?"

Colin paused midstir, casting me a glance of unameliorated amusement. "Ghosts?"

"You know, ghastly specters, headless horsemen, that sort of thing."

"Right. I'm afraid we're rather short on those at the moment, but if you would like to go next door, I hear Donwell Abbey has a few phantom monks to let."

"I didn't realize they were for hire."

"After Henry the Eighth confiscated the abbeys, they had to find some way to earn their keep. There's always a stately home in need of a specter or two."

"Who are Donwell Abbey's ghosts? I take it that there's more to them than just being monks."

Colin gave the contents of the pot a final gush and turned off the heat. "It's the usual story. Renegade monk breaks his vows, runs off with the lissome daughter of the local squire—plate, please."

I handed over a blue-and-white-patterned plate.

"Enter monk, pursued by squire?" I suggested, paraphrasing one of my favorite Shakespeare stage directions.

"Close, but not quite." Colin debonairly dislodged a large clump of goo from the serving spoon onto the plate. It looked a bit like dog food. I handed him the second plate. "The local squire didn't much care for his daughter, but he did scent an opportunity to turn a profit. With proper paternal outrage, he stormed over to the monastery—more?"

A laden serving spoon hovered in the air like a phantom hand at a séance. "No, thank you."

"The squire rushed over to the monastery and demanded a strip of land that ran between the abbey and his estate as repayment for loss of his daughter. The monks were not pleased. No one knows quite what happened that night, but the story has it that the monks caught up with the pair in a large field, not far from the abbey."

"What happened then?" I'm a sucker for a good ghost story.

"No one knows for sure," said Colin mysteriously, or as mysteriously as one can while waving a large ladle. "By morning, all that was left was the crumpled hood of a habit, lying discarded on the grass. Of the squire's daughter, there was no trace. But legend has it that he still looks for her on stormy nights, and you can see him, drifting endlessly through the grounds of Donwell Abbey, forever searching for his lost love."

Little prickles ran down my arms as I pictured the deserted heath, the pale rays of the moon illuminating their terrified faces. . . . A large blob of something brown appeared in front of my nose.

"Beans on toast?" said Colin prosaically.

It is next to impossible to maintain a ghoulish aura in the presence of beans and toast. It's more effective than waving garlic in front of a vampire.

The ghosts receded into the dusky darkness behind the window while we partook of beans and toast in the well-lit kitchen. Colin assured me it was his one culinary accomplishment.

"If that's a ploy to get me to leave, it's not going to work. Now that I've actually seen the archives, a steady diet of ashes couldn't drive me away."

"Hmm. Point taken. What about a ghastly apparition, all in white, hovering over your bed?"

"Too late. You already told me you don't have any ghosts."

Colin grinned a rakish grin that had an odd effect on the inside of my stomach—at least, I assume it was the grin, and not his culinary efforts.

"Who said I was talking about a ghost?"

Before I had quite puzzled out the ramifications of that statement, the door inched coyly open, and a feminine voice trilled, "Colin . . . Colin, are you home?"

Colin froze like a fox within sight of the hunt. Catching my eye, he made anxious shushing motions.

"Colin . . ." The door continued its inexorable swing inward, and a blond braid swung around the edge, closely followed by its owner, a tall girl in tight tan pants and a closely fitted jacket. Catching sight of her quarry, she stepped jauntily into the kitchen, booted heels clicking on the flagstones of the floor, riding helmet swinging from one hand.

"Colin! I thought I'd find you here. When I saw your car in the drive . . . Oh."

She had caught sight of me, sitting on the other side of the table. The riding helmet stopped midswing, and her jaw dropped. The expression didn't do much for her, bringing to mind portraits of some of the more heavy-jawed Hapsburgs. Or Red Riding Hood's wolf. Her teeth were very large, and very white.

"Hello," I said into the silence that followed.

The girl ignored me, her pale eyes fixing on Colin. "I didn't realize you had company."

"There was no reason why you should," said Colin blandly. He set down his fork on the edge of his plate. "Good evening, Joan."

With her mouth back in place, this time pursed in annoyance, the woman was not, I have to admit, entirely unattractive. Her mouth might have been a little thin and her nose a little on the pug side, but the overall effect of high cheekbones, endless legs, and sun-streaked blond hair against perfectly browned skin could have graced a Ralph Lauren advertisement. I was willing to bet that she was one of those annoying people who tan, not burn.

Her eyes, I noticed, were a little on the narrow side and a very pale blue. I don't usually notice people's eye color, but these particular eyes were still fixed on me in a decidedly inimical way.

"You haven't introduced me to your . . . friend." She looked like she was chewing on the ashes I had volunteered to eat.

"Eloise, this is Joan Plowden-Plugge; Joan, this is Eloise Kelly," provided Colin, lounging back in his chair.

"Hi!" I said brightly.

Joan continued to eye me with the sort of hostility better reserved for large insects that have invaded one's bed.

"Are you a friend of Serena's?" she asked, in the deadly tones of one knowingly asking a losing question.

"Well . . ." I had once held Colin's sister's head over a toilet bowl while she was violently ill, but I wasn't sure if that quite qualified as making us friends. "Not exactly," I hedged.

Joan looked daggers at me. I looked appealingly at Colin, but he was busy looking at no one in particular, while cultivating a façade of amused indifference. Some help he was. Obviously, I was going to have to take care of this little misapprehension on my own, or, as Shakespeare so eloquently put it, risk a predestinate scratched face.

"I'm a historian," I explained helpfully.

Joan looked at me as though I had just volunteered to introduce her to the Mad Hatter.

Okay, maybe it wasn't the most illuminating statement I could have made. I tried again. "Colin has been very generously allowing me the use of his archives," I clarified.

Joan's face cleared.

"Oh. You study dead people."

Clearly, she was of the Pammy school of history, where Genghis Khan hobnobbed with Louis XIV on Bosworth Field—all wearing hoopskirts. After all, if they weren't in the tabloids last week, it was all olden days, anyway. If it meant that she wasn't going to come after me with her riding crop, I really didn't care if she thought Attila the Hun had been one of the signatories of the Treaty of Versailles.

"You could put it that way. Right now, the dead people I'm studying happen to be related to Colin, so he was kind enough to give me the run of his library."

Libraries were evidently not a subject of abiding fascination to Miss Plowden-Plugge. With a swish of her braid, she dismissed me as an impediment of minimal importance, and returned to Colin. Given her position relative to the table, there was no way she could entirely cut me out of the conversation unless she were to stomp around the side of the table and stand between me and Colin, but she did her best, angling her body to maximize Colin frontage and minimize my presence. In profile, her nose appeared decidedly pug.

She rested her right hand against the table and leaned towards Colin. "How is darling Serena?"

Colin lazily tilted his head in my direction. "How would you say she is, Eloise?"

"You've seen her more recently than I have," I replied in bewilderment.

"But you were the one who took such charming care of her when she was ill the other night." Colin smiled beatifically at me before turning back to Joan, saying in a confidential tone, "We were at a party given by one of Eloise's friends the other night, and Serena felt a bit rough. But Eloise saw to her, didn't you, Eloise?"

There wasn't anything in that statement that one could point to as technically untrue. Pammy had thrown a party, Serena had been taken ill, I had hustled Serena off to the bathroom. Of course, what Colin had neglected to mention was that the party had been a huge PR extravaganza thrown in Pammy's professional capacity, not an intimate little cocktail party; Pammy had invited Serena, along with a whole group of her other old school chums; and I, in my role as Pammy's oldest friend in the world, had been tagging along after Pammy. I had been as surprised to see Colin and Serena as they were to see me. At the time, I had also been laboring under the misapprehension that Serena was Colin's girlfriend, but that was a whole other story.

Put the way Colin had put it, the whole thing did sound pretty damning—and it was clear that Joan was jumping to all the conclusions he wanted her to jump to.

"I thought you were here for the library," she said accusingly.

Colin stretched in that infuriating way men have and rested a casual hand on the back of my chair. It would have been funny if I weren't so miffed; I was sitting far enough away that the tips of his fingers barely brushed the chair back. As it was, he had to scoot slightly sideways in his chair to reach that far.

"Oh, I don't know. Eloise is more of a houseguest, really. Wouldn't you say, Eloise?"

What I wanted to say was unprintable. If there were any family ghosts in residence, I was going to sic them all on him. Headless cavaliers, wailing women in white, you name it. I never liked being the monkey in the middle. Especially when I had not been informed that there was a game in progress.

I directed an acid smile at Colin. "I would never presume."

Colin choked on a laugh. "Yes, you would," he said bluntly. "If there was a historical document in it for you."

Despite myself I started to chuckle. "It would have to be a really, really important historical document."

Thwomp!

Joan's riding helmet smacked down onto the middle of the table between me and Colin, jarring a piece of precariously balanced toast off my plate.

"I'll just be off then, shall I?" she said in saccharine tones. "Colin, you are coming to our little drinks party tomorrow night, aren't you?"

"I don't—" Colin began, but Joan cut him off.

"Absolutely everyone will be there." She began rattling off a list of names, clearly designed to convince Colin that he would be ragingly out of the loop if he didn't don a sport coat and sally forth. I retrieved my toast.

"Nigel and Chloe are coming, and they're bringing Rufus and his new girlfriend. And Bunty Bixler will be there—you do remember Bunty Bixler, don't you, Colin?"

Towards the end, I was convinced she was making up names, just to have more people I wouldn't know. From the look on Colin's face, he didn't recognize half the names, either, and I got the feeling that he wasn't overly fond of Bunty Bixler, whoever that unfortunately named person might be.

Sensing she was losing ground, Joan resorted to desperate tactics. "You can bring—" Joan looked at me blankly.

"Eloise," I provided helpfully.

"—your guest, if you like," she finished, in the tones of one making a great concession. Turning to me, she said hospitably, "Naturally, it won't be terribly amusing for you, not knowing anyone. I suppose you *could* talk to the vicar. He does enjoy going on about old things. Churches, and all that." I had been properly relegated to my place, doddering in the corner with the clergy.

After such a gracious invitation, how could I refuse?

"Thank you."

"Of course, if you're too busy in the library . . ."

I bared my teeth, which weren't nearly as large or white as hers. "I wouldn't miss it."

A muffled snicker emerged from the head of the table.

I looked pointedly at Colin.

"So sorry," he said blandly. "Bean in my throat."

Indeed.

His ill-advised humor had had the well-deserved side effect of refocusing Joan's attention on him. "We'll see you tomorrow then, yes? Don't forget, tomorrow night at half-seven."

The kitchen door slapped soundly shut behind her.

I stood, plunking my fork and knife onto my empty plate with a clatter. I had the feeling there was history there. Colin shifted in his chair behind me.

"No more beans, I take it?"

"No. Thanks." I lifted my plate and carried it to the sink, hearing the thud of hooves fade into the distance. I didn't think the phantom monk of Donwell Abbey would care to mess with her, not in that sort of mood. Outside the kitchen window, true dark had fallen, as it only does in the country. I could see my own reflection against the window, lips thinned in annoyance.

It wasn't any of my business, really.

In the window, I saw Colin approaching, plate in hand. Oh, the hell with that. If he was going to drag me into his amorous misadventures, it *was* my business. Especially since I was the one running the risk of being hunted down by an angry Joan on horseback. I'd rather take the phantom monk. At least the latter would make a better story when I got home.

Plunking plate and cutlery into the sink, I turned so rapidly that Colin nearly ran into me plate first. Objects in the window may be closer than they appear.

Leaning back against the sink to avoid a punctured midriff, I curled my fingers around the metal edge of the basin and said, "Look, I don't mind acting as a human shield, but, next time, a little advance warning would be appreciated."

Or, at least, that's what I meant to say.

What came out was "I'll do the dishes. Since you cooked."

Damn.

Colin took a step back and made an elaborate sweeping gesture. Having managed to put me on the spot instead of himself, he was in an infuriatingly good humor. "Go along. I'll wash up."

"Are you sure?"

"I don't mind. Go on." He gave me a light shove. "I know you must be eager to get back to the library."

"Well . . ." There was no disputing that statement.

Colin was already turning the faucets on. "You can cook tomorrow."

"Oh, but you're forgetting." I paused in the doorway. "Tomorrow, you're having drinks with Miss Plowden-Plugge. Good night!"

I swept out of the kitchen into the darkened hallway beyond, hoping I'd be able to find my way to the library. It would entirely spoil my exit if I had to turn around and ask for directions. As long as I could make it to the front hall, I could find my way from there.

It really did get dark in the country, without streetlamps and car headlights and lit storefronts all casting their friendly glow. I felt my way along the hall, one hand on the ribbed wallpaper, the other held warily in front of me, as though to ward off . . . well, not phantom monks. More small tables and that sort of thing, which have a habit of leaping out at one's shins in unfamiliar hallways. If I did start uncomfortably at a few shadows, and peer a little more closely than necessary through the odd doorway, let's just say I was glad that Colin wasn't there to see.

To take my mind off silly ghost stories, I directed it instead towards the Black Tulip. It was a name straight out of an old Rafael Sabatini novel, like Captain Blood, or the Sea-Hawk. Whoever chose it must have had a strong sense of the dramatic and, unlike Gaston Delaroche, a finely tuned sense of humor, to ape his rivals' noms de guerre so closely. There was no doubt in my mind that the Black Tulip's very name was a mocking riposte to the Scarlet Pimpernel and the Purple Gentian. It was a more grown-up, more clever version of the universal playground chant of "ha, ha, can't catch me."

If I were the Black Tulip, where would I look for the Pink Carnation?

I successfully skirted around a small table, and noticed with some relief that I had made it back to the front hall. From there I should be able to find my way back to the library . . . I hoped. My lack of sense of direction is legendary among anyone who has ever tried to travel anywhere with me. With any luck I wouldn't wind up in the attics or cellar by accident.

If I knew that the Pink Carnation had been a guest at Richard and Amy's wedding, the first place I would go would be the guest list. And since the guests, with the exception of Amy's countrified relatives from Shropshire, all hailed from the first stair of London society, I would want to insert myself into that milieu.

Of course, I reminded myself, the Black Tulip didn't need to be a member of the *ton*. There were hundreds of people who floated about on the fringes of society who could be reasonably assumed to have the same access—ladies' maids, valets, dancing masters, courtesans, bootmakers. Many a man's relationship with his tailor was more intimate than that with his wife; heaven only knew what he might reveal over the fitting of a new coat.

It was just so much less glamorous to think of the dreaded Black Tulip posing as a servant. Black Tulips weren't supposed to do things like bleach linen. They lurked in the corners of darkened hallways, swirling brandy snifters and twirling their mustaches. Or something like that.

Eeek! I staggered backwards as something moved in front of me, a misty form, shrouded in . . . oh. It was my own reflection in a darkened window. Ooops. A natural mistake, I assured myself.

If I didn't curb my imagination, I was going to be as ridiculous as that dim-witted heroine in *Northanger Abbey*, the one who pounced on a laundry list thinking it was going to be an account of ghostly goings-on. Colin would find me the following morning, hunched on the library floor in a gibbering ball of terror, moaning about clanking chains and eyes that burned out of the darkness where no eyes ought to be. Whatever had I been thinking to read all those ghost stories in my youth?

Taking my nerves firmly in hand, I continued onward to the library with a firm gait and a defiant gaze. All the same, despite my resolution to not think about ghosties and ghoulies and things that go bump in the night, I couldn't help but wonder . . .

What had Colin meant by that comment about apparitions by my bed?

Chapter Five

———— ❦ ————

Almack's Assembly Rooms: *a cunning ambush laid for unwitting English agents by a determined band of French operatives*

—from the Personal Codebook of the Pink Carnation

At precisely five minutes to eleven, Miles sauntered through the hallowed portals of Almack's Assembly Rooms.

Ordinarily, Almack's was not high on the list of Miles's favorite places to pass an evening. Given a choice between Almack's and a French dungeon, Miles would usually choose the dungeon. As Miles had complained to his valet earlier that evening, the company in the dungeon would be more congenial, the entertainment more entertaining, and, devil take it, the food was probably better, too.

"I'm sure it is, sir," said Downey, who was busily trying to tie Miles's cravat into something resembling a current fashion. "And if sir would refrain from speaking for just a moment . . ."

"The deuce of it is," Miles expostulated, chin crushing the fold Downey had just ever so carefully arranged, "I gave my word. What's a man to do?"

"If sir does not permit me to tie his cravat," pointed out Downey acerbically, yanking away the ruined cravat with enough force to make Miles's eyes water, "sir will be sufficiently tardy that he will not be allowed into the assembly rooms."

Miles considered his valet thoughtfully. Hmm. The portals of Almack's closed at precisely eleven o'clock, by order of the Patronesses, and woe betide the unfortunate man who rushed up to the doors a moment too late. Wouldn't that be a shame if he wasn't able to get inside and was instead forced by cruel necessity to go to his club and drink a few bottles of excellent claret?

Miles shook his head, ruining a third square of starched linen in the process. "It's an excellent idea, Downey," he said, "but it just won't wash. I promised."

There was the rub. He had promised Richard, and a promise was a promise. A promise to one's best friend was a vow on the order of a blood-signed pact with Mephistopheles. You just didn't violate that sort of thing.

"You will keep an eye on Hen for me while I'm away, won't you?" Richard had asked as he clasped his best friend's hand in farewell, preparatory to leaving for Sussex and married bliss. "Scare away the young bucks, and all that?"

"Never fear!" Miles had promised blithely, giving his friend a reassuring whack on the back. "I'll keep her closer than a cloister."

The reference to nunneries had struck precisely the right note; Richard had gone away reassured.

After all, how hard could keeping an eye on one twenty-year-old girl at the odd evening event be? Hen was a sensible sort of girl, not one to dash out on balconies with fortune hunters or moon over the first rake to look her way. All Miles had to do was bring her a glass of lemonade every so often, bend a leg in the occasional country dance, and loom threateningly over any importunate fop who got too close. Hell, he enjoyed the looming bit, and the dancing wasn't all that onerous, either. Hen hadn't trodden on his toes—on the dance floor, at any rate—since she was fifteen. How much trouble could it be?

Ha. Miles would have laughed bitterly at his own naïveté if it wouldn't have attracted too much attention. And attention was the last thing he wanted to attract. Miles resisted the urge to linger cravenly in the doorway.

There were all those . . . mothers out there. Mothers of the very deadliest kind. Matchmaking mothers. All of them determined to snare a viscount for their offspring.

It was enough to send a man running to Delaroche, begging to be put in a nice, safe cell.

Now, if he could just find Hen before someone spotted him . . .

"Mr. Dorrington!"

Damn, too late.

The sound came from a portly woman sporting a headdress with enough feathers to clothe a reasonably plump ostrich. "Mr. Dorrington!"

Miles feigned deafness.

"Mr. Dorrington!" the woman tugged at his sleeve.

"Mr. Who?" inquired Miles blandly. "Oh, Dorrington! I believe I saw him go into the card room. It's over that way," he added helpfully.

The woman's eyes narrowed for a moment, and then she laughed, whacking Miles so hard on the arm with her fan that Miles could have sworn he heard something crack. Probably his arm.

"La! You are droll, Mr. Dorrington! You don't remember me—"

If he had ever encountered her before, Miles had no doubt he would have remembered it. He would have had the bruises to remind him.

"—but I was a dear friend of your dear mama."

"How nice for you." Miles dodged another swipe of the fan.

"So of course the minute I saw you"—the fan swooped again, homing with unerring accuracy straight at Miles's nose—"I said to my darling daughter, Lucy—where did that girl go again? Oh, there you are—I said to her, 'Lucy'"—Miles sneezed violently—"'Lucy, we must simply go speak to dear, dear Annabelle's only boy.'"

"And now you have. Oh, look! There's an unmarried marquis looking for a bride!" Miles pointed in the opposite direction, and made a run for it.

Hen was going to owe him for this one. As soon as he found her.

Miles ducked behind a pillar, trying to simultaneously avoid that crazy woman with her bruising fan, and locate Henrietta. She wasn't on the dance floor; she wasn't at the refreshment table; and she wasn't in the card room. Miles couldn't see into the card room from his vantage point behind the pillar, but he didn't need to.

Above the chatter of voices, Miles heard a familiar laugh, and wheeled in the direction of the noise. There was something about that quality of frank amusement that couldn't belong to anyone but Henrietta.

Not an intrepid agent of the War Office for nothing, Miles successfully tracked the sound to its source. His eyes drifted past a bunch of Beau Brummell imitators who were staring people out of countenance through their quizzing glasses, past a lanky young lady who had clearly had an unfortunate accident with a curling iron, and finally settled on a familiar reddish-brown head adorned with a simple pearl clip. Henrietta and her two best friends, Penelope and Charlotte, were huddled in a corner, communicating in a combination of whispers, giggles, and agitated hand gestures. As Miles watched, Henrietta grinned and tossed a remark over her shoulder to Penelope, her hazel eyes alight with mischief.

An answering grin spread automatically across Miles's face, to be replaced by a frown as he noticed a young buck behind Henrietta also taking notice both of the infectious grin and the bare shoulder over which the remark had been addressed. Henrietta's shoulders and neck glistened in the candlelight, whiter than the pearls at her throat. Miles glowered, to little effect. The man raised his quizzing glass. Miles took a step out from behind his pillar, stretched to his full height, and cracked his knuckles. Then he glowered. Quizzing glass swinging from its riband, the man hastily hared off in the direction of the card room. Miles gave a satisfied nod. He was getting quite good at this chaperonage lark.

And a good thing, too. The number of amorous importuners who needed to be glowered out of countenance had increased recently.

From behind his pillar, Miles regarded Henrietta, her features more familiar to him than his own. Over his lifetime he had spent a great deal more time looking at Henrietta than in his mirror. Superficially, not much had changed. Same long brown hair, limned in red-gold where the light touched it. Same hazel eyes, sometimes brown-green, sometimes blue, tilted at the edges as though she were in constant thought. Same translucently fair skin, quick to freckle in sunlight and prone to rash from nettles, wool, or any other itchy substance, a fact of which he and Richard had taken shameless advantage in their reprehensible youth. Henrietta's hair was as long and brown, her eyes as tip-tilted, her skin as pale as when she had been nine, or twelve, or sixteen. And yet, when one put them all together, the result now was quite different from what it had been even a year ago.

Was she wearing her bodices cut lower? Her hair in a different way? She might not teach the torches to burn bright, but there was something glowing about her, something that made her stand out from Charlotte and Penelope. A new skin lotion, perhaps? Miles grimaced and gave up. Female fripperies eluded him. As for bodices, devil take it, she was his best friend's sister, committed to his care. He wasn't supposed to be aware she *had* a bodice. Of course, it would be bloody odd if she didn't have one, but the point remained. Anything under the neck was decidedly off limits. And his job was to make sure that every other man in the ballroom complied with that, too.

Looking up, Henrietta caught sight of Miles, and quite gratifyingly broke off whatever she had been in the process of saying to Penelope and Charlotte, her face breaking into a broad smile of welcome.

Miles saluted.

Henrietta tilted her head and squinched her nose in an expression of interest and incredulity clearly meant to convey "What on earth are you doing behind that pillar?"

There existed no facial contortions convoluted enough to explain that. Miles removed himself from behind the pillar, straightened his cravat, and strolled over towards Hen as debonairly as though he hadn't just been discovered standing behind a large piece of masonry.

"Who were you hiding from?" asked Hen, in some amusement, resting a gloved hand on his sleeve. She tilted her head back to look at him, both eyebrows raised at a droll angle. "Surely Monsieur Delaroche hasn't acquired a voucher to Almack's."

"Oh, no," Miles assured her. "Someone far, far more deadly."

Henrietta considered. "My mother?"

"Close," Miles said darkly. With appropriate hand gestures, he narrated his brief encounter with the fan-wielding, matchmaking mother from hell.

Henrietta's eyes widened with recognition. "Oh, I know her! She was after Richard all last Season. He actually knocked over a punch bowl just to create a diversion. He tried to make it look like an accident, but"—Henrietta shook her head with world-weary wisdom—"we knew."

"Someone"—Miles jabbed a finger at Henrietta—"might have warned me."

Henrietta fluttered her eyelashes in exaggerated innocence. "But that would have been unsporting."

"To whom?"

"To Mrs. Ponsonby, of course."

"You"—Miles narrowed his brown eyes at Henrietta—"are going to owe me for the rest of your life."

"You already said that last night. And the night before."

"Some things can't be said often enough," said Miles firmly.

Henrietta pondered that for a moment. "Like albatross."

"Albatross?" A lock of sandy hair flopped into Miles's eyes as he looked down quizzically at Henrietta.

"I just enjoy saying it," replied Henrietta cheerfully. "Try it. Albatross. It's even more fun when you draw out the first syllable a bit. *Al*-batross!"

"And Richard was so sure insanity didn't run in the family," Miles mused loudly.

"Shhh! Or you'll scare away my marital prospects."

"You don't think you already did that by shouting *albatross?*"

"I wouldn't call that a shout, precisely. More of a gleeful exclamation."

Miles did what any good rake would do when losing an argument. He favored her with a slow, seductive smile, the sort of smile that made maiden hearts flutter and worldly widows take to writing scented notes.

"Has anyone ever told you that you have a wicked way with words, Lady Henrietta?"

Product of two older brothers, Henrietta was proof against seductive smiles. "You, usually. Generally when I've outargued you over something."

Miles rubbed his chin in an expression of lofty thought. "I don't recall any such occasion."

"Oh, look!" Henrietta leaned confidentially towards him, the embroidered hem of her dress lapping at the toes of his boots. "I do believe you've been saved. Mrs. Ponsonby has latched on to Reggie Fitzhugh."

Miles followed the path of Henrietta's fan and noted with some relief that the crazy woman had indeed honed in on Turnip Fitzhugh. Turnip wasn't in the direct line for a title, but his uncle was an earl, and he did have an income of ten thousand pounds a year, enough to make Turnip a very attractive marital prospect for anyone who didn't mind a complete absence of mental capacity. That, from what Miles had viewed of this year's crop of debutantes, didn't look to be a problem. Besides, Turnip was a good chap. Not the sort of man Miles would want to see marrying his sister (there was little danger of that, as Miles's three half sisters were all considerably older, and long since legshackled), but he had a good hand with his horses, a generous way with his port, and a winning habit of actually paying his gambling debts.

He also had a positive talent for sartorial disaster. He was, Miles noted with mingled amusement and disbelief, dressed entirely à la Carnation, with a huge pink flower in his buttonhole, wreaths of carnations embroidered on his silk stockings, and even—Miles winced—dozens of little carnations twining on vines along the sides of his knee breeches. Turnip's recent sojourn on the Continent had clearly done nothing to improve his taste.

Miles groaned. "Someone needs to kidnap his tailor."

"I think it adds a touch of color to the evening, don't you? Our flowery friend will be so flattered."

Miles lowered his voice and made a show of toying with one of the ruffles of his cravat. "Be careful, Hen."

Henrietta's hazel eyes met his brown ones. "I know."

Since he was there *in loco fratensis*, Miles was about to say something wise and big-brotherly, when he was distracted by a familiar pounding noise.

It wasn't the headache—being a big, strong man, Miles never succumbed to such minor ills as the headache—and it wasn't French artillery, and as far as he knew, there weren't any giant-bearing beanstalks in the vicinity, so it could only be one thing.

The Dowager Duchess of Dovedale.

"I'll just get you that lemonade now, shall I?"

"Coward," said Henrietta.

"Why should two of us suffer?" Miles started to edge backwards as the duchess thumped forward.

"Because"—Henrietta caught hold of his sleeve and tugged—"misery loves company."

Miles looked pointedly at the Dowager Duchess, or, to be more precise, at the bundle of fur draped over the dowager's arms like a particularly mangy muff, and yanked his arm out of Henrietta's grasp. "Not this company."

"That hurts." Henrietta clasped a hand to her heart. "In here."

"You can pour lemonade on the wound," replied Miles unsympathetically. "Oh, hell, here she comes. And her little dog, too. Damnation!"

Miles fled.

"Hmph," said the dowager, stumping up to the three girls. "Was that Dorrington I saw fleeing?"

"I sent him to fetch me some lemonade," explained Henrietta on Miles's behalf.

"Don't try to fool me, missy. I know flight when I see it." The Dowager Duchess watched Miles's rapidly retreating back with some complacency. "At my age in life, making young men run away is one of the few pleasures left to me. Had young Ponsonby jump out a second-story window the other day," she added with a cackle.

"He twisted an ankle," Charlotte informed Henrietta softly. Having her grandmother in the vicinity had a considerably dampening effect on both Charlotte's spirits and her voice.

"Of course, it wasn't always that way," the Dowager Duchess continued, as though Charlotte hadn't spoken. She chortled in gleeful reminiscence. "When I was your age, all the young bucks were mad for me. I had no fewer than seventeen duels fought over me in my youth! Seventeen! Not one of them mortal," she added, in a tone of deep regret.

"Aren't you glad to know you weren't the cause of a good man's death?" teased Henrietta.

"Hmph! Any boy fool enough to fight a duel deserves to die in it! We need more duels." The Dowager Duchess raised her voice. "Reduce the number of half-wits clogging the ballrooms."

"What?" Turnip Fitzhugh ambled over. "'Fraid I didn't catch that."

"My point exactly," snapped the Dowager Duchess. "Speaking of half-wits, where's young Dorrington got to? I like that boy. He's a pleasure to torment, not like some of these young milksops." She glowered at poor Turnip, the nearest available milksop. "What's Dorrington doing, squeezing the lemons?"

"Probably hiding behind a pillar somewhere," suggested Penelope. "He's good at that."

Henrietta shot her best friend an exasperated look.

Charlotte came to the rescue. "There's usually a crush around the refreshment table."

The Dowager Duchess eyed her granddaughter without favor. "All this namby-pamby good nature came straight from your mother's side. Always told Edward he was weakening the bloodline."

Henrietta unobtrusively reached out a gloved hand and squeezed Charlotte's arm. Charlotte's gray eyes met hers in a look of quiet gratitude.

"Aha!" The dowager let out a crow of triumph. "There's Dorrington! Never made it as far as the lemons. But who's that hussy he's talking to?"

Chapter Six

———— ❦ ————

Orgeat: *1) an almond-flavored syrup commonly served at evening assemblies; 2) a deadly and swift-acting poison. Note: The two are almost entirely indistinguishable*
—from the Personal Codebook of the Pink Carnation

Miles wheeled off in the direction of the refreshments, taking care to put considerable distance between himself and the Dowager Duchess of Dovedale. And the Dowager Duchess of Dovedale's little yippy dog. Miles and that dog had an unhappy history—unhappy for Miles, at any rate.

Miles was just casting a backwards glance over his shoulder to make sure that the canine from hell hadn't scented him (it could move bloody fast when it wanted to, and it generally wanted to when Miles was in range), when there was a throaty "Oh!" and something warm and wet trickled down the side of his leg. Miles turned, expecting another pastel-clad debutante.

Instead, he found himself facing a sultry vision in black. Her dark hair was pulled simply back at the crown, and allowed to fall in long, loose curls that teased the edge of a bodice as low as anything being worn in Paris. The stark hairstyle illuminated the fine bones of her face, the sort of bones that in ladies more advanced in age were generally referred to as elegant, high of cheek and pointed of chin. But there was nothing aged about the woman in front of Miles. Her skin was orchid pale against the jetty loops of her hair, but it was the pallor of a carefully protected complexion, not illness or age, and her lips, so red they might have been rouged, arched in invitation.

Against the pink-and-white prettiness of the young girls in their first Season, she was as exotic as a tulip in a field of primroses, a stark study in light and shadow against a wall of watercolors.

"I'm so sorry," the same husky voice said, as Miles did an involuntary hop at the touch of the liquid, his shoes squelching in the sticky puddle of orgeat beneath his feet.

"Quite all right." Miles could feel the orgeat seeping between his toes. "I wasn't looking where I was going."

"But your breeches—"

"It doesn't signify," said Miles, adding gallantly, "May I fetch you another glass?"

The woman smiled, a slow smile that began at the corners of her lips and worked its way up through her cheekbones, but never quite to her eyes. "I'm not entirely displeased to be relieved of the stuff. I prefer my refreshments to be . . . stronger."

The glance she cast Miles's shoulders suggested that she was referring to more than just beverages.

"You've found yourself in the wrong place, then," replied Miles frankly. Almack's, after all, was known for its weak beverages and even more lackluster company. Unless one was passionately fond of Lady Jersey, and Miles didn't think this woman fell into the Lady Jersey idolizing faction.

Lashes as dark as her hair swooped down to veil bottomless eyes. "Every now and again, one finds exceptions to any general rule."

"That depends," Miles drawled, "on just how far one is willing to bend the rules."

"Until they break." The last consonant hung delicately in the air.

Miles favored her with his most rakish glance. "Like a maiden's heart?"

She drew a long-nailed finger delicately along the fringe of her fan. "Or a man's resolve."

On the other side of the room, Henrietta snatched the Dowager Duchess's lorgnette, and peered through the crowd. There, quite definitely, was Miles—his blond head was unmistakable. No one else's hair could attain quite that degree of disarray in an airless ballroom. And he was also unmistakably in conversation.

With a woman.

Henrietta held the lorgnette away from her eye, inspected it to make sure it was in proper working order, and then tried again. The woman was still there.

Henrietta was justifiably perplexed. Over the many times Miles had been dragooned into escorting her, a comfortable pattern had emerged. Miles would show up as late as decently possible; they would bicker a bit; Miles would fetch her lemonade, and some for Penelope and Charlotte, too, if he was in an accommodating mood; and then he would hare off to the card room with the other harassed brothers and husbands. He would pop out from time to time to make sure all was well, and fetch more lemonade, and dance whichever dance might be left empty on Henrietta's dance card, but otherwise, he kept carefully within the male sanctum of the card room.

He most decidedly did not speak to debutantes.

Of course, the woman in black—Henrietta squinted through the lorgnette, wishing she had an opera glass instead—didn't much look like a debutante. For one thing, debutantes didn't wear black. And their necklines, for the most part, tended to be somewhat more modest than that sported by Miles's companion. Good heavens, did that dress even have a bodice?

Henrietta fought down an unreasonable surge of pure dislike. Of course, she didn't dislike the woman. How could she dislike her? She hadn't even met her yet.

But she *looked* dislikable.

"Who is she?" Henrietta asked.

Pen gave a very unladylike snort. "A husband-hunter, no doubt."

"But aren't we?" Henrietta countered absentmindedly as the woman laid a black-gloved hand on Miles's arm. Miles didn't seem to be making any move to divest himself of the appendage.

"That," decreed Penelope, "is beside the point."

"I would prefer my future husband hunt me," sighed Charlotte.

Penelope grinned mischievously. "He'll lurk beneath your balcony and cry, 'My love! My love! O love of my life!'"

"Shhh!" Charlotte grabbed one of Penelope's outflung arms. "Everyone's staring."

Penelope squeezed Charlotte's gloved hand affectionately. "Let them stare! It will only increase your mystique, don't you agree, Hen? Hen?"

Henrietta was still staring at the dark woman with Miles.

The dowager slapped Henrietta's hand.

"Ow!" Henrietta dropped the lorgnette straight into the dowager's lap.

"That's better," muttered the dowager, lifting her eyepiece. "Ah."

"Yes?" prompted Henrietta, wondering if it would be possible to ever so casually wander over there and eavesdrop a bit without looking like she had done so on purpose. Probably not, she decided ruefully. There was nothing large to hide behind except Miles, and his companion would probably catch on if she saw Henrietta peeking out from behind Miles's back. She would undoubtedly mention it to Miles. And Henrietta, wicked way with words though she might have, would have a great deal of trouble explaining that one away.

"So that's who it is! Whoever would have thought she'd be back in London?"

"Who?" asked Henrietta.

"Well, well, well," tutted the duchess.

Henrietta directed an exasperated look in the direction of the Dowager Duchess, but knew better than to speak. The more interest she expressed, the longer the dowager would take to get to the point. Making gentlemen jump out ballroom windows wasn't her only source of pleasure. Tormenting the young of any gender fell into the same category. Young being interpreted as anyone between the ages of five and fifty.

"If it isn't little Theresa Ballinger! I thought we'd seen the last of that girl. Good riddance, too."

"Who was she?" asked Pen, leaning over the duchess's shoulder.

"She was the reigning beauty of 1790—the men were all mad for her. Men!" snorted the duchess. "Sheep, the lot of them. *I* never liked her."

Henrietta had always known the Dowager Duchess to be a woman of discernment and extreme good sense.

"She married a frog—a titled one."

"A frog prince?" Henrietta wasn't able to resist.

"A frog marquis," corrected the duchess. "Not that she would have turned down a prince if she could have gotten one. That girl always had an eye for the main chance. I wonder what she's doing back in London?"

The other outraged onlookers viewing Miles's little flirtation had no doubts on that score. It was altogether too clear what the beautiful Marquise de Montval was doing in London—snaring a viscount. Viscounts being a rare commodity, her progress was regarded with more than a little distress by a sizable portion of the ballroom.

"She had a husband already!" one girl complained huffily to her mother. "And he was a marquis! It's not fair!"

"There, there, dear," clucked her mother, glowering in the direction of Miles and the marquise. "Mummy will find you another viscount. There's that nice Pinchingdale-Snipe boy. . . ."

Their consternation was all for naught. Miles wasn't interested.

Well, he wasn't entirely uninterested—he was male, after all, and between mistresses at the moment, and that was quite a respectable expanse of bosom being presented for his delectation. He just wasn't interested enough. The offer was flattering, but there was an old adage about not fouling one's own nest. If he was going to dally, it wouldn't be among the *ton*.

So instead of tipping his head towards the nearest exit, Miles took the gloved hand that was offered him and tilted his torso in an elegant bow. Just for good measure, just so she wouldn't feel like all her wiles had been wasted, he turned her hand over and pressed a kiss to her gloved palm. It was a gesture he had picked up years ago from an elderly Italian fellow named Giacomo Casanova. It never failed to please.

"Madam, it has been a pleasure."

"Not the last of its kind, I hope."

"Aren't the best pleasures unexpected ones?" Miles prevaricated. It struck him as a rather clever way of avoiding setting up an assignation.

"Sometimes anticipation can be as pleasant as surprise," countered the marquise. She closed her fan with a meaningful snap. "I ride in the park tomorrow at five. Perhaps our paths will cross."

"Perhaps." Miles's smile was as meaningful—and as meaningless—as hers. Since everybody rode in the park at five, the odds of their encountering each other were high, the odds of it being deliberate less so.

It had occurred to him that as the widow of a French marquis, she might be of some use in exploring the possibility of a spy lurking among the French émigré community, but she had mentioned, in the course of their brief, if innuendo-laden, conversation that she had returned from France two years previous, and spent the intervening time living quietly in Yorkshire in the first flush of mourning for her husband. Miles had better-informed contacts in the émigré community—even if less attractive ones. Besides, his best point of departure on this assignment still seemed to be the agent's employer, Lord Vaughn.

The object of Miles's speculation was, at that very moment, moving in the direction of the group of young ladies clustered around the formidable Dowager Duchess of Dovedale.

Henrietta regarded the newcomer with interest. He wasn't precisely tall—not as Miles was tall, at any rate—but his lithe frame gave the impression of height. Unlike the more adventurous of the *ton*'s young blades, who had decked themselves out in colors ranging from Nile green (as unfortunate to the complexion as it had been to Bonaparte's ambitions) to a particularly virulent shade of puce, the gentleman approaching was dressed in a combination of black and silver, like midnight shot through with moonlight. His hair carried out the theme, a few silver strands frosting rather than disguising the original black. Henrietta wouldn't have been surprised if he had silvered them intentionally, just to match his waistcoat; the confluence of colors was too perfect to be anything but planned. In one hand he carried a silver-headed cane. It was clearly intended for show, rather than use; despite the slight lacing of silver in his hair, he moved with a courtier's sinuous stride.

He looked, thought Henrietta, rather as she had imagined Prospero. Not Prospero in his island wilderness, but Prospero in all the decadence of Milan in his days of power—elegant, unreachable, and more than a little bit dangerous.

As he approached, clearly intent on joining their party, Henrietta noticed the silver serpent that slithered along the body of the cane, its fanged head constituting the handle. It was an ebony cane, of course. Henrietta had no doubt that, as he drew closer, the silver squiggles on his waistcoat would also resolve themselves into the twining, writhing bodies of snakes.

Silver serpents, for goodness' sake! Henrietta bit her lip on an impertinent chuckle. That was taking trying to look wicked and mysterious just a little too far. The mysterious verged so easily onto the ridiculous.

She controlled the impulse to laugh just in time; Prospero had reached them, and stood smiling before the duchess, one leg slightly bent, like an actor about to declaim.

"Vaughn, you old rogue!" exclaimed the duchess. "Haven't seen you about this age. So you've decided to come back, have you?"

"How could I not, when such beauty awaited me at home? I see that during my long absence, the Three Graces have removed from Olympus to brighten the dreary ballrooms of London."

"And who am I, the Gorgon?" The dowager cocked her powdered head. "I always fancied turning men to stone. Such a useful talent for dull parties."

Lord Vaughn bent over her hand. "You, as always, your grace, are a Siren, born to fright men from their wits."

"As well delivered an insult as I've ever heard! And I've delivered quite a few in my day. You always were a smooth-talking rogue,

Vaughn. But I'll present you to these young chits, anyway." The duchess waved her cane dismissively at Charlotte. "My granddaughter, Lady Charlotte Lansdowne."

Charlotte sank into a dutiful curtsy. Lord Vaughn's quizzing glass passed over Charlotte's bowed blond head without interest.

"Miss Penelope Deveraux." Pen sketched the merest gesture of a curtsy. The quizzing glass rested on Penelope's clean-boned face and flaming hair for a moment, then continued its inexorable sweep onward.

"And Lady Henrietta Selwick."

"Ah, the sister of our gallant adventurer." On Lord Vaughn's lips, the word "gallant" sounded more insult than praise. "His fame has reached even the more remote corners of the Continent."

"I imagine they don't have much else to talk about," Henrietta said tartly, coming up out of her curtsy. "Being quite so remote."

For the first time, Lord Vaughn looked her full in the face, a flicker of interest in his heavy-lidded eyes. He let the quizzing glass dangle and took a step closer.

"Would you teach them more interesting topics, Lady Henrietta?" he asked silkily, in a tone meant to make a lady's heart beat faster and her cheeks flush.

Henrietta's pulse picked up—with annoyance. Having grown up with two rakes-in-residence, namely Richard and Miles, she didn't fluster easily.

"The study of ancient literature is always a worthy pursuit," she suggested demurely.

Vaughn's quizzing glass dipped in the direction of the neckline of Henrietta's gown. "I prefer natural philosophy myself."

"Yes, I can see that." Some internal imp prompted Henrietta to say, "I could tell just by looking at the adorable serpents on your waistcoat, my lord."

Lord Vaughn cocked an eyebrow. "Adorable?"

"Um . . . yes." Blast that internal imp. It always got her into trouble. Henrietta cast about for a suitable response. "They're so . . . slitheringly sinuous."

"Perhaps your taste in waistcoats runs more to flowers?" he suggested smoothly.

Henrietta shook her head. Since she had gotten herself into this ridiculous conversation, she decided she might as well go on with it. "No, they're too insipid. What a waistcoat needs is a nice mythical beast. I'm particularly partial to gryphons."

"How unusual." Lord Vaughn eyed her with a slightly bemused expression, as though trying to ascertain whether she was exceptionally clever or some sort of entertaining oddity like a parrot who could recite Donne. "What are your sentiments regarding dragons?"

Henrietta cast a pointed look in the direction of the Dowager Duchess of Dovedale. "I'm quite fond of some of them."

"If your fondness extends towards the Oriental varieties, I have a modest collection of Chinese dragons in my possession. They would be, I am sure, quite different from any you have seen."

"I will admit my experience with dragons has been limited, my lord," Henrietta hedged warily. Over Lord Vaughn's shoulder, she could see her mother bearing purposefully across the room, looking uncommonly irked. "One encounters so few. They are nearly as elusive as unicorns."

"Or the Pink Carnation?" suggested Lord Vaughn lightly. "I'm giving a masked ball at my home in two days' time. If you would grace the event with your presence, I would be more than pleased to make you known to my dragons."

"I hope they're not in the habit of eating tender young maidens," Henrietta quipped, hoping to direct the subject back to the general and inconsequential, and away from her putative attendance at Lord Vaughn's masquerade. "I hear dragons have a tendency to do that."

"My dear young lady"—Lord Vaughn's long-fingered hand stroked the serpentine head of his cane—"I can give you my best assurance that—"

"Hello!" Miles rudely burst in on the conversation. "Do hope I'm not interrupting. Hen, your lemonade."

"Thank you." Henrietta greeted Miles with some relief and peered dubiously into her cup, which contained about half an inch of yellow liquid. The rest, judging from the stickiness under Henrietta's fingers, had evidently sloshed over the sides during Miles's enthusiastic progress from the refreshment table. "Lord Vaughn, do you know Mr. Dorrington?"

"Vaughn, did you say?" Miles perked up inexplicably; then his face relaxed into a big grin. "Vaughn, old chap!" Miles pounded Lord Vaughn on the back. "Care for a hand of cards?"

Henrietta hadn't known that Miles was acquainted with Lord Vaughn. Clearly, neither had Lord Vaughn, who was regarding Miles as though he were a strange stick insect who had crawled out of his ratafia.

"Cards," he repeated delicately.

"Excellent!" enthused Miles. "Nothing like a good game of cards, eh, Vaughn? Why don't you tell me about your travels on the Continent . . . ?" Taking the earl by the arm, he propelled him in the direction of the card room, passing Lady Uppington on the way.

"That was well done of Miles," commented Lady Uppington with approval. "Your father would have done the same."

"Well done?" repeated Henrietta incredulously. "He all but kidnapped the man."

"He did just as he should. Lord Vaughn," pronounced Lady Uppington, in her best "I am your mama and therefore know everything" voice, "is a rake."

"Isn't Miles?" countered Henrietta, remembering several tales she wasn't supposed to have heard.

Lady Uppington smiled fondly at her daughter. "No, darling. Miles is a dear make-believe rake. Lord Vaughn," she added disapprovingly, "is the real thing."

"He is an earl," teased Henrietta.

"Darling, if I ever turn into one of those sorts of mothers, you have my permission to elope with the first bounder who comes your way. Provided he's a good-hearted sort of bounder," Lady Uppington added as an afterthought. "Not that I wouldn't mind your marrying an earl, but the most important thing is that you find—"

"I know," Henrietta broke in, in her best wearisome-youngest-child voice, "someone who loves me."

"Whoever said anything about love?" countered Lady Uppington, herself the rare possessor of one of the *ton*'s few love matches, a marriage so sickeningly happy that it had led to decades of raised eyebrows and envious stares. "No, darling, what you want to look for is a good leg."

"Mother!"

"So easy to shock," murmured Lady Uppington, before saying seriously, "Be on your guard around Vaughn. There are stories. . . ." Lady Uppington stared in the direction of the card room, a distinct furrow appearing between her elegantly arched brows.

"Stories?" prompted Henrietta.

"They're not appropriate for your ears."

"Oh, but assessing a gentleman's legs is?" muttered Henrietta.

Lady Uppington pursed her lips. "I don't know what I did to deserve such impertinent children. You're as bad as your brothers. Brother," she corrected herself, since everyone knew Charles was a model of decorum. "But just this once, Henrietta Anne Selwick, I want you to listen to me without an argument."

"But, Mother—"

"Miles won't always be around to extricate you from awkward situations."

Henrietta opened her mouth to make a snide comment about that being Miles's one purpose in life. Lady Uppington cut her off with one raised hand.

"Take your wise old mother's advice, and stay well away from Lord Vaughn. He is *not* a suitable suitor. Now, aren't you supposed to be dancing with someone?"

"Bleargh," said Henrietta.

Chapter Seven

———— ❦ ————

Cards, Game of: *a battle of wits waged against an inscrutable agent of the Ministry of Police. See also under* Hazard

—from the Personal Codebook of the Pink Carnation

"What say you, Vaughn? Care for another hand?" Miles fanned the deck of cards out temptingly on the tabletop.

He still couldn't quite believe his luck in stumbling across Vaughn at Almack's, of all places. Clearly, someone somewhere was smiling on his efforts. Had Vaughn not been speaking to Henrietta at just that moment . . .

He would have tracked Vaughn down eventually, anyway. It just would have taken longer. Miles had evolved, over the course of the afternoon, a very logical plan of action for stalking Vaughn, involving finding out which clubs the older man belonged to, at which hours he tended to frequent them, and where he might be best waylaid. This was much easier.

The only problem was, none of Miles's probing questions had obtained the slightest result. Miles had tried commenting casually on the difficulty of finding good footmen nowadays. Lord Vaughn had shrugged. "My man of business takes care of that for me."

No "Dash it all, they're always dying on me!" No "Funny thing, one of my footmen just happened to snuff it this morning." One might expect some reaction—incredulity, annoyance, distress—from an innocent employer whose footman had recently been murdered. There hadn't been any sudden guilty start or any shifting of eyes, either, but Miles found the absence of reaction just as suspicious as Vaughn's failure to mention the incident.

References to the gallant exploits of our flowery friends, the difficulty of traveling on the Continent in this time of troubles, and the shocking rise of crime in the metropolis (especially murder) over the past few weeks had elicited equally little more than polite murmurs. In fact, the only topic in which Lord Vaughn showed the slighted interest was the Selwick family. Lord Vaughn had asked several questions about the Selwicks. Miles, in his role of tiresome young man, had bombarded him with inconsequentialities, like the color of Richard's curricle, and the fact that the Selwicks' cook made exceptionally good ginger biscuits, none of which seemed to be quite what Vaughn was looking for.

Suspicious, decided Miles. Highly suspicious.

Unfortunately, he had nothing to confirm his suspicions. Almack's, alas, was not ideally suited to spying. There was no strong liquor with which to coax Lord Vaughn into a state of gregarious inebriation, and the stakes allowed in the card room were too low for Miles to contrive to lose enough that Miles would have to give Vaughn his vowels (thus cleverly necessitating a visit to Vaughn's house). So far, Miles had lost precisely two shillings and sixpence. There could be no hope of convincing Lord Vaughn that he didn't have the blunt.

"Another hand?" Miles repeated.

"I think not." Lord Vaughn pushed back his chair, adding dryly, "I shall have to forgo that pleasure."

If Miles hadn't been so sure that the man was a deadly French spy, he would have almost been sorry for him about then. But since the man was quite likely a deadly French spy, Miles had no compunction whatsoever about being as annoying as possible, in a performance based on Turnip Fitzhugh at his less endearing moments.

"Oh, are you going to your club? I could—"

"Good *night,* Dorrington."

Miles bit down on an entirely inappropriate urge to smile, and tried to look suitably rebuffed. "Ah, well," he said, subsiding into his chair with what he hoped was a mournful air. "Some other time."

The cane beat a staccato retreat. Miles waited until the echoes had faded and then, cautiously, rose from the table. He peered out the door of the card room. Vaughn was making a leg to Lady Jersey, Lady Jersey was shaking her finger at him, and . . . Lord Vaughn was exiting the ballroom.

Miles followed.

He followed at a suitable distance, making sure to keep hidden within the doorframe as Vaughn climbed into his sedan chair. It was a large chair, and as elegant as everything else about Vaughn. The walls were covered with black lacquer chased in silver that shimmered in the torchlight. Two liveried bearers held the poles at either end.

Most likely Vaughn was just going home, or to his club (Miles didn't take his disclaimer a moment before as reliable; hell, if he'd been Vaughn, he'd have lied, just to get rid of him), or to a bawdy house, or anyplace else one might conceivably go of an evening for purposes that had nothing whatsoever to do with espionage.

But what if he wasn't?

It didn't hurt to follow him. Just in case.

Miles hurried over to a line of sedan chairs for hire sitting in a row on the opposite side of the street. They did a brisk business, since so many areas of London were unsafe to walk after dark, with streets too narrow for even the skinniest of phaetons, much less a regular carriage. The chairmen were chatting desultorily as they waited for custom—recounting the gorier details of yesterday's cockfight, from what Miles could hear.

Miles didn't wait to hear which bird had won. He strode up to the sturdiest-looking of the chairs, a battered box that had once been painted white but was begrimed to gray, and cleared his throat loudly enough to cause a gale in Northumberland. Two men reluctantly detached themselves from the mob of bird-baiters, and came forward.

"You want a ride, gov'ner?"

Vaughn's chair was swaying around a corner. In a moment, it would be out of sight. Miles climbed hastily between the poles, folding his large frame into the small chair.

"Follow that chair!"

"That'll be extra if you want me to run," the bearer in front informed him laconically.

Miles plunked a half crown into his hand. "Go!"

The chairman jerked a finger towards his colleague in the back. "And for me friend."

"If," Miles clipped out, "you get me there on time and unseen, I will give you both double that. Now *go!*"

The chairmen lifted him and went. Over the chairman's shoulder, Miles thought he could just barely make out a corner of Vaughn's chair as it tilted around a corner, but it was too hard to see. Miles leaned to the side, causing the chair to sway perilously, and earning a muttered epithet from the chairman in back, who grappled with the poles to keep the chair upright.

Miles settled back down into the center of the seat, staring fixedly at the chairman's shoulder blades. It really wasn't much of a view.

Deciding that they were far enough behind that Vaughn's men wouldn't notice, Miles lifted the hinged roof of the sedan chair and peered over the top. Vaughn's chair was so far ahead that he could just make out the glint of the linkboy's lantern, bobbing up and down before Vaughn's chair like a will-o'-the-wisp in the darkness.

Wherever it was going, Vaughn's chair was taking the most circuitous route possible. Miles's bearers twisted down narrow alleys where the houses leaned drunkenly towards one another, past riotous taverns and quiet churches, around abrupt corners, and through busy thoroughfares. For the most part, Vaughn's bearers chose the less traveled paths, back alleys where the tops of the chairs jostled against lines of laundry and the chairmen had to slow to keep from slipping in the refuse that fouled the ground. They slowed, but they did not falter, picking up the pace to something near a run whenever the terrain permitted.

Miles tried to rein in his rising excitement. Vaughn might just be eager to meet a mistress . . . but what man kept a mistress in this part of town? Although the streets were unfamiliar to Miles, his internal compass was spinning merrily away, and had landed unerringly on southeast; they were heading, in their roundabout way, away from Mayfair, away from Piccadilly, towards the river and the more rough-and-tumble areas to the east. Clearly, they were not making for Vaughn's townhouse in Belliston Square.

On a street of shuttered shops and seedy taverns, Vaughn's chair began to slow. His chairmen obediently trotted around a corner, and paused in front of an alehouse whose sign creaked idly in the evening breeze.

Miles jabbed the chairman between the shoulder blades. "Stop here!"

The chairman skidded to a rib-crushing halt just before the turn. At least, Miles's ribs felt like they had been crushed. They had whacked right into the chairman's head. Wheezing, Miles vaulted out of the chair, clapped some coins into the chairman's hand without stopping to count them, and flattened himself against the corner of the building.

Miles watched as Vaughn waved away the hand offered him by one of his bearers, and climbed out of his chair. At least, Miles assumed it was Vaughn. The figure who emerged from the chair was entirely swathed in a large black cloak. Only the serpent-headed cane marked the phantom figure as the same man whose footsteps Miles had dogged. Pausing to arrange something with his chairmen—most likely the time at which he wished to be collected, as the neighborhood was not one in which a gentleman would wish to go on foot—Vaughn disappeared into the tavern.

Miles squinted at the faded sign above the door. Depicted below a ducal coronet were a pair of broad-topped boots of the type worn by the cavaliers of a century ago. Miles could just barely make out the faded legend. THE DUKE'S KNEES.

The entire place had a seedy aspect, an air of long decay compounded by drooping shutters and peeling paint. Despite its run-down aspect, it seemed popular enough. A trio of men, swaying together in song, had just staggered out the door, unleashing a hint of the hubbub within—and a strong reek of spilled ale—before the door teetered closed again.

As an afterthought, Miles leaned down and unclipped the jeweled buckles from his shoes, slipping them into his waistcoat pocket. In this neighborhood, they shone like a beacon, if not to his quarry, then to the thieves and footpads who waited to prey on inebriated gentlemen after dark. If Miles could have also stripped himself of his white silk stockings and knee breeches, he would have, but somehow, he thought he'd arouse more attention striding in there buck-naked than he would clad as though for a court audience.

What he needed was a cloak, one of those big, all-enveloping sorts that Vaughn had been sporting. Damn! Keeping to the shadows, Miles cursed himself for not having thought of it. Of course, he hadn't realized that he was going to be playing the intrepid spy tonight as well as the bored escort; had he known, he would have dressed accordingly. Not in black—since no one wore unrelieved black except spies and parsons, and Miles had no desire to be taken for either—but various dull shades of brown that would blend into the scenery and render him eminently unremarkable.

As luck would have it, there was a brown cloak of exactly the type required walking Miles's way. Unfortunately, it was attached to a very large individual, with a crooked nose and scars on his face that proclaimed he wouldn't look amiss at a brawl. There was a female creature in dirty flowered cotton and tattered lace clinging to his arm—secondhand goods by the look of them, both the clothing and the woman.

Miles stepped out in front of the pair. "Hello," he said, with a winning smile. "I'd like to purchase your cloak."

"My cloak?" The man looked like he'd sooner punch him than negotiate with him. "What do you want with me cloak?"

"It's chilly, don't you think?" Miles improvised. He rubbed his arms and feigned a shudder. "Brrrrrr!"

"Awww, gi' it to 'im, Freddy," cooed the little doxy, hanging on his arm like a squirrel off the branch of a tree. "I'll keep ye warm."

"A charming sentiment," Miles applauded. "And now for the price . . ."

The mention of money had its desired effect. Miles walked away several shillings the poorer, proud possessor of a smelly piece of brown wool. A voluminous, hooded, smelly piece of brown wool. Never again would he leave home without one, he vowed.

No time to muse on the functionality of cloaks. He had wasted too much time already. How long had Vaughn been in there? Swirling the cloak about him, Miles strode rapidly towards the Duke's Knees. Miles gingerly pushed open the door, which lolled drunkenly off its frame, held in place by a makeshift hinge at the top. From the splintering in the wood of the frame, it looked like the door had been broken off its hinges, and more than once. Charming clientele this place boasted.

Holding his cloak close about him to hide his telltale white stockings and knee breeches, Miles kept his back hunched and his head low. The taproom was full. Uncertain light wavered over the proceedings from the hearth in the left-hand wall and the battered pewter sconces on the wall. A gang of rowdies in rough shirts and unkempt hair was playing a complicated game with a knife in one corner of the room, the object of which seemed to be not getting one's fingers sliced off.

Miles could safely say Vaughn was not of their company.

In another corner, men were dicing, flinging ivory cubes from a battered tin container. A busty barmaid squirmed on the lap of a red-nosed patron, slapping at his hands and squealing protests with more form than force. Definitely not Vaughn. A steep flight of stairs in one corner led out of the taproom, to private rooms upstairs, no doubt, the sort of rooms designed for clandestine meetings of the amorous kind. Or of the treasonous kind.

Miles started towards the stairs. But there was another corner of the room left. His eyes had initially skirted over it because the little nook sat entirely in shadow, too far from the hearth for any light to reach. The candle on the wall had gone out—or been blown out, by someone aiming to discourage prying eyes.

Tucked away behind the curve of the bar, wedged in the far right-hand corner, there was room for just one small table. At that table were seated two men.

Vaughn. There could be no question. Although the hood was pulled down as far as it would go, covering his forehead and shadowing his eyes, there was no mistaking that aquiline nose, or the elegant aesthete's hands that sat so incongruously on the scarred wood of the table. Those were not the hands of a laborer.

Miles sidled closer, under pretext of getting a drink from the bar.

His companion, too, was cloaked and hooded. Hoods, thought Miles with a wry twist of the lips, appeared to be popular this season. The two were seated on a slight diagonal, with Vaughn nearer the bar, slightly turned away from the main room, and the stranger wedged in the crook between the join of the walls. With the second man's face turned out, Miles should have been able to make out his features, but the lack of light transformed his visage into something out of one of the novels Hen was so fond of, a hooded horror with nothing but emptiness where the face ought to have been. Dramatic rubbish, thought Miles, inching nearer.

There was a slightly darker shadow that might have been a mustache. . . . Miles bumped into the corner of the bar, and bit back a startled *oomph*.

Since he was there, Miles seated himself on a stool. He hunched over the bar, yanking his hood farther down over his brow, and proceeded to listen.

"Do you have it with you?" Vaughn was asking tersely.

"So hasty!" The other man's voice was lightly accented, with a familiar lilt. It might have been French; Miles was too far away to tell, and while the cloak did wonderful things for hiding his features, it had a distinctly annoying tendency to muffle sound. "While we are here, a drink perhaps?"

"What d'ye like?"

The voice was not Vaughn's. It was high-pitched, feminine, and came from a region roughly in the vicinity of Miles's left ear.

"Hunh?" Miles jerked his head around to encounter a truly alarming quantity of flesh overflowing a low-laced bodice.

The barmaid heaved a long-suffering sigh, making the mounds of flesh swell to perilous proportions. "What d'ye like? I ain't got all night. Though for you, sweet'eart"—her voice lowered suggestively, as her bosom lurched an insistent inch closer to Miles's nose, bringing with it an odor of sweat and cheap scent—"I might be persuaded to change me mind."

"Uh . . ." Choking on the reek—that would be something to explain to his friends and relations, asphyxiation by bosom—Miles scooted back as far as the stool would allow. What did they drink in places like this? Not claret, that much he remembered. It had been so long since Miles had explored the seedier side of London.

"Gin," he said decisively, pitching his voice gruff and low, just in case Vaughn was listening. Vaughn seemed quite involved in his own conversation, speaking in a low, authoritative tone, but one never knew. Miles turned his attention back to his quarry, assuming the barmaid would hare herself off to riper regions.

No such luck. The barmaid waved a hand at the barkeep. "Oy, Jim! A glass of blue ruin for our friend 'ere!"

"What was 'at, Molly?" Jim cupped a hand over his ear. "I can't 'ear ye!"

"Blue ruin!" bellowed the barmaid, loud enough to be heard clear across the Thames. "For this 'andsome 'unk of man 'ere."

So much for being inconspicuous.

Miles could only be glad that his back was to Vaughn and his companion. Even if they turned to stare, all they would see would be an expanse of brown wool.

". . . utmost discretion," Vaughn was saying behind him.

"Sooooo"—Molly trailed a hand along Miles's shoulders, her cloying voice in his ear cutting off whatever it was Vaughn was trying to be discreet about—"would ye be fancyin' anythin' else with that drink, sir?"

"Just the gin," Miles mumbled, trying to keep an ear cocked in Vaughn's direction. What had he just said? Something about . . .

Plonk! Miles caught the edge of the bar to keep from tumbling over backwards, right into Vaughn's table, as Molly flung herself down on his lap. "Aw, don't be shy, sir."

"This is very flattering"—Miles attempted a small shove, but Molly wasn't moving—"but I'm not interested."

Damn, damn, damn. The voices behind him had dropped a notch, implying conversation of a highly confidential, and thus highly interesting, nature. And he couldn't make out a word of it. If he could just find some way to move a little closer . . .

"If ye 'ave a problem, like, we can work on it."

"I don't have a problem," Miles gritted out. At least, not that sort of problem. "I have a mistress." Well, he didn't at the moment, actually, but he had had up until last week. The details were unimportant.

Molly removed herself from his lap with an irritated flounce. "Well, 'oity-toity, aren't we? Too good for the likes of us . . ." Her voice receded to a droning buzz in the distance. Miles scarcely noticed. All of his attention was focused on the conversation taking place behind him.

"And the rest?" Vaughn was demanding in a low voice.

Miles risked a glance back, on pretext of leaning over to straighten the hem of his cloak. Vaughn's pose was nonchalant, relaxed, but his knuckles were white on the head of his cane.

"By next week. I assure you, everything will be arranged to your satisfaction."

Vaughn's grip eased. "See that it is."

"Would I betray you?"

"Most likely," Vaughn said grimly.

The hooded figure laughed. "Milord amuses himself."

"Milord," countered Vaughn, "has scarcely been less amused. Let's get on with this, shall we? I do assume you brought it with you?"

"But, of course!" The accented voice rose on a note of wounded dignity. "You think me incompetent, perhaps?"

"Oh, no." Vaughn's voice was laced with irony. "Not that."

"Here." If his companion noticed the implied insult, he ignored it. Miles heard the whisper of fabric, the crackle of paper. "I have it for you."

"Thank you."

Miles turned just in time to see a folded note change hands, disappearing beneath Vaughn's cloak. He hastily reoriented himself to face the bar, as Vaughn levered himself to a standing position, bracing both hands on the small, round table.

"I shall arrange with you through the usual channels regarding next week's . . . installment."

Miles heard the scrape of wood on wood, as the second man stood in his turn. A swishing noise followed, which might have been a bow, or the abstraction of a handkerchief, or just the sweep of Vaughn's cloak against the edge of the table. "I shall not fail you, milord."

"I sincerely doubt that," Vaughn murmured, so softly that Miles, practically back-to-back with him, barely caught the words. "I bid you good night," he said crisply.

Acting on impulse, Miles swung down from his stool just as Vaughn began to move away, jostling the older man.

"Sorry, so sorry, me lord," he grunted in a gruff baritone, in tones that he hoped leaned more towards the dockyard than Oxbridge. He started patting Vaughn's chest with clumsy motions, as though checking for broken limbs. "I'm so sorry. Be yer lordship unhurt?"

"Quite"—Vaughn forcibly removed Miles's hand from his person—"all right, my good man."

"Aye, yer lordship. Thank 'ee, yer lordship." Miles bowed and scraped backwards until he felt his backside hit the bar, taking care to keep his head well around the level of Vaughn's waistcoat. He would have tugged his forelock, but that did seem to be overdoing it a bit. Besides, his hands, like Vaughn's, were too clearly those of a gentleman. He had been taking risk enough in his assault on Vaughn's waistcoat.

But he had achieved exactly what he had sought. Under cover of the hood, Miles permitted himself a small, self-satisfied smirk.

Just to be safe, Miles remained in his groveling position until the click of Vaughn's cane and the scurrying footsteps of his companion had receded across the floor, until the door had swung open and shut, until the sound of Vaughn's voice giving orders to his chairmen could be heard through the open windows.

Then, and only then, did Miles permit himself to rise from his crouch.

It might be wise to give Vaughn and his companion some time to remove themselves from the area (the other man might still be lurking about), so Miles took the glass of gin the affronted barmaid slammed in front of him and, calling for a candle, retreated to the secluded table Vaughn and his companion had just vacated.

He absentmindedly took a gulp of the gin, wincing at the sharp taste of it on his tongue. Nasty stuff. He could understand how a few daily pints of it could turn someone blind.

Miles pushed the glass away, just as Molly, his no-longer-so-friendly barmaid, slapped the requested candle down on the table in front of him. It was the merest stub, stuck to the saucer by its own wax, and from the looks of it, it had only a half hour left in it at best.

Miles didn't care. He didn't intend to be there quite that long.

With a sense of gleeful anticipation, he drew out from under his cloak the folded note he had abstracted from Vaughn's waistcoat pocket. The man hadn't a clue, Miles thought complacently, examining his prize. The paper had been folded into tiny squares, the better to be passed from hand to hand, and, from the looks of it, never sealed. There was no writing on the exposed folds, no name, no direction.

Anonymity was, after all, the hallmark of espionage.

What could it be? Directions, perhaps, mused Miles. Instructions from the Ministry of Police to their trusted spy, conveyed via a recently arrived operative. The other man's accent had sounded as though it might be French.

Nudging the candle closer, Miles slowly unfolded the page and held it up to the uncertain light. His eye caught the word "burn" heavily underscored.

Good God, had he stumbled upon a plan to burn Parliament? It would be just like Guy Fawkes, only without King James I.

Miles moved the note nearer to the candle, so close that the flame lapped dangerously at the edge of the fragile paper. He squinted at the spiky writing, which had been inconsiderately rendered in a pale brown ink.

"I burn for your touch," read the phrase in its entirety.

Damn. That didn't sound like a plan to blow up the houses of Parliament.

Miles returned his attention to the letter. "Every night, I dream of your embrace; I yearn for your voice at the window, and your hands on my—"

No, definitely not a plot to immolate the members of Parliament. Fiery, yes. Treasonous, no.

Miles moved on to the next paragraph, which contained more of the same. It could, he rationalized desperately, be merely a ploy in case the missive fell into the wrong hands. Make it look like a love letter and then slip in the pertinent information somewhere in the middle.

With an expression of great determination, Miles read the letter through from start to end. By the last line, he could safely say that there were no troop movements hidden in there. It might be in code . . . but it would take one perverse mind to come up with a code that detailed, that convincing, that graphic. Some of the descriptions made Cleland's *Fanny Hill*, a favorite piece of contraband among Miles's set at Eton, look positively restrained, even prim. Delaroche's mind was certainly perverse, but it didn't move in those particular channels.

The signature was entirely illegible, a long squiggle that might have been anything from Augusta to Xenophon. As for the salutation . . . well, "Dearest Love" was seldom a proper name.

Oh, hell.

A look of grim disgust spread across his face as he came to an unfortunate but inescapable conclusion. Miles dropped the paper onto the table, resisting the urge to follow it with his head, preferably banged very hard, several times in a row. Of all the idiot things to do! Since smiting himself was out, Miles reached for the gin instead. He had stolen the wrong bloody note.

Chapter Eight

Fashion Papers: *the private files of the former Assistant to the Minister of Police*
— from the Personal Codebook of the Pink Carnation

Midnight shrouded Delaroche's study. Dark lay heavy as dust on desk, cabinet, and chair, on the rough flagstones of the floor, and on the unadorned surface of the walls. The former assistant to the Minister of Police had, himself, departed half an hour before, closing his cabinets and realigning his chair in the cavity of his desk with mathematical precision. All was still in the office of the tenth-most-feared man in France.

Except for a quiver of movement along the far wall.

Like a waterbug skimming the surface at the edge of an algae-ridden lake, so subtly that it barely disturbed the enshrouding darkness, a tiny point of metal inched along the central join of the room's one small window. The sliver of metal encountered the hook that latched the window closed, and paused. Another moment and the metal continued to rise, like mercury in a barometer, carrying the hook with it.

The metal disappeared. The windowpanes, which had not been opened since the early days of the reign of Louis XIII, slid outward with an ease that bespoke hinges newly oiled. The quiet surface of the room rippled as a shadow, darker than the rest, oozed over the windowsill and swung neatly into the room. The windowpanes were, once again, eased closed, and latched for security. A length of cloth made its way from the intruder's shoulders over the uncurtained window. This night's work needed light to proceed, and light might call unwanted attention. A similar, smaller piece of thick-woven black cloth covered the small grille in the door.

Preparations complete, the silent figure drew out a small, shuttered lantern, and gently coaxed the flame into life. There was no fizz, no smoke, no crackle from the wick, just darkness one moment, and a gentle light the next.

The black-clad figure nodded in approval, and followed the subdued light in the direction of Delaroche's desk.

The chair, so carefully arranged a mere half hour before, was lifted gently back, and placed, with equal care, a short distance away, leaving just enough space for the dark figure to kneel under the desk, feeling with long black-gloved fingers along the back wall. A prick of wood, no larger than a splinter, and like Sleeping Beauty falling softly into slumber, a panel of wood slipped back, revealing a cache just large enough to hold one file.

In one fluid movement, the black-garbed intruder backed out from under the desk, rising seamlessly to place the file on Delaroche's pristine blotter. One gloved hand tilted the little lantern closer, providing a steady stream of light as the other hand flipped quickly but steadily through the contents of the file, committing them to memory.

With two pages left to go, the lantern trembled, sending wavy lines of light dancing about the walls. The Pink Carnation quickly steadied the lantern, but her eyes, narrowed in concern, never left the closely written page.

So it had come to this, had it?

In the file, looking as innocent as only a piece of paper can look, sat a draft of Delaroche's latest instructions to the Black Tulip. And there, in the middle of the page, blazed the name "Lady Henrietta Selweecke."

The misspelling, the Pink Carnation knew, provided no hope of misdirection; it was merely an indication of Delaroche's contempt for the English, expressed through a willful misuse of the alphabet. The Black Tulip was, directed Delaroche, to allocate particular attention to Lady Henrietta Selweecke and M. Miles Doreengton, associates both of the perfidious Purple Gentian. Either would be in a position to make use of the former Purple Gentian's resources, his League and his contacts, to bedevil the French Republic. Any methods were acceptable. "Any methods" was heavily underscored.

The Pink Carnation scanned the page, mind working rapidly as her eyes moved across the rat's nest of Delaroche's handwriting, as familiar to her by now as her own.

If she had been of a different temperament, the Pink Carnation might have slammed the file shut or cursed or clasped her hands together to stop them from shaking. Because she was Jane Wooliston, her pale complexion turned a shade paler, her spine became a tad straighter, and her lips thinned.

This wouldn't do at all.

She had—if her messengers had survived the journey—already apprised both Henrietta and the War Office of the presence of the Black Tulip in London. They would have to be warned immediately of this new development. She would send off a letter in code tonight. There was no need to break off contact with Henrietta; Delaroche suspected Henrietta only through her relationship to Richard, not her unusual volume of correspondence with France.

Wasn't that, thought Jane primly, returning the file to its hiding place, just like Delaroche to suspect the right person for all the wrong reasons?

It would have to be stopped. She would not have Henrietta falling into danger. Jane chose not to dwell on that ominous phrase "any methods," or the even darker stories she had gleaned of the Black Tulip's former activities. That wouldn't be of the slightest use to Henrietta or Mr. Dorrington. Jane moved her mind, instead, into more useful channels.

Jane could, of course, create some sort of diversion in France, moving suspicion away from Henrietta and Mr. Dorrington, and necessitating the recall of the Black Tulip to the Continent. But Jane had larger plans brewing, of which immediate action was not a part. It did not in the least serve her purposes for the fanatical former assistant to the Minister of Police to learn that the Pink Carnation remained in France.

Her attention had recently been drawn to the possibility of an Irish rising being organized out of Paris; Delaroche's files confirmed that a meeting was planned between Bonaparte's Minister of War, General Berthier, and Addis Emmet, a representative of the United Irish. The meeting needed to be infiltrated, and French use of Ireland prevented. Then there was the matter of the generals. Disaffected generals, currently in Bonaparte's pocket, but beginning to find Bonaparte overbearing and subservience suffocating. All they needed was a gentle hand urging them in the right direction. Jane had only just begun the series of gentle nudges that might topple them into treason. Having Delaroche's attention directed across the Channel had been an unexpected boon, and one she was not yet prepared to relinquish.

False intelligence could be planted, and brought to Delaroche's attention, intelligence directing the Black Tulip's attention to . . . whom? A suitably vague description, Jane decided. Something that could apply to half a dozen pinks of the *ton,* but would most decidedly not apply to either Henrietta or Mr. Dorrington. Ever since Sir Percy Blakeney's successful masquerade as a fashion-mad fop, the French had been decidedly twitchy about those who professed to immerse themselves in fashion. A few mentions about the cut of waistcoats this season, slipped into "reports" designed to be intercepted, should sufficiently agitate the French intelligence community. Jane had two double agents on her payroll for just this sort of assignment. They came dear, but they were worth every penny.

As a precautionary measure, it was worth pursuing, but it wasn't enough. No agent of the Black Tulip's caliber would allow himself to be put off by such a tepid report. He might set about garnering extra information, but, at best, his attention would be diluted, not diverted.

Jane frowned as she perfectly realigned Delaroche's desk chair.

Removal to the country would be equally futile, in fact, perhaps more dangerous than not. So many accidents could happen in the country. A horse could shy; a shot could go awry; the wrong sort of mushroom could be added to a sauce. No. Henrietta would be safer in town, where the rules of society dictated the presence of a chaperone.

Having neatly assessed and dismissed most of the viable options in her head, Jane Wooliston settled on the only acceptable plan. They would simply have to find the Black Tulip.

It would take Delaroche some time to replace an agent of that skill. Until he managed to do so, Henrietta and Mr. Dorrington would be free from molestation, and Jane could proceed with her master plan. It would all serve very well.

There was nothing for it but to remove the Black Tulip.

Word would be sent to Henrietta and the War Office, labeled for the highest of alerts. Her own men in Paris would be sent to ferret out any scrap of information they could find relating to the identity of the Black Tulip. Fouché's files would have to be looked into.

There was no reason, resolved Jane, that they shouldn't have the Black Tulip enjoying His Majesty's hospitality within the next fortnight. It was all a matter of applying oneself logically to the problem.

A furrow appeared between Jane's pale brows. It could all be quite simple—if only the Black Tulip didn't make his move first.

Jane squelched worry as neatly as she had rifled through Delaroche's files. Her courier could be in London by the day after next. Within the next thirty-six hours, Henrietta would be warned, and, Jane hoped, modify her behavior accordingly. There were only the next thirty-six hours to be got through, and, surely, a spy so newly arrived in London would wish to survey the field before resorting to darker methods.

Having arranged the matter to her satisfaction, the Pink Carnation shuttered her lantern. She retrieved her cloak from the window and her scrap of cloth from the door. She oozed out into the night as silently as she had come, leaving Delaroche's office once again swathed in slumber, exactly as he had left it.

Chapter Nine

———— ♥ ————

Jealousy: emotional warfare waged by an agent particularly cunning in the ways of human nature; an attempt to prey on the sentiments and derail one from one's mission
—from the Personal Codebook of the Pink Carnation

"Hen!" exclaimed Penelope in annoyance. "You aren't paying attention!"

"What?" asked Henrietta vaguely, looking up from the amber swirls in her teacup.

Penelope scowled. "I just asked you if you wanted arsenic in your tea, and you said, 'Yes, two, please.'"

"Oh. Sorry." Henrietta put her teacup down on the inlaid wood of her favorite table in the morning room, and smiled apologetically at her oldest friend. "I was thinking of something else."

Penelope rolled her eyes. "That much was obvious."

Henrietta succumbed to the urge to direct yet another glance at the dainty china clock on the mantelpiece. It was nearly noon. And Miles hadn't stopped by yet. Miles always stopped by on Thursday mornings. Every Thursday, Cook made ginger biscuits, for which Miles held a regard tantamount to that of Petrarch for his Laura. For Miles not to appear on a Thursday morning was tantamount to the bells of St. Paul's refusing to chime. It just didn't happen.

Unless Miles was otherwise occupied. In the arms of a dark-haired beauty, for example.

It wasn't like Miles to disappear from Almack's without stopping by to say good-bye. And yet he had done just that. Usually, he left with the Uppingtons, riding with them as far as his lodgings on Jermyn Street, and taking his leave with a joke and a tug of one of her curls. Henrietta found the latter habit decidedly less than endearing and had remonstrated with Miles about it on several occasions. But without him there . . . the evening felt oddly incomplete.

That Woman had disappeared around the same time.

Coincidence? Henrietta deeply doubted it.

Not that it mattered one way or another. Miles was a grown man, and it wasn't as though he hadn't had mistresses before; Henrietta wasn't *that* naïve. It was simply, Henrietta rationalized, that it would be very tedious if Miles took up with someone nasty. After all, with Richard away in Sussex, and Geoff hideously preoccupied with that vile Mary Alsworthy, Miles was her primary source of lemonade and banter at the nightly social events deemed de rigueur by the *ton*. If he started dancing attendance on some cold-eyed temptress, it would just be inconvenient—that was all. There was certainly nothing more to it than that.

"Oh, Pen!" Charlotte's cry broke into Henrietta's reverie. Charlotte's large gray eyes grew three sizes larger. "You weren't out on the balcony with Reggie Fitzhugh?"

"Oh, Charlotte!" mocked Penelope, adding with a wicked twinkle in her eye, "He does have ten thousand pounds a year. Surely you can't disapprove of that."

"And the mental capacity of a turnip," put in Henrietta dryly, allowing herself to be diverted from her decidedly less-than-pleasing speculations.

Charlotte giggled. "I suppose all that gold does rather gild the turnip."

Penelope eyed her askance. "Gild the *turnip?*"

"You know, like gilding the lily. Only he's a turnip."

Henrietta shook her head to clear it of unfortunate images, and looked pointedly at Penelope. "Back to the matter at hand . . ."

"Don't fuss, Hen. What's the worst that could have happened?"

"Disgrace?" suggested Charlotte.

"Marriage to Mr. Fitzhugh," warned Henrietta.

"Ugh," said Penelope.

"Exactly," said Henrietta crisply.

Henrietta was about to drive the point home, when she was distracted by the sound of booted footsteps in the doorway. Jerking her chair around, she saw the object of her earlier speculations leaning winningly against the doorjamb. He had clearly made the kitchen his first stop; he held one of Cook's ginger biscuits in either hand and was alternating taking bites from both.

"Good morning, ladies," he pronounced with a winning smile, only slightly marred by bulging cheeks.

"You do know Richard doesn't live here anymore?" snapped Penelope.

Henrietta waved a languid hand. "Oh, that doesn't make the slightest difference to Miles. He just comes here . . ."

". . . for the meals," Miles obligingly finished for her, swallowing a final mouthful of ginger biscuit.

Henrietta cocked her head. "You're in good spirits this morning."

"How could I not be, with three such pulchritudinous ladies arrayed before me?" Miles swept an elaborate bow.

Charlotte blushed.

Penelope snorted.

Henrietta narrowed her hazel eyes suspiciously. "Last night it was 'Run along, children; I'm flirting.'"

Miles clasped his hands behind his back and gazed up at the elaborate plasterwork of the ceiling. "I don't know what you're talking about."

"You have a new mistress?" Henrietta fished.

"Hen!" Charlotte exclaimed.

Miles wagged a finger, and pronounced, "You aren't supposed to know of such things."

Henrietta noticed that he didn't deny the allegation. "Don't you mean 'such women'?"

"Such states of affairs," Miles corrected loftily.

"Affairs are precisely what I was referring to," Henrietta said, rather more sharply than she had intended.

"Richard," Miles said ominously, "tells you altogether too much."

"If you knew half of what was whispered in the ladies' retiring room, your ears would fall off in shock."

"Might be an improvement," muttered Penelope.

"I don't think ears fall off just like that," put in Charlotte thoughtfully.

"Whose ears are falling off?" inquired Lady Uppington, sweeping into the morning room in a rustle of emerald silk.

"Miles's," said Penelope pointedly.

"Not before this evening, I hope. You will be coming with us to the Middlethorpes' ball tonight?"

"Uh . . ."

"Good. We'll call for you at those dreadful bachelor lodgings of yours at ten o'clock. That's ten o'clock, mind you. Not five to eleven."

"I had a problem with my cravat," protested Miles defensively.

Lady Uppington emitted one of her infamous harrumphs. "Don't think I don't know your tricks by now, young man."

Henrietta smothered a chuckle.

She failed to smother it well enough. Lady Uppington's shrewd green eyes lighted on her daughter. "Henrietta, darling, the lime green silk, I think, for tonight. I've just heard that Percy Ponsonby will be there—"

"I don't like Percy Ponsonby."

"—with Martin Frobisher."

"And Martin Frobisher doesn't like me."

"Don't be silly, darling. Everyone likes you."

"No, he really doesn't like me."

"She spilled ratafia all over his new coat last week," explained Pen, exchanging an amused glance with Henrietta. "It was completely ruined," she added with relish.

"Pure sacrilege, ruining a coat by Weston," muttered Miles.

"He said things no gentleman should say." Charlotte rose to her friend's defense.

"What did he say?" Miles asked darkly.

"Nothing like that!" snapped Henrietta. "He just made a suggestion regarding the balcony and placed his hand somewhere where his hand was not supposed to be."

"If he tries it again—" began Miles, just as Lady Uppington said frowningly, "When I see his mother at the Middlethorpes' tonight . . ."

"Oh, no," Henrietta groaned. "This is just why I didn't tell you. Mama, please don't speak to his mother about it. It would be too humiliating. And you"—she pointed at Miles—"whatever you were thinking about doing, just don't. I'm *fine*."

"Unlike Martin Frobisher's coat," giggled Penelope.

"Shhhh!" Charlotte tried to kick Penelope but hit the claw foot of Penelope's chair instead, subsiding back into her own chair with a little cry of pain.

"Didn't you have shopping to do before tonight?" asked Henrietta pointedly of her former best friends, casting them an "I am never telling you anything ever again" look.

"Oh, goodness!" Lady Uppington clapped her hands together. "Charlotte, I promised your grandmother I would deliver you both to the modiste by noon. Come along now—chop-chop. No dawdling, Penelope."

"I'll stay home," interjected Henrietta. "I have some letters to write." Or at least, she could find some letters to write. To someone. She just didn't feel like picking over ribbons and squealing over flounces this morning. A nice gloomy, horrid novel would be just the thing.

Lady Uppington cast Henrietta a sharp look, but her maternal eye failed to note any flush of fever, so she hustled Penelope and Charlotte out of the room in a flurry of flounces and rustle of petticoats, issuing orders all the while.

"Don't forget, Miles! Ten o'clock!"

Miles wandered out into the hallway. "How does she do that?"

"Black magic," replied Henrietta frankly, rising from the settee to join him just outside the morning room. "Eye of newt and toe of frog, with just a dash of essence of hedgehog."

"I heard that!" came Lady Uppington's voice from the other end of the hall.

"That also explains," added Henrietta confidentially, "her exceptionally good hearing." The front door clicked shut, cutting off the cacophony of female voices. Henrietta cocked her head to look up at Miles. "I need a favor of you."

Miles casually rested a hand against the wall above Henrietta's head. "I'm listening."

They had stood that way a hundred times before—Miles liked leaning on things and against things and over things—but for the first time, Henrietta felt uncomfortable. Crowded. She was acutely aware of the stretch of Miles's arm next to her head, the muscles outlined against the well-tailored sleeve of his jacket. The warm, distinctly Miles scents of sandalwood and leather filled the space between them. He was so near that she could see the minuscule blond hairs on the underside of his chin, so near that to sway even slightly forward would bring her into his embrace.

Embrace and Miles were not concepts that went together; Henrietta found the thought distinctly unsettling.

So she did what any mature, poised young lady would do in such a situation. She poked him in the chest. "Do stop looming."

"Ouch!" Miles jumped back. "Don't I loom well?"

Henrietta moved quickly away from the wall. "Yes, splendidly, but it's very frustrating trying to carry on a conversation with the bottom of your chin. Valet nicked you shaving, did he?"

Miles's hand went protectively to the bottom of his chin.

She felt much better standing three feet away, with the black-and-white checks of tiled floor separating them. Much more like herself.

"About that favor . . . ," she began.

Miles's eyes narrowed. "What sort of favor do you have in mind?"

Henrietta shook her head in exasperation. "Nothing as onerous as all that."

" 'Onerous,' " Miles said darkly, rubbing his abused waistcoat, "is a highly relative term."

"Will you dance with Charlotte tonight?"

"Why?" asked Miles suspiciously.

"What sort of nefarious ulterior motive could I possibly have?" Miles cocked an eyebrow.

"You don't think . . . I'm not trying to matchmake!" Henrietta was surprised by the vehemence of her own reaction. "You're not Charlotte's type at all."

"Well, that's reassuring," muttered Miles. "I think."

"Oh, for goodness' sake," sighed Henrietta. "Charlotte was very cast down at Almack's last night because no one—except the most obvious fortune hunters—asked her to dance. She didn't say anything, but I could tell. It's been like that all Season."

"She's very quiet," Miles said, attempting to exonerate his sex.

"That doesn't mean she doesn't have feelings," countered Henrietta. "It's very lowering for her having to spend the evening standing next to her grandmother."

"If I had to spend the evening standing next to her grandmother, I'd be low, too. The woman is a menace to society."

Henrietta looked at Miles expectantly. "Well?"

"Tell her to save me the first quadrille."

"You really are a dear." Henrietta beamed, standing on tiptoe to press a quick kiss to Miles's cheek. His skin was warm beneath her lips, and surprisingly soft. If he turned his head just a little bit to the right . . .

Henrietta clunked back down onto her heels with such celerity that she staggered.

"I know," Miles said smugly.

"Toad," countered Henrietta, wrapping the insult around herself like an old and beloved blanket.

"Come for a drive with me this afternoon?" Miles asked.

Henrietta shook her head regretfully. "I can't. My new voice teacher is coming at five."

"New voice teacher?" Miles strolled with Henrietta in the direction of the door. "What happened to Signor Antonio?"

An elusive dimple appeared in Henrietta's right cheek. "He and Cook had an artistic disagreement."

"An artistic disagreement?"

"Signor Antonio thought that a true artiste didn't need permission to help himself to Cook's biscuits. Cook disagreed." Henrietta glanced up at Miles. "Cook, as you know, has a formidable way with the rolling pin."

"Not with me," said Miles smugly.

"Braggart."

Miles stepped aside as a footman trotted forward to open the front door for him. "Jealousy does not become you, my dear."

Henrietta skidded to a stop just before the open door. "Who said I was jealous?"

"Don't try to hide it," Miles said knowingly. Too knowingly. "You know Cook likes me best."

"Oh. Right. Cook." Hen took a deep breath. "Of course."

"Are you all right, Hen? You seem a bit flustered."

Henrietta mustered up a smile. "Fine. Perfectly. Just a little . . . um, well . . ."

Miles clapped his hat on his head. "See you tonight, then! Tell Cook I adore her."

The door slammed shut behind him. Henrietta stood there, in the marble foyer, staring at the inside of the door. She stood there so long that the footman shifted uncomfortably and asked if she wished him to open the door again. Henrietta shook her head, not altogether sure what he had asked, because her mind was somewhere else entirely, finishing that last sentence. She wasn't sure she liked the result. In fact, she was quite sure she didn't.

Just a little . . . jealous?

Chapter Ten

———— ❦ ————

Poetry, Romantic: *a detailed report provided by an agent of the War Office*

———from the Personal Codebook of the Pink Carnation

Miles bounded cheerfully down the front steps of Uppington House. His cheek still tingled where Henrietta's lips had pressed against it, and Miles lifted a hand to rub absently at the spot. The scent of her toilet water—some flower or another, Miles never could keep them straight—tickled his nostrils. It smelled nice. Like Henrietta. Settling his hat more firmly on his head, Miles pushed the thought aside and contemplated the sun-dappled street. Just past noon, and the rest of the day still ahead of him.

It was, considered Miles complacently, shaping up to be an exceptionally fine day. Downey had manipulated his cravat into a Waterfall after only three ruined squares of linen; Cook's ginger biscuits were, as always, the epitome of gingery goodness; there were rumors of a new soprano at Haymarket (Miles being, at the moment, lamentably between mistresses); and he had a spy to catch.

Shaking a floppy lock of blond hair out of his eyes, Miles looked back at Uppington House with a smile. Even now that he had London lodgings of his own, it still felt more like home to him than anyplace else in the world.

The first time he had ever gone up that shallow flight of steps, he had been a terrified eight-year-old with nowhere to go for Christmas. His parents had been on the Continent, his old nurse had been called away to take care of her ailing sister, and Miles had been left at loose ends until Richard suggested he accompany him home.

Richard took his friend by the collar and tugged him forward. "I've brought Dorrington home," he announced helpfully.

Lady Uppington, with fewer gray hairs, but just as imperious a disposition, bustled forward. "Does Dorrington's family know he's here?" she asked.

This consideration had, indeed, eluded both Richard and Miles. Richard considered a moment. "No."

Her worst fears about her son's career as a kidnapper confirmed, Lady Uppington looked sternly at her wayward offspring. "You are going to have to return him."

"It's all right," said Miles matter-of-factly, just as a chubby toddler in a frilly dress waddled into the room. "They don't want me returned."

Before Lady Uppington could react to that startling statement, the toddler thrust the grubby doll in her arms at Miles. The china head wobbled ominously and bits of stuffing escaped out the neck. "Play."

Miles decided that if he was going to spend the holidays here, they were going to have to get a few things straight. "Boys," he informed the tot grandly, "do not play with dolls."

The toddler looked decidedly unimpressed. She shoved the doll at him again. "Play."

"I say, Selwick? Does your sister have any toy soldiers?"

And that was that. Miles was firmly ensconced in the Uppington household. Lady Uppington did, early on, write a letter to the Viscountess of Loring, on the theory that the viscountess might somehow resent the appropriation of her only offspring, but the reply that returned was so riddled with references to *Les Noces de Figaro* and so devoid of the slightest mention of Miles, that Lady Uppington muttered a few very uncomplimentary things in the general direction of Italy, and set about relabeling Miles's trunks. Miles received an extra-large helping of trifle that night, and a good-night hug that put him in imminent danger of asphyxiation.

After that, it was simply understood that Miles's Christmases and summers and anything that might come up in between were to be spent at Uppington House. Lord Uppington took him fishing and shooting, and instructed him in the rudiments of estate management. Lady Uppington scolded him and cosseted him and dragged him, squirming and complaining, to be outfitted for school. Every so often, Miles would receive a box from Europe, filled with murky bottles of mineral water, folios of sheet music, and tiny lederhosen that might have fit him when he was two, but in all ways that mattered, his true home was at Uppington House.

And there were those ginger biscuits.

Miles considered going back for another handful, but decided twelve was really quite enough for one day. Besides, he had a job to do.

With a light step and a cheerful whistle, he set off in the direction of his club. Last night, after the fiasco with the note, Miles had sat for a long while at that secluded table. After a few searing sips of gin, Miles had stopped muttering imprecations to himself, and abandoned tempting visions of self-flagellation. By halfway through the glass, he had come to the conclusion that, really, it had all turned out quite well. After all, now he had proof that Vaughn was up to something dodgy, whatever that dodginess might be. An innocent man didn't have clandestine meetings in seedy parts of town.

As for the note . . . well, no one really needed to know about that, did they?

Besides, what was one note compared with the prospect of getting whole folios of evidence? By that point, Miles was three-quarters through the glass of gin and feeling decidedly sanguine, even though the candle had guttered and gone out, and Molly the barmaid was conspicuous by her glower. Instead of resting on one note, resolved Miles, he would gather enough evidence to make a full case against

Vaughn and rout out any little cronies Vaughn might have scuttling around the city.

That one note, had he managed to steal the right one, might have been enough to implicate Vaughn—Miles squinted wistfully at the level of gin in his glass at that point, and took another swig—but it wouldn't have done anything to smoke Vaughn's accomplices out of their burrows. Where there was one mysterious hooded man, there were bound to be others; spies generally carried on their nefarious undertakings through means of an elaborate network.

By the time the glass was empty, Miles had come up with a plan, and he would have tried to put it into execution immediately if he hadn't been just a bit not at his best at the time. He wasn't foxed, not on one glass of blue ruin—or had it been three? He couldn't remember. At any rate, he was just a little . . . tired. That was it. Tired.

His trouble locating the doorknob as he exited from the tavern convinced him that his plan was best mulled upon overnight and executed in all its fullness the following day. When he could walk in a straight line again. Besides, he needed an accomplice, and he knew just where to find one.

Turning down St. James's Street, dodging an inexpertly driven phaeton on the way, Miles strode briskly towards White's, in search of a large brandy and a partner in crime.

It was at moments like this that Miles missed Richard. It wasn't something that Miles would ever admit to—aloud, at least—but White's felt oddly empty without his oldest friend around. Richard would have been the logical choice for accomplice in this endeavor; the two of them even had their own code, developed during their schooldays and never cracked by even the most determined of French agent. But no, Richard had to go and fall in love. Dashed inconsiderate of him.

It wasn't that Miles disliked Amy. She seemed nice enough. Reasonably pretty, bright, clearly devoted to Richard. Not Miles's type, but that was probably a good thing, since he could imagine few things more disturbing and dishonorable than harboring an illicit passion for one's best friend's wife—except perhaps harboring an illicit passion for one's best friend's sister. So it didn't distress Miles that he couldn't quite see just what Richard saw in Amy. He couldn't have wished for better for his best friend.

But this whole having-a-wife-around business changed a man. No matter how unobjectionable the wife in question was. Dash it all, in the old days, Richard would have been at White's. They would have split a bottle of claret, exchanged manly quips about outwitting Bonaparte, thrown a few darts, plotted the downfall of Lord Vaughn, and headed off to Gentleman Jackson's for a quick mill. And where was Richard now? Rusticating in Sussex, that was where. It was a damned waste.

Ah, well, at least Geoff was still in town, and free from feminine leg shackles. Miles went in search of his second-oldest friend. Until recently, Geoff had been in Paris with Richard, serving as second in command of the League of the Purple Gentian.

Now he was conveniently back in London, and just the man Miles needed to help him unmask that French spy. Miles caught sight of the back of a familiar-looking head at a small table at the back of the room, and strolled in that direction.

"Geoff?"

The head, with its close-cropped dark hair, remained bent over the table, a quill tapping restlessly against the scratched surface.

"Pinchingdale-Snipe?"

Still no response.

Miles drew closer. A low droning noise emerged from the vicinity of the tabletop, punctuated by the tapping of the quill.

"If—*tap*—to love me—*tap, tap*—I could thee—*tap, tap*—entice . . ."

" 'It would be very, very nice'?" suggested Miles.

Geoff's head snapped up. "What are you doing here?" he demanded, with less than the show of pleasure one might reasonably expect from one's second-oldest friend.

Miles regarded the splotchy piece of paper with some amusement. "Not what you're doing, clearly." He leaned an elbow on the table and scanned the verses inscribed in Geoff's tidy handwriting.

" 'Oh peerless jewel in Albion's crown/I would I had thee for my own'?"

"Don't you have someplace else you would rather be?" gritted Geoff, clamping an ink-stained hand down over the piece of paper.

"Not particularly." Miles leaned over to peer between Geoff's fingers. "Are you sure that scans, old chap?"

"Don't you have a mistress you could go annoy? Somewhere far, far away?"

"Not at the moment." Miles abandoned Geoff's literary attempts and propped himself casually against the table, stretching his booted legs out in front of him. "I gave Catalina her congé last week. I was late for dinner and she broke an entire tea set over my head."

Despite himself, Geoff's lips twitched. "Sugar bowl and all?"

"Down to the last saucer," confirmed Miles. "Artistic temperament is one thing, but having china shards underfoot all the time was growing a bit wearying. Not to mention painful."

Miles grimaced at the recollection. It had taken hours to pick the fragments of porcelain out of the folds of his cravat. His valet, Downey, had been decidedly unamused by the process. And when it came down to a choice between his valet and his mistress . . . well, there was no question. No one kept linen quite as fresh as Downey.

"Then shouldn't you go find a new one?" Geoff suggested, keeping a protective hand over his maligned verses. "I hear there's a new French opera singer performing at Haymarket tonight. If you hurry, you might be the first to proposition Madame Fiorila."

"I've gone off opera singers for the moment. Too temperamental. Besides, I'm consigned to perdition in the form of the Middlethorpes' ball this evening. I promised Richard I'd keep an eye on Hen while he's in Sussex. Keep the young bucks at bay, that sort of thing."

"Isn't that a bit like setting the wolf to guard the henhouse?" Geoff winced. "Damn. I didn't mean it to come out like that."

"I don't know which is worse, your puns or your poetry."

"I'll pretend you didn't say that."

"That's because you know I'm a better shot than you are," Miles replied equably.

Geoff cast his friend an exasperated look, but refrained from comment. "I'll see you at the Middlethorpes' tonight."

"That's exactly what I was hoping you would say." Miles clapped his friend on the shoulder, then lowered his voice. "I need your help."

Sensing the change in Miles's tone, Geoff set down his quill, took a quick look around the room to make sure it was empty, and modulated his own tone accordingly. "With what?"

"I need you to make sure someone remains in the ballroom while I burgle his house."

"May I ask whose house you're planning to burgle, or is that a secret? And why? This isn't for a wager, is it?" Geoff asked in long-suffering tones.

Hmph. That had been eight years ago. And he'd given the chamber pot back after he'd won the wager. Trust Geoff to bring that up.

Miles refused to let himself be diverted onto the thorny pathways of self-justification. "What do you know of Lord Vaughn?"

Geoff's dark brows drew together in thought.

"Vaughn . . . He left for the Continent under mysterious circumstances while we were still at university, something to do with the death of his wife. She was an heiress, and upon her death, all of her wealth devolved to him." Geoff looked grim. "Vaughn had expensive tastes. Something didn't smell quite right about it. He put it out that she died of smallpox, but there was something dodgy about it."

"Go on," urged Miles. "Anything else?"

"There were other rumors, too, the usual sorts of things, about the Hellfire Club and various other secret societies. Pure hearsay, you understand. Nothing was ever substantiated."

"Would any of those secret societies be dedicated to revolutionary activity?" Miles asked eagerly.

There had been several revolutionary societies about in the late eighties and nineties, devotees of Tom Paine's works who had cheered on the events in France as the dawn of a brave new age. Many of the groups had been infiltrated and egged on by French operatives who sensed a breeding ground for sedition. The government had done a pretty good job of clamping down on the noisier groups, but it was, of necessity, a piecemeal process, and several had slipped through their fingers. It would tie in so neatly . . . .

Geoff shook his head, dashing Miles's clever theory. "No. The focus was debauchery, not politics."

"How do you know all this?"

Geoff raised an eyebrow. "It's my business to know all this."

Miles scowled. That eyebrow thing was deuced infuriating and Geoff knew it.

"I take it Vaughn is under suspicion?" prompted Geoff.

"Up to his neck," confirmed Miles.

"Let me know what I can do, and I'll do it."

Geoff turned back to his poetry, and began tapping away with his quill. As far as Miles could tell, all he was creating was a charmingly abstract pattern of little dots.

So much for that bottle of claret and some sparring at Gentleman Jackson's.

"Some of us have a country to save," Miles muttered at Geoff's hunched back, but Geoff was too immersed in trying to get "entice" to rhyme with "delight" to notice or care.

It wouldn't be quite so bad, reflected Miles, if Geoff were going to write lovelorn poetry, if he would at least write *good* lovelorn poetry. Which begged the age-old question, was there such a thing as good lovelorn poetry? Probably not, concluded Miles. Either way, it seemed like a bloody waste of time.

Had Cupid availed himself of Bonaparte's artillery? Next thing he knew, even Reggie Fitzhugh would be google-eyed over some chit of a girl. Perhaps it was a new French tactic, mused Miles darkly. The French had slipped something into their brandy to induce otherwise reasonable men to turn into lovesick jackanapes so busy mooning over the composition of poetry—poetry!—that they wouldn't even notice a French army trooping across the Channel. Only he, Miles Dorrington, remained unaffected, the sole hope and prop of England.

Rolling his eyes, Miles set off to find himself a nice, comfortable leather chair, where he could sit and scheme without being assaulted by iambs.

Tonight, he would search Lord Vaughn's house. Tomorrow, he would avail himself of the registers at the Alien Office regarding recent arrivals from the Continent. Theoretically, every foreigner in London was supposed to register with the Alien Office upon arrival in the city. Vaughn's contact might have slipped in illicitly (in fact, there was a high probability that he had), or he might have been in London for several months already, relaying messages brought by someone else, more recently arrived. Even so, it was the logical place to start searching for a mysterious man with a foreign accent.

After all, *someone* had to protect England.

Chapter Eleven

Quadrille: *a deadly dance of deceit*
——from the Personal Codebook of the Pink Carnation

By eleven o'clock that evening, Henrietta was in a state of intense irritation with both herself and the world.

She was irritated by the silly fop who had just escorted her back to her mother (whoever had told him that a puce waistcoat was becoming with a chartreuse jacket?); she was irritated by the footman who offered her a glass of champagne; she was irritated with the cloying smell of lilacs that pervaded the ballroom; and she was irritated with the lace fringe on her cap sleeve that scratched against her arm and made her want to twitch like a demented bedlamite.

Mostly, she was irritated with herself.

It had been an irritable sort of day. She had spent the afternoon starting letters and crumpling them up; picking up books and putting them down again; staring sightlessly out the window; and being generally restless, purposeless, and cross. It had occurred to her, belatedly, that she probably would have been better off going to Charlotte's fittings with her, just to have something to do. The reflection, coming as it did three hours too late, only made her crosser.

Most of all, more than anything else, she was irritated with herself for her detailed knowledge of the movements of one blasted Miles blasted Dorrington. Henrietta had danced ten dances, sat out another chatting with Mary Alsworthy's younger sister, Letty, pulled Pen back from the verge of the balcony and ensuing social ruin, and had a long discussion with Charlotte about the novels of Samuel Richardson and whether Lovelace was a romantic hero (Charlotte) or a treacherous cad (Henrietta)—all the while noting Miles's each and every movement.

Since their arrival at the ball, Miles had brought her lemonade, retreated to the card room, returned half an hour later to see if she wanted anything, and engaged in a long discussion with Turnip Fitzhugh about horses. She knew that he had gone out on the balcony for twenty minutes with a cheroot and two friends, danced a duty dance with Lady Middlethorpe, and very vividly acted out bits of yesterday's boxing match for the edification of the Middlethorpes' seventeen-year-old son.

It was infuriating; it was idiotic; it was . . . Was that Miles over there?

No. It wasn't. Henrietta realized the strange gnashing noise she heard was her own teeth.

She was behaving, Hen told herself firmly, like a great big ninny.

What she needed, she decided, twitching irritably as that diabolical ruffle brushed her arm, was distraction. Obviously, she must be quite, quite bored, or she wouldn't be playing silly games with herself over Miles, of all people. This was, after all, Miles, Henrietta reminded herself for the fiftieth time this evening. Miles. The man who had once balanced a chamber pot on the spire of St.-Martin-in-the-Fields. He'd nearly been excommunicated for that one. He was also the same man who had managed to fall backwards into the duck pond at Uppington Hall while playing catch with Richard's now-defunct corgi. True, he had been thirteen at the time, but Henrietta chose to remember the splashing and swearing and squawking (the last from the ducks, not Miles) instead. Not to mention his memorable performance as the Phantom Monk of Donwell Abbey. Henrietta had had nightmares for a week.

To be fair, he'd also snuck her into the boys-only tree house, smuggled her her first champagne, and given her her favorite stuffed animal, Bunny the bunny (Henrietta had not been the most creative of small children). But Henrietta didn't want to be fair. She wanted to regain her ability to ignore Miles. She had never thought of it as a specific talent until now.

Clearly, she needed occupation. Looking for the French spy would be the ideal diversion—Henrietta perked up a bit at the thought—but she hadn't the first notion of where to start looking. Jane's letter, after all, had merely signaled the presence of a new operative, not anything distinguishing about him. Henrietta had, in a moment of desperation that afternoon, considered tackling her contact in the ribbon shop in Bond Street on that topic, but her instructions on that score had been clear: She was never to have any more conversation with the ribbon seller than that necessitated by the purchase of ribbons. To do otherwise could jeopardize the secrecy of the whole enterprise. Besides, for all she knew, the ribbon seller was just as much in the dark as she was.

No, her only hope was Amy, who was bound to have some sort of idea as to where she should start. Amy always had ideas. Henrietta engaged in some desperate calculations. Even assuming that Amy sat down and replied to her letter the instant she received it—of course, it was easily possible for Amy to be distracted, leave it on her writing desk, and rediscover it a month later, but Henrietta refused to entertain that possibility—but, assuming the best, assuming Amy wrote at a speed at which no woman had written before, and handed it back to the courier before he could do more than gulp a glass of ale in the kitchens of Selwick Hall. Assuming the courier had fresh horses lined up along the way and rode as if ten highwaymen were dogging his heels. Assuming all that . . . it would still take at least another day, Henrietta concluded glumly.

Blast.

"Oh, look!" exclaimed Lady Uppington, poking Henrietta in the arm. Henrietta rubbed irritably at the spot. Splendid. Now she was itchy *and* bruised. "There's Miles dancing with Charlotte. Isn't that sweet of the dear boy?"

"Perishingly," said Henrietta sourly, following the direction of Lady Uppington's punitive finger towards the dance floor, where Miles was pacing the elegant figures of the quadrille with Charlotte.

One could see—or, at least, Henrietta could see—that he was making a valiant effort to make conversation with Charlotte, even though he hadn't the slightest idea what to say to her. She could tell from the way his eyes narrowed ever so slightly at the corners, and the way his brows drew together in concentrated thought, as if he were working very hard on a complicated philosophical theorem. He must have devised something, a comment about the weather, most likely, because his entire face cleared with relief. His eyebrows went up, his mouth opened, and a big, engaging smile spread across his face.

Henrietta's heart clenched in a way it had no business clenching over Miles.

Over Charlotte's shoulder, Miles caught Henrietta's eye and grinned.

Henrietta started, blushed, and swallowed half a glass of champagne the wrong way.

Those bubbles up her nose *hurt*.

When Henrietta had gotten over the worst of her coughing fit, Lady Uppington turned an inquisitive eye on her wheezing daughter. "You know, darling, you don't appear to be in a very good mood this evening."

Henrietta repressed the urge to growl, partially because it would be undignified, and partially because her throat felt like it had been stripped raw by the champagne.

"I'm *fine*."

"Darling." Lady Uppington gave her a deeply reproachful "don't try to lie to your mother" look. "What's wrong?"

"Nothing! I am having a brilliant time. Brilliant. Utterly, *absolutely* brilliant." Henrietta flung out her arms, which had the unfortunate side effect of giving the ruffle full rein along the sensitive underside of her arms. Henrietta scowled. "My sleeve itches."

"I told you not to choose that lace," Lady Uppington said unsympathetically, waving to an acquaintance.

Was twenty too old to put oneself up for adoption?

As Henrietta watched, Miles returned Charlotte to her grandmother, made a manful effort to dodge the dowager's deadly pug dog, and beat a hasty retreat. Right in their direction. Henrietta snatched down the hand that had automatically risen to smooth her hair.

Someone else had clearly been monitoring Miles's movements as well, because as Miles moved towards their party, a dark figure glided out to intercept him. Today she was wearing smoky purple instead of black, but the figure inside the dress was unmistakable. It was That Woman. Seen up close, she was even more infuriatingly beautiful— why couldn't she have a bad side? Or spots? A nice red spot would stand out so well on that perfect white skin.

It wasn't fair to hate her just because she made every other woman in a fifty-foot radius look like a troll, Henrietta scolded herself. After all, look at Helen and Aphrodite, made miserable by their very beauty—and, frankly, without much else to recommend them. It must have been very difficult to look like that. Hated by women, pursued by men for all the wrong reasons. Maybe she was shy.

Hmph. Even Henrietta couldn't make herself believe that one. There was nothing shy about the way the marquise was draping herself over Miles's arm. At that rate, why didn't she just fling her arms around his neck and have done with it? As if she had read Henrietta's thoughts, the marquise chose just that moment to lift a gloved hand to Miles's cheek.

Oh, for goodness' sake! Henrietta had had enough of standing gawking on the sidelines like a spectator at a bad play. She was really supposed to be dancing with Turnip Fitzhugh, but if Turnip hadn't come to claim his dance, there was no reason she shouldn't amuse herself by chatting with her old friend Miles.

With a bright social smile fixed upon her lips like a shield and a champagne glass held aloft like a cavalry officer's baton, Henrietta marched determinedly over to Miles, and placed herself at his arm.

"Hello!" she said brightly.

"Uh, hello," said Miles, blinking at her sudden appearance.

Resolving to give the horrid woman a chance, Henrietta turned to the marquise with the friendliest smile she could muster, and said in her warmest voice, "I have been admiring your gown all evening. The lace is exquisite!"

The marquise eyed her rather as she would an importunate ferret. "Thank you."

Henrietta waited for the requisite return compliment. It did not materialize. Henrietta experienced a certain grim satisfaction at the knowledge that the woman was just as dislikable in person as she was from a distance. Good. Now she didn't have to try to be nice to her.

Miles belatedly remembered his duty. "Madame de Montval, may I present Lady Henrietta Selwick?"

"Selwick?" The marquise pursed her lips becomingly in thought.

Was there any gesture the woman used that wasn't becoming? Henrietta would have willingly wagered the entire contents of Uppington House, including three Canalettos, assorted Van Dycks, and the family tiara, that the marquise had practiced her entire range of facial expressions in front of a mirror.

"Oh, of course!" The marquise unfurled her fan with a little trill of laughter. "The noble Purple Gentian! Are you related?"

"My brother," said Henrietta shortly.

"Those of us, my dear, who suffered in the late unpleasantness know only too well what a debt we owe him. But you would have been far too young to remember."

"In the nursery, crawling around on all fours and drooling," Henrietta agreed, so sweetly that Miles glanced at her sharply. She was tempted to make some comment about the marquise's advanced age, but nobly declined to sink to her level. Besides, she couldn't think of a clever way to phrase it.

In Henrietta's moment of hesitation, the marquise turned her attention back to Miles, placing a gloved hand caressingly on his wrist. "I so enjoyed our drive in the park today," she murmured.

It was all Henrietta could do to keep her jaw from dropping in indignation. Their drive in the park! But . . . but . . . that was *her* drive. Of course, she'd been the one to turn the invitation down, but that reflection did nothing to alleviate the sting.

"I never knew the Serpentine could be so enthralling," the marquise continued, looking up at Miles from under long dark lashes.

What could possibly be enthralling about the Serpentine? It was a body of water. With ducks.

"It all depends on what angle you look at it from," said Miles modestly.

Preferably, thought Henrietta, from within the water, while being violently pecked by maddened warrior ducks.

"Or," countered the marquise with a sultry smile, "on one's companion."

Miles made noises of humble denial.

The marquise begged to disagree.

Hen clamped down on the urge to wave a hand in front of their faces and trill, "Hello! I'm here!"

"I personally prefer to ride in the Row," she said loudly, just to have something to say.

"No, you don't," said Miles.

Henrietta glowered at him. "It is a recently formed opinion."

"You hate the Row. You said that only pretentious fops and over-dressed—"

"Yes!" Henrietta intervened. "Thank you, Miles."

"In the young," interjected the marquise understandingly, somehow managing to look down on Henrietta even though they were roughly of a height, "opinions change so quickly. When you grow older, Lady Henrietta, you will become more settled in your tastes."

"Yes." Henrietta nodded just as understandingly. "I imagine that's what happens when one can't get about as much. Do you suffer much from stiffness of the joints? My mother has an excellent remedy for it if you do."

The remark had been petty and childish and not terribly clever, but it hit its mark. The marquise's eyes narrowed ever so slightly. The expression did nothing to improve her looks. It brought out little crow's-feet on either side of her eyes. Henrietta hoped Miles was looking closely.

"So kind." Dropping her hand from its permanent perch on Miles's arm, the marquise snapped her fan shut with an audible click and re-garded Henrietta narrowly. "Tell me, Lady Henrietta, do you share your brother's interests?"

Henrietta shook her head. "No, my mother won't let me go to gaming halls. It might interfere with my bedtime."

Miles nudged her. Hard.

Henrietta nudged back. Harder.

"What in the hell is wrong with you tonight?" muttered Miles.

The marquise didn't like being ignored. "I'm sorry, Mr. Dorring-ton. Did you say something?"

"Nothing!" chorused Henrietta and Miles, just as the great clock in the hall began striking midnight.

One could barely hear the chimes over the din of the crowd—hundreds of voices talking and laughing, musicians playing, booted feet tapping across the parquet floor—but the faint echo of sound held Miles arrested.

Damn, if he wanted to burgle Vaughn's house, he should be about it now, before Vaughn grew bored with the insipid entertainment on offer in the Middlethorpes' ballroom and wended his way home. Most likely, he would stop off at other affairs before seeking his bed, but Miles would feel safer if he knew Geoff was keeping an eye on him here.

"Shall we continue our exploration of the park tomorrow, Mr. Dorrington? There are so many paths still undiscovered."

"Um, certainly," said Miles, with no idea what he was agreeing to. Miles bowed to a point somewhere in between Hen and the marquise. "If you'll excuse me, ladies, I just remembered something I promised Pinchingdale-Snipe. Dreadfully sorry, but needs must, and all that."

"Quite all right," said the marquise smoothly. She extended a gloved hand at such an angle that Miles couldn't do anything but kiss it. "Until tomorrow, Mr. Dorrington. Good evening, Lady Henrietta. It has been a singular pleasure."

"Words cannot convey the extremity of my rapture," replied Hen-rietta politely. She waggled her fingers at the marquise's departing back.

"What was that all about?" Miles demanded, turning to face Henrietta.

Henrietta drew herself up on her tiptoes, stuck her bosom out, and draped one hand languidly over Miles's arm. "Oh, la, Mr. Dorrington, how utterly enthralling you are! I declare I shall swoon from the ecstasy of your presence."

"Is it so bizarre that someone should appreciate me?" Miles inquired.

Henrietta snorted. "If she appreciated you any more, you'd both be banned from the ballroom."

"Aren't you supposed to be dancing with someone?"

"He forgot."

"Ah," said Miles. "So that's what put you in such a foul mood."

"I'm not in a foul mood."

Miles cast her a highly sardonic look. "Shall we simply say that you are not your usual vision of charm and good cheer?"

Henrietta glowered.

Miles backed away with exaggerated alarm. "Or I can just not say anything at all and leave quietly."

Hen flapped her hands at him. "Oh, just go away. I'm going to go find a nice little hole to crawl into."

Miles wondered if he ought to stay, making offerings of lemonade and quadrilles, but the hands of the clock were steadily inching past midnight. Besides, Hen in a bad mood was a rare and frightening occurrence. So Miles simply grinned a comradely grin, kept an eye on her until he saw her fall in with Charlotte, who, from the disgruntled look on Hen's face, immediately inquired into her foul mood—Miles could faintly hear an irate "Why does everyone keep asking me that!" floating from the other side of the ballroom—and went off in search of Geoff, to implement part one of his cunning plan.

Geoff's dark head was easy to spot among the crowd; he stood out several inches over the dumpy dowagers and diminutive debutantes (the male population of the room had already begun a steady but inexorable progression to the card room and the refreshment table). But Geoff, Miles noted with a grimace, was otherwise occupied. He had persuaded that peerless jewel in Albion's crown, otherwise known as Mary Alsworthy, the biggest flirt this side of the English Channel, to partner him for a quadrille, and was gazing down at her dark curls with the devout reverence of a Crusader first sighting the Holy Land.

Miles stood on the side of the dance floor, and made subtle gestures at Geoff. Geoff's eyes remained fixed adoringly on the crown of Mary Alsworthy's head. Miles abandoned subtle. He waved his arms about and jerked his head in the direction of the door. Geoff caught his eye and grimaced. Miles couldn't tell if that was an "I'll be with you in a minute" grimace, or a "Stop waving your arms about because you're embarrassing the hell out of me" grimace. Either way, there wasn't much more Miles could do, short of bodily dragging Geoff off the dance floor, so he retreated to the side of the room with less than good grace, and leaned against the wall with arms crossed.

"You waved?" commented Geoff ironically, striding over to join him as the set on the dance floor dissolved and a new round of couples took their place for a lively country dance.

Miles decided to ignore the irony. Springing from his languid pose against the wall, he announced grandiloquently, "The time has come!"

"To embarrass me in front of Mary Alsworthy?"

"Oh, for the love of God!" The lady in question was already surrounded by five other swains. Miles forbore to point that out, not wanting to precipitate Geoff's departure. "There's a war on, remember? Can we concentrate on that for a moment?"

"Oh. Right." Geoff had already sighted Mary's entourage for himself and was looking that way with a worried line between his brows.

Witchcraft, Miles concluded. There had to be black arts involved somehow. This, after all, was Geoff, who had spent the past seven years capably taking care of the administrative end of the League of the Purple Gentian while Richard undertook the more daring bits. Nothing short of diabolical intervention could explain it.

England was long overdue for a good witch burning.

"You know," Miles said cunningly, "maybe if you avoid her for a few hours, it will pique her interest in you. Hen tells me women respond to that sort of thing."

Geoff shook his head. "Doesn't make any sense."

"Which is just why it might work," Miles said sagely.

"Hmm, there is that."

Miles decided he had pressed that ploy as far as he could without raising Geoff's suspicions. Of course, given his current state, he could probably tell Geoff that King George had just turned into a giant rutabaga, and Geoff would nod and agree.

"The person in question is over there, by the large statue of Zeus throwing thunderbolts," said Miles in a conversational tone so that no one walking by would suspect anything clandestine. "I need about an hour. If you see him take his leave before then, think of some way to detain him. I'm counting on you, Geoff."

"An hour?"

"More would be better, but an hour will do."

Geoff nodded. "Good luck."

Miles grinned, executed a fancy little fencing move against the air, just for the hell of it, and turned to go. At the last moment, another thought struck Miles. He poked Geoff in the shoulder. "One last thing."

"What might that be?" asked Geoff warily.

It was a sad day when one's friends turned all suspicious. "Just keep an eye on him and Hen, will you? I didn't like the way he was hovering over her last night."

"Simple enough," agreed Geoff with relief. "I can always spirit her off onto the dance floor. Maybe if I could make Mary jealous . . ."

"Knew I could count on you, old chap!" Miles whacked Geoff on the shoulder before he could complete the thought, and strode cheerfully out of the ballroom with the comfortable sense of one who has done his duty.

Loping down the front steps, Miles drew in a deep, restorative breath of night air—and nearly gagged. Miles's face twisted in disgust. The smell was unmistakable, as were the noises that accompanied it. Someone, coattails sticking up in the air and head in the shrubbery, was casting up his accounts right into the Middlethorpes' carefully trimmed shrubbery.

As Miles passed, the retcher stood up, stumbled, landed with one hand under the bushes—Miles winced—and levered himself up again so that the lantern light fell full on his pasty face. Miles stopped dead in his tracks. Here was someone he'd been meaning to speak to. It wasn't the best of timing, but Miles would rather get this particular interview over with as quickly as possible. The stench only provided extra incentive.

Taking hold of a mercifully clean part of the man's cravat, Miles helped haul him upright.

"Frobisher," he drawled. "I've been wanting to speak to you."

"Honored, Dorrington." Frobisher swayed on his feet as he attempted a bow. He grimaced at the ground as though he suspected it of trying to attack him. "Pleasure, don'tcha know."

Miles couldn't echo the sentiment. Miles sidestepped to get out of the way of the blast of brandy fumes that emerged, like flames from a dragon, when Frobisher spoke. The man's cravat hung askew, his jacket gaped open, revealing streaks of Miles didn't want to know what on his waistcoat, and his bloodshot eyes narrowed with the sheer difficulty of trying to focus on Miles.

This inebriated cretin had had the gall to touch Henrietta. Miles's nostrils flared with distaste—a mistake, since it allowed in more of Frobisher's disgusting reek. When not in his cups, Frobisher was a perfectly presentable specimen, but any man of his age who would let himself get in such a state didn't deserve to be in the same room as Hen, much less drag her out onto darkened balconies. The man needed to be taught a little lesson in manners, starting with keeping his scurvy hands off Miles's best friend's sister.

Calm, Miles reminded himself. Just a little man-to-man chat. It didn't do to pound one's acquaintances silly—it made social life dashed awkward. He just needed to make sure the man knew that if he so much as looked at Henrietta again, he'd better bloody well start thinking about emigrating to the remoter bits of the Americas.

Miles crossed his arms over his chest. "I hear you had a little difference of opinion with Henrietta Selwick."

"Damn disagreeable chit," slurred Frobisher. "Goin' about, cutting
up stiff just because—" He catapulted back into the bushes.

Miles grasped the back of his waistcoat and hoisted him out again.
If he held him dangling in the air just a moment longer than necessary, Frobisher was foxed enough not to notice. Nor did he suspect
that Miles was considering replacing his hand with a boot and testing
just how far one drunken degenerate could be kicked.

Regretfully, Miles dropped Frobisher. He had a message to deliver
first. Kicking would have to wait.

"Thanks, Dorrington." Frobisher brushed ineffectually at his
waistcoat. Some substances did not respond kindly to brushing. Frobisher scowled at the ruin of his gloves. "Dashed decent of you."

"About Lady Henrietta," Miles began menacingly, eager to say his
piece and be done with it.

"Don't know what she was so upset about." Frobisher shook his
head at the vagaries of women. "Jus' a little cuddle. Girl's in her third
Season. You'd think she'd be thanking me."

"She'd *what*?"

Did the man have a death wish? Miles concentrated on the possibility he had misheard. The man was drunk; he wasn't speaking
clearly.

"Last prayers, y'know," Frobisher elucidated helpfully. "On the
shelf."

Miles's fragile hold on his temper snapped.

"Would you care to say that again," Miles clipped, "at dawn?"

Chapter Twelve

Duel *(n.)*: *1) a desperate struggle in a darkened room; 2) a means of emptying crowded ballrooms*
—from the Personal Codebook of the Pink Carnation,
with annotations by the Dowager Duchess of Dovedale

Martin Frobisher might have been drunk, but he wasn't stupid. At least, not entirely stupid. He knew enough to be very, very afraid.

Dorrington's skill with an épée was unparalleled, his marksmanship legendary, but the prospect of being skewered or shot faded to insignificance before the far more immediate menace of Miles himself. Miles's hands were flexing in a way that had nothing to do with Queensberry rules. Frobisher backed away, bumped into the shrubbery, and steadied himself with one hand against the wall.

"I say, Dorrington . . ."

"Yes, Frobisher? What exactly do you have to say?"

"Never meant it like that," he stammered, sliding down the wall to sit heavily in a puddle of his own making. "Damn fine girl. Anyone would want 'er. Tits like—urgh . . ."

Frobisher's head snapped back with the force of the blow. His eyes bugged out in horror as Miles seized him by the cravat and hauled him upright.

"You will not touch Lady Henrietta Selwick ever again. You will not dance with her. You will not kiss her hand. You will not cuddle, fondle, or otherwise defile any part of her anatomy. Is that clear?"

"Won't touch her," Frobisher dutifully gurgled. Struck by a sudden inspiration, he looked anxiously at Miles. "Won't even talk to her!"

"Even better," said Miles grimly. Opening his hand, he let Frobisher drop—right back into the pile of his own filth. Frobisher sprawled half under the bushes, clasping his throat and panting with relief. "Frobisher!"

"Yes?" a cracked voice said from the bushes.

"If I were you, I'd refrain from mentioning any of this to any of your little friends. Speak Lady Henrietta's name with anything but respect, and I'll thrash you within an inch of your miserable life and sell you to the press gangs. If they'll have you," added Miles with a disparaging glance at the crumpled pile of soiled fabric curled up under the bushes. "Good night, Frobisher."

A faint moan followed Miles as he clumped purposefully off down the street.

The triumphal hero was feeling less than pleased with himself. He had, he knew, massively overreacted. Massively. The man had been drunk, he'd been in no condition for a fair fight, and, to be just, he hadn't even meant to be offensive; he just was. All Miles had to do was calmly and coolly deliver a warning, gentleman to gentleman, to alert Frobisher that Henrietta wasn't unprotected and she wasn't fair game. Simple enough. Instead, he had lost his head, flexed his muscles, mouthed threats like some thickheaded numbskull fresh from the countryside. It was sheer dumb luck that no one had been watching.

But there was something about Frobisher, about the thought of him pressing his attentions on Hen, that made Miles want to stomp back and finish what he'd started. How dared he refer to Henrietta in those terms?

Miles scowled. Frobisher's careless words had brought back a memory that Miles had been doing his best to repress for the past month. He'd nearly managed, too. There had been an incident. An incident involving Henrietta and a nightdress. A bloody indecent nightdress. Weren't innocent young virgins supposed to be bundled up in yards of woolly fabric to prevent shocking the sensibilities of any bachelors who might happen by? If they weren't, they should be.

Henrietta had come running down the stairs in a nightdress that gave whole new meaning to the word "diaphanous." To be fair, Miles wouldn't have noticed if Lady Uppington hadn't made a sharp comment and ordered Henrietta upstairs to change, but once he'd started noticing, it had been hard to stop. When in the hell had she grown breasts like that? The candlelight through the thin lawn of her nightdress had left very little to the imagination, and Miles rather doubted even imagination could improve upon . . .

Miles clamped down on the memory before it could go any farther. As far as he was concerned, Henrietta wasn't supposed to have a body. She was a head on legs. Hmm, those had been very nice legs he'd seen outlined through . . . No. There were rules about lusting after your best friend's sister. Hell, forget rules, more like immutable laws of nature. If he broke them, there would be strange eclipses of the moon, and the sheeted dead would rise and gibber in the streets. It was unnatural—that was what it was. Unnatural and wrong.

But so well shaped, for something so wrong.

Devil take it! Miles picked up his pace, striding furiously in the direction of Belliston Square. He had a house to burgle, and, thanks to that idiot Frobisher, he had already lost another ten minutes of his allotted hour. Fortunately, Vaughn's residence was a scant five blocks from the Middlethorpes'; Miles's long legs covered the distance in minutes.

Just outside Belliston Square, he forced himself to slow and reconnoiter. This was, after all, where the operative had been murdered, and Miles wanted to take a look around outside as well as in. Staggering a bit, a gentleman well in his cups making his way home after one too many social events, Miles swaggered slowly into the square, looking keenly about under the guise of an idly lolling head.

The square was shadowed on one side by the shuttered bulk of Belliston House, a grand mansion in the Palladian style erected early in the previous century. The current duke was an avid sportsman who seldom came to London. There would be a skeleton staff in residence, to maintain the premises and guard its priceless collections, but the odds of anyone in Belliston House taking notice of dubious goings-on in the square (including Miles's) were slim. The other three sides were identical; each boasted a large house in the center flanked by two smaller houses on either side, rather in the manner of a triumphal arch. Vaughn's was one of the former, nestled on the south side of the square. An immense triangular pediment supported by three Doric columns dominated the façade, lending the structure a fashionable air of the antique. More important, all the lights were out.

There was a party in progress in one of the houses, a musical evening, from the liquid syllables that spilled out the window. In front of another, a footman was teasing a little maid, who giggled and colored under his attentions. Miles stopped and stretched; he leaned against a gate, gazed at the moon, fiddled with his stickpin. No one took the slightest notice. Miles continued on his way, his theory confirmed. The maples planted in the middle of the square meant anyone standing in front of Vaughn's house would be blocked from the view of the houses opposite; as for the other houses, as long as the murderer looked like he belonged in the square, and moved quickly enough, he could be almost sure of escaping detection.

Ducking around the back of the square and into an alley, Miles donned the concealing garments he had brought along for just this occasion. They weren't elaborate, nothing like the complicated costume Richard used to wear for his escapades as the Purple Gentian, but there was only so much Miles could stuff into his pockets. Unfastening his diamond stickpin, Miles yanked off his white cravat, bundled his equally white gloves into it, and stuck the lot beneath a convenient bush. Downey would be none too pleased, but what was a scrap of linen more or less in a good cause? Replacing the white gloves with thin black ones, Miles drew out of his pocket a square of black cloth. Miles eyed it with disfavor. He really wasn't looking forward to this part.

England, he reminded himself. Rule Britannia and God Save the King, and all that.

His jaw fixed in an expression of extreme stoicism, Miles knotted the black cloth bandanna-style around his head, hiding his fair hair, and covering a good chunk of his forehead as well. Miles caught a glimpse of himself in a dark window and grimaced. Hell, put an earring in his ear, and he'd look like a bloody pirate. All he needed was a tattoo on his arm and a wisecracking parrot.

There was worse yet to come. Over the bandanna, Miles tied a thin black silk mask, the sort worn by ladies who wished to preserve their reputations and the roués who preyed on them. Now he looked like a pirate with a yen for anonymity. Miles the Bashful Pirate, Scourge of the High Seas. If Hen ever saw him in this getup, he'd never hear the end of it.

Ah, well. Miles shook his head at himself. At least if anyone discovered him, he could claim he had been on his way to a fancy dress party, and had wandered into Vaughn's garden in pursuit of his runaway parrot.

Feeling like a prize dimwit, Miles slipped unnoticed through Vaughn's garden gate. The windows on the first floor were all dark. Inching through the midnight garden, the air heavy with the scents of roses and lavender, Miles could see a faint glint of light from below stairs. Vaughn's valet would, naturally, be waiting up for his master. From the sounds of merriment emerging from the open window, he had company. Good, thought Miles, the more they were entertaining themselves, the less likely they were to hear the dark shadow who slipped soundlessly into the house.

Ouch! He had whacked right into an ornamental bench that some diabolical mastermind had placed right up against the wall. Miles swallowed a bellow of pain, cursing silently, which wasn't nearly as satisfying as cursing noisily.

Rubbing his shin, the black shadow limped along, examining his options. Up three shallow steps stood a balcony, with French doors that gave onto the garden. The steps, of course, were right in the center of the garden, in plain view of anyone in the house. The ornamental shrubs that marked out the patterns of the parterre would provide no concealment; they came to Miles's knee at best.

Easily enough remedied, thought Miles with a roguish grin. Placing one black-gloved hand on the corner of the stone balustrade, he vaulted over the railing, landing in a supple crouch on the balcony. Standing, Miles flexed his arms smugly.

Back against the wall, he edged his way to the French doors, and with one cautious, gloved hand, tried the handle. It turned smoothly. Once inside, Miles didn't let himself stop to gloat; he had worked out a plan of action last night, and intended to stick to it. He had already wasted enough time giving that revolting reprobate Frobisher the what-for.

Miles jerked his mind back to the matter at hand before it could stray into dangerous territory.

Vaughn's study would be the obvious place to search—which was precisely why he wasn't going to do so. If Vaughn was the ruthless spy he supposed him, he would have anticipated the possibility of midnight callers, and hidden his papers accordingly, planting false information in the more obvious spots, such as locked desk drawers and hollow globes. Besides, Vaughn had only recently returned from his travels; he would have gotten in the habit of keeping his most sensitive papers close by him, ready to be packed up and moved along at a moment's notice. And when a gentleman wanted something kept close at hand, he kept it in his bedroom. The same principle applied for both documents of a sensitive nature and mistresses.

Even Delaroche, that half-mad fanatic, kept his more sensitive documents under his pillow—or had done, until Richard cleared out the lot.

Vaughn's house was a connoisseur's dream and a spy's nightmare, filled with tottering vases and unexpected statues. Miles nearly fell back into one of the former as he rounded a corner to encounter a fourteen-foot-high Hercules guarding the front stairs. A very dispirited-looking lion crouched underneath Hercules's foot, and the club in Hercules's hand seemed to be pointed directly at Miles.

"Hello, old chap," murmured Miles as he placed one foot warily on the first step, balancing on the balls of his feet to keep his heels from clicking tellingly against the marble. Rugs. That was what this house needed, decided Miles crossly. Lots and lots of rugs. It would make creeping about much easier.

Hercules continued to watch him as he climbed, the stairs circling around the statue. "Keep an eye out for the staff for me, would you?" Miles asked. He had always felt something of a rapport with Hercules ever since that incident with the determined countess. And he shared the man's dislike for snakes, an antipathy obviously not echoed by Vaughn. They figured prominently in his decorating scheme. Sconces encircled by writhing reptiles reposed at regular intervals along the walls.

Crossing his fingers for luck, Miles selected a room at random, slipping soundlessly inside, shutting the door again behind him. With the heavy drapes closed, the room was in complete darkness. Rather than blundering about, Miles decided to risk striking a match. In the momentary flare, he saw flowered wallpaper, a dainty writing desk, and an embroidered fire screen.

Not the earl's bedchamber—but the countess's?

Miles made it to the window just before the match burned down onto his fingers, and nudged the drapes aside just enough to allow in sufficient moonlight to see by. Everything was a little blurry, but it was safer than another match, and what he saw confirmed his guess. The room was dainty and feminine, and nothing in it dated to later than a decade ago. Dried-up bottles containing cosmetics and perfume still sat on the dressing table, and an old-fashioned sacque was draped along the end of the bed, as though its owner were expected to return and don it at any moment.

More important, there were doors in both walls, and where there was a countess's suite, there was bound to be the earl's. Much easier than blundering around the hallway, poking his head through more doorways. One never knew who might be on the other side.

The door on the far left yielded what Miles sought. He was in Vaughn's bedchamber. And quite a bedchamber it was. The room was dominated by an immense bed, placed on a raised dais in the French style, and adorned with innumerable swags of rich blue velvet. Two shapely nymphs held up the headboard, an immense shell that Venus would be proud to call her own. The carvings on the bedposts carried out the aquatic theme; dolphins disported themselves with water nymphs while Triton supervised from above. Miles gave the posts a careful tap—the dolphins' tails looked like excellent latches for a secret cache—but came away with nothing more than a bruised knuckle.

The small cabinet beside the bed likewise refused to yield up any vital secrets, containing nothing more exciting than a chamber pot. Determined to be thorough, Miles removed the item. After all, what more devious place to hide secret documents? An exceedingly quick inspection put paid to that theory. Sometimes, a chamber pot was just a chamber pot.

By the time he had rooted through all the bed linen, inspected Vaughn's armoire, gone through his collection of silver-headed canes, peered underneath an embroidered footstool and up the chimney, some of Miles's initial enthusiasm began to fade. He hadn't been expecting a folio volume to be sitting upon Vaughn's pillow, helpfully engraved with the legend MY CAREER AS A CUNNING SPY AND OTHER SHORT STORIES, but *something* would have been useful. A letter in cipher, perhaps. Or a mysterious bit of crumpled paper. There had to be something. Clearly, he just wasn't looking in the right places.

Trying to scrub a hand through his hair, but foiled by the bloody bandanna, Miles turned to glare at Vaughn's bed. What had he missed? There was no room to hide anything in the shell, and the nymphs were completely solid; Miles had checked, with special attention to the fleshier bits. The cabinet beside the bed held nothing but that chamber pot . . . and a book. How had he overlooked the book?

Skidding on a small Persian carpet, Miles bounded back up onto the dais and snatched up the book from the top of the cabinet. It was Edmund Burke's *A Philosophical Inquiry into the Origin of Our Ideas of the Sublime and Beautiful*, and it wasn't hollow. Damn. But there was a piece of paper folded into it, marking the page.

It was too big to be the note he had seen change hands last night; Miles noticed that straight off. Sticking a finger in the book, so as not to lose Vaughn's page, Miles yanked out the folded piece of paper and shook it open. Damn, damn, damn. Nothing but a bloody playbill. No wonder Vaughn was using the thrice-blasted thing as a bookmark.

Miles started to return it to its place—and froze. Slowly, with a dawning excitement, he held it back up to the meager moonlight.

Not just a playbill. A French playbill.

If he hadn't been in Vaughn's house under decidedly suspicious circumstances, Miles would have jumped up and down and hooted. As it was, he gave an involuntary start of excitement that sent the book tumbling. Miles caught it before it could hit the ground and dumped it unceremoniously on the bed. The hell with marking the page—he had his man.

France! Vaughn had been in France! And, recently, too. The date on the playbill was only a fortnight ago, well after Bonaparte had broken the Peace of Amiens, and booted all Englishmen out of the country as potential enemy agents. Any Englishman found in the city was subject to instant imprisonment. Jane had only slipped beneath the notice of the Ministry of Police because she was a woman, and the first cousin of Edouard de Balcourt, a toadyish hanger-on at the First Consul's court. Vaughn had been not just in France, but in Paris, heavily patrolled Paris, where the Ministry of Police was all aquiver with anxiety over the Pink Carnation. Vaughn had been in Paris, attending a bloody operatic performance, in plain sight of Bonaparte's watchdogs. The whole thing reeked to high heaven.

Miles could have kissed that playbill, but he didn't want to smudge the ink.

Bringing it over to the window, he examined the document more closely in the moonlight. It announced the performance of one Madame Aurelia Fiorila, Queen of the Operatic Stage. The name niggled at Miles; he knew he had heard it before, and recently. He could chase down recollection later; right now, something else claimed his attention, an address, scribbled in the lower-right-hand corner of the playbill: 13 rue Niçoise. Their operatives in France would have to follow the lead. It might be innocent, the home of an acquaintance, or a shop that specialized in ebony canes . . . or it might not be.

Miles was just folding the paper when he heard the sound. A sound that wasn't the rustle of leaves in the maple trees, or the faint crackle of embers from the banked fire, or the steady tick of the gilded clock on the mantelpiece. The lilting lines of melody from across the square had long since ceased. In the silence, Miles heard the stealthy slide of feet moving deliberately across the floor behind him.

That was all the warning Miles had before reflected silver flashed in the window. Acting on instinct, Miles dodged out of the way, and the serpent's fangs plunged through the glass instead of Miles's head, spewing shards with a hideous clatter. Miles's assailant raised the cane to strike again.

Whirling, Miles grabbed the cane and struck out with one booted foot. He heard something crack, and a high-pitched yelp of pain. His opponent abruptly released his grip on the cane, sending Miles sprawling back into Vaughn's armoire. By the time Miles had shaken his head clear and sprung back to his feet, his assailant had wrenched open the connecting door to the countess's chambers and disappeared into the darkness beyond.

Miles cursed fluently. Grabbing up the abandoned cane, he started in pursuit, until a new noise made him still in his tracks.

Make that lots of noises.

The broken window had done its work; the household had been awakened, and were after the intruder in full cry. Miles could hear masculine shouts of alarm, the shrill squeals of housemaids, and, far more ominous, the pounding of feet thudding down the hall to the earl's chambers.

Miles whirled grimly from the connecting door to the countess's chambers, through which his assailant had disappeared, to the doorknob of Vaughn's bedchamber, which was already beginning to rattle. The lock would only hold his unwitting pursuers for so long. There was, unfortunately, only one path to take.

Praying that his old skills had not entirely deserted him, Miles put one hand on the sill and vaulted out of the window—into a decidedly prickly hedge.

Some things never changed.

Assaulted by a hundred tiny stings, Miles crawled through the underbrush, yanking off mask and bandanna as he went. A few more yards and he would emerge from the shrubbery into the square, brush himself off, and stroll calmly out again in his guise of inebriated man about town. The servants would be looking for a footpad, not a bon vivant. Miles was just bracing himself to spring forth from the shrubbery, when, with all the perversity of memory, the answer hit him.

He knew where he had heard that name before.

Despite a bruised knee, a twisted wrist, and scratches on parts of his anatomy he didn't even want to think of, a cocky grin spread across Miles's unmasked face.

Tomorrow, he was going to the opera.

Chapter Thirteen

―――― ❦ ――――

"I t's locked," said Colin.

Feeling like a heroine from a gothic novel caught out in some mischief, I pulled away from the padlock I had been examining. The padlock was attached to a very thick oak door, which in its turn was attached to a large stone tower.

After a morning spent in the library poring over the Selwick archives, even my dedication had begun momentarily to flag. Henrietta's handwriting was perfectly legible, and Jane's a historian's dream, but Miles's was all but indecipherable. Besides, outside the library window, the sun was shining, the birds were chirping, and the larks were on the thorn.

Or was it the snails who were supposed to be on the thorn while the larks were on the wing? Either way, it didn't much matter. I wanted to be out there with them. Good weather in England in November is too rare not to take advantage of it.

Packing everything neatly away into their little acid-proof cases, I'd returned to my room to don my multipurpose Barbour jacket and the most sensible of my shoes. Unfortunately, given the nature of my shoe collection, they weren't terribly sensible, a pair of Coach stacked loafers with improbably narrow heels. They worked very well on the streets of London, and looked excellent extending under the hem of a pair of pants, which had been my primary consideration to date. I didn't think they'd fare all that well in crossing a patch of lawn.

I looked longingly at the spare pairs of Wellies lying about next to the kitchen door as I let myself out—there were some that didn't look too far from my size—but since I had already invaded Colin's home, it seemed like pushing it a bit too far to appropriate his sister's boots. At least, I assumed they were his sister's boots. Goodness only knew how many women flitted in and out of Colin's kitchen. I'd only been there three hours when the first one appeared. That could explain the large number of boots in the entryway.

Scolding myself for being silly, I made my way out of the kitchen and along a little stone path that someone had conveniently laid out once upon a time. The irregular stones were separated by broad swathes of creeping thyme and other greenery I couldn't recognize; the effect was too charmingly natural not to be deliberate. I picked my way from stone to stone, my heels and I giving sincere thanks to whoever had had the bright idea of putting something between their feet and the turf.

The path led around the side of the house, into the gardens. They were, for a modest gentleman's residence, fairly extensive gardens. I was lost within five minutes. Mind you, I have managed to get lost two blocks away from my own apartment, so that isn't saying much. In my meager and not very convincing defense, the gardens were laid out not in the formal French mode, where you can see for miles and even I have trouble losing my way, but in an English wilderness style, designed to lead the hapless wanderer down meandering paths into unexpected cul-de-sacs. Excellent for assignations among the shrubbery. I wondered idly if that was one of the reasons they had caught on in the eighteenth century. It was very hard to sneak out for a surreptitious smooch among flat parterres.

There was no hermit's cave complete with hermit and tortoise, *à la Arcadia,* but I did stumble across a faux Roman ruin, featuring larger-than-life-sized heads of miscellaneous emperors, and artistically arranged fallen columns. At least, I assumed it was faux. Had the Romans ever made it to Sussex? They might have; they tended to pop up in the most unexpected places (to fall back on the standard academic disclaimer, it's not my field), but I rather doubted they'd traveled with their favorite statues. Besides, Marcus Aurelius had a decidedly French look about the nose. I abandoned the classical folly for a pretty summer house entwined with vines, whose glossy dark leaves suggested they might become roses at some more promising point in the year.

I kept an eye out for a familiar blond head as I made my way along the pathways. I hadn't seen Colin at all since the previous evening, when I had left him doing the washing up. When I had gone down to the kitchen that morning, there had been a note propped against the sugar bowl, saying, "Out. Help yourself. C."

One had to admire the economy of language. Hemingway would approve. Dr. Johnson wouldn't.

Wherever "out" was, it wasn't in the gardens. The closest I came to a human form was a very smug Apollo playing his lyre above a fountain flanked by fawning naiads, like Elvis surrounded by swooning teenyboppers. I had a nice little chat with Apollo, much to the distress of the naiads, and clambered up on the rim of his fountain to try to get a better vantage point. These ramblings were all very amusing, but I did have a goal, of sorts, and if I was going to get there before the weather changed its mind about not raining, I needed to start being a bit more purposeful about it.

Ever since the car had pulled up the drive last night, I had been hankering to explore that hunk of stone in the distance. The library window provided an exceptionally fine view; the eye was drawn over the gardens, and straight to the noble monument on the hill, with its jagged outline of crumbling stone. It might merely be another folly, like the charming faux Roman fountain—there had been an eighteenth-century vogue for Gothic ruins as well as classical ones—but it seemed a bit massive and unadorned to be a mere garden decoration. Whatever it was, I wanted to explore.

An open expanse of field separated the gardens from the little tower mound. It was a longer walk than it looked, mostly uphill. I left a little trail of heel-shaped holes in my wake. More effective than bread crumbs for finding one's way home, I reassured myself.

The tower stood at the top of its own little summit. It was larger than it appeared from the house, constructed of massive stones that gave me the same dwarfed feeling I had the first time I'd been taken to the Temple of Dendur in the Met as a small child. Slowly, I paced the circumference of the structure, running a hand along the rough stone of the wall as I went. It was completely solid, without any apertures for the curious to peer through—or the covetous to besiege. Higher up, there were the thin shadows of arrow slits, but from ground level the place was entirely impermeable. It would have made a fine prison for Rapunzel.

The only way in was a thick door on the south side of the tower. There were no metal studs or intricate iron bolts or little grille set high in the door, or any of the other trappings of fairy tale. This door was a simple, workmanlike affair, with one purpose: to keep people out. It clearly wasn't the original door; the old timbers must have rotted long ago. Someone, fairly recently, had put in this sturdy contraption of oak. Just in case intruders—like me—didn't get the hint, it had been fastened shut with a padlock the size of a small handbag.

The padlock was very shiny, and very new. And very definitely locked.

That was where Colin came in. I turned to face him, squinting against the sunlight.

"I can see that it's locked, but what is it?"

Colin stood up very straight, locked his hands behind his back, adopted a vacant stare, and said in a credible tour-guide voice, "You see before you, miss, the first keep what was built by the Selwick family in the time of William the Conq'ror. That'll be four pounds fifty for entry."

"Really?"

Colin dropped the pose. He was wearing a faded pair of jeans with that soft sheen jeans get when they're on the verge of disintegrating in the next wash, and a battered green jacket. He looked relaxed. Happy. They were not attributes I associated with Colin. Tense and edgy were usually more like it.

"All right, then, five pounds."

"Does this really date back to the Conquest?"

Colin laid an affectionate hand on the rough stone of the wall, like a farmer slapping the rump of a prize cow.

"Probably not. Fulke de Selwicke was granted this land by the Conqueror in 1070 or thereabouts, but his original stronghold was most likely built of wood. Most of them were, you know," he informed me. I hadn't known, but I nodded knowledgably, anyway. "This keep probably dates to the twelfth century, at best."

I shoved my hair out of my eyes. The wind had picked up, and my hair was at that awkward length where it's not long enough to pull back effectively, but just long enough to be a nuisance.

"Can I go inside?"

I love old castles. For a while, I had considered studying the Middle Ages, just to have an excuse to clamber through crumbling old keeps. But then I discovered that you needed years of intensive training just to make out the handwriting. Not to mention that my reading Latin was still purely at an eighth-grade level. The eighteenth century was much easier. But I had never quite lost my fascination with castles, the more decrepit the better.

Colin shook his head. "Sorry, no visitors."

"Why not?"

"The place is falling apart. It's a huge insurance liability."

"Oh." I must have looked as disappointed as I felt, because Colin took pity.

"There's not much to see. The upper floors have entirely disintegrated. It's really nothing but a hollow shell."

"With arrow slits," I said wistfully. Arrow slits always conjure up images of Technicolor extravaganzas with Errol Flynn manning the battlements, and a fighting friar swigging ale somewhere in the background.

"We used it to store farm equipment," Colin said ruthlessly, "until a piece of coping crushed the back of a tractor."

"Have you no romance in your soul?" I demanded.

"There is nothing romantic," countered Colin, "about good equipment being ruined."

"Serves you right for putting farm equipment in there. It was probably the ghost of Fulke de Selwicke getting back at you for desecrating his keep."

"We don't have any ghosts, remember?" Colin took my elbow in one hand, and clamped his other arm across my back to steer me away from the tower. I automatically jerked away. Colin dropped his arm. I wasn't sure whether to be relieved or disappointed.

Relieved. Definitely relieved.

To hide my momentary confusion, I asked a question that had been idly floating about in my head. "If this isn't the principal seat of the Selwick family"—that was Uppington Hall in Kent, home to the current Marquis of Uppington, and favorite destination of tourist buses—"why is the original tower here?"

"Shouldn't it be the other way around?" Colin asked, with an amused sideways glance.

I threw him an exasperated look. "You know what I mean."

"There's nothing mysterious about it," said Colin, walking easily, hands in his pockets, as I braced myself against the downwards slope of the hill. I was beginning to be a little sorry I had shaken off his steadying hand. "The family wasn't elevated to the peerage until 1485. We backed the right side on Bosworth Field, against old Crouchback—"

"You mean when Henry Tudor stole the throne from poor, good King Richard? Richard had a much better claim to the throne than Henry." I sent him an arch glance that was only somewhat spoiled by my tripping over a malevolent rock. The rock was obviously a Tudor supporter.

Colin grabbed my arm to steady me, and let go again as soon as it became clear I wasn't in imminent danger of tumbling down the hill. "I wouldn't go repeating that if I were you. We're quite fond of good King Henry. He gave Sir William Selwick an estate confiscated from one of Richard's supporters near a little town called Uppington."

"Ah," I said. "Hence the title."

"Hence the title," Colin agreed. "It was only a barony at the time, but after the Restoration, Charles the Second elevated the baron to earl."

"For his loyal service to the Crown during the Civil Wars?" I guessed, conjuring up an image of a dashing cavalier in plumed hat.

"That," Colin said, with a suggestive lift of his eyebrows, "was the official story. The earl also had an exceptionally beautiful daughter."

"She didn't!" I exclaimed, easily caught up in the gossip of several hundred years ago. Charles II had been known for his roaming eye— and for his generosity in handing out titles to those who had warmed his bed.

"We'll never know for sure," Colin said tantalizingly, "but Lady Panthea bore a very swarthy son just eight months after her father was invested as earl."

"Lady Panthea was fair?" I guessed.

"Precisely," said Colin.

We nodded at each other in complete historical complicity. His hazel eyes caught mine. That look was an entire conversation in itself, one of those odd moments of unspoken communication when you know beyond a doubt that you're on the exact same page.

My damnable fair skin turned red with a thought that had nothing whatsoever to do with Charles II.

"What about the marquisate?" I asked awkwardly, pretending great interest in the flagstones beneath my feet. We had started up the little path to the kitchen door, and I made a show of stepping from stone to stone. "When did that come in?"

Colin shrugged. "It's not nearly as engaging a story. The earl at the time had some success as a general in the Wars of the Spanish Succession. Queen Anne raised him to marquis."

Colin stopped to open the kitchen door for me, waiting for me to precede him into the house. "I'd show you around the house, but I have some paperwork I need to get sorted before tonight."

I shook my head, feeling my tousled hair shift around my face. "That's all right. I should be getting back to the library anyway. But, listen, about tonight . . . if it's going to be weird for you having me at that party, I don't mind staying here on my own. I won't feel left out or anything."

Colin grinned. "Not looking forward to an evening with the vicar, are you?"

I bristled at the imputation of faintheartedness. "No! It's not that! I just—thought I might be butting in," I finished lamely.

"Trust me," said Colin dryly, "I don't resent the intrusion."

Now was the time to ask what the story was with Joan, and what the hell he thought he was doing using me as a human shield. "But Miss Plowden-Plugge might. I don't want to be nosy or anything, but—"

"Reading other people's letters isn't?"

"Not when they've been dead two hundred years," I retorted, before realizing that I'd just been cleverly rerouted. Damn, was I that easy to manipulate?

"One wonders whether they would agree," mused Colin.

I refused to be drawn in further. "About tonight—"

"If you don't have anything to wear," cut in Colin smoothly, "you can take a rummage around Serena's wardrobe."

How did he do that? Belligerently, I opened my mouth.

"She won't mind," Colin reassured me. "It's all several years out-of-date, anyway."

"Thanks," I muttered. "I think."

"Splendid! I'll leave you to it, then, shall I?" He strolled out, whistling.

Not surprising that he should whistle, I thought indignantly. He had just assured himself of a walking, talking buffer zone.

It wasn't that I minded, I told myself, clomping out of the kitchen and down the red-papered hall to the front stairs. It was just being conscripted without being asked that bothered me. And maybe, just a little, the notion that he wanted me along for something other than my charming company.

I took the stairs very, very slowly, pondering that thought. If I was to be honest with myself—which is really a highly overrated thing to do—it did rankle, just a little, to know that it wasn't my sparkling eyes and effervescent wit that had spurred him to press the invitation. I understood quite well that I had only been asked along to fend off Joan Plowden-Plugge. I made an effort to look at the situation with detached amusement. After all, romantic peccadilloes are always quite entertaining when one isn't at the center of them, and I should have been happily snickering into my sleeve at the thought of Colin hiding behind me to escape a predatory blonde. There was plenty of prospect for good old-fashioned slapstick.

Somehow, it wasn't quite as funny as it should have been.

I stopped and glowered at one of Colin's ancestors, who stared superciliously at me from a heavily gilded frame on the second-floor landing. You, I scolded myself, are refining too much on a look and a smile. So, fine, a moment ago, walking back, there had seemed to be just the tiniest bit of a spark there. And, all right, maybe I had been the tiniest—just the tiniest bit—intrigued. After all, he was handsome, if one liked that clean-cut, fair-haired, Prince William sort of look. He was clever, and amusing, and engaging—when he wanted to be. Not to mention that there are very few men out there who can bandy about English monarchs in conversation. That, to me, was more lethal than any number of washboard abs.

For goodness' sake! I was clearly letting Henrietta's mood infect my own. So far, in my limited acquaintance with Colin Selwick, he had been impossibly rude in a letter, followed it up by being even more insufferable in person, and only in the past day or so had thawed into normal human behavior.

Besides, even if this warm, friendly, relaxed Colin was the real thing, it was a horrible idea to get involved with someone whose archives I was using, almost as bad as an office romance. What if we started something (I pulled my disobedient mind back before it could go into too-detailed contemplation of what that something might be, complete with dialogue), it ended rapidly, and I still had several thousand pages' worth of manuscript to read? At best, it would exceedingly awkward. At worst, it might mean the end of my access to his library. Men come and go; manuscripts remain constant. Or something like that.

But there were those sideways glances. . . .

I clumped off down the hall in the direction of the library, as if by creating a clatter I could drown out the irritating hum of my own thoughts. On the verge of taking out the manuscripts, I paused. In this sort of mood, I could stare at the same page for half an hour without reading a word. And communing with Colin's ancestors was probably not the best way to take my mind off Colin.

Instead, I fished in my pocket and dug out my mobile. What I needed were voices, nice, modern, human voices. Like my little sister Jillian's. She would soon set me straight. But—I consulted my watch—it would only be nine-thirty in the morning back in the States, and Jilly wouldn't appreciate being woken up before noon on a Saturday. Nor, for that matter, would her roommates, who would all be sleeping off their Friday night revels. Last call for brunch in the dining hall wasn't till one o'clock, so why get up before twelve-forty-five? Ah, college.

Oh, well, I could always call Pammy. I scrolled through my list of contacts for her number. While she might not be any good at delicate emotional crises, Pammy was excellent at telling me I was behaving like a dimwit.

Wandering over to the window, I pressed SEND.

"Ellie!" squealed Pammy. The diminutives come of having known one another since we were five, along with a revolting wealth of embarrassing personal information. "How's Sussex?"

"I'm being a dimwit," I said, one eye on the window.

"What did you do?"

"Nothing . . . yet." Was that a flash of green jacket over there at the edge of the garden? No. It was a plant of some sort. They have those in gardens, I reminded myself. "I caught myself considering snogging Colin. Silly, no?"

"Why not?" yelled Pammy. "He's cute. You're single. Go for it!"

"You're supposed to tell me that I'm being ridiculous!"

"When was your last real date?" asked Pammy pointedly.

I did some quick mental calculation. That blind date back in March didn't count, nor did that June dinner with a colleague that was supposed to be platonic until the guy tried to grope me in the cab on the way back. A whack on the offending hand convinced him of the error of his assumptions. The truth was, I just hadn't met anyone who seemed worth expending the time and effort of dating. As a place to meet eligible men, a university campus (unless you're an undergrad, in which case it's like having your own private buffet) ranks just slightly above convents and concerts of folk music. And since I'd moved to London . . . well, there's always an excuse, isn't there?

"Last December," I muttered. The date of my highly publicized and messy breakup with Grant.

"That's pathetic!"

"I love you, too, Pams."

"Listen, there was an article in this month's *Cosmo*"—a rustle of papers in the background as Pammy shuffled through her extensive magazine collection—"here it is! 'Ten Easy Ways to Seduce the Pants off Him.'"

"But I don't want—"

Pammy kept going full steam ahead. "Wear something sexy tonight. No tweed. Do you have a bustier?"

"No!" I yelped.

"Oh, I'd loan you mine, but the Sussex thing is kind of a problem. How about—"

"Don't even think of it," I said grimly. Pammy occupied the fringes of the fashion world. Combine that with an absolute lack of a) taste, and b) shame, and you had the red leather bustier, the dress made out of multicolored feathers, and the hot pink snakeskin pants. Thursday night she had tried to persuade me into an outfit constructed entirely out of two handkerchiefs.

I was saved by the agitated bling of Pammy's landline.

"Uh-oh! Gotta go. Good luck tonight! I want all the juicy details tomorrow, and I mean all! Mwah!"

"There won't be any—grrr." The line had gone dead.

So much for Pammy setting me straight. Oh, the hell with it all! I jammed my phone back into my pocket. I was going back to the nineteenth century, where at least no one printed articles about seducing the pants off idiot men one didn't want to seduce, anyway, even if one owned a bustier, which one didn't.

Maybe I should take Colin up on that offer to raid Serena's wardrobe. She was a little skinner than me, and a little taller, but in a cocktail dress, surely that didn't matter that much, did it? And if it were a little tighter and shorter than it was supposed to be, well . . .

Urgh! Dammit, I wasn't going to tart myself up, and I wasn't going to seduce anyone, and I wasn't going to go all weak-kneed over high cheekbones and an opportune reference to Charles II. That way madness lay, complete with huge signs warning, "Here be dragons." One dragon in particular. Prone to sudden flares. Probably gobbled up the odd village maiden in his spare time, leaving only the Wellies behind.

Dragging out the collection I had been working with before, I unlooped the string holding the box together, and forced my mind back to more important problems, like long-dead French spies.

If the drinks party from hell wasn't starting until seven-thirty, and it was only two-thirty now, I should still be able to get several hours of work in. It wouldn't, I told myself firmly, take me that long to dress. There was no reason to make any special effort, and there was every reason to stay longer in the library. I still had no inkling as to the identity of the Black Tulip, although for Henrietta's sake, I wouldn't have minded if it turned out to be the Marquise de Montval.

Of course, there was still Vaughn's mysterious behavior to be reckoned with, and Miles's midnight assailant. I had gone over his letter to Richard describing the incident three times, hoping to find something I'd missed, an asterisk or a postscript giving some inkling as to the appearance of the figure who had swung at him with the cane, but there was none. Either he hadn't caught much of a glimpse, or he hadn't thought what he saw worth noting.

Unlike that playbill, about which he had gone on for several paragraphs in tones of increasing excitement. Personally, I thought he was refining too much on a bookmark—goodness only knows I'm prone to grabbing up whatever piece of paper is lying nearest at hand—old movie tickets, the phone bill, postcards—and wedging it between the pages. Vaughn's being in France was interesting, but not necessarily damning.

As for the opera singer . . . like Miles, the reference niggled at my memory. I knew I'd come across something similar before, during my early pre-England days of dissertation research, when I was reading whatever I could get my hands on in Harvard's libraries, from old periodicals preserved on microfilm to whatever contemporary correspondence had made it into scholarly editions. There had been something about an opera singer, I recalled with mounting excitement. Rumors of a connection with Napoleon. Accusations of espionage. And her name had ended with A.

Just like every other opera singer in existence, I reminded myself dryly.

Damn. I could practically *see* the page in my head, scrolling across the grimy screen of the microfilm reader in the basement of Lamont. It had been a gossip column of some sort—and had it been the opera singer who was accused of being a spy, or her husband? Of course, this could all be made quite simple by opening my laptop and using the FIND feature on my notes, but, no, that would make it all too easy. I was embarked on a personal grudge match with my memory.

Catalani. That was her name. Fine, so it didn't end with an A. It was a vowel, wasn't it? And there were two As in the name, so, really, it was a more than reasonable mistake.

Damn. It would have been so convenient if the opera singer in question had been Mme. Fiorila.

Come to think of it, the entire incident had been much later, too, not until . . . 1807? 1808?

Maybe, I thought wildly, there was a whole spy network out there, composed entirely of opera singers!

Maybe I was being entirely ridiculous.

Definitely the latter.

With a little grimace at my own folly, I retreated to my favorite chair, and unwound the string from the acid-free box that contained Henrietta's diary and correspondence for the year 1803. Hopefully Henrietta's meditations were proving more fruitful than mine.

At least she wasn't wasting her time staring off into the gardens in the hopes of a glimpse of a certain man among the shrubbery! Manuscripts, I reminded myself firmly. I was here for manuscripts, not men.

With that salutary kick in the pants, I tore my eyes away from the window, and directed them firmly towards the closely written pages of Henrietta's diary.

Chapter Fourteen

———— ✿ ————

Bookshop *(n.)*: *a den of espionage, intrigue, and sedition*
—from the Personal Codebook of the Pink Carnation

"There!" announced Penelope. "You just did it again."

Browsing among the new stock at Hatchards Bookshop, Henrietta shook herself out of a daydream involving Miles, a white horse, and herself in a charmingly flowing gown. "Did what?"

She glanced from the novels she was examining to her friend, who stood glowering over the display like a wicked stepsister come to life out of the pages. Charlotte was two feet away, immersed in a new import from France that promised to be a dashing tale of love and intrigue. Hmm, love. Intrigue. Miles. Henrietta's lips curved in a secret smile.

"Ha!" Penelope jabbed a finger at her, causing her reticule to swing straight at Henrietta like a medieval mace aimed to maim. "That . . . *smile*. You've been smiling like that all morning."

"Really." Henrietta tried to look like she had no idea what Penelope was talking about. She picked up a book at random and began leafing idly through the pages.

It hadn't been *all* morning. She had been perfectly composed through breakfast, and only done one impromptu twirl in the upstairs hallway, which didn't count, because no one had seen.

Last night, Henrietta had retired early from the Middlethorpes' with a torn flounce—how that flounce had come to be torn was a matter of mystery to the matrons in the ladies' retiring room, who were quite used to seeing young ladies rush in with snagged hems, but seldom ripped sleeves—and an equally ragged temper. There was nothing to do for it but go early to bed and hope the mood went away. If sleep could knit raveled sleeves of care, it could certainly whisk away a bout of ill temper. She would go to bed, Henrietta told herself, and when she woke up, the world would have readjusted itself along comfortable, familiar lines, and all would be happy again.

There was only one problem with that plan. She couldn't sleep. Every time she closed her eyes, there, imprinted on the back of her lids like a garish billboard, stood Miles. Miles grinning, Miles eating biscuits, Miles dancing with Charlotte, Miles spilling lemonade.

Miles looming close enough to kiss.

Henrietta experimented with opening her eyes, but that was even worse, because open eyes meant wakefulness, and wakefulness meant thinking, and there were too many things that Henrietta was doing her best not to think about, like Miles driving with the marquise, or, even worse, why on earth it should matter to her that Miles was driving with the marquise. It wasn't, after all, as though his taking the marquise driving presented a personal inconvenience to Henrietta. She had a lesson with Signor Marconi at six o'clock tomorrow that effectively precluded her afternoon drive with Miles, which meant that she couldn't have ridden with him even if she'd wanted to.

But she still didn't want the marquise there in her place.

Henrietta groaned and rolled over onto her stomach, inadvertently squishing Bunny in the process. "Sorry, sorry," she whispered urgently, scooting over and yanking Bunny out from underneath her.

Bunny regarded her reproachfully from under floppy cloth ears. "I'm being an idiot," Henrietta informed Bunny.

Bunny didn't argue. Bunny never argued. That was usually one of Bunny's great charms as a confidante. Sometimes a girl needed a bit of unconditional agreement.

"It shouldn't matter to me at all who Miles chooses to take driving,"

Henrietta said firmly. "Why should I care who he takes driving? It's of no matter to me. Well, it *isn't*."

There was a highly sardonic gleam in Bunny's black glass eyes. "Urgh!"

There was no point in arguing with inanimate objects if they were going to get the better of the argument without even saying anything.

Henrietta flung off the bedclothes and stomped over to the window, where the full moon silvered the plants in the garden and glinted off the windows of the neighboring houses. It was a moon for lovers' trysts, for clandestine kisses in gardens, for murmured endearments. Somewhere, under that same moon, Miles was off . . . with the marquise? Playing cards with Geoff? Alone in his bachelor quarters? Henrietta left off trying to pretend to herself that it didn't matter. It did. She wasn't sure why, but it did.

Henrietta sank down onto the chaise longue next to the window, and tucked her feet up under the embroidered hem of her nightdress. Wrapping her arms around her legs, she rested her chin on her knees and thought back over the past couple of days, when the world had begun to fall out of joint.

She couldn't blame it on her courses; those had come and gone a week ago, with their attendant stomach pains, spots, and snippiness. That would have been too easy. This was a distemper of the mind rather than the body, and it had begun with the arrival of the marquise. No, Henrietta corrected herself with brutal honesty. Not with the arrival of the marquise. With Miles's lingering to speak to the marquise.

Henrietta banged her forehead against her knees. There was really no escaping it, was there? She was jealous. Jealous, jealous, jealous. Miles was supposed to be *her* escort, *her* permanent cavalier.

Where there was jealousy . . .

Henrietta jerked her head up so quickly that she nearly tumbled off the chaise. She couldn't have fallen in love with Miles. The very term, with all of its poetic resonance, conjured up something grand and dramatic. There was nothing whatsoever grand or dramatic in the way Henrietta felt about Miles. It was a very simple concept, really:

She just didn't want to share him with anyone. Ever. She wanted to be the person his eyes sought out in a crowded ballroom, the person he nudged when he had a really smashing joke he just had to tell, the first person he saw when he woke up in the morning, and the last person he spoke to when he went to bed at night. She wanted to be the one whose ear he whispered in at the opera, and the one perched next to him in his alarmingly tottery phaeton when he drove in the park at five.

Love, Henrietta told herself with a decisiveness she was far from feeling, was something of a different caliber entirely.

Before their first Season, she and Penelope and Charlotte had spent endless hours eating whatever biscuits were left after Miles raided the tray, and discussing Love. Love with a capital letter, that would swoop down with shining wings and carry them away to realms of enchantment hitherto undreamed of. Love, of course, would be properly attired in tight tan buckskins, wear an immaculately tied cravat, and have a vaguely rakish air. His arrival would be heralded by violins in the background, an impressive fireworks display, and the odd clap of thunder, all signaling to her instantly that the love of her life had come to her. And here she was, without a thunderbolt in striking distance, musing over Miles, Miles who had been there nearly all of her life, without any sort of emotional pyrotechnics taking place.

It was ludicrous. If she did harbor deeper feelings for Miles, wouldn't she have known sooner? Wouldn't she have felt odd constrictions of the heart as he snatched biscuits out from in front of her, and turned cartwheels into the duck pond? All the books were quite clear on that point: When one's true love turned up, one was supposed to *know*. Immediately.

Of course, she had been not quite two when Miles first showed up at their door, and her vision of love at the time had a lot to do with warm milk.

Henrietta turned her head to stare thoughtfully at the moon. By all the classic measures, she couldn't be in love with Miles. But how did one account for the fact that the very thought of him driving with someone else filled her with bitter wormwood and gall? As for the thought of him marrying someone else . . . the idea was too harrowing to even contemplate.

Miles. The name tasted right on her tongue.

Henrietta chuckled in the darkness. Of course it did! She had been uttering it in various tones of assertion, annoyance, and affection for the past eighteen years. Eighteen years. Henrietta let her chin sink back to her knees and thought about eighteen years of Miles. She thought about the way his cravat never stayed tied and his hair never stayed brushed, and the way his smiles always seemed too big for his face.

Millions of memories of Miles crowded one after the other in glorious chronological disorder. Miles letting her take the reins of his curricle and drive his beloved bays, breathing down her neck all the while—hmph, she had been nowhere near that tree. Miles popping out of her wardrobe as the Phantom Monk of Donwell Abbey, but ruining the effect by yanking the sheet off his head the minute she screamed. The scream had been one of indignation, rather than fear (she wasn't simpleminded; she'd seen the black shoes poking out under the edge of the habit), but it seemed a shame to inform Miles of that when he was so busy apologizing. There was the summer she was thirteen and had climbed too far up the old oak in the back of Uppington Hall. It had seemed a good idea at the time, a floating faerie tower in which to read and daydream, but less of a good idea once she was up there, perched precariously on a tree limb, book tucked into her sash, and the ground a long way away. Henrietta was not a tree-climbing sort of girl. Richard had gone for a ladder, but Miles, grumbling all the way, had scaled the tree trunk and helped her down, branch by shaky branch.

There could be worse things than falling in love with one's oldest friend.

A slow smile began to spread across Henrietta's face. It lingered there while she slept, returned when she woke, and crept back at intervals throughout the morning.

Penelope yanked down the book Henrietta was holding in front of her face. "Do stop trying to hide. Why all the smiling?"

"It's Miles."

"What has the big oaf done now?"

"Miles isn't an oaf," Henrietta replied tolerantly. They had been through this before.

"No, he's a *big* oaf."

An unexpected chuckle rose from behind Charlotte's book. "Have you ever heard of a little oaf?"

Henrietta decided to intervene before they wandered irreversibly off on that fascinating tangent. "I have," she said, running her finger along the spine of the book, "developed a bit of a *tendre* for Miles."

"You've developed a what?" yelped Penelope.

"I think she said *tendre*," filled in Charlotte helpfully.

"Don't be ridiculous," argued Penelope. "It's Miles."

Henrietta assumed the sort of beatific expression more commonly associated with wings, halos, and Renaissance altar paintings. "Miles," she agreed.

Penelope stared at her closest friend in horrified disbelief. In desperation, Penelope flung out a hand to Charlotte. "You say something to her!"

Lowering her book, Charlotte shook her head, a small smile flitting about her lips. "I can't say I'm surprised. I *had* wondered. . . ."

"Wondered what?" inquired Henrietta eagerly.

Charlotte lowered her voice confidingly. "Has it never struck you as odd that the minute you walk into a ballroom, the first person you gravitate towards is Miles?"

"She likes the lemonade?" suggested Penelope.

"I don't think it's the lemonade." Charlotte turned back to Henrietta. "It's always been you and Miles. It just took a long time for you to notice."

"How do you know that?" countered Penelope crossly. "This isn't one of your silly romantic novels. Just because Miles is always loafing about doesn't mean that he's . . . that they're . . . you know!"

Henrietta ignored her. "When you say it's always been me and Miles, do you mean it's always been me following along after Miles, or something else?"

Charlotte considered. "He does seek you out," she said after a pause that lasted several agonizing years. Henrietta felt her spine relax. Then Charlotte had to spoil it by adding, "I don't think there's anything romantic about it, though. At least, not yet."

"Blast." It was nothing Henrietta hadn't considered herself, but it still wasn't pleasant hearing it. "How do I get him to stop thinking of me as a little sister?"

"Never speak to him again?"

"Pen! I'm serious about this!"

"You're sure there's not someone—"

"Quite sure," Henrietta cut her off. "Ouch!"

She staggered as someone squeezed past her along the narrow aisle, treading on her toes and jerking her reticule loose in the process. The little bag tipped sideways, spilling coins, several new hair ribbons, and a spare handkerchief across the floor.

"Oh, for heaven's sake!" Henrietta dropped to the floor, pouncing on an adventurous coin before it could spin merrily away underneath the table. Charlotte ran for another, which, in the miraculous way of fallen currency, had already managed to bounce several yards away. Henrietta spared a moment to be thankful that she had dropped off her latest report at the ribbon shop before joining her friends at Hatchards. Somehow, she didn't think Jane would approve of it drifting about the floor of the bookstore, even properly swathed in code.

Penelope plunked to her knees on the floor next to Henrietta, as Henrietta shoved her belongings back into her bag.

"All right," Penelope muttered, lunging under the table to grab one last shilling that had tried to make its escape and poking it into Henrietta's reticule. "I'll help. But I still think he's an oaf."

"A big oaf?" Henrietta used the tabletop to lever herself to her feet, and pressed a kiss to her best friend's cheek. The offer might have been graceless, but she knew how long Penelope had disliked Miles and how hard-won that small concession had been. Yanking open her reticule just wide enough for Charlotte to slide one last coin through, Henrietta wound her bag tightly around her wrist. "Thank you, Pen. Now, ideas?"

Charlotte stared dreamily off into space. "In *Evelina*, she wins Lord Orville through her innate sweetness and good nature."

Pen vented some of her thwarted irritation by sending Charlotte a withering look.

"Well, she asked if I had any ideas!" protested Charlotte.

"How does one portray innate sweetness and good nature?" inquired Hen.

"If you have to think about it, you probably don't have it," said Charlotte thoughtfully.

Henrietta grimaced. "Thanks, Charlotte."

"Oh, no!" Charlotte dropped her book in her distress. "I didn't mean it that way! You're one of the sweetest people I know."

"Here." Penelope dragged both of them over to a rack of magazines in the corner of the store. "None of this inner sweetness rot. You need to take a more practical approach."

She yanked down a copy of the *Cosmopolitan Lady's Book* and began leafing through.

Henrietta pointed to one of the headlines. "You might want to take a look at that one, Pen."

Penelope turned it over to see "Humiliation on a Balcony! The Five Minutes That Ruined My Life."

"Oh, ha, ha. Hmm, that's not a bad idea, though . . . if you got Miles out on a balcony, and arranged for a witness—that would be me—to burst indignantly onto the scene, you could be married within the week."

Henrietta shook her head decisively. "I don't want to trap him. If he marries me, I want it to be because he loves me, not because he's forced into it."

Charlotte nodded furiously in agreement.

Penelope rolled her eyes. "All right, if you want to go about it the hard way."

Huddled in a corner of Hatchards they went through "Use Your Eyes to Tell Him He's the One" (Henrietta went cross-eyed trying to gaze meaningfully into Penelope's eyes); "Ten Tricks for a More Flirtatious Fan" (three books tumbled to the floor); and "Ravish Him with Roses," which wasn't nearly as titillating as it sounded, having to do mostly with flower arrangements.

"Brilliant," said Hen disgustedly. "I can stun him into immobility by going cross-eyed, knock him senseless with my fan, and stick a rose in his teeth while he's unconscious. Nothing says 'I love you' quite like a mouthful of thorns."

"Maybe if you held your wrist just a little lower while flicking open the fan?" suggested Charlotte.

"It's no good," said Henrietta, rubbing the offending joint. "I'm not going to turn into a ravishing seductress overnight. Besides, that role has already been filled."

Penelope looked perplexed.

Charlotte grimaced in comprehension. "The Marquise de Montval."

"The very one," said Henrietta.

"Oh, no," breathed Charlotte.

"I know." Henrietta grimaced. "It's hopeless, isn't it?"

"No," Charlotte hissed, flapping her hands in agitation. "It's not that. She's right there. To your left. Don't . . ."

Henrietta and Penelope both swiveled sharply to the left.

". . . look," Charlotte finished weakly.

The marquise bent a casual glance on Henrietta and her companions, then continued on her way to the till, book in hand.

"Who knew she could read?" muttered Henrietta.

"Shhhh . . ." Charlotte cast an anxious glance back at the marquise, shepherding Henrietta and Penelope towards the back of the store, out of earshot.

"She all but propositioned Miles last night." Henrietta fumed, glowering around the bookshelves in the general direction of the marquise. "In front of me!"

"But did he accept?" asked Charlotte quietly.

"Maybe you should just leave him to her," broke in Penelope. "If he's the sort of man who'd succumb to a woman like that, why would you want him?"

"What man wouldn't succumb to a woman like that?" returned

Henrietta wryly. Even in profile, across the length of the store, the marquise's flawless complexion shone like the legendary beacon at Alexandria.

Usually, Henrietta was quite pleased with her own appearance. She knew she'd never set off a flotilla of ships, but she liked the oval face reflected in the mirror. She liked her thick brown hair with its reddish glints; she liked her high cheekbones and her small nose; and she was especially fond of the almond-shaped eyes that tilted at the corners in a way that Charlotte had fondly assured her lent her an exotic air.

Next to the marquise, Henrietta felt about as exotic as sticky toffee pudding.

As she watched, the marquise tucked her purchase into her reticule and swayed gracefully out of the shop.

"Even her *walk* is a poem," groaned Henrietta.

"I'm not sure Miles is quite as susceptible as you think," said Charlotte, running a finger along the spine of one of the novels on the table next to her. "He didn't seem eager to linger at her side."

"He didn't have to," Henrietta said reluctantly, refusing to allow herself the false comfort of Charlotte's words. "They're driving together today. The marquise was the one to suggest it," she added, before Charlotte could ask. "But Miles could have refused."

"There's only one way to find out, isn't there?" Penelope leaned forward, reticule swinging, amber eyes gleaming.

"What do you mean?" Henrietta asked warily.

"We could follow them. We'll lie in wait in Hyde Park and wait for them to drive by. If Miles is fending off her advances"— Penelope's tone suggested she thought that highly unlikely—"then you'll know he's worthy of your attention. If not . . ." Penelope shrugged.

"How perfectly romantic," breathed Charlotte. "Like the wife of the Green Knight testing Sir Gawain."

"It's a dreadful idea!" protested Henrietta. "And didn't Sir Gawain fail the test?"

Charlotte's cheeks turned a guilty pink.

"Ha!" Penelope pointed a finger at Hen. "You don't want to go along with it because you're afraid you'll see something you don't want to see."

"Nooooo." Henrietta plunked her hands on her hips. "I don't want to go along with it because it's a horrible idea. It's entirely impractical. First, we have no idea which route Miles is taking. Second, how do we see him without his seeing us? Third . . . uh . . ." Blast, she didn't have a third. She knew there was one—and most likely a fourth, fifth and sixth as well—but none was popping to mind, other than a generalized sense of outraged misgiving, which she doubted Penelope would take as an acceptable argument.

"Which way does Miles usually drive?" asked Penelope.

"Along the Serpentine," muttered Henrietta.

"And does he ever deviate from this route? In all the years you have been driving with him?"

"He might!"

"We'll disguise ourselves," said Penelope enthusiastically. "We can hide behind a hedge—or even better, up a tree! And when he comes along we'll just look down and—"

"Never," said Henrietta decisively. "Absolutely out of the question. I would never stoop that low."

"Is it really low if you're up a tree?" asked Charlotte.

"I CANNOT BELIEVE I'M DOING THIS," muttered Henrietta three hours later.

She stooped behind a bush in Hyde Park with Penelope crouching beside her on one side, and Charlotte on the far side of Penelope. They were dressed all in green—to blend into the scenery, Penelope had explained with relish—and resembled nothing so much as a troupe of lost leprechauns, or a bunch of frogs who had misplaced their lily pad.

Henrietta adjusted the green bandeau in her hair. "I don't know how I let you talk me into this."

"Did you have a better idea? Let's think about that. No, you didn't."

Hmm. There was that. Henrietta subsided back beneath the bush. After a moment, she popped up again. "How do we even know they'll come this way?"

"If they don't, we'll just go home again."

"Why don't we just go home now?" Henrietta started to struggle to her feet.

Penelope grabbed her by the sleeve and yanked her back down. "Sit!"

Henrietta sat down hard in a patch of wet grass.

"I cannot believe I'm doing this."

A sudden squeal came from Charlotte, green and silent on the other side of Penelope. "Shhhhh! I see them! I see them!"

Henrietta sprang up again, just far enough that she could see over the edge of the shoulder-high hedge. "Where?"

"There!" Charlotte pointed down the beaten dirt track that wound along the Serpentine. There, unmistakably, was Miles's pale blue high-perch phaeton, drawn by his two matched bays. The woman seated next to Miles was equally unmistakable; she wore a driving dress of deep gray, banded in purple, which despite its high neck nonetheless managed to draw attention to all the attributes one might want noticed if one had seduction on the agenda. Instead of trying to impersonate a hedge.

Miles, Henrietta noticed a bit smugly, was wearing his blandest man-about-town face, which, translated, meant he wasn't listening to a word the marquise was saying. Every now and again, he would remember he was supposed to be engaged in a conversation, paste a momentary smile on his face, nod slowly, and murmur something in that low grumble that passed for conversation among men. Henrietta knew that look well. Miles didn't use it on her anymore, because he didn't like being poked in the ribs.

It did not, however, seem to be deterring the marquise one whit. Henrietta's warm glow of satisfaction faded. Despite the fact that they were in public, the marquise was making herself shamefully free of Miles's person. She had turned on the seat so that her body was perpendicular to Miles, her face, under the slightest wisp of a bonnet, near enough to kiss. She was smiling into Miles's abstracted face, while one hand trailed across his chest. Good heavens, was that woman reaching under Miles's jacket? Henrietta stared in fascinated disgust.

Miles twitched distractedly.

Henrietta ought, at that point, to have ducked behind the hedge. But she was too busy staring at Miles's torso, trying to figure out what on earth the marquise was doing with her hand, and whether there was any way to dislodge it—a subtly thrown rock, perhaps?—without making her presence known, and spooking the horses in the process. Instead of seeking cover, she stared straight at Miles, her gaze moving up from his blue-and-yellow-striped waistcoat to his face, to see how he was reacting to this bold assault upon his person.

Her eyes lifted in the direction of his—and caught.

Henrietta froze, horror beginning to wash over her from the tips of her toes, past the ant that was crawling up along her leg, all the way up to her wide, startled eyes, which were so inextricably locked with a very familiar pair of brown eyes that were moving steadily closer as the horses trotted along. Oh, no. He couldn't be looking her way. He couldn't.

Henrietta could have smiled and waved. She could have pretended she was just on a walk. She could have strolled calmly the other way as though she hadn't recognized him. She could have done any number of perfectly plausible things that would have sufficed to allay the suspicion of a person of the male persuasion.

Henrietta took one panicked look at Miles, and flung herself face-down behind the bush.

Chapter Fifteen

————— ❧ —————

Phaeton *(n.)*: *1) Apollo's son, chiefly famed for destroying his father's chariot; 2) a silly sort of vehicle favored by sporting enthusiasts; 3) spectacular failure in one's mission. See also under* Crash *and* Burn

—from the Personal Codebook of the Pink Carnation

"Quite." Miles cast a winning smile in the general direction of the woman sitting next to him. "Absolutely."

To say that Miles was slightly preoccupied would have been akin to saying that the Prince Regent had a slight penchant for spending money. Despite the lavish charms of the woman next to him, his mind was on other things entirely. An opera singer, to be precise.

True to his resolution, Miles had made his way to the opera house in Haymarket that afternoon, to have a little chat with the newly arrived Madame Fiorila. A little bit of preliminary intelligence gathering had netted Miles the information that her first performance had taken place three nights before, to a packed house. The previous night, she had been engaged for a private party—not, Miles's informant had hastened to add, *that* kind of private party. It had been an evening of song arranged by an elderly noblewoman with musical pretensions.

Decking himself out in his most dandified attire, Miles had set out for the opera house in the guise of eager swain, prepared to woo out of Madame Fiorila any information she might have about Lord Vaughn, Paris, and the mysterious address in the rue Niçoise. In one hand he carried an elaborate bunch of flowers, in the other, a playbill from Tuesday night's performance (acquired from the ever-obliging Turnip Fitzhugh), to add verisimilitude to his story that he had seen her sing and been overcome by her beauty and charm. Dash it all, he hoped she was beautiful; otherwise his story might be somewhat lacking. If she was a matronly woman with a bosom like a feather bolster, his smitten state might be somewhat harder to explain.

It never came to that point. Madame Fiorila, the porter informed him, was receiving no callers. She was indisposed. A sixpence failed to change the porter's message. A half crown didn't do any better, but did elicit the information that Madame Fiorila had abruptly canceled her performance for that night and all of her engagements for the next week. She was, reiterated the porter, indisposed. Miles had left the flowers, along with his card, urging the porter to inform him if there were any change in the lady's condition.

Another lead lost. Of course, there were still her lodgings to locate and inspect, and numerous other avenues he could explore, but it was a dashed nuisance not being able to see her in person. At least then he might have a better idea of whether Vaughn's interest was professional or amorous.

A stop at the Alien Office to discover the identity of Vaughn's hooded companion had proved no more fruitful. It had not been, Miles reflected, the best of days. Madame Fiorila had proved elusive, the Alien Office barren, and he still had no inkling at all as to the identity of last night's assailant.

Miles's first assumption, based largely on the sight of a silver-headed cane plowing towards his head, had been that his attacker was Vaughn. But Geoff, confronted at Pinchingdale House at an ungodly hour of the morning (before noon, at any rate), had decisively denied that possibility. Several times. With increasing emphasis. No, he hadn't let Vaughn out of his sight. No, he was really quite sure. No,

Vaughn couldn't have left the room without his knowing. Would Miles like him to find a Bible somewhere to swear on?

Miles had politely turned down the offer of a Bible. Really, Geoff was dashed touchy these days.

Geoff had also mentioned, as proof of his complete concentration on the movements of Vaughn, that Vaughn had indeed approached Henrietta, solicited her hand for a dance, and reiterated his hopes that she would grace his humble abode that evening.

Too many bloody men were showing interest in Henrietta. First Frobisher, now Vaughn. If Miles had known that keeping her out of the arms of her amorous suitors was going to be a full-time job, he would have told Richard to keep an eye on her himself. All that was needed was for Prinny to take an interest in Hen, and then they'd really be in for it.

Could she just try to be a little less attractive?

For a start, she could pull her hair back more sternly. Those little wisps at the nape of her neck practically invited caresses. Then there were her gowns. The gowns definitely had to go. Miles jerked harder than he'd intended on the reins. Not like that. The gowns definitely had to stay on. There would be no mental removing of clothing. None at all. He'd just pretend that little thought sequence hadn't happened. What he meant was the gowns needed to be replaced, preferably with something of a thick, heavy material that wouldn't cling to her legs when she walked. And whatever it was, it had better bloody well button straight up to the neck. Dammit all, what was Lady Uppington thinking, letting Hen go around half-exposed like that?

Miles tugged at his cravat.

"Unseasonably warm day for May, isn't it?" he said to the marquise.

At least, that was what he opened his mouth to say to the marquise. Miles's mouth remained open, but no sound came out. As he'd turned to look at his companion, his eye caught a glimpse of a very familiar forehead.

Good God, was that . . . Henrietta? Miles blinked a few times, wondering if there was any truth to the old wives' tale that if you thought about a person hard enough they'd appear. She certainly looked pretty solid for a figment of his imagination. And green. Very green.

As Miles tried to puzzle that one out, Henrietta's eyes met his. Her hazel eyes widened, and an expression of indescribable horror flashed across her face. Before he could lift his hand in greeting, Henrietta's forehead disappeared. Just like that. One minute it was there; the next minute it wasn't.

Pulling back on the reins, Miles drew his team to an expert stop.

"Is something wrong?" inquired the marquise, with just a bit of an edge to her voice.

Miles didn't answer right away. He was too busy leaning as far as he could over the edge of the phaeton without tipping the whole contraption over. He had seen Henrietta, hadn't he? At least, a small piece of Henrietta, poking over the edge of that bush. Miles peered more closely. Now, the bush just looked like . . . a bush. Green. Bushy. In fact, it bore a remarkable resemblance to that prickly thing he'd tumbled into last night. It didn't in the least bit resemble Henrietta.

Miles frowned. Had he descended to imagining things? True, he wasn't his usual well-rested and collected self—Miles ignored the little voice in his head that snorted at the latter half of that statement; it was bad enough to conjure Hen up behind bushes without her voice joining in, too—but, seeing people who weren't there? Maybe he should cut back on the claret.

Just as Miles was about to consign himself to a dark little hole in Bedlam, he saw it. A shape that could not possibly belong to shrubbery. In fact, it looked remarkably like a well-rounded derriere.

The possessor of the attribute in question hunched facedown behind the hedge, clinging desperately to the timeless delusion that if she couldn't see anyone, no one could see her.

"I," muttered Henrietta through a mouthful of grass, "am an idiot. I am a great big idiot."

She spat out a small bug that had ventured into her mouth, and continued her litany of misery in tight-lipped silence. Maybe, she told herself, maybe, if she was truly fortunate, Miles hadn't seen her after all. Maybe, she thought, on a tide of rising optimism, he had been too preoccupied with the horses to notice. Maybe, even if he had noticed, he would convince himself he had imagined it. People were, after all, very good at not seeing what they didn't expect to see, and goodness only knew Miles wouldn't expect to find her crouching behind a bush. Maybe . . .

Two sets of hooves clomped to a halt right in front of Henrietta's hedge.

Maybe she should emigrate to Australia under an assumed name. Preferably within the next five seconds.

"Why, Mr. Dorrington!" the marquise exclaimed in tones of alarming sweetness, "Isn't that your little friend behind that hedge?"

Someone groaned. Henrietta realized it had been her.

Farther down the hedge, loyal Charlotte had already popped up, and was saying brightly, "Hello, Mr. Dorrington! How lovely, and, um, unexpected to see you."

Henrietta tentatively tilted her head. With the one eye that wasn't buried in the grass, Hen could see Charlotte's hand, under cover of the foliage, making little flapping motions, urging her to stay down. Seeking reinforcements, Charlotte dragged Penelope up by the arm.

"Penelope and I were just . . . um . . ."

Henrietta couldn't see what was going on in the curricle, but just picturing it made her wince. The marquise's brows arched in an expression of supercilious disbelief. Miles, half amused, half confused. Penelope and Charlotte standing there behind the hedge like a leprechaun honor guard.

"Would you be so kind as to tell Henrietta I'm here?" Miles was saying politely.

Oh, blast. Blast, blast, blast.

Henrietta rose very slowly, brushing grass and dirt and debris off her knees, fervently hoping she didn't have any twigs in her hair, or dirt smudges on her cheeks, just to make her humiliation complete.

"Hello," she said hopelessly. It was just as she'd imagined: the marquise in all her perfection eyeing her as she would an oversized insect, and Miles, blast him, with a look of barely contained amusement pasted all over his transparent face. "We were . . ."

"I know," Miles helpfully filled in for her. "Just, um. Charlotte told me. By the way, you have a twig in your hair."

"How unique," contributed the marquise.

Henrietta lifted her chin. The twig came unmoored and bobbed distractingly against her cheek. "We were just on a nature walk," she said brightly, brushing away the twig. "To look at . . . um . . ."

"Nature!" finished Charlotte.

Penelope, the traitor, snickered into her green lace handkerchief.

Hmph. If Henrietta didn't know better, she might have suspected Penelope of setting up the entire humiliating fiasco as a means of making sure that Miles couldn't see her without doubling over in laughter. Being discovered upside down behind a bush was not exactly conducive to inspiring burning passion. But Penelope wasn't capable of anything that devious. Was she?

"Nature," repeated the marquise, who had clearly not had any truck with that particular commodity. Her eye dwelled tellingly on the green smears marring Henrietta's kid gloves.

Taking a deep breath and gritting her teeth, Henrietta patted the side of the hedge, and said in her best governess voice, "Did you know that this is an exceedingly rare species of bush?"

Miles looked quizzically at the prickly green mass. "Really?"

"Yes! It's called, um . . ."

"Shrubbus verdantus!" supplied Charlotte eagerly.

"Is it any relation to *Hedgus pricklianus?*" inquired Miles.

"Don't be silly," said Henrietta loftily. "There's no such thing as *Hedgus pricklianus.*"

"Right." Miles nodded very solemnly, but Henrietta could see his lips twitching with suppressed laughter. "Not like *Shrubbus*—what was it again?—*victorious*, that well-known botanical wonder."

Would it be an impediment to their future married bliss if she clouted him over the head with a fallen tree branch?

Miles was starting to make little snorting noises, like a dragon about to blow. "How"—*sputter*—"clever of you to disguise yourselves so that you don't scare away the shrubbery."

"Touchy things, hedges," agreed Henrietta.

The snorts and sputters took over. Even the horses joined in, bucking and snorting, until Miles recovered enough to grab for the reins, still clutching his ribs with his spare hand. Henrietta caught Miles's eye as he rolled with mirth, and reluctantly grinned back.

Oh, fine, so it *was* funny.

Penelope gave her a "This is what you want to fall in love with you?" look.

"What in the blazes are you really doing out here?" asked Miles, when he'd calmed the horses. "Aren't you supposed to be having a voice lesson?"

"Oh, no." Henrietta fell back a step, one grass-stained hand to her lips like an actress in a bad melodrama. "What time is it?"

Penelope fished the pretty enamel watch she wore on a chain around her neck out of her bodice and flicked it open. "Six-fifteen."

"Oh, no, oh, no, oh, no," repeated Henrietta. She looked frantically from side to side, as though a magic carpet might suddenly appear out of the air and whisk her back to Uppington House. "I was supposed to be home fifteen minutes ago."

Miles leaned over the side of the phaeton, hair flopping in typical disarray across his face. "I can drive you home, if you'd like."

Next to him, the marquise emitted a delicate but forceful sniff.

That decided it. "Thank you," said Henrietta firmly. "I would be most grateful. Unless . . ."

She looked quizzically at her two best friends.

Penelope shook her head and flapped a hand at her in a gesture of dismissal. "You go ahead." She looked at Charlotte. "We'll finish our nature walk."

"So many shrubs still unexplored!" chimed in Charlotte.

Thank you, Henrietta mouthed, as Miles swung down from the phaeton. With a hand on her elbow, he boosted her up into the high equipage next to the marquise, who was studiedly looking the other way, as though engrossed in the glories of the landscape.

Having gotten Henrietta settled in the curricle, Miles climbed up to resume his seat. There was just one problem. There was no seat to resume. The phaeton had been designed for two, not three.

"Could you scoot over?"

Henrietta slid down the seat the half inch or so that separated her from the marquise, leaving a grand total of three inches for Miles. "I don't think there's any more room to scoot," she said apologetically. "I can always get out and walk."

The horses were beginning to grow restless at being kept standing so long.

"Never mind." Miles plunged into the seat. Henrietta let out an unintentional whoosh of air as she careened into the marquise. The marquise said nothing, but her lips got very tight and her eyes very narrow.

"See? All cozy," said Miles heartily, twitching the reins to set the horses moving. Hen gave him a wry look. The marquise sat very straight, and arranged her violet-gloved hands in her lap, looking anything but cozy. Scrunched between the two of them, Henrietta felt like a recalcitrant child who had been caught eavesdropping and was being hauled home. Which, she admitted unhappily, wasn't all that far from the truth. The thought was not an uplifting one.

"What lovely gloves," Henrietta ventured, in an attempt to paint a thin veneer of sociability over the situation. She scrunched her own grass-stained gloves into the folds of her skirt, hoping the marquise wouldn't notice. "Did you bring them with you from Paris?"

"I brought very little with me from Paris," replied the marquise frostily. "Revolutions leave one little time to pack."

"Oh," said Henrietta, wishing she had never spoken at all. "Naturally."

"Everything was taken from us—the château, the townhouse, the paintings, even my jewels. I fled Paris with barely the clothes on my back."

On the marquise's lips, her flight sounded more sultry than sordid, conjuring images of artfully tattered rags fluttering from barely concealed curves, Venus in distress fleeing her shell. Henrietta's heart sank somewhere beneath the horses' hooves, each thud of their shoes against the cobbles a pressure against her chest. How could she have hoped to compete?

"It sounds dreadful," Henrietta said woodenly. "How did you contrive to escape?"

To add injury to insult, the marquise's hip bone was sharper than any hip bone had a right to be, and, wiggle though she might, Henrietta couldn't seem to get away from it. Every time she managed to evade the marquise, there was Miles on her other side, glowering at the reins as though they had done something to offend him.

As Henrietta struggled to maintain a polite conversation with the marquise—and avoid being skewered—Miles went from quiet to cross to surly. If they were alone, Henrietta would have poked him, and demanded to know what was wrong. As it was, she couldn't get her hand free to poke him even if she wanted to. It was stuck somewhere between her skirt and Miles's thigh. The strap of her reticule bit into her fingers, which were rapidly growing numb.

Henrietta gave her hand an experimental tug.

Miles growled.

"Did I scratch you?" Henrietta said over a description of the charms of the dead marquis and the dead marquis's châteaux.

"No," grumbled Miles, somehow managing to utter the syllable without ever opening his mouth.

"Are you all right?" Henrietta twisted in her seat to look at Miles. Miles continued to look at the reins.

Miles was having a difficult time remembering the meaning of "all right." He was broiling in his own private hell. For once, it was nothing to do with the French. It was entirely Henrietta.

Devil take it, he'd ridden with Henrietta dozens of times before—hundreds! He'd never had the slightest bit of difficulty keeping his mind out of uncomfortable places that made his cravat—and other bits of his attire—feel suddenly too tight. Of course, on those other rides, there hadn't been three people in a seat meant for two. On those other rides, Henrietta hadn't been pressed intimately against him, so intimately that he could feel every curve of hip and thigh outlined with burning accuracy against him. Miles tried scooting, subtly, to the side, but there was nowhere at all to scoot; they were welded closer together than a pickpocket to a purse.

Just when Miles thought that there was nothing more unbearable than the feel of her jammed up against his side, the blasted vehicle swayed. A warmly rounded bit of Henrietta's anatomy brushed against his left arm. Then she wiggled again.

And Miles realized it could get worse. Much worse. He was in that peculiar circle of Dante's Inferno reserved for those who had been caught thinking lustful thoughts about their best friends' sisters. True, he couldn't recall Dante mentioning that one specifically, but he was certain it had to be in there. This was his punishment for dwelling on certain details of Henrietta's appearance that he shouldn't have been dwelling on. In fitting punishment, measure for measure, breast for breast, he now had to endure their proximity in excruciating detail, and the worst of it was, he couldn't do a single thing about it.

The five-minute drive to Uppington House had never felt longer.

"Ungh," Miles responded, which Henrietta, from her long exposure to the vagaries of male communication, took as "No, I'm in a vile mood, but I can't admit it, so leave me alone."

Henrietta had the unhappy feeling she knew the cause of his ill humor. And it wasn't the horses, the reins, or the state of the war with France. It was an unwanted presence in the middle of his curricle, separating him from the seductive marquise and her roving hands.

Henrietta would have complied, and left him alone—if there was any way she could have fled the curricle entirely that wouldn't have involved a suicidal leap and a painful death being crushed by carriage wheels, she would have done so—but just then she felt something slip from her squished fingers and fall with a dull thud on the footrest.

Oh, blast, that was her reticule.

There was no way she could unobtrusively lean down and scoop it up. Even if her right hand wasn't trapped between her and Miles, it would be uncouth to bend over like that in an open carriage in the middle of a well-traveled street. On the other hand, she didn't want to just leave it lying there. What if the carriage swerved abruptly, and it fell out? Her mother would never let her hear the end of it. Maybe if she just managed to slide her foot through the loop, then she could ever so subtly lift her foot until it was at a level where she could quietly pluck it up with no one the wiser.

Henrietta started feeling around the baseboard with one booted foot. It would be much easier if she could look down, but between her skirts and the marquise's, she couldn't see anything, anyway.

The marquise was commenting on the beauties of the spring, and Henrietta, exploring a likely shaped lump with her toe, made an equally banal response. For all of her beauty, the marquise was really an incredibly *boring* woman. Maybe, Henrietta thought absently, feeling around the lump, it was all because she was beautiful; she'd never had to try to be interesting. If only she could impress the fact of the marquise's dullness upon Miles in a way that didn't come out sounding hopelessly spiteful. That would be a conundrum for later; for now, she was fairly sure she'd found her reticule, and just needed to try to jolt it around so that she could get her foot through the loop. But it wasn't moving.

Maybe it was stuck against something.

Blast it all, the loop had to be somewhere. Henrietta started feeling for the top of the little bag.

Miles leaped halfway out of his seat.

Ooops. Maybe that hadn't been the reticule.

"What in the name of Hades do you think you're doing?" Miles roared. A nearby horse reared. Heads turned in passing carriages. Curtains twitched.

The marquise looked like she wished she were in anybody else's carriage.

"I dropped my reticule," Henrietta said, somewhat breathlessly. Miles had landed on her. "I was trying to pick it up."

"With your *foot*?" Miles slid off Henrietta's lap and shoved himself as far against the opposite side of the carriage as he could go.

"My hand was stuck," explained Henrietta reasonably, wiggling the erring appendage.

"Ungh," said Miles.

Henrietta wasn't quite sure how to interpret that grunt.

"I think," said the marquise darkly, "I should like to go home now."

"Don't worry. You're next," Miles said shortly. His curt tone would have done much to raise Henrietta's spirits if it hadn't been the exact same tone he'd been using with her.

Miles yanked the horses to a stop in front of Uppington House and leaped out of the phaeton with all the alacrity of an early Christian martyr dodging a lion. He grabbed Henrietta around the waist and swung her down from the carriage, setting her down in front of her house with a jarring thud. Leaning back into the carriage, he snatched up the offending reticule.

Henrietta took the reticule from him, saying very carefully, "Thank you for the ride home."

Miles unbent enough to give her a sheepish half-smile. Henrietta's heart stirred and ached with thwarted affection.

"'S'all right," he said. "I'll see you tonight. Aren't you late?"

Oh, blast, she kept forgetting about her music lesson. Calling a quick good-bye over her shoulder, Henrietta scurried up the steps of Uppington House. As Winthrop opened the door for her, she heard the sound of Miles's horses resuming their journey. Hopefully straight to drop the marquise off at home.

Henrietta didn't let herself dwell on the thought. She dropped her reticule on a table in the hall, and rushed into the music room. The harp loomed uncovered and unused; the pianoforte, with its intricately painted lid and golden legs, sat mute. There was no sign of Signor Marconi.

Henrietta glanced at the gilded clock on the mantel. Both hands were pointing delicately at the six. She was half an hour late. He'd probably given up and left. Blast! Just over from the Continent, Marconi was in great demand, and she'd counted herself lucky to secure lessons with him. Now, with her romantic folly, she had probably just convinced Miles she was mad and lost her voice teacher all in one fell swoop. Urgh.

Making annoyed noises at herself, Henrietta scurried back out into the hall.

"Signor Marconi?" she called, just in case he might have been shown into one of the drawing rooms to wait.

There was a rustle of sound from the morning room. Expelling her breath in a long sigh of relief, Henrietta raced down the hall and careened around the doorframe, babbling breathlessly, "Signor Marconi? I'm so dreadfully sorry to be so late! I was delayed in—"

She broke off abruptly. Henrietta's surge of relief was replaced by confusion as the source of the rustling noise became clear.

The black-garbed figure of Signor Marconi was bent over her opened escritoire, papers in each hand.

Chapter Sixteen

———— ❦ ————

Flattered: *under suspicion by the Ministry of Police; subject to intense scrutiny, and possibly attack. See also under* Signal Honor

—from the Personal Codebook of the Pink Carnation

Henrietta stumbled to a halt, physically and verbally.

Marconi hastily shoved the papers back into the cavity of the desk. Straightening, he flung both arms wide.

"I look-a for dee—how you say? Dee paper. I look-a for dee paper to write you dee note to tell you I no wait longer. But now"—Marconi shrugged, as though that solved everything—"you are here. So I no need dee paper."

"I'm so sorry to be late," Henrietta repeated, gathering hold of her scattered wits.

Moving past him, she shut the lid of the escritoire, and turned the key. It wasn't as though there were anything terribly secret in there—all of her letters from Jane and the little codebook she kept upstairs in her room, hidden, with her diary, in an empty chamber pot under her bed—but it was her private space, and she preferred her private space to remain private. Hence, the lock.

But Signor Marconi didn't know that, so Henrietta simply said, "Next time, if you need writing implements, just ask Winthrop, and he'll bring them to you."

"About dee lesson"—Signor Marconi tugged at his little black mustache—"I have-a dee udder engagement."

"Dee . . . ?" Henrietta shook her head to block out visions of cows. Nothing made any sense today. Wildlife, herbiage . . . It was all a distressing blur. She needed a cup of tea.

"Dee udder engagement," repeated Signor Marconi patiently.

"Oh, another engagement! Of course." Henrietta wasn't feeling terribly swift at the moment. From the look on Signor Marconi's face, he shared that opinion. She added anxiously, "You will come back next week, though, won't you?"

Signor Marconi pursed his lips and nodded solemnly. "For your voice, milady, I come-a back."

It was nice to know she had something to recommend her.

A determined click of heels on the parquet floor made her turn. It was her mother, bustling across the room with the attitude of a woman with a mission. She left off her determined beeline towards Henrietta long enough to spare a glance for the music teacher.

"Signor Marconi! Leaving so soon?"

"He has an udder engagement," Henrietta informed her mother, who didn't so much as blink. Something was clearly wrong.

Lady Uppington waved a dismissive hand vaguely in Marconi's direction. "Good evening, signor. We'll expect you next Wednesday. Henrietta, darling, I've had dreadful news."

Marconi bowed. Neither lady noticed. He bowed again. On the third bow, he gave up, swept his cloak about him, and left.

"Little Caroline and Peregrine have come down with mumps," declared Lady Uppington distractedly, flapping the letter in her hand for emphasis. "The baby hasn't caught it yet, but, really, with mumps it's just a matter of time, and poor Marianne is beside herself."

Henrietta emitted noises of distress. Her little nieces and nephew were the most adorable creatures in the history of the world—Caroline three years old, Peregrine two, and the baby just over six months—and they weren't supposed to get sick. It just wasn't in the proper scheme of the universe.

"The poor babies!"

"I," announced Lady Uppington, tucking a strand of silver-gilt hair into her unusually disheveled coiffure, "am going down to Kent tonight." There was a clatter in the hall. "Ah, that will be Ned with the trunks."

"Is there anything I can do? I could come, too, if you think that would help," offered Henrietta, trailing behind her mother into the hall.

"The last thing I need is your getting mumps, too. No, no. You'll stay here. Keep watch over your father. Make sure he eats and doesn't stay up all night in the library. Cook will come to you with menus in my absence, and if there are any problems with the staff—"

"I can manage," Henrietta said tolerantly. "Don't worry."

"Don't be ridiculous," said Lady Uppington. "Of course, I'll worry. When you are a mother, then you'll know what worry is."

"Shouldn't you be going, Mama?" Henrietta intervened, before the maternal lecture could gain momentum. "Before it gets too dark?"

She was not entirely successful. Lady Uppington paused in ordering trunks loaded and calling for her cloak—no, not the velvet one, the simple traveling cloak—to look sharply at her youngest child.

"About the masquerade tonight," Lady Uppington began ominously.

Henrietta waited. She knew her mother would have liked to forbid her to go to any event hosted by Lord Vaughn, but to do so would go against Lady Uppington's most strongly held Principles of Mothering. Henrietta had heard them all often enough to know all of the main ones by heart. High on the list was Thou Shalt Not Forbid, since, as Lady Uppington was fond of pointing out, if Lady Capulet had only been sensible, and not forbidden Juliet to see that Romeo boy, Juliet probably would have married Count Paris and borne lots of darling little grandchildren instead of dying hideously in the family crypt.

Henrietta had used that theory several times to her advantage.

She could tell her mother had just replayed the Lady Capulet cautionary tale in her head, because Lady Uppington said sternly, in the tone of one who wanted to be saying more, "Be sure to stay close to the Dowager Duchess."

"Yes, Mama."

"Don't wander away from the ballroom, or go into the garden, or let yourself be drawn into any dark alcoves."

"I know, Mama. We've been through all this before. Remember? Before my first party."

"Some things don't stale with repetition, darling. Miles will be there to keep an eye on you. . . ."

Henrietta thought of the departing pair in the carriage. "Who'll be keeping an eye on Miles?"

"The duchess," replied Lady Uppington promptly.

"The duchess?" repeated Henrietta. Hmm, now there was an image. A little wisp of a smile curled around Henrietta's lips as she imagined setting the duchess on the marquise. There was no doubt as to who would emerge victorious.

"Yes. I've sent a note to her telling her she's to take you with her and Charlotte tonight, and I've sent a note to Miles warning him to be on time, and I sent another message to the duchess to send to Miles to make sure he doesn't forget."

Henrietta's head reeled under the profusion of notes.

"Good night, darling." Lady Uppington kissed her quickly on both cheeks. "Be good, and don't let your father tire himself writing speeches all night."

Henrietta trailed along after her mother towards the door. "Give my love to the little ones. . . . Tell Caro that I have a present for her if she gets well quickly, and tell Peregrine that he's the bravest outlaw in the forest, and give the baby an extra kiss for me. Are you sure you don't want me to come along?"

The door had no sooner closed behind Lady Uppington than Winthrop sidled up, a silver tray in his hands.

"Yes, Winthrop?"

"Your post, my lady." Winthrop bowed, extending the tray.

Despite sore feet, sore head, and a sore heart, Henrietta felt a little flicker of excitement as she took the three letters from the tray. After arranging for a pot of tea and some biscuits to be brought to her, she took her booty to the morning room, collapsed on her favorite settee, and prepared to examine her spoils.

The first was a brief note from her sister-in-law Marianne. The children had mumps, but the doctor said it wasn't a bad case, the baby seemed fine, and Henrietta wasn't, under any circumstances, to allow Lady Uppington to go haring off to Kent.

Ooops. Too late.

Henrietta put the note to the side, resolving to write Marianne a quick letter of apology before she dressed for the masquerade tonight.

The second letter was from Amy. And it was thick. Henrietta tore open the seal with a surge of anticipation. That had been fast; Amy must have sat down with her quill and a stack of paper as soon as she received Henrietta's note. Settling back against the settee, Henrietta skimmed rapidly. Amy was delighted, wished she could help in person, was overjoyed to offer her expertise, blah, blah, blah. Ah, the good bit! Henrietta sat up straighter. Amy had jammed in four closely written pages of advice. Some, Henrietta took mental note of, such as the tips regarding ways to bind one's breasts without experiencing excruciating pain, and how to listen at a keyhole without being squashed if the door opened unexpectedly. Others, such as the suggestion that she burgle the War Office at dead of night in case they had extra information, Henrietta discarded out of hand. Spying on one's own side just seemed so . . . unpatriotic. And no one could accuse Henrietta of lack of patriotic zeal. She knew all seven verses of "Rule Britannia" by heart, even the obscure ones about Muses still with freedom found and manly hearts to guard the fair.

Henrietta put Amy's bulky letter aside for further perusal later. There were some bits that required deeper scrutiny. The diagrams on lock-picking, for example, were not the sort of things one could memorize in just one viewing.

Even better, in a cramped postscript jammed onto the very bottom of the very last page, Amy had added an invitation. A week hence, she and Richard were having several people to stay for an intensive training session. The brilliance of it was, wrote Amy blithely, that it would look to be no more than a simple country house weekend. If anyone asked, there would be all the usual entertainments: hunting and fishing for the men, a jaunt to a nearby Norman ruin for the women, and a trip to the village shops. In actuality, they would be learning the subtleties of disguise, the art of eavesdropping, and several other thrilling things. Though Henrietta could still go to the shops if she liked.

Henrietta smiled to herself as she reached for the next letter. It was all so like Amy. And quite, quite perfect. Her mother would never object to her spending a weekend with Richard, "chaperoned" by Amy. She wondered whether Miles would be present. As Richard's best friend, one would think he would be . . . Henrietta ruthlessly dragged herself away from the dangerous realm of daydream, and hastily broke open the lumpy seal on the final letter.

The last letter was from Jane.

Henrietta peered at the familiar signature, held it out at arm's length, frowned a bit, and stared at the signature again. It was still from Jane.

Henrietta regarded the battered piece of paper in some confusion. There was no way at all, even with fleet horses and favorable winds, that Jane could have received her own letter and penned a reply already. Henrietta's own epistle had been nothing to excite so speedy a response even if it were possible; she had reassured her that Uncle Archibald had been informed of the presence of the new horrid novel and was sure to snap it up as soon as he could locate a proper bookshop. The rest of the letter had been filled with trivialities, such as her conversation with Lord Vaughn, Miles's unprecedented attentions to the marquise, and the Dowager Duchess harrowing Percy Ponsonby out a second-story window.

Jane's missive was more a note than a letter. Her tiny, precise writing filled less than half the folded sheet. It was, Jane wrote, just a quick message to her dearest cousin, to let her know that she had

attended yet another Venetian breakfast that morning and a gentleman unknown to her had asked after both Henrietta and Mr. Dorrington. She believed this gentleman must know them both through
Henrietta's darling brother, but had been unable to ask. Surely, Henrietta must feel this signal honor, and would be accordingly flattered.

Henrietta sat very still, edging around the ramifications of Jane's
brief note. She should, she supposed, go upstairs to her room and
fetch the codebook and make sure of the contents. But she had a
dreadful suspicion she already knew what it meant. Jane had gone on
another late-night raid to the Ministry of Police. There she had found
that someone had ordered inquiries into the movements of both Henrietta and Miles, most likely due to their proximity to Richard. Blast.
What other interpretation could there be?

Henrietta moved slowly to the escritoire, releasing the lid with a
dull thump. The papers Signor Marconi had dropped were still scattered about in disarray, but Henrietta didn't bother to sort through
them. Henrietta reached for a clean sheet of paper, her inkpot, and a
quill, to write . . . what?

There were too many questions teeming through her mind. If she
and Miles were under scrutiny, what about Geoff? The Ministry of
Police most likely already had a file on him, based on his long sojourn
in France with Richard. There were also her parents to be considered.
They had all visited Richard in Paris in April, just before his capture
and speedy escape. Her mother, in fact, had played a key role in
springing Richard from the dungeons of the Ministry.

Then there were the even more important questions, such as why
the Ministry had suddenly developed an interest in them. Henrietta
tapped the dry quill against the blotter. She supposed it made a certain
amount of sense for them to track down the connections of the former
Purple Gentian. While the Gentian himself might now be permanently out of the spying business, thanks to the dramatic revelation of
his identity (not to mention marriage and the prospect of small children), it stood to reason that the disbanded members of his League
might continue in their fight against France. And the most logical way
to smoke out those members was to investigate those closest to

Richard. She and Miles were both closer to Richard than pretty much anyone—well, in her case, one had to be when one lived in the same house for all those years—and they had both been in France within the past month. To a paranoid French agent, a description that neatly summed up Gaston Delaroche, those facts might add up to something very sinister indeed.

Something cracked. Looking down, Henrietta realized she had pressed so hard against the quill that the nib had fractured.

Henrietta put the quill down. There was no point in writing to Jane, begging for answers, when she wasn't even sure what she wanted to ask. The logical person to speak to just now was Miles. He needed to be warned.

The danger to herself, Henrietta discounted. She wasn't sure why her name had popped up in the pending files of the Ministry of Police, but she was fairly certain they wouldn't scrutinize her too closely. Bonaparte was notorious for underestimating women—it was one of the reasons Jane's plans had succeeded quite so spectacularly—and, aside from her current employment, Henrietta had never played any role in the hostilities against France other than the passive one of pesky younger sister to the Purple Gentian. If they investigated her actions, all they would find was a list of books borrowed from the lending library, five refused offers of marriage, two volatile voice teachers, and an inordinate number of ribbon purchases.

Henrietta dipped her broken pen absentmindedly in the ink, pulling the sheet of paper towards her.

Miles, on the other hand, was the perfect target. His work with the War Office, while certainly not bandied about town, was no secret— how could it be, with Miles openly going there at intervals for the past several years? His connection with Richard was also common knowledge. If the Ministry of Police were looking to eliminate those who might prove a danger to Bonaparte's ambition . . . Henrietta looked down to see a spreading pool of brownish ink on the formerly pristine piece of paper. In the dim light, it looked like blood.

For goodness' sake! Henrietta crumpled the spoiled piece of paper.

No blood was going to be spilled. Miles should be warned, but not by note. It wasn't the sort of thing one wanted falling into the wrong hands, and she and Miles had no code. A thousand private witticisms and shared memories, but no secret cipher.

She could go to his lodgings. Henrietta cocked her head and grimaced. Blast, this was the problem with knowing oneself too well. She knew that her main motive for wanting to go to Miles's lodgings wasn't to warn him of potential danger; it was to make sure that he was home. Alone.

Henrietta took a deep breath, and shoved back her chair. Right. She wasn't going to stoop to that. Yes, she knew she had said that about the hiding-behind-the-hedge plan, too, but this time she meant it. She was making a new resolution: no more skulking about. Except in the interest of England, of course. But when it came to Miles, they had been friends too long to play those sorts of games. If she wanted to know the nature of his relationship with the marquise, she would ask him straight out, not pop into his lodgings at strange hours like the jealous husband in a French farce.

Besides, from a strategic point of view it was a dreadful idea. Aside from all the nasty things it could do to her reputation if she were discovered, if she and Miles were being watched by French agents, her slipping hooded into his apartments would only convince the secret police that they had something to hide, thus increasing the danger of Miles being shot, stabbed, or otherwise permanently maimed.

Miles would have to be warned, but she would do it in person, tonight. It was well past seven already, and he was under orders from two of the most fearsome matriarchs in Britain to put in an appearance at Lord Vaughn's masquerade no later than ten o'clock tonight. The masquerade would provide the perfect setting for a clandestine meeting; among the masked and tipsy revelers, she could draw Miles off to a secluded alcove for a private meeting.

After all, Henrietta rationalized to herself gleefully, her mother's stricture about disappearing into alcoves couldn't possibly apply to

Miles, since Miles was the one who was supposed to be keeping an eye on her.

Yes, Henrietta decided, shutting the lid of the escritoire with a definitive click, her conversation with Miles would have to wait until tonight.

What could possibly happen between now and ten o'clock?

Chapter Seventeen

———— ✿ ————

Carousing: *engaged in a mortal struggle with Bonaparte's minions*

—from the Personal Codebook of the Pink Carnation

Miles didn't remember leaving his sitting room such a mess. He didn't remember flinging his books across the room, he didn't remember yanking down his drapes down off their rods, and he certainly didn't remember slashing open the seat of his settee.

"What in the *hell*?" exclaimed Miles.

Miles had to grab hold of the doorframe to keep from tumbling over a small table that had been upended right in front of the door. In front of him, chaos reigned. Tables lay on their sides, paintings hung crookedly on their pegs, and a broken decanter of claret leaked its contents into the warp of the Axminster carpet. Dash it all, he had liked that decanter. He'd been pretty fond of its contents, too, before they'd soaked into the rug. Porcelain fragments from a broken urn dappled the floor, warring for space with tumbled books and crumpled bits of paper. The fabric covering his settee and the two matching chairs hung in tatters from their gilded wooden frames.

Miles took a cautious step over the fallen table and heard shards crunch beneath the heels of his boots. Leaning over, he picked up a book, automatically smoothing the pages. The other contents of his bookshelves also occupied the floor, lying at odd angles throughout the room, some flat on their backs, others bent open, as though someone had flung them out of the bookshelf one by one. Crunching his way across the room, Miles stuck Livy's *Commentaries* back on the empty shelves, where, of course, it promptly toppled over onto its side for lack of companions.

This was absurd! Unspeakable! A man left his lodgings for, what, five hours at most—no, more than that. He had gone out at eleven to badger Geoff, lunched at his club, toddled over to the opera to question Mme. Fiorila, browsed among the boots at Hoby's, shot at targets at Manton's, and finally driven along to the marquise's townhouse on Upper Brook Street to take her driving, cooling his heels in her drawing room until she had finally condescended to emerge, perfumed, powdered, and pouting. Still, even an eight-hour absence didn't justify the complete and utter destruction of a man's abode.

Clutching his head, Miles stared out across the room. Who would have done such a thing? This was clearly not the work of a band of thieves, since as far as Miles could tell from the drawing room, nothing had been taken. A valuable silver snuffbox lay in plain view next to one of the upended tables, too tempting a plum to be left by anyone with a quick profit on the agenda. Besides, what thieves in their right mind would expend that much energy in destruction when their best hope of success lay in grabbing and running?

Crazed vandals? Escaped Bedlamites? An angry ex-mistress?

Miles froze guiltily. No. Surely even Catalina wouldn't . . . well, he wouldn't be quite so sure about that. Flinging things about for the sheer fun of watching them go smash was very much Catalina's style, but doing it in private wasn't. Catalina liked an audience. She only smashed crockery when there was someone to smash it at. Then there was the added fact that Catalina, experienced courtesan that she was, hadn't shown any signs of tearing rage or towering passion at their parting. She had clung to his leg a bit, flung her arms about, and expostulated in Italian, but the tears in her eyes had been rapidly replaced by a greedy gleam when Miles had presented her with a farewell parure of diamonds and rubies. Miles decided he could safely rule out his ex-mistress. Which only left a far more disturbing possibility. The French.

Damn.

The condition of the room made no sense for thieves, but perfect sense for someone who was searching for something—and lost their temper when the search proved fruitless. They really hadn't missed a spot, had they? His books had been rifled, his furniture slashed through; even the bookshelves had been moved away from the wall and the paintings shoved aside in case of secret caches behind. Miles didn't even want to know what his bedroom must look like.

Damn, damn, damn.

Somehow, he must have alerted this new band of operatives that he was on to them. Miles couldn't think of any other reason for Bonaparte's minions to be reducing his lodgings to a shambles. What were they looking for? An unfinished dispatch, perhaps? If they—Miles was beginning to severely dislike that pronoun—were desperate enough to tear apart his home, he must have stumbled onto something important, something they didn't want him to find.

Vaughn. A grim satisfaction pervaded Miles's weary frame. Ha! It had to be Vaughn. He must have been recognized leaving Vaughn's house last night. Could one of Vaughn's henchmen have seen him strolling out of Belliston Square, trying to look like a man who'd just had a bit too much to imbibe, and put two and two together? It might equally well have been that, despite his ridiculous costume, he'd been recognized by his attacker in Vaughn's bedchamber. Or . . . some of Miles's satisfaction began to fade as he considered the number of times he might possibly have revealed his identity to his adversaries. Or he might have been spotted at the Duke's Knees that night. True, Vaughn had given no sign of recognition, but an experienced spy wouldn't, would he?

Then there was his trip to the opera this morning. Miles whacked his head with the back of his hand. If Vaughn was in league with Mme. Fiorila . . . well, leaving his card with Mme. Fiorila had not been the brightest of ideas. Pity, that. It had seemed such a sensible course of action at the time.

Why did this sort of thing never happen to Richard? Of course, Richard had been captured by the French secret police, which did tend to even the score a bit. That thought made Miles feel better. Almost.

Heedless of escaping stuffing, Miles groaned and flopped down on his mutilated settee. He didn't want to contemplate crazed French spies, he didn't want to contemplate his own mistakes, and he certainly didn't want to contemplate the amount of time it was going to take before his lodgings were livable again. It had been a long, tiring, and—Miles's unregenerate mind presented him with a tactile reenactment of Henrietta's foot inching up his leg—*frustrating* day, and all he wanted was to sprawl out on his sofa, imbibe a glass of claret, and vent to Downey. Miles glanced down at the claret-colored stain on his carpet, glinting with the crystal fragments that had once been glasses. Not bloody likely.

Where in the hell *was* Downey, for that matter? Or Mrs. Migworth, his housekeeper, cook, and maid of all work? True, Mrs. Migworth was slightly deaf, and tended, once her morning rounds of cleaning and tidying were done, not to leave her domain in the kitchen, but one would think someone would have noticed the odd whirlwind flashing through the flat.

Miles heaved himself off the sofa, shedding little tufts of horsehair as he dragged himself upright. Grinding glass into the carpet as he went—the carpet was going to have to be thrown out, anyway, so he might as well get the satisfaction of making loud, crackling noises— Miles stomped off in search of his staff.

"Downey!" he shouted. "Where in the blazes are you?"

There was no answer.

Miles stalked off into the dining parlor, noting grimly the silver that had been upended on the sideboard, and the pictures that had been torn off the wall.

"Downey!" Miles roared. "Where are you, man?"

Of all the times for his valet to take an unauthorized afternoon off! Miles came to an abrupt halt in the middle of the room, scowling at the smashed pile of fragments that had once been his dinner service.

That was when he heard it. A low moan, little more than an exhalation of air. Miles whirled, seeking the source of the sound.

"Hello?" Miles said sharply. It might have been nothing more than a draft of air from an open window, or a mouse in the skirting board—though Miles didn't think mice sighed. No, this sound had been human in origin. Miles's eyes rifled across the room, darting past the table, over several chairs ... and under the sideboard, which boasted, in addition to its own four legs, a black-shod foot protruding where no foot ought to be.

Miles flung himself to his knees on the parquet floor. There lay Downey, sprawled facedown beneath the sideboard, a dark stain marring the back of his coat.

"Oh hell, oh hell, oh hell," muttered Miles. "Downey? Downey, can you hear me?"

Another faint moan emerged from the valet's crumpled form.

"It's going to be all right," Miles said with more determination than he felt. Yanking the cravat from around his throat—Downey, after all, was in no state to protest—he fashioned a rough dressing over the hole in Downey's back. From the way the blood was caked on Downey's coat, the wound appeared to have mostly stopped bleeding, but moving him would undoubtedly open it again. He must have been lying there for some time.

Being as gentle as he could, Miles eased Downey out from under the sideboard, eliciting another wordless moan.

"Sorry, old boy," Miles muttered. "It'll just be a moment, I promise ...."

"Thieves," croaked Downey, in a barely audible whisper.

"Shhh," said Miles, feeling like one of the world's lowest sort of crawling creatures. "Don't try to talk."

"Couldn't ... stop ..."

"No one could have done more," Miles reassured him, his voice rough with remorse. "You just lie here, while I—"

"Couldn't ... see ..."

"Don't say another word. I'm going to get a surgeon. You just stay here."

Not giving his fallen valet time to object, Miles raced through his chaotic sitting room, vaulted over the table blocking the doorway, and took the stairs three at a time. Storming into the street, he collared a young boy he recognized as a page from the neighboring establishment.

"Go to the nearest surgeon and tell him to come here at once—at once, do you hear?"

The boy shrank away, eyeing Miles's bloodstained hands with pop-eyed alarm.

Miles dug in his waistcoat and yanked out a silver crown. "Here." He slapped it into the boy's palm. "There'll be another for you if you're back here within the next ten minutes."

"Yes, sir! Yes, indeed, sir!" The boy set off running.

Within half an hour, Downey had been moved to the settee—a liberty he would have protested had he not been unconscious at the time—examined, and pronounced very lucky to be yet among the living.

"An inch lower," pronounced the surgeon grimly, "and your man would have been skewered straight through the heart."

Several hours and two glasses of brandy later (the brandy having been consumed mostly by Miles), Downey was propped up on pillows, partaking of hot broth, and being fussed over by Mrs. Migworth.

"Not but what if I'd known, I wouldn't have gone to market this day," said Mrs. Migworth for the tenth time, shaking her graying head. "It's that sorry I am, Mr. Downey."

"That makes two of us," muttered Miles, pacing the ruined carpet. "Downey, I can't tell you how sorry I am that this has happened."

Downey looked as gratified as a man swathed in bandages with a spoon stuck in his mouth could contrive to look.

"It's . . . no matter . . . sir." Downey suddenly started up in alarm, sending Mrs. Migworth into a whole new agony of fussing and pillow-fluffing. "Sir! Her ladyship . . . Lady Uppington . . . left a message."

"Calm yourself, Downey." Miles perched himself on an only slightly slashed chair. "It can't be that important."

"But her ladyship said . . . the masquerade. . . ."

"Oh, no. I'm staying right here with you. I don't care if the Prince of Wales himself is throwing it, I—oh. Oh, *no*." Miles uttered a word that made Mrs. Migworth bristle with disapproval.

Miles didn't notice. Miles didn't care. Miles was staring off into space with a fixed look of horror in the manner of Hamlet being confronted with his father's ghost. Only this was far, far worse than any number of spirits from beyond the grave. The masquerade was being hosted by Lord Vaughn, held at Lord Vaughn's townhouse, entirely under Lord Vaughn's control and direction.

Hen was there. With Vaughn. In Vaughn's house.

Everyone would be masked, the more fantastical the costume the better. The *ton*, safely disguised behind feathery masks and elaborate wigs, would have seized the opportunity to indulge in a bit of licentious revel. Champagne would flow, sharpening voices and numbing wits. In the midst of them all would be Henrietta, meandering innocently along like a lamb among wolves. How hard would it be to yank her away, out of the throng of partygoers? Vaughn could slip a drug into her drink; he could back her into a dark corner; he could even sweep her up and toss her over his shoulder and anyone who saw would simply assume it was all part of the fun, a bit of playacting to enliven the evening.

And once Vaughn had isolated Henrietta from his guests . . . Miles's blood ran cold. The man had just stabbed Miles's valet with no more thought than Miles would give to crushing an ant.

"What time was I supposed to be there?" Miles demanded hoarsely.

"Ten o'clock," said Mrs. Migworth briskly, rubbing her hands on her apron. "Is aught wrong, sir?"

"Ten o'clock," Miles repeated. The tall cabinet clock in the corner was missing its glass fronting, but behind the jagged break, the hands still faithfully ticked off the minutes. It was nearly half past eleven.

Miles bolted for the door.

A faint whisper rose from the couch. "If sir would divest himself of bloodstains before leaving . . ." Downey managed, before his head dropped back onto the pillow.

It was too late. Miles was already halfway down the stairs, doing his damnedest not to think about all the things that might be happening to Henrietta at this very moment, and failing miserably.

MILES WAS LATE.

Henrietta peered into the crowd of masked revelers overflowing the spacious reception chambers of Lord Vaughn's London mansion, searching for a familiar blond head. Given the number of powdered wigs, feathered hats, and shuttered medieval helmets in evidence, the task was proving less straightforward than usual. In front of her, a self-satisfied Marc Antony, resplendent in breastplate, tunic, and Roman helmet, strolled arm in arm with a very scantily clad Diana the Huntress, whose arrows lay abandoned in their quill as she simpered up at the Roman general. Definitely not Miles.

Henrietta heaved a sigh. The heaving was a mistake, since the sudden inhalation of air brought her ribs into contact with her tightly laced stomacher with a force that would have made her double over had she had the capacity to double over. Henrietta scowled in the direction of her stomach, and got a curl in her eye for her pains. Nasty, silly costume. Yet, so becoming, which was really the point of the whole exercise.

Since she had only two days in which to plan for Lord Vaughn's masquerade, Henrietta's choice of costume had been limited. She had wanted something that would make her seem alluring, mysterious, irresistible, something that would bring Miles to his knees. "I don't think they have costumes for that," Charlotte had commented. Penelope had suggested that, if that was what she wanted, why not just be direct about it and come as Nell Gwynn, with her bodice open to her waist, and a basketful of oranges holding suggestive messages. Neither comment had been appreciated.

In the end, Henrietta had done some rummaging, and appropriated one of the dresses from her mother's own long-ago debut, a shimmering thing of greenish blue brocade, trimmed with gold lace around the low, square neck. The overdress laced tightly over a white silk stomacher embroidered with tiny sprays of flowers before opening out again over an underskirt embroidered in the same pattern. It had to be lengthened, of course, since Lady Uppington was a good five inches shorter than her daughter, but otherwise the old-fashioned style suited Henrietta perfectly, making the most of her small waist, and hiding a set of hips that were rather too lavishly curved for current fashion. She only hoped Miles appreciated it.

Where was the blasted boy?

Henrietta dropped her golden mask (her arm was beginning to hurt from holding it up) and turned to Charlotte, who was standing beside her. "Would you care to take a turn around the room with me?"

Taking a firmer hold on her crook, Charlotte shook her head miserably, setting the little bows on her cap waving. Charlotte had wanted to dress up as the Lady of the Lake, clad in a gown of flowing white samite, but her grandmother had dismissed the notion with a derisory snort as namby-pamby nonsense. Instead, she had squeezed Charlotte into a short, tightly laced shepherdess costume, complete with striped stockings, ribbon-bedizened crook, and even a stuffed sheep.

"I'd prefer to hide here, if you don't mind," sighed Charlotte, nudging her sheep gloomily. "Maybe Penelope would go with you?"

The two girls turned to look at Penelope.

Penelope had come dressed as Boadicea, draped in a length of blue plaid that had the dual benefit of flattering her complexion and annoying her mother into a rapid departure. Lady Deveraux had last been seen heading towards the balcony, bemoaning the hard lot of a mother cursed with a difficult daughter to a very sympathetic King Lear. The Dowager Duchess had very little use for Penelope's mother, and thought the costume was a brilliant idea; her only objection was that Penelope had neglected to include a war chariot. The dowager had rapidly appropriated Penelope's spear, and was amusing herself and Penelope by poking unwitting fops in sensitive parts of their anatomy.

Henrietta and Charlotte exchanged a resigned glance.

"I don't think Penelope will want to join me. If your grandmother asks, will you tell her I went to the ladies' retiring room to, uh . . ."

"Fix your flounce?" suggested Charlotte, with the first hint of a smile she had shown all evening. "Give my regards to Mr. Dorrington when you find him."

Henrietta impulsively leaned over to hug her, her wide skirt whapping into Charlotte's panniers.

"If I find any amorous shepherds, I'll send them your way."

Charlotte flapped the stuffed sheep at her in farewell.

Henrietta maneuvered past a Henry VIII who looked like he needed very little extra padding for his doublet, and a morose Katherine of Aragon clutching a rosary. Henry made a perfunctory grab for Henrietta's waist as she twisted past him, and Katherine whacked him with her beads. Henrietta kept going.

There, to her left, was Turnip Fitzhugh, dressed as . . . good heavens, was he a giant carnation? The mind boggled. He was chatting with a woman draped mysteriously in black, who, at first glance, Henrietta thought might be the marquise. She started forward to take a closer look, but two Pierrots surged in front of her, clinging to each other for balance and breathing brandy with every breath. Henrietta yanked her wide skirts out of the path of the swaying men, scanning the crowd for Turnip's pink petals, or the black lace of the woman beside him, but they had disappeared into the masses of people milling through Lord Vaughn's reception rooms like so many drops of water into a pond.

Henrietta had her own reasons for wanting to locate the marquise.

It had occurred to her, as she whiled away the hours before the evening's entertainment, that if a spy was trailing along after her and Miles, it stood to reason that this individual would be someone who had recently begun paying a great deal of attention to them.

Henrietta entertained the fleeting thought that a truly talented spy would be quite careful not to pay marked attention to his prey, but she quickly dismissed the notion as unhelpful. Even if it were true, what use was it? Trying to sift through the number of people who hadn't singled her out recently was the sort of pointless task imposed upon heroines in fairy tales. They at least had fairy godmothers to help them sort through stacks of beans or spin straw into gold.

The marquise had certainly made no secret of her interest in Miles; she had dogged his footsteps—or something else—at every opportunity.

Of course, there was the slight problem that the marquise had everything to lose and nothing to gain from the Revolution. She had itemized it all in the phaeton. The houses, the paintings, the clothes . . . and her husband. The marquise still wore the dark hues of mourning for her husband, but Henrietta harbored the ignoble suspicion that her wardrobe choices arose less from affection than because she knew the colors suited her better than pastels. Love wouldn't win the marquise's loyalty, but a château in the Loire Valley, a wall full of Van Dycks, and a treasure trove of family jewels certainly could.

Blast. Henrietta would have so dearly loved for the marquise to be engaged in something underhanded.

Unless . . . Henrietta brightened. Unless the marquise had come to an agreement with the French government, whereby she got to keep her jewels and her châteaux in exchange for a wee bit of treason in her native land. As a theory, it didn't have much to recommend it, but it was the best Henrietta could come up with. She would have to keep an eye on the marquise. For the good of England, of course.

Just before she left the house that evening, Henrietta had penned a quick note to Jane, asking her to look into the background of the marquise. She did feel more than a little bit foolish about using the resources of the Pink Carnation on what was most likely a personal grudge, but . . . just in case.

But, aside from the potential sighting with Turnip, she had only caught one glimpse of the marquise that evening, engaged in entirely unsuspicious behavior. The marquise had been dressed as Isabella of Spain, swathed in an elaborate Spanish mantilla, but through the swirls of lace, Henrietta had seen the glint of blue-black hair that proclaimed its owner as unmistakably as the conscious grace of her movements. She had been deep in conversation with Lord Peter Innes, a scapegrace second son who had installed himself as an intimate of the Prince of Wales by dint of excessive drinking, gaming, and (although Henrietta wasn't supposed to know about such things) wenching. Try as she might, Henrietta couldn't find anything the least bit sinister in their conference. Ill-advised, if the marquise's purpose was to replenish her coffers through an advantageous marriage—the prince's intimates were not the marrying kind, and the state of their coffers didn't bear commenting upon—but not treasonous.

All the same, Henrietta kept her eye out for a black lace mantilla, just in case.

Nor had Henrietta yet encountered her host. Henrietta added Lord Vaughn to her little list of suspects. His attentions to her had been as sudden as they had been assiduous. He had fetched her champagne at the Middlethorpes' ball last night—and Lord Vaughn struck Henrietta as the sort of man who seldom fetched anything for anyone without good reason. Henrietta just didn't know whether his reasons were amorous or otherwise. She didn't delude herself that she was the sort of woman who drove men wild with uncontrolled passion, but Lord Vaughn was of an age when he might well be seeking a second wife and an heir rather than letting the estate and title devolve to some vile fifth cousin twice removed (distant cousins who stood to inherit were invariably vile). Henrietta made excellent heir-bearing material. She was the daughter of a marquis, and possessed of a ready wit, pleasant features, and no history of insanity in the family.

On the other hand, he had only settled his quizzing glass upon her after the topic of Richard's escapades had arisen.

"Lady Henrietta! You honor me with your presence."

There had to be something to the old adage about summoning the devil by thinking of him; Henrietta nearly tripped over her hem as the object of her speculations appeared before her.

She plunged into a curtsy to cover her confusion, her wide skirts collapsing around her, only just managing the combination of unfamiliar hoops and tottery heels. "Good evening, Lord Vaughn."

"For shame, Lady Henrietta," Vaughn chided smoothly. "At a masquerade one is never oneself."

"Should I have said Signor Machiavelli, then?"

In a doublet of rich black satin, Vaughn was dressed as a Renaissance grandee. The sleeves were slashed with silver tissue, and a school of writhing sea serpents wound its way around hem and neck, looking for all the world as though they were searching for a ship to sink. A heavy golden chain of office, like those worn by important officials in Elizabethan portraits, hung around his neck. The pendant was not a seal, but a falcon, with ruby eyes.

Lord Vaughn laughed, the ruby eyes of the falcon glinting with the movement of his chest. "Do you praise my acumen or insult my morals?"

That came a little too close for comfort. "Neither. I was simply guessing based on the time period."

"And Machiavelli's was the first name that came to mind?" Vaughn arched an eyebrow. "You have a devious turn of thought, Lady Henrietta."

Was he flirting with her, or baiting her?

"Though not nearly so keen an eye as you have," Henrietta prevaricated hastily. "I'm quite impressed that you recognized me through the mask on so slight an acquaintance."

Lord Vaughn made a courtly leg. "Can beauty mask itself?"

"A mask," replied Henrietta matter-of-factly, lowering hers, "often provides the best illusion of beauty where there is none."

"Only for those who need such subterfuge." Lord Vaughn proffered a crooked arm, leaving Henrietta, trapped within a web of manners, no choice but to take it. "I believe I promised you mythical beasts."

"Dragons, in fact," agreed Henrietta, rapidly reassessing her situation. Her proximity to Lord Vaughn, while unsought, might yet prove useful. If she could ask him suitably leading questions—suitably subtle leading questions—she might eke out of him enough to determine whether or not he had turned traitor in his years abroad. A careless comment about having been frequently in France, perhaps, or an excessive familiarity with the workings of Bonaparte's court.

With Henrietta on his arm, Vaughn moved at a measured pace through his masquerade, bowing to acquaintances as they passed. For the first time, Henrietta blessed the wide skirts she had been tripping over, jamming into doorframes, and mentally consigning to perdition all evening. The skirts might be a blasted nuisance, but they kept Lord Vaughn a safe distance away, as they walked with their arms raised in courtly fashion over the gap, her fingers resting lightly on his outstretched hand.

"Your home is lovely, my lord," Henrietta ventured, by way of starting a conversation. "How could you bear to stay away from it for so long?"

Underneath her fingers, Vaughn's hand stiffened, but his voice contained nothing more telling than urbane indifference as he answered, "The Continent has its own pleasures, Lady Henrietta."

"Yes, I know," Henrietta said enthusiastically. "I was in Paris with my family just before the end of the peace"—that much, after all, was public knowledge, so it would do no harm to tell him what he already knew—"and was amazed by the beauty of the architecture, the excellence of the food, and the quality of the theater. Despite recent events, it is really a most charming city. Do you find it so, my lord?"

"It has been many years since I have found Paris anything or anything in Paris," said Vaughn dismissively, turning to bow to a passing acquaintance.

Henrietta's pulse picked up beneath the despised stomacher. "You mean," she asked, in tones of exaggerated innocence, "that you find Paris dull these days?"

"I haven't been to Paris for some time. War does tend to impede one's freedom of movement." Vaughn's face was bland, his voice equally so.

Henrietta didn't believe a word of it.

"How very inconvenient," she murmured, just to have something to say.

"One must sometimes put up with a spot of personal inconvenience for the sake of world affairs, Lady Henrietta," Vaughn replied dryly. "Or have your brother's exploits not yet taught you that lesson?"

Another reference to Richard, noted Henrietta suspiciously. Those were dangerous waters, replete with sea serpents—rather like those portrayed on Vaughn's doublet. Hmph, she was supposed to be questioning Lord Vaughn, not the other way around. This incongruent interest in her brother's exploits could be an indication of Vaughn's involvement in Bonaparte's spy network. Or it could be no more than common curiosity. Over the past few weeks since her brother's unmasking, Henrietta had been pestered for information about her brother and his exploits by any number of people whom one could not possibly suspect of being French spies, Turnip Fitzhugh foremost among them.

"Richard was so seldom at home," Henrietta said vaguely, adding, by way of changing the subject, "Have we much farther to go before I meet your dragons?"

Having reached the end of the string of reception rooms, Lord Vaughn led her out of the throng along a sparsely populated corridor, ill lit after the thousands of candles that illuminated the reception rooms. Henrietta held her golden mask more closely to her face. Aside from a Harlequin and a medieval maiden locked in amorous embrace, the hallway was deserted. Henrietta had the feeling that this was the sort of thing her mother had meant when she had cautioned her against secluded alcoves. As Lord Vaughn placed his hand on the latch of a closed door, Henrietta wrestled with a craven desire to turn and flee back to the security provided by lights and companionship.

No. Henrietta made a wry face at herself behind Lord Vaughn's back. She wouldn't get very far in her plan to catch Jane's spy if she bolted back to safety at the first hint of danger! Richard, Henrietta was quite sure, would have gone forward. Richard, on the other hand, was not a medium-sized female in danger of being compromised. It did add a whole new level of complication to this spying business, considered Henrietta, but if Jane could manage, so could she.

It was too late to turn around even if she had wanted to. The handle turned, the door swung inward, and Lord Vaughn ushered her ahead of him through the portal.

"Welcome to my cabinet of treasures."

Henrietta turned in a slow circle. Candles placed on lacquered ledges illuminated a small octagonal room. Each of the eight sides of the octagon was paneled in rosewood, edged with an intricate design worked in gold. Set at irregular intervals in seven of the eight panels were roundels containing pictures painted on Oriental porcelain, depicting men in little boats, ladies lounging before pagodas, and even the promised dragons. In the eighth panel, delicate vases and curious porcelain figurines posed on a red-veined marble mantelpiece. Little lacquered benches with odd Oriental lions at their feet were scattered at regular intervals along the walls, padded with silken cushions of crimson shot through with gold.

The pattern of the parquet floor drew the eye inward, toward a small table in the center of the room. On it, ranged around a silver carafe, someone had laid out a repast to make a glutton gloat: ripe clusters of grapes piled upon platters, custards whipped to melting smoothness, delicate madeleines, and drifts of dates glinting with sugar. There were peaches and apples carved into fanciful shapes, mountains of chocolate bonbons, and, in their own small silver dish, like garnets loosed from a necklace, a shimmering pile of pomegranate seeds.

Henrietta was quite sure she didn't like the idea of playing Persephone to Lord Vaughn's Hades.

On the other hand, she might have no choice. The door clicked shut behind Lord Vaughn, only there was no door anymore, simply a rosewood panel edged in gold, identical to all the other rosewood panels. There was no sign of knob or lock or hinges. The small room was doorless, windowless, exitless.

There was no way out.

Chapter Eighteen

——— 🙶 ———

Lair, Dragon's: *the innermost interrogation chamber of the Ministry of Police (also commonly referred to as the Extra-Special Interrogation Chamber); a windowless cell equipped for torture*

—from the Personal Codebook of the Pink Carnation

"What do you think?" asked Vaughn. He rested a casual arm against the mantel, but his eyes never left her face.

I think I'm in over my head, thought Henrietta, repressing the very strong urge to bang on the wall in search of an exit. Schooling her face to an expression of bright interest, she said instead, "It's very cunning, my lord. But don't you find the lack of windows somewhat oppressive?"

"Not at all. Sometimes, one needs to get away from the world, don't you think, Lady Henrietta?"

That phrase had a highly ominous ring to it, especially in light of the pile of pomegranate seeds. Henrietta devoutly hoped that when he spoke of getting away from the world, he didn't mean permanently.

As much for herself as Vaughn, Henrietta quoted lightly, " 'The world is too much with us,' do you mean?"

"You read Wordsworth, Lady Henrietta?"

"Occasionally. A friend of mine recited that particular poem to me not long ago, and the phrase caught." Henrietta conjured Charlotte's familiar image, and found it helped to keep the nerves at bay.

"I prefer Milton, myself," replied Vaughn. Striking an attitude, he recited in resonant tones, "'Which way I fly is Hell, myself am Hell.'"

It was a trick of the light—that was all. A trick of light, and tone, and costume. Against the marble bulk of the fireplace, his hands twisted behind him and his head flung back, with the sparse candlelight flicking along his archaic clothes, turning the gold chain about his neck into a living necklace of flame, Lord Vaughn made far too plausible a Satan, chained in agony to his own adamantine rock.

"I've always found that line a bit melodramatic," said Henrietta firmly. "It's pure self-indulgence on Satan's part. There is no reason at all for him to go on wallowing like that. All he had to do was acknowledge his error, beg God's pardon, and he could have returned to Heaven and his old glory. He chose to continue to rebel against God; it wasn't as though anyone pushed him to it."

Vaughn's heavy-lidded gaze fastened intently on her face.

"Would you lift him from the depths, Lady Henrietta?" he asked mockingly. "Would you make an angel of him again?"

Henrietta was quite positive they were no longer discussing Milton, theology, or anything to do with the Prince of Darkness. As to what they were discussing, she had no idea. Could it be that he was repenting of his treason, and wished to confess? Perhaps this was her cue to boldly step forward and promise expiation if he would only cut his ties with France and return to the fold. But she had no power to promise any such thing, and no proof that he was, indeed, a French spy. And his tone repelled overtures as much as it invited them. Henrietta felt as though she were picking her way from stepping-stone to stepping-stone across a dangerous swamp on a moonless night. Blindfolded.

"I believe"—Henrietta stepped delicately out into the swamp—"that each man must make the choice to be lifted by himself. I certainly wouldn't presume to claim redemptive powers for myself!"

"Pity," said Vaughn lazily, stirring from his pose by the mantel. "But I apologize! You must think me a poor host, to offer you no refreshment." Vaughn crossed deliberately to the small table in the middle of the room. "Champagne?"

A denial rose to Henrietta's lips.

In the center of the room, Vaughn waited, one hand on the neck of the bottle. In the candlelight, his eyes gleamed as silver as the detail on his doublet.

"Yes," she said demurely. "Thank you."

If he were trying to drug her, better not to arouse his suspicions by refusing the wine. With a bit of cunning and a great deal of luck, perhaps she could feign drinking. It was not, she admitted to herself, going to be easy. Vaughn's eyes hadn't left her face. How much of a drug did one have to ingest before it began working?

Vaughn poured the liquid into two tall glasses made of amber-tinted Venetian glass. He had poured both portions from the same bottle, and surely he wouldn't poison himself, Henrietta reasoned with herself. But the presence of the large silver bucket in the middle of the table effectively hid his hands from view as he picked up both glasses. His Renaissance garb included several large rings. Henrietta entertained alarming recollections of Lucrezia Borgia and Catherine de' Medici, of whispers of poison dispensed by means of a cunningly designed ring. It would be a moment's work to flick open the face of the ring and release its powder into her glass.

Henrietta smiled brightly as she accepted the glass Lord Vaughn offered her across the table.

Vaughn raised his own goblet; Henrietta eyed the bubbles critically as they oscillated and burst. Was it just her imagination, or was the liquid in her glass slightly darker than his?

"To what shall we toast?" asked Vaughn.

"To your masquerade, my lord."

Good heavens, the habit was catching. Now even she was speaking in innuendo. She wasn't sure she liked it. She felt like someone in an old tale, dicing with the Devil, afraid to go on, but even more afraid to stop.

Vaughn lifted his eyebrows at her. "Shall we say, rather, to *un-masking*?"

Just whom did he intend to unmask? Her own mask sat discarded on one of the little benches at the side of the room, though she didn't delude herself that Vaughn meant anything quite that literal.

"By all means," Henrietta said, with a sudden spurt of irritation at this ridiculous verbal game they played, this dance of half-understood meanings. "Let us drink to Truth. They say it will out, you know."

Vaughn tilted his glass against hers, the crystalline click echoing in the small room like the chimes of the celestial spheres.

"It *is* your toast, Lady Henrietta, and it would ill become me to deny you. But you will learn, as time goes by, that Truth is a malleable mistress."

Henrietta set her glass down decisively on the table, using the motion as an excuse to tip the glass so that some of the liquid spilled onto the tray of grapes.

"I can't agree," she said bluntly. "Something is either true or false. Men may misuse appearances, but Truth remains constant. For example," she continued daringly, "treason is always treason."

Vaughn took an abrupt step away from the table, and Henrietta wondered if she had gone too far. Well, there was nothing she could do about it now. Henrietta took a firmer grip on her wineglass. It wasn't much of a weapon, but broken it might do enough damage to . . . to do what? Keep Lord Vaughn at bay?

It was all she could do to keep herself from falling back as Lord Vaughn advanced, his face still and watchful, his gaze fixed on her like a hawk plummeting down upon its prey. The ruby eyes of the falcon on his chest glittered hungrily in the candlelight.

"And what of you, Lady Henrietta?" he asked silkily. His fingers grasped her chin and tilted her face mercilessly up towards his. "Would you remain *constant*?"

The word reverberated in the little room, rebounding off the walls, the china roundels, the silver carafe, all the silent objects frozen into listening silence.

"C-constant?" Henrietta played for time, while her mind raced anxiously ahead in fifteen different directions. One part of her mind insisted on dwelling unpleasantly on how tight Vaughn's grip was, and how easily his fingers might move from her chin to her throat. Another wondered detachedly whether Vaughn was trying to urge her to turn traitor, and if she was more likely to be strangled if she answered yes, or no, or if the question was rhetorical and she wasn't supposed to be saying anything at all.

Vaughn's fingers tightened around her chin, his gaze speculative.

Into the terrible silence crept a noise no louder than the scratching of a rat in the wainscoting. Vaughn's hand dropped from Henrietta's face and he strode abruptly towards the sound.

Henrietta drew a deep, ragged breath.

A panel of the wall opened tentatively inwards, detaching itself smoothly from the rest. So that was how it worked, thought Henrietta, taking careful note of the door's location. The outline of the entryway was concealed by the golden grillework, while a cleverly placed jade and coral plaque masked the line left by the top of the door.

"Enter!" Vaughn directed harshly.

Only the manservant's face appeared around the edge of the concealed door, floating halfway up like the disembodied head in a horrid novel. Where disembodied heads in horrid novels generally tended to err on the side of glowering and threatening, this one was a very alarmed, very apologetic disembodied head. Henrietta bit down on a sudden crazy urge to laugh, and discovered that her legs in the tottery heels weren't quite so steady as she'd thought them to be.

"Begging your pardon, your lordship," said the floating head anxiously, "I know you said as how you wasn't to be disturbed, but—"

"What is it, Hutchins?" Vaughn broke in impatiently.

"A message, your lordship. Most urgent, they said it was."

"Lady Henrietta." Vaughn turned to her with a smooth smile, every inch the regret-ridden host, as if that last interlude had never transpired. Henrietta's hand surreptitiously crept up to her chin, as though she might still find the marks of his fingers there. "I regret I must abandon you for a brief moment, but I trust you will find sufficient to amuse you until my return."

Unable to believe her luck, Henrietta smiled giddily and waggled her fingers at him. "Don't worry. The dragons and I will no doubt have plenty to discuss." Such as where they had hidden the door handle.

Vaughn bowed in a courtly way utterly at odds with his previous behavior, and exited, shutting the door deliberately behind him. Skirts bunched in her hands, balanced on the very balls of her feet, Henrietta tiptoed over to the panel through which Vaughn had just departed. She paused for a moment, ear against the wall, listening to the sound of footsteps recede along the corridor, Vaughn's stride swift and assured, the other's a limp and a shuffle, scurrying to keep up.

Good. Vaughn was well and truly gone. For how long he would remain so was another matter entirely.

Hazel eyes narrowed in concentration, Henrietta examined the wall panel, with its porcelain pagodas and gilded dragons. Henrietta didn't care how much fire they breathed; she was determined to find the secret catch that opened the door before Vaughn returned.

Reaching up, she ran her fingers along the gilded frame of a painted porcelain scene, and yanked her hand back again in surprise. The china was set into the wall itself, the frame a trompe l'oeil illusion designed to give the impression of substance. The curls and protrusions that appeared so ripe for manipulation were nothing more than brushstrokes in gilt against the wood of the wall, as useless to her as the mask that lay discarded by her side.

Henrietta schooled her breathing, concentrating on drawing air past the ridges of her corset. Calm, she had to stay calm. Taking deep, exaggerated inhalations, she lifted both hands, palm up, and ran them down the length of the wall. If all else failed, at least now that she knew where the proper panel was, she could lie in wait for Vaughn's return. For him to enter, as he must, the panel would have to open, and she could bash him over the head with the heavy silver carafe he had used to cool the champagne.

Henrietta's lips twisted in a slightly hysterical smile. Miles would approve. He was a great advocate of head-bashing.

But it hadn't come to that yet, she reminded herself, squaring her shoulders. At least, not quite yet. The porcelain panels yielded no cracks or protrusions that might hide the mechanism that bolted the door. One boasted a dragon as part of the scene; the dragon was, appropriately enough, bearing off a hapless village maiden to parts unknown. The maiden didn't seem all that unhappy to be borne. Perhaps Chinese dragons were kinder to their prey than their European counterparts, mused Henrietta irrelevantly, pressing hard upon the body of the dragon. Nothing budged. Dragon and maiden remained endlessly journeying, flat against their fragile base, forever in flight.

Forever. Funny how she had never found that word quite so sinister until now. Shivering in a way that had nothing to do with the temperature in the little room, Henrietta dropped to her knees, feeling around the base of the panel with hands that were increasingly unsteady. Finer than a brushstroke, she could see the crack that marked the join of the door, taunting her with its presence.

"Why won't you open?" she hissed.

The door, smug and silent, forbore to answer.

Unfortunately, not everything was as silent. Oh heavens, were those steps she heard in the hallway? Spurred by panic, Henrietta jammed a fingernail desperately at the divide. The nail broke. The door remained stubbornly shut. If she couldn't even wiggle a nail into the space, how could she hope to lever it open with anything more substantial? She settled back on her haunches, staring sightlessly ahead of her. It would have to be the carafe, wouldn't it? There was nothing else she could do, nothing else she could try. She had pushed and prodded every inch of the door, run her hands over every panel, yanked on every protrusion. She was, she admitted to herself hopelessly, well and truly caught.

The two dragons, propping up their velvet bench, sneered at her in gilded smugness, twin Cerberus to her Persephone.

Dragons! Of course! Henrietta rocked back on her heels, a new burst of optimism firing her veins. They were so far below eye level that she had never thought of them, but if one was designing a secret lever, wouldn't one want to make it as unlikely as possible? It was, at least, a chance, and a better one than attempting to bludgeon Vaughn senseless with the carafe.

She poked them in their round, staring eyes. She yanked on their little pointed ears. She prodded their paws. She tugged on their lolling tongues. And then, just as she was about to consign them to perdition and herself to an undignified tussle with her host, the tongue of the dragon on the right shifted as she pulled. A movement! It had moved, hadn't it? Half-afraid to hope, Henrietta heaved harder. The long tongue curled forward and forward again, until deep in the recesses of the door something clicked.

With a sound like a spring being released, the door slid smoothly forward.

MILES BURST INTO THE FRONT HALL of Vaughn's mansion, nearly careening into a scowling Black Death. Black Death swirled his tattered draperies out of the way as Miles barreled by, searching for Hen. Dash it all, where was she? Miles fought his way through a dizzying throng of masked revelers. They eddied around him like a medieval painter's dazed nightmare, men with heads like birds, women in huge, feathered masks, all laughing and dancing with frenetic gaiety. Miles twisted past, looking, searching, blotting out the high-pitched voices and blur of shapes, focused entirely on finding Hen.

Miles experienced a spurt of relief as he spotted Penelope's familiar red head towards the back of the second room. Where there was Penelope, there was usually . . . no. Henrietta wasn't there. Miles skidded to a stop, panting, in front of Penelope.

"Have you seen Henrietta?" he demanded.

The Dowager Duchess poked him with a bronze-headed spear. "You're late!" she cackled.

"Henrietta?" snapped Miles dangerously, slapping away the spear. "You were supposed to be bloody chaperoning her!"

There was a tug on his sleeve. "She went looking for you." Charlotte bit her lip. She, at least, Miles noticed, had the good sense to look worried. "She didn't find you?"

Miles leaned forward earnestly, not even flinching when the dowager prodded his ribs with her instrument of torture. "Which way did she go?"

Charlotte pointed down the room, towards the open French doors that led into the music room, thronged, as was the ballroom, with masked revelers. "She went off that way. But it was some time ago."

"You're a good man, Lady Charlotte." Miles clapped her on the back and bounded off in the direction indicated.

"Mr. Dorrington! Wait!"

Miles skidded to a halt.

"She was wearing a blue *robe a l'anglaise*," said Charlotte rapidly. "With a gold mask."

Miles nodded his appreciation and plunged back into the crowd. He didn't stop to ask Charlotte what a *robe à l'anglaise* was. Some sort of dress, no doubt. Any additional explanation would be superfluous, time-consuming, and largely incomprehensible.

He saw red and white dresses and yellow dresses worn with enough gold masks to re-cover the dome of St. Peter's; he saw blue dresses paired with silver masks and black masks and masks of molting feathers, but no blue dress with a gold mask and no Henrietta. By the time he had made his way to the last of the reception rooms, Miles had passed frantic and was on his way to desperate. She wasn't anywhere downstairs. No one remembered seeing her. Nor, for that matter, could anyone recall having seen their host for quite some time.

Miles's mind teemed with unpleasant possibilities. Could Vaughn have kidnapped her, and carried her off to the cellars, bound and gagged? Had she been smuggled out through a window and carted off to some deserted hunting lodge in the countryside? Or had Vaughn simply taken Henrietta upstairs? Miles blanched, remembering that large canopied bed, with its cavorting nymphs. With the noise generated by five hundred squawking guests, no one would hear Henrietta scream.

Miles turned to bolt for the front hall and the stairs to the upper regions, when a familiar hand settled on his arm.

"Dorrington!" exclaimed Turnip Fitzhugh. "Smashing party, eh, what?"

Miles shook Turnip's hand off. "You haven't seen Henrietta Selwick about, have you?"

"Lady Henrietta? No, I can't say that I have, but I did see Charlotte Lansdowne, and she looked absolutely smashing—dressed as a shepherdess, you know, with a little sheep. I say, your costume's not quite the thing! What are you supposed to be, old chap?"

"An incompetent duelist," clipped Miles. "Look, have you seen—"

"An incompetent duelist . . ." Turnip mulled it over. "Ha! Very clever. An incompetent duelist! Wait till I tell—"

"Fitzhugh!" Miles roared over Turnip's chuckles.

"What?"

"Have. You. Seen. Lord. Vaughn?"

"Oh, our host? You don't have to worry about paying your respects; it's such a crush, the man'll never know the difference. I—"

"Have you seen him?" Miles gritted out, reminding himself that it wasn't at all the done thing to strangle old school friends just because they were nattering on while Henrietta could be being attacked or tortured or . . . Maybe strangulation wasn't too extreme. Why was he even wasting his time? "Never mind," he said curtly. "I'll see you later."

"Vaughn went that way," said Turnip amiably.

"What?" Miles spun back around on his heel.

"You were looking for Lord Vaughn, weren't you? Don't know why you'd want to, but—"

Miles grabbed Turnip by the shoulders. "Was there a woman with him? A woman in a blue dress with a gold mask?"

"Easy there, old chap! There was, at that. Toothsome piece, too. Dorrington?"

Miles was already elbowing his way through the throng in the direction Turnip had indicated, with only one thought in his mind. To find Hen. Right away.

A door at the end of the room took him into an ill-lit hallway, eerily dark and silent after the hubbub behind him. Damnation. Miles picked up speed. He had a feeling he knew what he'd find at the end of the corridor—a concealed stair leading up to the upper regions. And once he got there . . .

Miles didn't have much time to figure out exactly how he was going to reallocate Vaughn's anatomy (and to hell with keeping him in one piece for interrogation purposes), because at that very moment he barreled into something small and human that let out a very feminine-sounding "Ooof!" as it banged into him.

Acting on instinct, Miles grabbed her by the shoulders to keep the woman from toppling over. They tottered together for a moment. The woman's mask tumbled to the ground, and her head tilted back to reveal a very familiar pale, oval face, just as she blurted out, "Miles?"

"Hen?" Miles exclaimed incredulously, tightening his grip on her shoulders, as though he were afraid she would disappear if he let go.

His brown eyes roved anxiously across her face, across those wonderfully familiar tip-tilted hazel eyes, that small, straight nose, the lips that had fallen slightly open in surprise and delight.

"Dammit, Hen, do you know how worried I was?" he said thickly, and, before he could think better of it, before he could remember that she was his best friend's sister and they were in the middle of a corridor in the house of a potentially deadly French spy, before he could remember anything other than that she was Hen, and she was safe, and he was so damn relieved he might bloody well burst with it, Miles wrapped his arms around her as tightly as they would go and captured her lips with his.

Chapter Nineteen

———— ❦ ————

Assignation: *a rendezvous with a fellow agent under pretense of amorous dalliance*

        —from the Personal Codebook of the Pink Carnation

It took Henrietta a moment to realize that she was being well and truly kissed by Miles. His lips moved across her own with a fervor born of anxiety, molding the contours of her lips to his, squeezing her so tightly that the dreaded corset bit into her back and any air that might have remained in her lungs thought better of staying. Henrietta didn't care. She wrapped her arms around Miles's neck, clinging as tightly to him as he was to her, glorying in the feel of his warm skin through the thin linen of his shirt, the scent of sandalwood and cheroots, the soft ends of his hair tickling her fingertips.

"God, Hen," he murmured, pressing little kisses along the corner of her mouth, as if he couldn't bear to move away for even so long as it would take to speak, "you had me so worried. When I thought"—*kiss*—"what that man could"—*kiss, kiss*—"be doing to you . . ."

Henrietta cut off whatever he was about to say by the simple expedient of rising on her tiptoes and stopping his mouth with a kiss. His mouth tasted slightly of brandy, salty, intoxicating—not that Henrietta needed any inebriant; she was as deliciously light-headed as she had been that night when Miles snuck her that first glass of champagne.

Miles rapidly lost any interest in continuing what he had been about to say, his lips slanting to meet hers, and his hand tangling in her hair, tilting her face to meet his. His roving fingers dislodged one of the large pearl combs that decorated her old-fashioned coiffure. It clattered on the parquet floor, the sound reverberating through Miles's dazed brain like the tolling of a thousand warning bells.

Releasing her, Miles staggered back, eyes glazed and heart hammering.

Meanwhile, his brain, returned from its brief vacation, was loudly screaming, Oh hell, oh hell, oh hell. Certain other parts of his body were also clamoring for attention, but Miles ignored them. They had gotten him into enough trouble already. Oh, hell. He hadn't really just kissed Henrietta, had he? It could have been a daydream, a hallucination. Miles caught sight of Henrietta's gleaming eyes and swollen lips. That would have had to have been one bloody convincing hallucination.

"It's, um, good that you're safe," he said lamely, sticking his hands in his pockets.

"Mm-hmm," agreed Henrietta, beaming up at him with her head tilted up towards him at an angle that practically invited . . . Miles took an extra step back; he would have made the sign against the evil eye, too, if he'd thought it would do him any good. God help him, all he wanted to do was kiss her again. Miles found himself addressing his Maker on terms of intimacy he hadn't employed for many a year.

Since God didn't seem to want to be obliging about sending thunderbolts or the like to serve as a diversion—Miles thought glumly that he probably deserved at least one of those thunderbolts through his own thick skull—Miles took refuge in indignation.

"What," he demanded, as Henrietta stooped down to retrieve her fallen accoutrements, "were you doing wandering about by yourself like that?"

"Looking for you," she said gaily, smiling up at him.

"You couldn't have waited with the duchess?"

"Have you seen the duchess tonight?" Henrietta rocked back on her heels and stuck her pearl comb haphazardly back in her hair. "I preferred to take my chances here, thank you very much. Um, do you think you could help me up? These hoops are a nightmare."

Miles looked down. It was a mistake. From his current vantage point, all he could see was breasts. Lots and lots of breasts. Beautiful, ripe, tempting breasts mounding over the top of her square bodice. What was she trying to do, kill him?

"You were very lucky it was me," Miles said sternly, yanking her unceremoniously up off the floor. "If someone else had come upon you, they might have—"

"Kissed me?" Henrietta supplied mischievously, shaking out her skirts.

"Um, yes. I mean no. I mean . . ." Henrietta's grin widened. Miles scowled. Exactly when had he lost control of this conversation? "Dammit, Hen, what if it had been Martin Frobisher? Or Lord Vaughn?"

"But it wasn't," Henrietta said cheerfully.

She couldn't bring herself to spoil the moment just yet by bringing up the alarming interlude with Lord Vaughn. After all, it wasn't every day that one was delightfully and thoroughly kissed by the man one had been daydreaming about. She hadn't even had to ravish him with roses.

Henrietta chuckled to herself at the thought, utterly delighted with the world and everything in it.

Miles's scowl deepened. "I don't think you're taking this seriously enough, Hen."

"Can I be serious tomorrow instead?"

Miles had to pace rapidly back and forth across the hallway to keep himself from grabbing her. Just for good measure, he locked his hands behind his back, since he didn't trust them to behave themselves. Just look what his lips had been doing with absolutely no direction from his brain—well, not that brain, anyway—just moments before. Miles's lips thinned.

"Dammit, Hen, this isn't a joke. You could have been killed."

He really was adorable when he was trying to be manly and commanding. Henrietta was so busy reveling in the familiar way his hair flopped across his brow and the way his muscles moved against the thin linen of his shirt as he paced, while her mind chortled, "Mine! All mine!" that it took her a moment to register the slight incongruity in the verb.

"Killed?" she repeated, wrinkling her brow. "Don't you think that's a bit of an exaggeration?"

Admittedly, there were moments when she had feared for her life in Vaughn's Chinese chamber, but the more time elapsed, the more ridiculous her worries seemed. Surely no peer of the realm would strangle a marquis's daughter in the midst of his own party, even if he were a French spy. It would be in poor taste, both socially and strategically.

Besides, Miles didn't know about any of that. She would tell him, of course. Eventually. To tell him now would add far too much credibility to his side of the argument. And Henrietta really didn't want to have a serious discussion just now. She wanted to bask in the aftermath of her first kiss (her first kiss that counted, at any rate), giggle for no reason, and maybe twirl in circles a bit for good measure.

She also wouldn't have minded kissing Miles again, but Miles's concerted glower seemed to imply that he was not currently amenable to further dalliance.

"Yes, killed," Miles repeated decisively.

He paused for a moment, thinking rapidly. Hen was a bright girl—and a stubborn one. He knew her well enough to know she wouldn't be impressed by vague warnings of danger. The War Office wouldn't like it, but . . . Henrietta's safety came first. Of course, that still begged the question of who would be keeping her safe from *him*.

Miles raked his fingers through his hair. "I probably shouldn't be telling you this, but if that's what it takes . . . Listen, Hen"—Miles lowered his voice—"there's a dangerous French spy on the loose."

"You know about that?" exclaimed Henrietta.

"*What?*" Miles's head snapped up.

"The spy." Henrietta made sure to keep her voice suitably low. She drew closer to Miles, her wide skirts brushing his breeches. Miles side-stepped like a skittish colt.

"I was going to warn you tonight, when I found you, but circumstances intervened." Henrietta rather wished those particular circumstances—the ones to do with Miles kissing her—would materialize again, but since they showed no sign of doing so, she continued. "According to my sources, there is an extremely dangerous new spy in London."

Miles sat down heavily on one of the small gilded benches placed against the wall. Since when had Henrietta had sources?

"I won't even ask," he muttered.

Henrietta made a wry face, and joined him on the bench, her skirts frothing over his legs. "It's probably best you don't."

"Do you know anything else about this . . . new development?"

"All I know is that you and I are both under scrutiny, most likely in regard to our connection with Richard."

"And you still wandered off alone?"

"I needed to warn you," Henrietta said in the most sensible tone she could muster. She hurried on before Miles could plunge back into lecture. "And I also took the opportunity to do a spot of detecting along the way."

"Does your mother know about this spot of detection?" asked Miles darkly.

"That," said Henrietta, "was unkind. Mama is in Kent with the children, and what she doesn't know won't hurt her."

"No, just when you turn up dead in a ditch somewhere."

"Why a ditch?"

Miles made an inarticulate noise of extreme frustration. "That's not important."

"Then why did you mention it?"

Miles responded by banging his head into his knees. Hard.

Henrietta decided it was time to change the subject. "How did you know about the spy?"

"Some of us," commented Miles in a muffled tone, "happen to work for the War Office. Some of us aren't naive young girls who are courting death and disaster by playing with things that they should *not be involved in*."

"Don't you even want to know what I found out?" Henrietta wheedled.

Still doubled over, Miles eyed her warily. "I'm going to regret this, aren't I?"

"Lord Vaughn," Henrietta began, "has been behaving very oddly."

"He's been doing more than behaving oddly," Miles said grimly. "He stabbed Downey."

All the amusement fled from Henrietta's face. "Is Downey all right?"

Miles let out a deep breath and slumped back against the wall. "The surgeon says he'll make it, but it was close." He closed his eyes, reliving the memory of his valet on the floor, covered in blood. "Someone tore up my flat today, looking for something. Downey was in the way. If I had been home—"

"He still might have been stabbed. You just can't know that."

"If he hadn't been working for me—"

"He might have been attacked by a footpad, or knifed by a thief. These things happen."

"They're far more likely to happen when there are French spies involved," muttered Miles. "I brought this on him. You don't understand. I was careless, Hen. If I hadn't attracted the attention of the spy . . ."

"But don't you see?" Henrietta twisted to look at him, gasping as the boning stabbed her in the ribs. "You didn't. At least, not by any action of your own. You were already being watched simply by virtue of having been friends with Richard all these years. If it's anyone's fault," she continued, warming to her theme, "it's Richard's, for being so successful. There. You see?"

As she had known he would, Miles grimaced at her. "That makes no sense, Hen."

"Neither do you, so we're even."

"Thanks," he said gruffly.

"Of course," Henrietta said softly.

Looking at him sitting there, slumped on the bench, no jacket or cravat to speak of, waistcoat unbuttoned, shirt rumpled, disheveled, derelict, and dejected, she had to clamp down on an overwhelming surge of affection. She wanted to smooth back that permanently disordered bit of hair at his brow and kiss away the worried wrinkle just over his nose.

Wise in the ways of Miles, Henrietta did none of those things. Instead, she asked neutrally, "How do you know it was Lord Vaughn who stabbed Downey?"

"He didn't leave a calling card, if that's what you're asking," Miles said with all the snippiness of a male who has just been bamboozled into revealing emotion.

Henrietta gave him a "don't be an idiot" look. "It just doesn't seem the sort of thing Lord Vaughn would do."

"You don't think him capable of murder?"

"I wouldn't say that. But can't you more easily picture him slipping someone a thimbleful of poison?" Henrietta refrained from bringing in her own personal experience in this regard. After all, she had no proof the wine had been poisoned. "Stabbing someone is just too . . . crude. Lord Vaughn likes the subtle, the arcane. If he were going to kill someone, he would set about it more inventively."

Miles frowned in thought. "Point taken. I don't know whether he did it personally or sent a lackey, but he seems the most likely instigator, if you would prefer to look at it that way."

"Why would he want to ransack your flat?"

Miles took a quick look down either side of the hallway, and dropped his voice to a mere thread of sound. "We have reason to believe he might be the agent we're looking for. One of our agents was recently killed—also stabbed—in a way that suggested a connection to Vaughn."

"That would explain a great deal," Henrietta said slowly, thinking back over his unexpected interest in her once the Purple Gentian's name was invoked, his odd behavior in the windowless chamber. Something nagged at her, though. Something didn't quite add up, and she couldn't figure out why. She made a wry face at herself; Miles wasn't going to lend much credence to woman's intuition. Nor would she if their situations were reversed. Nonetheless, she ventured, "But what would he have to gain?"

Miles shrugged. "Money? Power? Settling a personal score? A man could turn traitor for any number of reasons."

Henrietta shivered.

Miles risked a glance in her direction, trying very hard to keep his eyes above her neck, and almost succeeding. "Are you cold?"

Henrietta shook her head, grimacing. "No. Just alarmed by human nature."

"You should be," Miles said grimly. "They knifed Downey with no more consideration than if he had been a—"

"Rabid dog?"

"I was thinking more a bug, but something like that."

Miles looked soberly at Henrietta, cursing himself for being ten times a fool. He should have grabbed her by the arm and hauled her straight back to the dowager the moment he had barreled into her. There was no excuse for his behavior—either of his behaviors; this last interlude had been just as self-indulgent and just as dangerous as that damnable kiss. He had been swept up in the relief of having someone to talk to, to confide his guilt over Downey, to trade ideas about the progress of the mission, someone he could trust. But that was no excuse. He knew Henrietta well enough to know exactly how she would react. This was, after all, the girl whose favorite phrase as a toddler had been "me too."

To have Downey hurt by his carelessness was bad enough; for anything to happen to Henrietta . . . it was unthinkable. Miles considered dragging out some of the past exploits of the Black Tulip, including his charming habit of carving his calling card into the flesh of his victims, but prolonging the discussion would only make matters worse. The more he said, the more intrigued Henrietta would be, and the more intrigued Henrietta was . . .

His voice came out harsher than he had intended. "Stay out of this, Hen. This is no parlor game."

"But, Miles, I'm in it already. Whoever it is, he's looking for me, too."

"All the more reason for you to be even more careful. Have you considered joining your mother in Kent for a few weeks?"

"And catch the mumps?"

Miles stood abruptly. "The mumps are the least of my worries."

Henrietta stood, too, looking mutinous. "The best way to secure all of our safety is to catch the spy."

"Don't worry." Miles started off down the corridor. "I will."

Henrietta trotted along after him. "Don't you mean, *we* will?"

"*You* are going back to the duchess. That woman is better protection than a citadel."

In front of them, Henrietta could hear the hubbub of voices that betokened the more populated parts of the party. She yanked on Miles's arm, eager to have her say before they once more joined the throng.

"Miles, I'm not going to sit idly by while you do all the work."

Miles didn't say anything. He just looked stubborn.

Ha! thought Henrietta, clapping her golden mask to her face and following her glowering escort in the direction of the dowager. Miles didn't know the first thing about stubborn. She would talk him around tomorrow, she decided confidently. She would ply him with tea and ginger biscuits. (Cook would surely be amenable to whipping up an extra batch.) And if that failed—Henrietta's lips curved into an anticipatory smile—why, then, she would just have to kiss him into compliance. A hardship, but such were the sacrifices one had to undergo for the sake of one's country.

Henrietta grinned all the way back to the dowager.

Miles glowered all the way back to the dowager. Miles glowered the length of three rooms. Miles glowered as he deposited Henrietta with the Dowager Duchess, and sternly advised them all to go home. Miles glowered particularly forbiddingly as the Dowager Duchess pinked him with Penelope's spear.

"I'll see you tomorrow," called out Henrietta, waving her mask at him like a triumphal banner.

Miles grunted in response. Then he resumed glowering.

Appropriating a glass of champagne, he retreated to an unoccupied alcove where he could glower at Henrietta from a safe distance. At least, he thought darkly, rubbing his bruised posterior, she would be free from harm so long as she was with the Dowager Duchess; the woman provided a better deterrent to would-be assassins and abductors than an entire Greek phalanx. Hell, ship her over to France and Napoleon would surrender within the week.

France. Miles stared grimly into the sparkling liquid in the crystal goblet. He had to find enough to conclusively prove Vaughn's guilt. The War Office wouldn't act without proof. They also wouldn't act if it meant damaging their chances of rounding up the rest of Vaughn's contacts first.

The War Office and Miles had slightly different priorities at the moment.

Across the room, he heard a high, clear, utterly unmistakable laugh, and winced in a way that had nothing to do with French agents.

Maybe if he asked nicely the War Office would send him on assignment to Siberia.

Chapter Twenty

Excursion: *an intelligence-gathering mission undertaken in some form of disguise*
Excursion, delightful: *an intelligence-gathering mission of no little success*
See also under Jaunt, pleasant
—from the Personal Codebook of the Pink Carnation

"What do you want?"

A woman with a glaringly white fichu draped over her ample bosom glowered from the open doorway of 13 rue Niçoise.

"A room," said the girl standing on the stoop. Her lusterless dark hair was pulled severely back beneath a neat cap, but the rest of her appearance showed signs of neglect; her collar and cuffs drooped limply, and there was a weary look about her gray eyes. "Not for me," she added hastily, as the door began to close. "For my mistress. She heard you had rooms to let."

"Your mistress," repeated the woman in the doorway derisively, her sharp eyes roaming over frayed cuffs and scuffed boots. The starched fabric of her apron rustled against the wood of the doorframe. "What's your mistress doing looking for rooms here?"

"She's a . . . widow," explained the girl earnestly. "A respectable widow."

The woman's eyes narrowed at the telltale pause. "I know her kind, and we don't need none of that sort around here."

The girl twisted her hands in her apron. "But I was told . . ."

"Told!" the woman snorted. "I know what you was told. But you can just put it right out of your mind. I run a respectable house, I do. Not like her as was here before."

"Here before?" the maidservant echoed in a small voice, her eyes darting longingly past the bulk of the proprietress to the painfully clean foyer beyond.

"Madame Dupree." The woman spat the name out as though it tasted foul. "Take anyone, that one would. The goings-on in this house! Enough to make a respectable woman blush, it was. Gentlemen callers coming and going, cigar stains on the sheets, wine spilled on the carpets."

"Even Englishmen, I heard," the maidservant ventured timidly.

"English, Prussian, all manner of riffraff." The woman's white cap rustled as she shook her head over past depravity. "Didn't matter none to her so long as they payed their rent proper. I had my work cut out for me cleaning it out, I did."

"Where did they all go?" asked the maidservant, wide-eyed.

"No interest of mine." The woman's lips hardened into a determined line. "So you can just tell your mistress she'll have to look for lodging elsewhere."

"But—"

The maidservant staggered back as the door thudded shut. Through an open window came the sound of a mop being vigorously applied.

As she moved out of sight of the house, the girl's dejected slump disappeared, and her pace accelerated to a brisk walk. The black hair dye made her head and eyebrows itch mercilessly, but Jane Wooliston resisted the urge to scratch as she made her way rapidly from the rue Niçoise back to the Hotel de Balcourt, looking to all the world like an anxious servant on an errand for a demanding mistress. She would be able to doff her costume soon enough; she had found out what she wanted to know.

Number 13 rue Niçoise was a boardinghouse. In an unfashionable neighborhood, it currently catered to the poor but respectable, to hardworking clerks and maiden aunts eking out the end of their days on meager savings. The hall had been as painfully whitewashed as the proprietress's linen; any speck of dirt would no doubt be pounced upon and eliminated as soon as it crossed the threshold.

It was not at all the sort of establishment one would expect Lord Vaughn to patronize.

From the woman's tone, Jane surmised that the boardinghouse, until recently, had served a clientele of another sort entirely, dubious characters living on the fringe of the demimonde, a haven for runaways and rendezvous. That, decided Jane, made a good deal more sense. The illusion of assignation could provide an excellent pretense for meetings that had more to do with policy than paramours. No one would think anything of a gentleman haring off to the seedier parts of the city for a bit of illicit amusement.

She would, determined Jane, weaving her way around a dray cart blocking the street, have to discover how long ago the boardinghouse had come under its current management. The former proprietress would be located, and discreetly questioned as to the prior inhabitants of the house. It was a pity Dupree was such a common name, but Jane had no qualms about her ability to locate her. Beneath her serene countenance, a plan began to form. She would send one of her men, in the guise of an anxious brother seeking a sister who had fled from the bosom of her family. Naturally, the concerned brother would be anxious to know not only the whereabouts of his "sister," but any people with whom that ill-fated and fictitious female had come in contact, especially men who might have taken advantage of her youth and innocence. It would make a most affecting tale.

Head down, shoulders bowed, Jane crossed the last few yards to her cousin's house. If Lord Vaughn had been using 13 rue Niçoise as a base for nefarious activities, the boardinghouse could be the key to unraveling an entire network of agents.

Her mind rapidly working over this new piece of information, the Pink Carnation slipped in through the servants' entrance of the Hotel de Balcourt. She had dye to rinse out of her hair, orders to issue, a coded report to send to Mr. Wickham, a supper party to attend, and a meeting of the United Irishmen to infiltrate. Unseen, the Pink Carnation ascended the servants' stairs to her own room and, efficiently divesting herself of her servile garb, prepared to don her third disguise of the afternoon—that of elegant young lady.

Chapter Twenty-One

—— ◆ ——

Accident, an: *an event causing harm or inconvenience brought about by the agency of malignant French operatives; generally designed to give a spurious appearance of inadvertence*

—from the Personal Codebook of the Pink Carnation

"Henrietta! You're finally here!"

Henrietta's diminutive sister-in-law Amy barreled down the front steps of Selwick Hall like a muslin-clad cannonball, catching up her skirts as she ran towards the hired traveling chaise. Two immense torches lit the front entrance of Selwick Hall, casting odd glints off Amy's short, dark curls, and the horses' trappings.

The six-hour trip had stretched to eight, thanks to a broken axle barely an hour out of London. Fortunately, the accident had occurred as they lumbered along behind a crowded mail coach on Croydon High Street; they had been moving at barely more than a walk when the wheel began to tilt ominously, and the chaise with it. Henrietta and her maid had exited the conveyance with more speed than grace, taking refuge at the Greyhound, one of the town's chief posting houses, where a new chaise was hired, the luggage all reloaded, and the tired horses refreshed.

Enveloping Henrietta in an enthusiastic hug, Amy all but dragged her down the folding steps of the traveling chaise. Tugging her towards the front door, Amy exclaimed, "How are you? Did you have a frightful trip from London? We were so worried about you! Do you want to freshen up? Just wait until you hear the plans for the weekend!"

Henrietta hugged Amy back, made the requisite number of delighted squealing noises, and submitted to being tugged.

"Where is Richard?" she asked, as a footman bowed them into the front hall. The footman, like everyone else in the house, was a devoted participant in her brother's undercover activities. No one was employed at Selwick Hall who had not been proven entirely trustworthy. A mistake in judgment could prove fatal. It had, after all, been a French operative, posing as a lady's maid, who had caused the demise of one of her brother's closest friends. "Doesn't he love me anymore?"

"Oh, he'll be along," said Amy, helping to divest Henrietta of her bonnet and shawl. "He was supervising the footmen setting up the targets and climbing walls for Saturday. You won't believe all the wonderful things we have planned!"

Targets? Climbing walls? That sounded ominous. Henrietta didn't mind aiming at targets—in fact, there was a certain large, blond target she wouldn't much mind taking a shot at about now—but wall climbing? She couldn't even climb a tree. And those had branches.

Putting alarming thoughts of physical exertion aside, Henrietta broke into Amy's spate of words to edge towards what she really wanted to know. "Who else will be here this weekend?"

Amy abandoned alarming explanations about walls and steel picks. "There's Mrs. Cathcart," she said, naming a cheerful widow of middle years and ample proportions, who had made her debut with Lady Uppington in the latter's mythical youth, "and Miss Grey . . ."

"Miss Who?"

"Grey," said Amy, herding Henrietta into a small drawing room at the front of the house. "She was a governess. And then the Tholmondelay twins—I know they haven't a brain between them, but Richard is quite taken with the idea of identical agents."

"Is that all of us?" asked Henrietta, trying not to sound as disappointed as she felt. The Tholmondelays, pronounced, in the mysterious way of English nomenclature, Frumley, were not the men she had in mind.

"Geoff was supposed to join us, but he was unavoidably detained." Amy rolled her eyes. "Can't you guess by whom? Oh, and then there's Miles, of course."

"Of course," echoed Henrietta, dropping down onto a blue-striped settee. "Is he here yet?"

"Miles?" Amy had to stop and think for a moment. "Not yet. He was supposed to be here hours ago. Richard wanted his help with the ropes course."

Ropes course? Henrietta didn't even want to think about it. Wasn't being a spy supposed to be a mental exercise, involving deep ratiocination? Ratiocination she could do; ropes were another matter entirely.

"Is there any tea?" she asked hopefully.

"No, but I can ring for some," replied Amy. "I'll have Cook send up some biscuits, too. Have you had anything to eat?"

"We had a light meal at the Greyhound while we were waiting for the chaise to be repaired."

"Oh, good," said Amy. "The others should be arriving tomorrow morning, just in time for the seminar on French geography. Did you know that Richard knows more than fifteen escape routes to Calais? After that, I'll be coaching everyone on local dialects. My favorite is the Marseillaise fishwife."

"The Marseillaise fishwife?" Henrietta echoed, looking longingly at the door in the hopes a tea tray would materialize.

"You get to screech a lot for that one," explained Amy enthusiastically, checking herself momentarily as she added, "Although the smell *is* dreadful. Oh, Stiles! Tea for Lady Henrietta?"

Henrietta could see why Amy had ended on an interrogative. Richard's butler had clearly already entered into the spirit of the weekend. He was wearing a striped jersey and a black beret, and had slung an odiferous necklace of onions around his neck. He looked far more likely to hit someone over the head with a bottle of Bordeaux in a rough seaside tavern than carry in a tea tray.

"Eeef eet eez posseeblah, madame," he hissed in an impenetrable accent that the Frenchest of Frenchmen wouldn't be able to understand, flung his onions more securely over his shoulder, and stalked out.

Henrietta's incredulous gaze met Amy's and the two burst into laughter. It had seemed to Richard a fine idea to incorporate an out-of-work actor into the League of the Purple Gentian, until he had realized there was one slight hitch. Stiles had a good deal of difficulty divorcing role from reality. This had, occasionally, worked in Richard's favor, but it was very hard to discern who Stiles was going to be from one moment to the next. He had a marked fondness for tragic Shakespearean heroes of the toga-wearing sort. There had been a brief, but lamentable, Macbeth phase, involving haggis on the tea tray and bagpipes at odd hours of the night.

"Even with the onions, it's an improvement on his last incarnation," pointed out Amy cheerfully.

"I don't know," mused Henrietta. "I rather liked the pirate impression. The parrot was darling."

"Oh, no, you missed the last one—he was a highwayman for a full two weeks. He put up wanted posters all over the house, and took to calling himself the Silver Shadow."

"Why silver?"

"The dye from his octogenarian phases hadn't grown out yet. We wouldn't have minded so much if he hadn't kept insisting that we stand and deliver."

"Deliver what?" asked Henrietta practically.

"Our money or our lives, of course. On the bright side"—Amy's big blue eyes took on a reminiscent gleam—"it did keep the house clear of guests during our honeymoon."

Henrietta adored her sister-in-law and her brother and had done all she could to facilitate their nuptials (since Richard had, of course, made a proper muddle of it), but in her present mood, honeymoons were the last thing she wanted to think about. After the glorious rapture of Friday night, Henrietta's own romance had taken a rapid turn for the worse.

On Saturday, Henrietta had put on her most becoming frock, arranged herself attractively on the settee in the morning room, and waited for Miles to call. She had, over a sleepless night spent mostly in rapturous reliving of the Kiss, gone over Amy's spying advice, and drawn up a comprehensive plan to pin down Vaughn and ferret out his spy ring. She knew Miles would initially be difficult—he tended to be a little overprotective where she was concerned—but had no doubt he could be talked around. After that, maybe a walk in the park together, strolling among the fragrant spring flowers, her hand tucked away in the crook of his arm, while he soulfully recited poetry . . . all right, maybe not the poetry. Henrietta wasn't quite infatuated enough to abandon reality entirely. Besides, she liked Miles the way he was, even if his conversation did tend more towards horses than heroic couplets.

There was just one slight problem. Miles didn't appear.

Miles didn't appear Saturday, and he didn't appear Sunday, and he didn't appear Monday, even though Henrietta cleverly spent the entire day out shopping, on the grounds that the moment she happened to be out was the moment he would choose to call. He didn't.

"Are you sure no one called?" Henrietta asked Winthrop, just a little shrilly. It had, after all, been three days at that point. "Perhaps someone could have come up to the door and left again without your seeing? Are you *quite* sure?"

Winthrop was quite sure.

By Wednesday, there was only one possible solution. Miles had to be ill. In fact, he had better be very, very ill. Henrietta delegated her maid, Annie, who was niece to Miles's Mrs. Migworth, to discover the state of affairs at *chez* Dorrington. Annie, face flushed from running, returned to report that Mr. Dorrington was quite well, in fine form, in fact. Mr. Downey, Annie added, blushing, was also recovering nicely, and looked to be about his duties within the week.

Henrietta suspected that Annie was sweet on Downey. She considered delivering a pithy warning on the perfidy of men, but didn't want to disillusion Annie. Annie would find out on her own soon enough, when Downey kissed her as though he never wanted to let her out of his arms, and then didn't bloody call for five blasted days, while she sat there in emotional agony waiting for a knock on the door that never came and her heart slowly turned to a leaden lump of bleak despair within her chest. Or something like that.

"He may have just been busy," suggested Charlotte.

"He wasn't good enough for you," pronounced Penelope.

"Bleargh," said Henrietta.

Clearly, the kiss had meant far less to him than it had to her. Henrietta could accept that (she told herself, gritting her teeth). But to kiss her and then disappear for an entire week? Did she mean that little to him after eighteen years? One would think that he owed her some sort of explanation, even if it was only one of those hideous speeches that began with "You are a lovely person," and inevitably ended with "Someday, you'll find someone who really loves you." At least that would show that he held her in enough regard to take the time to crush her heart in person. But, no, he couldn't even bother to do that.

Even a *note* would have been preferable.

"Oh, there Miles is!" exclaimed Amy, pointing out the window. A smart curricle and four drew into the little circle of light before the door. As Henrietta watched, Miles handed the reins down to a groom and swung easily off the box. "I'll just go tell Richard. Would you mind playing hostess for a moment?"

Assuming that the answer would be positive—and why, after all, should Amy assume otherwise?—Amy darted off before Henrietta could answer.

The long delay in Croydon had provided Henrietta ample time to resolve how she would behave upon seeing Miles. Cool and distant, Henrietta reminded herself as she rose slowly from the settee. Icy elegance. Impenetrable calm.

She was just making her cool, icy, and dignified way across the threshold of the drawing room, when Miles bounded energetically through the front door.

He saw her, and checked himself midstride. "Uh, Hen," he said, with the trapped look of a fox run to earth. "Hello."

Cool and distant ceased to be a possibility.

Henrietta marched up to Miles and looked him dangerously in the eye. "Do you have something you would like to say to me?"

"Your hair looks nice today?" Miles ventured.

Henrietta's lips clamped together. "That," she snapped, "was *not* the right answer."

Turning on her heel, she stalked off.

Miles clamped down on the urge to go after her. If he did that, he would defeat the entire purpose of this past week's exercise in absence. At first, he had meant to go see Henrietta. But Downey had been feverish on Saturday, which provided an excellent excuse for inaction. By Sunday, Downey's temperature was down and there was no impediment in the way of Miles's trotting straight over to Uppington House—except that he couldn't figure out what to say. The "You're a lovely person and someday you'll find someone who really loves you" speech just wouldn't work for Henrietta. He thought of sending a note, but what would it say? "Unavoidably detained; sorry about that kiss. Miles." Somehow, he didn't see that being awfully well received, either.

The more he had stayed away, the better an idea it had seemed. After all, if he didn't encounter Henrietta, there was no danger of his libido betraying his brain and engaging in a repeat of Friday night's indiscretion. One kiss was bad enough, but two? He really couldn't explain away two. Hell, he couldn't even explain away the one, which brought him back to his original problem of not knowing what to say to Henrietta.

He knew he should have stayed in London.

"What the devil did you say to Henrietta?" Richard strode into the front hall, absently rubbing his arm. "She nearly knocked me over on the garden path."

"Something about her hair," Miles hedged.

Richard shrugged. The ways of little sisters were indeed a mystery no grown man could hope to plumb. "How about a glass of claret and something to eat, while you tell me the news from London?"

"Excellent idea," said Miles with relief, matching his stride to his friend's as they moved in the direction of the dining room. A glass of wine, some sustenance, and a soothing conversation about homicidal French agents. It was exactly what he needed to keep his mind off the far more alarming topic of a certain irate female.

Thwack!

Both men started at the sound of stone crashing against stone. It had come from the direction of the garden.

Richard frowned at Miles. "What in the blazes did you say about her hair?"

"Owwwwww ..."

Henrietta clutched her sore shoulder and glowered at the shattered bust of Achilles. Pieces of his helmet littered the garden path, his nose was wedged up against a hedge, and one large, staring eye had rolled under a rosebush. The pillar on which he had perched lay on its side, having dragged half a rosebush down with it. And just who had decided the edge of the rose garden would be a good place to put a top-heavy bust? Oh, goodness, that *hurt*. She supposed it could have been worse. It could have fallen on her foot.

Henrietta dropped down on a nearby bench before she could cause more devastation.

"I am a walking disaster," she muttered.

She really hadn't handled that very well, had she? When she saw Miles, she was going to put him in his place by treating him with icy dignity, not storm out like a demented two-year-old on a rampage. Like a *destructive* two-year-old on a rampage, she amended, glancing at the remains of the bust. She would have to apologize to Richard for the decimation of his garden ornament tomorrow.

He did deserve it, though; no one could deny that. Miles, that was, not Achilles. Of course, if there were a bust of Cupid anywhere within reach, Henrietta might be tempted to do violence to it. It really didn't seem quite fair of Cupid—or Destiny, or Fate, or whoever was in charge of these sorts of things—to place love blissfully, gloriously within her reach and then yank it away, jeering, "Ha, ha, thought you had a chance, did you?"

Henrietta yanked a leaf off a neighboring bush and started to shred it.

Blaming Cupid didn't solve anything. Miles owed her an explanation. Not because he had kissed her—with two older brothers, Henrietta had grown up knowing quite well that a kiss was seldom a promise—but because they were, or at least they had been, friends. Friends didn't kiss friends and then go off for seven days. Friends didn't kiss friends and then try to brush them off with weak compliments. Your hair looks nice today? Ha! Did he really think he could placate her with that?

"What sort of a ninny does he think I am?" Henrietta grumbled to the quiet night air.

Only the crickets answered, with sympathetic clicking noises. Henrietta didn't have the heart to tell them it was a rhetorical question.

Around her, the garden was dark and still, silent as only the country could be. The scent of the lavender and hyssop that bordered the path hung heavy in the air, warring with the heady aroma of the roses that had been trained over a trellis to form an arch above. Henrietta sat there for a very long time, shredding leaves and brooding, while the marble seat grew cold and clammy under her twill skirt.

She was in the midst of a long and complicated conversation in her head with Miles, and was just up to the point where Miles confessed that he had only stayed away because he was paralyzed with fear by the strength of his own emotions for her (this followed the equally long and complicated conversation in which Miles caddishly declared that kisses were commonplace, and Henrietta blistered his ears with a scathing tirade rivaled in length and eloquence only by a Ciceronian oration), when she heard the sound of a foot stepping on a fallen twig just outside her little bower.

Right. Henrietta sat up straighter on her little bench. If that was Miles come to find her, she was going to tell him exactly what he could do with his meaningless compliments and equally meaningless kisses.

A second footfall followed the first, and a dark shadow paused at the opening of the path.

It was not Miles.

Henrietta instinctively shrank back into her bower as a hooded figure hovered in front of the trellis, a tart rejoinder frozen unuttered on her lips. In profile, the overhang of the hood seemed to encase only empty air; beneath the long robe that fell straight to the ground, sleeves tucked one into the other, there was nothing to suggest a human form. The apparition's coarse woolen robe swept the stone path with a low swishing noise, as the hooded figure swiveled in the direction of the house.

Henrietta's hands clenched around the marble seat of the bench, little goose prickles running up her arm. In the darkness, the breeze that had seemed so pleasant before turned chill, the clammy chill of the grave.

Swish, brush. Swish, brush.

Slowly, deliberately, the dark figure paced up the path towards the house, its tasseled belt swinging with each measured movement. It glided smoothly up the three shallow steps to the veranda, pausing once again before the French doors to take stock of the terrain before lifting one robed arm to the door handle. Quietly, seamlessly, the hooded figure slid into the empty drawing room, drawing the door soundlessly shut behind.

Henrietta sat frozen on her bench, eyes fixed on empty veranda.

The Phantom Monk of Donwell Abbey had just stolen into her brother's house.

Chapter Twenty-Two

———— ❦ ————

"**I**s there really a Phantom Monk of Donwell Abbey?"

The vicar grinned at me as he dumped a very unclerical portion of gin into his glass. "Has someone been bending your ear with that old yarn?"

I waved a hand in the direction of Colin Selwick, who stood several little groups of people away in the heavily Victorian drawing room of Donwell Abbey, eyes glazing over under the conversational onslaught of Joan Plowden-Plugge. He must have sensed he was being talked about, because his head turned in our direction, and he lifted his wineglass in an infinitesimal salute.

I looked hastily away.

The vicar, bless him, seemed not to notice. He was on his second drink ("Hazard rations, my dear," he had informed me, as he went for the second), and over the past twenty minutes we had become great chums. Joan had pounced the moment I entered the room. "You'll want to talk to the vicar," she announced with a tug on the arm, towing me in the direction of the drinks table. With me safely deposited, she had marched back off to the doorway to reclaim her spoil of war, i.e., Colin.

I didn't mind terribly much. For one thing, there was a certain amusement in watching an ambushed Colin glance distractedly around the room for means of escape. For another, the vicar was the most delightfully un-vicarlike vicar I had ever met.

Admittedly, I hadn't encountered a wide range, but anyone raised on a steady diet of British literature has a pretty good idea of what a village vicar is supposed to be like. I had expected someone spare and white-haired, with pale, veined hands, and a saintly aspect. The sort of vicar who putters through old village records, writes long treatises on the local flora and fauna, and spends his spare time in gentle labor in his garden, contemplating God's purpose as revealed through His creation.

Instead, I found myself shaking hands with a rangy man in his late thirties, with a crooked nose and equally crooked smile. He had, he explained, played rugby for Durham University until a dodgy knee forced him to abandon sport. Nothing daunted, he had presented himself to a talent agency in the hopes of a career in film. Two commercials and several stints as an extra in costume dramas later ("The Regency cravats were sheer hell, you know."), he had given up acting, acquired an M.Phil. in History of Architecture at Cambridge, tried his hand at journalism, written for a gossip column, and taken up sky-diving. It was that last, he informed me, which had led him to theology, since "There's nothing like plummeting towards the ground to make a man reconsider his relationship with his Maker." His predecessor, he assured me, had served the parish since 1948, and been the very model of an aged village vicar. "They're still getting used to me," he informed me with an unregenerate grin.

It took us most of his first gin and tonic—heavy on the gin, light on the tonic—to make our way through his life story. The preparation of the second provided a breathing space for me to ask what I really wanted to know: just what the story was with the Phantom Monk of Donwell Abbey.

Of course, I didn't really think that Henrietta had seen a ghost flit into her brother's house. Among other things, drawing on the immense supernatural knowledge gained by several informative evenings with History Channel specials on the subject (after all, if it's the History Channel, it counts as career development), why would a ghost use the door? Shouldn't it be able to drift through walls?

I sensed a human agency at work.

I sensed a human agency with an interest in Selwick Hall, the Purple Gentian, Miles, Henrietta, or all of the above. A human agency that worked for the French. Any spy who chose a name like the Black Tulip wouldn't scruple at playing a bit of dress-up. What better costume than that of a phantom monk? The habit provided complete concealment, and if anyone spotted the dark figure drifting through the grounds, as Henrietta had, they would simply chalk it up to the unquiet spirit of the Phantom Monk, endlessly searching for his lost love.

On the way over to Donwell Abbey, I had compiled a mental list of questions. Topping the charts was how widely spread the local ghost story had been in 1803. Was it, for example, the sort of information that would have been available to a French operative based in London? One assumed friends of the Selwick family would have heard the ghost story, as well as anyone who came from that part of Sussex. The Marquise de Montval originally hailed from Yorkshire, which meant that if the story was an entirely local affair, she was out, as was Mme. Fiorila, the Italian opera singer.

Damn, I had no idea where Vaughn's family seat was. I wondered if Colin's library boasted a suitably antiquated copy of *Debrett's Peerage and Baronetage*.

"They tried the local ghost story on me when I took the parish," said the vicar confidentially, as we wandered away from the drinks table to let others partake, "but I must say, there have been little in the way of manifestations so far."

"I can't imagine that a ghost would last long in this house," I commented, looking around at the heavy dark woodwork and clusters of little tables crammed with silver-framed photographs. "He'd probably be afraid of bumping into something."

The vicar chuckled. "Or he's run off in aesthetic distress."

I grinned. "Do you think he's tried to engineer an exchange with another ghost? Can't you just see the want ads? Phantom Monk, 550 years old, seeks drafty castle for hauntings, howlings, and long country walks."

"Why be so old-fashioned?" asked the vicar, with a swig of his drink. "What d'you say we propose a special edition of *Changing Rooms* for the spirit world?"

"I love it!" I sputtered into my largely untouched glass of wine. We waxed more than a little silly plotting out the first two episodes. There's nothing like having the Hound of the Baskervilles redesign the House of Usher—after the fall, of course.

Colin's head turned, seeking the source of the hilarity. I gave a little wave.

"Should we go rescue your bloke, d'you think?" asked the vicar, swirling the dregs of his gin and tonic.

"He's not my bloke," I replied quickly. I glanced back at Colin and Joan; Joan was glowering at me again. "Although that does seem to be the general misapprehension around here."

"Hmm," said the vicar.

I started to put my hands on my hips, and remembered just in time that that was not the brightest thing to do while holding a glass of wine.

"Nothing like that!" I protested. "I'm just using his archives."

"Ah," commented the vicar, "so that's what they're calling it now."

"Don't," I said. "Just don't. Are you coming with me on this rescue mission, or do I have to go over the top alone?"

"I'll be along"—the vicar rattled his ice cubes and beamed beatifically—"just as soon as I top up my drink."

I looked reproachfully at him. "Whatever happened to that crusading spirit?"

"Go with God, dear child," he said in sepulchral tones, making me laugh as I headed off on the Colin Rescue Expedition.

Joan looked less than thrilled to see me back so soon; I suppose she had been hoping the vicar would keep me safely by the drinks table.

She made the best of a bad situation by giving my borrowed cocktail dress a condescending once-over. It was a wrap dress of the sort that had been popular a couple of years before, with black, green, and white blocks of color overlapping in a vaguely geometrical pattern. I hadn't felt quite so bad borrowing something that had been left behind as clearly out-of-date; not to mention the main joy of wrap dresses—they aren't quite one-size-fits-all, but it was certainly better than trying to wiggle into one of Serena's old sheath dresses, which clearly came from a scarily skinny phase as well as from an era of higher hems. They would have been too tight, too short, or both. Pammy would certainly have approved, which was more than enough reason for not wearing them.

"What a charming frock," Joan commented, with a disdainful smirk. "I had one like that, too—two years ago."

"It's on loan from Serena's closet," I explained innocently. "She has excellent taste, don't you think?"

It was almost too much fun watching Joan squirm. Taking pity, I said, "You have a lovely home."

I regretted my charitable impulse almost immediately, as Joan embarked on a long monologue about country pursuits clearly designed to make me feel like an ignorant outsider. What it did accomplish was making me wish I hadn't resolved to be alcoholically abstinent this evening; Thursday night's revelry (or, more accurately, Friday morning's hangover) had been enough to make me swear off overindulgence forever. Half an hour of Joan, however, would have sent Carrie Nation fleeing for the bottle.

"Do you ride?" Joan asked, in the tone of one who expects— indeed, hopes—the answer will be negative.

I had ridden, actually, years and years ago, in the grips of the inevitable "I want a pony" phase that attacks eight-year-old girls as inevitably as the chicken pox. One bout of lice had cured me of the riding bug, combined with the realization that I wouldn't be allowed to ride bareheaded through the fields, leaping over things like in *National Velvet*.

I saw no reason to go into this with Joan. Among other things, I had the sneaking suspicion that any admission of equestrian ability would prompt her to arrange for us all to go riding—I had no intention of falling into that trap, and finding myself falling, quite literally, into a ditch somewhere. I like my collarbone where it is, thank you very much.

"Usually the bus," I replied cheerfully.

Joan looked at me uncomprehendingly. "What an unusual name."

It was my turn to look uncomprehending. Was there a crucial piece of British slang I had missed?

"That *is* what they're usually called."

Next to me, Colin started making little gurgling noises.

Joan seized the opportunity to pound him on the back. "Quite," sputtered Colin, "all right. Don't"—*sputter, choke*—"mind me."

Joan was all solicitude. "We must get you some water," she gushed, employing her patented towing technique. Whatever athletic activities she engaged in, they had developed some very strong arm muscles; she had Colin off to the other side of the room before he could regain his breath.

I found myself standing entirely alone in a roomful of strangers.

"Lovely to see you, too," I muttered under my breath.

A girl with long, wavy hair who had been standing about a foot away, observing, crossed the distance with a friendly smile. "Hello."

A human! Addressing me! I could have hugged her. There's nothing more demoralizing than standing alone at a party—unless it's tagging along after someone who palpably doesn't want you there. I'd be damned if I was going to trail along after Joan and Colin to the drinks table. If he wanted to extricate himself, he could bloody well do it himself.

He didn't seem to be trying all that hard.

Following my gaze, my new companion said, "Don't mind Joan. She's been out of sorts ever since Colin chucked her."

"Was it recent?" I tried not to sound too interested.

"About twenty years ago—Joan was eight at the time, and she's been impossible to live with since." She stuck out a hand. "I'm Sally, Joan's sister."

"Oh," I said guiltily.

"And you," continued Sally, eyes gleaming with mischief, "must be Eloise."

"How did you know?"

Sally ticked off the points on her fingers. "Let's see. American, red hair, with Colin."

"Not exactly *with* Colin," I pointed out with some asperity. I had always found the gossipy insularity of Jane Austen novels—where everything made the rounds of the neighboring gentry within five minutes—utterly charming, but I was beginning to reconsider. Why did everyone in the room—in the entire county of Sussex, for all I knew—assume I was going out with Colin? All right, I was staying at his house, but it was a sad, sad day when one couldn't even have a houseguest of the opposite gender without imputations of improper behavior.

I really had been living in the Regency too long. Next I'd be going on about needing a chaperone or being compromised.

"You are staying with him. . . ."

"I really am just here for the archives," I said, half-apologetically.

Maybe I should put up a billboard. Although, really, they were all imagining such lovely prurient things that it seemed almost a shame to disappoint them. Perhaps I should hint at wild orgies. In the library. With manuscripts.

I decided it was time to change the subject.

"Have you lived at Donwell Abbey long?"

"Since I was five." Sally grinned at the surprise on my face. "You mustn't let Joan know I've told. She likes to pretend we're to the manor born."

"Here since the Conquest, you mean?"

As I remembered that afternoon's discussion with Colin, my cheeks turned an unexpected pink—damn these fair complexions! I light up like Rudolph's nose at the least provocation—but, fortunately for me, Sally must have put the flush down to the wine, since she went on without reference to the damning blush. And why should she? Why would anyone blush about the Conquest? Why in the hell was *I* blushing about the Conquest?

There are times when I make no sense even to me.

"Exactly. My father," Sally added conspiratorially, "is actually a rather successful solicitor."

"Does that count as being In Trade?" I asked, warming to the Austen-ish theme.

"Don't let Joan hear you say that! She'll snap your head off. She works so very hard to be horses and hounds." From the tone of Sally's voice, and the trendy nature of her attire (more Warehouse than Jaeger), I gathered it was not an aspiration Joan's little sister shared.

"Who lived here before?" I asked, glancing around the dark living room, with its age-spotted photographs and claustrophobic cluster of antiques.

"The Donwells of Donwell Abbey. Who else? The portraits came with the house," Sally added.

So there was the answer to one question. Were the Donwells the sorts of people who would harbor a French spy? In 1803, Selwick Hall would have been at least six or seven hours from London by coach—much faster if one posted down by curricle, but still not the sort of drive one wanted to undertake twice in one day—so the Black Tulip would presumably be staying somewhere in the area, either at an inn or with neighbors. Unless . . . no, none of Richard and Amy's other houseguests had arrived, which removed the possibility that one of the other spies in training was, in fact, the Black Tulip. Besides, why would a legitimate houseguest bother to deck himself out as the Phantom Monk, when he could just pretend to have taken a wrong turn on the way to the convenience, everyone's favorite age-old excuse. Had there been houseguests at Donwell Abbey on the first weekend of June 1803?

Unfortunately, while much nicer than her sister, Sally didn't seem the sort to know. Joan most likely would—or would, at least, know where to look—but . . . did historical fervor extend that far?

Probably. If it came down to it. With any luck, a bit more rooting about in Colin's archives would remove the need to resort to Joan.

I would, I admitted to myself, be very disappointed if Henrietta never discovered the identity of the Black Tulip. It would be a nice little twist to my dissertation—I could add a chapter on "The Dark Mirror: French Counterparts to English Spies"—but mostly, I just wanted to know, because if I didn't it would nag at me, like the question of what happened to the poor little Dauphin, or who killed the Princes in the Tower.

I decided to give Sally a shot, anyway. "Are there any old stories attached to the house?"

Sally shook her head. "You would have to ask Joan," she said apologetically.

"Ask Joan what?"

I started, spilling some of my wine, as Colin materialized at my elbow.

Fortunately, it was white wine. And no one noticed. At least, I hoped they didn't. My muddled brain was too busy processing Colin's sudden reappearance. One minute I was talking to Sally; the next, there he was, floating in the air above me like the Cheshire cat. I had to turn and tilt my head to look up at him; he stood next to me, but a little behind, so that if I leaned back, just the slightest bit, my back would fit very comfortably against his side.

I stood straight enough to satisfy the most exacting headmistress, and took a little step to the side, which had the added benefit of putting me right over the spilled wine patch.

"I was just asking Sally if there are any old stories about Donwell Abbey," I said brightly.

"Are you planning to go root about in someone else's archives?" teased Colin. "Should I be jealous?"

Maybe I had been better off with him slightly behind me. The force of that smile, faced full on, was dazzling. Stop it! I told myself sternly. He was just relieved to have escaped from Joan. That did not count as flirting with me. At least, not in any way that meant anything.

He was, however, wearing a very pleasing aftershave.

"He doesn't even have any ghosts," I said to Sally dismissively.

"Shall we swap?" suggested Sally to Colin.

"You take Eloise, I get the ghost? No, thanks."

"The ghost eats less," I pointed out. "And it's quieter."

"But can it do the washing up?" asked Colin.

"You'd have to ask it," said Sally solemnly. "Have you taken Eloise down to the cloisters yet?"

Colin sent Sally a sardonic look. "And leave the party?"

"Your fault for saying yes," scolded Sally.

"There are some consolations," countered Colin.

"Cloisters?" I piped in.

Colin groaned. "It's like dangling a bone before a dog."

"I resent that," I said without heat.

"Would you prefer a carrot in front of a mule?"

"Even worse." I turned to Sally. "So there are still bits of the old abbey?"

"Would you like to see?" suggested Sally. She glanced at Colin. "You don't mind?"

Colin raised an eyebrow, looking like James Bond about to demand his martini shaken, not stirred. No one could look that debonair without working at it. "Why not?"

Giggling like naughty schoolchildren (at least Sally and I were giggling), we snuck out of the drawing room. Joan was in the midst of a group of people who all seemed to be talking and drinking with evident enjoyment, and didn't see us go. She was smiling in a genuine way that reduced her teeth from Red Riding Hood's wolf to somewhere near normal size, and the thought struck me that when not defending her territory, she probably wasn't half-bad.

Then Sally, whose tugging abilities were as well developed as her sister's, yanked on my hand, and I popped out of the drawing room into a tortured maze of back hallways. Selwick Hall was a miracle of eighteenth-century symmetry in comparison. Sally's house seemed to have been designed by the Mad Hatter in conjunction with a paranoid mole; everything was narrow and dark and had more turns than necessary. I wandered along after Colin and Sally, who were bickering amiably about a mutual acquaintance, who had some sort of weekly column that was either a load of codswollop (Colin) or an insightful commentary on modern mores (Sally).

They seemed to be on very easy and amiable terms—which did make sense, since they lived next door to one another. I wondered if Sally was Colin's usual buffer from Joan's less-than-subtle advances. And if the presence of the older sister had prevented anything from happening with the younger.

Sally really was quite pretty. Although they both possessed the same lanky frame, Sally didn't have the glossy photo-shoot perfection of her older sister; Sally's hair was an indeterminate brown to her sister's determined blond (and just how much of that difference came out of a bottle was open to speculation), long and curly where Joan's was sleek and straight, her brow wider and her features broader. All the same, there was something much more attractive about Sally's frank, open face. She possessed that timeless girl-next-door quality that endears itself to women as well as men.

Of course, I reminded myself, she was the girl next door. Quite literally. I concentrated on keeping track of where we were, and regretted not having packed breadcrumbs in my purse. By the time it struck me that miniature Certs might fulfill the same function (and be less likely to fall prey to woodland creatures than the comestibles in the story), we had already come to a halt by a side door.

It must have once been, like the narrow back hallways, part of the servants' domain in the *Upstairs, Downstairs* days. Now, the back entrance was cluttered with muddy boots, old raincoats, and various other odds and ends, including a broken tennis racket and some very dirty garden gloves.

Colin glanced out the door at the midnight black sky. It couldn't have been much past eight, but sunset comes early in November; it had been full dark since five.

"Torch?"

"On the shelf." Sally pointed to a large gray flashlight banded in maroon, the sort with a bulb the size of a fried egg, and a wide flat handle. This one looked like it might have once been white, but years of dust and grimy handprints had taken their toll.

"Is it far?" I asked belatedly, gathering my borrowed pashmina around my shoulders. The air from the open door bit through the thin material of Serena's dress, and made me wish I'd thought to put on stockings. I was beginning to wonder what I was getting myself into. I hadn't seen any sign of ruins as we'd driven up to the house earlier that evening, and while my enthusiasm for crumbling structures is extreme, it waned a bit in conjunction with thin fabrics, impractical heels, and the prospect of tripping over things in the dark. And, trust me, if there was something to trip over, I would find it.

Sally looked to Colin.

Colin shrugged.

"Not very," he said, in that uninformative male way that could mean anything from just down the block to somewhere in the Outer Hebrides, reachable only by snowbound mountain passes.

To do him justice, he might have been about to elaborate, but any further description was cut short by a click of heels, and a voice calling, "Sally?"

"Maybe if we ignore her?" I suggested.

"Oh, the innocence of youth," murmured Colin. I whacked him on the arm with a stray corner of pashmina. When had I developed these tendencies towards casual violence? First a glow stick, then a pashmina . . . Of course, there was a perfectly good explanation, but I didn't like it, so I ignored it.

Joan's voice was not as easily ignored. And it was getting closer.

"Sally!"

"Oh, bother," said Sally, throwing back her shoulders in a resigned way. "I wonder what it is now. You go on without me."

"Are you sure?"

Sally flapped her hand in dismissal. "Colin knows the way. I'll be along as soon as I can get away. Coming, Joan!"

"It's just us, then," said Colin, switching on the torch. A ghostly circle of yellow light appeared on the ground about a yard ahead, highlighting dead blades of grass with eerie precision.

"And the ghost," I pointed out.

"As a chaperone," Colin replied, shutting the door behind us, "he is not very substantial. Shall we?"

Did he feel the need for a chaperone? I decided not to inquire further; it might sound too much like flirting, and if he were already lamenting the lack of a chaperone, the last thing I wanted to do was give him the impression I was flinging myself at him.

To give him his due, he was really being more than decent to an unwanted houseguest. I had twisted his arm for an invitation, and he would have been well within his rights to leave me alone in the library. He hadn't had to make me dinner or join me for a walk or take me along to the party with him. When it came down to it, he was behaving exceptionally well, and I . . . well, let's just say that I wasn't all that proud of my own performance thus far.

So I let the chaperonage comment pass, and said simply, "Let's."

The thin beam of light wavered in front of us, a narrow link to warmth and light and civilization. I thought briefly, longingly, of the drinks table. But how often does one get to follow a ghost to his lair? Wrapping my borrowed pashmina more tightly around me, I stumbled along beside Colin towards the lonely cloister of the Phantom Monk.

Chapter Twenty-Three

——— ♥ ———

Phantom *(n.)*: *an agent of unusual stealth and skill; the most deadly kind*

—from the Personal Codebook of the Pink Carnation

Ghosts did not have feet.

It took Henrietta the space of a moment to realize that what she was seeing was not, in fact, a ghastly apparition from the spirit world, but, instead, a human with skulduggery on the mind. Despite Miles's and Richard's protestations to the contrary, there was not a phantom monk. If there were one, she rather doubted it would jaunt over from Donwell Abbey to visit the neighbors, and it would most definitely not step on twigs.

If Miles was reprising his famous appearance as the Phantom Monk of Donwell Abbey . . .

Henrietta levered herself off her bench and stalked towards the house, her dark blue twill traveling dress blending well with the shadows.

By the time she had made it out of the protective covering of the rose arbor, common sense had returned. It couldn't be Miles. One could make oneself seem larger, but seldom smaller, and the figure she had seen poised outside the drawing room doors had definitely been smaller and slighter than Miles.

And if it wasn't Miles . . . oh dear.

In her indignation over Miles, Henrietta had nearly managed to forget that they were under the surveillance of the French Ministry of Police. It would have been much less worrisome if the hooded figure had been Miles.

Hideous images of deadly French operatives rose to taunt her, and with them, a certain indignation that the French would have the gall, the unmitigated gall, to follow them here to Selwick Hall, where they had always been safe and peaceful. It was one thing to go hunting spies; it was quite another for those spies to invade one's home. Henrietta set her chin in a stubborn expression that boded ill to Napoleon's secret police. The spy's temerity in following her here did have one advantage, though. It made him easier to catch.

Henrietta slowed her steps, making sure to stay to the shadows. She crept softly up the shallow flight of stairs up to the veranda, balancing on the very toes of her kid half-boots. Her choice of footwear had been quite sensible for a long journey, but less so for hunting Phantom Monks. The heels had an unnerving tendency to click against the stone of the veranda. Henrietta would have stopped to take them off, but the Phantom Monk had already had far too much of a head start. So she tiptoed as best she could, turning the handle of the French doors with painstaking slowness, grateful for the Axminster carpet that covered the floor of the Long Drawing Room and muffled her steps.

Henrietta paused for a moment in the middle of the Long Drawing Room, which, true to its name, ran three-quarters of the length of the back of the house. Despite its size, it was sparsely furnished, with groupings of little, light chairs and tables that could be pushed easily to the sides of the room for an impromptu dance. Henrietta's gloom-accustomed eyes surveyed the room, and found no shapes there that ought not to be. The drapes lay flat against the walls, and the low, backless settees with their scrolled ends were too flimsy to hide anyone larger than a well-fed midget. The cloaked figure had certainly not been midget-sized.

If she were a French spy, where would she hide? Henrietta had always had her doubts as to the efficacy of that line of reasoning. How could she know where a French spy would hide unless she knew what the spy wanted? If he were after Richard's correspondence, he would most likely head for either study or bedroom; if he were after either her or Miles . . . Henrietta nipped that thought before it could go any farther. Making herself anxious wouldn't do anyone any good, except, possibly, the spy.

On the right, a door opened into the music room; on the left, another drawing room. Henrietta didn't waste time searching, either. She went straight to the flimsy white-and-gold doors directly across from the garden entrance, and gently pulled one just far enough to slip through into the front hall, blinking in the unaccustomed light. The candles in the gilded sconces in the wall had not yet been extinguished for the night. Henrietta hovered for a moment in the shadows beneath the overhang of the stairs.

She could hear male guffaws from the small family dining room on the left side of the hall. Miles and Richard were probably lingering over their port. Relief that they were safe transmuted rapidly into indignation. Good to know they were making themselves useful while French spies stalked the corridors of Selwick Hall, thought Henrietta tartly. And they called women the weaker vessel? Hmph. Napoleon's army could troop through the front hall, and Miles and Richard would probably go on obliviously exchanging salacious stories until they ran out of port.

On the other side of the hall, the rooms were all dark—but not entirely silent. Henrietta heard a slight rustle. It might be the breeze rustling through the curtains, or it might be something, or someone, else.

The sound had come from Richard's study.

It was all Henrietta could do not to jump up and down with excitement, but since that would defeat her ultimate purpose (jumping up and down not being a particularly stealthy activity), she controlled the impulse. Moving carefully across the marble floor, Henrietta began creeping towards Richard's study. Pressed against the wall, she crept past the dark doorway of the small drawing room where she had sat with Amy earlier, past Ethelbert, the suit of armor who lived next to the stairs, until she could see the door to Richard's study, ever so slightly ajar.

The door was so close to closed that Henrietta wouldn't have even noticed the gap, had it not been for the thin outline of light that shone weakly through the narrow gap. Richard might, of course, have simply left a candle burning, either through forgetfulness, or in preparation for a later return. He could have left a fire burning in the grate against the chill of the early June evening. From time to time, Amy liked to appropriate Richard's study for work of her own, curling up in Richard's own big chair with a proprietary air. There were half a dozen perfectly innocent explanations for that pale flicker of light.

Henrietta didn't waste time on any of them.

Backtracking slightly, Henrietta caught up a heavy silver candelabrum from a marble-topped table in the hall, hurriedly snuffing the candles. She wanted it for its bludgeonlike qualities, not light. A fireplace poker would have been even better, but she couldn't count on one being easily within reach in Richard's study. She had thought of borrowing Ethelbert's sword, but even if she did manage to remove it without knocking over Ethelbert, she wouldn't have the slightest idea of how to use it.

Henrietta made her slow and careful way just to the verge of the study door. No, this was much better. With any luck, she could sneak up on the intruder from behind and—

"—fell right out the window!"

"No! Not in the middle of St. James's Street!"

"And then Brummell said, 'My dear young man, if you must be a sartorial disaster, kindly refrain from making a further spectacle of yourself.' I thought Ponsonby was going to soil himself!"

The door to the small dining room on the other side of the hall burst open, unleashing a spate of loud footsteps and masculine laughter. Under the study door, the brief glimmer of light abruptly disappeared.

No!

Henrietta abandoned subtlety and sprinted for the study, yanking open the door. After the light of the hall, all her eyes perceived was a sheet of unmitigated blackness. In her headlong rush, she barreled stomach-first into something sharp and hard and nearly dropped her candelabrum. Had she been run through by a Frenchman's sword?

An exploratory mission revealed that it was, in fact, only the edge of Richard's desk, and there was no loss of blood involved. But it *hurt*.

Gasping, Henrietta forced herself to uncurl, but it was all too clear that she was too late. The lingering smoke from a recently snuffed candle tickled her nose, but the snuffer of the candle was nowhere to be seen.

As her eyes acclimated, the black blobs scattered about the room resolved themselves into recognizable pieces of furniture, chairs and tables, several busts on narrow pedestals, and the vindictive desk. Flailing wildly with her foot in the area under the desk failed to unearth a crouching spy, and other than two wing-backed chairs there was no other piece of furniture in the room large enough to hide convincingly under or behind. Bookshelves lined the walls, containing nary a single secret passage so far as Henrietta knew—and if she didn't know, the Phantom Monk wouldn't, either. Henrietta was about to look behind the chairs, just to be thorough, when she spotted something that made her quite sure the effort would be entirely wasted.

On the far side of the room, the draperies swayed in a way that suggested the open window had recently been put to good use.

Blast.

Henrietta dashed to the window, but the intruder had disappeared as thoroughly as though he had been the phantom he impersonated. Under the impartial moon, the park was silent and empty. The Phantom Monk had had plenty of time to make his escape while she grappled with Richard's desk.

Henrietta scowled at herself. She really wasn't making a terribly good showing as an intrepid spy, was she? Of course, she still thought that if it hadn't been for those two loud, raucous *men*, she could have taken the intruder by surprise.

Henrietta realized she was still holding the heavy silver candlestick and set it down on Richard's desk with a disgruntled thump. Blasted noisy, interfering men. Addlepated great galumphing creatures. True, they made good dance partners—when they remembered to turn up for their assigned dance, that was, and didn't clomp on her foot like a dinosaur with a direction problem—but other than that, the Amazons had it right. They were more trouble than they were worth, and when it came down to it, she could bloody well dance with Penelope.

A heavy footfall in the door made Henrietta jump; she whirled to face the door, the desk at her back. The glare momentarily blinded Henrietta, so all she could see was a nimbus of light in the darkness.

For heaven's sake! One Phantom Monk was enough for any night; she didn't need more supernatural apparitions. Henrietta blinked irritably and the light resolved itself back into a candle flame.

"Who's there?" she demanded.

"Hen?" replied a startled masculine voice.

"Oh," she said flatly, as Miles stepped into the room. Reminding herself of the Amazons, she lifted a hand to shield her eyes from the glare of his candle. "It's you."

Miles looked quizzically around the dark room. "What are you doing in here, in the dark?"

"Nothing you would care to know about." Henrietta stomped towards the door before she gave in to the urge to use the candlestick on him. That would be just how she wanted to end the day—explaining to Richard and Amy how she had come to give Miles a concussion. "Good night."

Miles grabbed her by the arm before she could stalk past, and hauled her to a stop. With one foot, he kicked the door closed and placed himself between her and it.

"Hen, don't do this."

"Don't do what?" Henrietta twitched her hand out of his grasp.

Miles scrubbed a hand through his hair. "You know."

"No," Henrietta said flatly, "I don't know. Maybe I would know if someone had bothered to stop by or send a note instead of disappearing for an entire week——" Henrietta heard her voice rising and hastily clamped her lips shut before she started screeching like the Queen of the Night on a bad day.

Well, she was justified, she reminded herself. It *had* been a bad day, and a long one, between broken coaches and ghastly apparitions and idiot men who first hid from you when you did want to see them, and then wouldn't let you leave the room when you didn't. Henrietta glowered fiercely at Miles.

Miles held his ground manfully under the force of that glare.

"I need to speak to you."

"And you were unavoidably detained by armed maniacs for the past week? Tied to a chair, perhaps? Deprived of writing implements? Bound, gagged?"

Miles swallowed hard. "I was a cad?"

"No argument," said Henrietta tightly, reaching for the doorknob.

Miles looked a little frustrated. "What I'm trying to say is, I'm sorry."

"Well, that's very nice," muttered Henrietta. One little *I'm sorry*, for six—no, seven, if one counted most of today—days of sheer heart-scraping agony? Ha.

Miles either didn't hear her or chose not to.

"I miss you," he said earnestly. "Life is just . . . flatter when you're not around. I miss talking to you. I miss our rides in the park."

"Hmm," said Henrietta noncommittally, but her hand fell away from the doorknob.

"It's not the same when you're not there." Miles paced back and forth. "Hell, I even miss Almack's. Can you credit it? Almack's!"

He sounded so confused and indignant that, despite herself, despite all the waiting and disappointed hopes and angry diary entries, Henrietta felt her temper begin to melt away. This was her Miles again, not a distant stranger in her head, and there was something about his disgruntled tone that made her oddly hopeful, in a way no poetic declaration ever could.

"Lady Jersey will be flattered," said Henrietta cautiously, but a hint of a smile began to tug at the corners of her lips.

"Lady Jersey can go hang," said Miles with a vehemence that would have deeply distressed Lady Jersey had she been there to see it.

"That's not very charitable of you."

"*Hen,*" Miles groaned, looking as though he was one moment away from banging his head against the door. "Will you let me get on with this?"

Henrietta promptly subsided, a strangle elation taking hold of her, stealing her breath and sending little tingles straight down to the tips of her fingers. She didn't even notice that Miles's perambulations had taken him well away from the door, leaving her path clear. Suddenly, storming out no longer seemed quite so imperative.

"All right," she said breathlessly.

"This rift between us." Miles waved his hands about expressively. "I don't like it."

"Neither do I," said Henrietta in a voice she scarcely recognized as her own.

"I can't do without you," Miles pressed on earnestly.

He couldn't do without her. This was Miles, Miles saying he couldn't do without her. She would have pinched herself to see if she were dreaming, asleep in the garden among the lavender and roses, with crickets chirping a lullaby, only if she were to dream such a moment, it would have been in an elegant gown of sky blue satin, with her hair arranged in charming ringlets, and Miles would be on his knees in the summer garden, not pacing like a maniac in her brother's darkened study. Yet, here she stood in her travel-stained twill, with her hair straggling limply around her face, a spot on her chin, and Miles was saying he couldn't do without her. It had to be real.

Henrietta's heart began to pound out the Hallelujah Chorus with full instrumental accompaniment.

She was in the midst of a particularly soaring high C, two seconds away from flinging her arms around Miles and bringing the chorus to crescendo with a resounding kiss, when Miles added, as though it summed up everything, "You're almost as important to me as Richard."

The orchestra broke off with a discordant screech; the chorus stuttered to a halt mid-hallelujah; and Henrietta's heart plummeted down from the vicinity of the pearly gates to land, with a loud thump, in the midst of yesterday's garbage.

"Oh." It was an effort to force even that one little syllable through her suddenly swollen throat.

You're almost as important to me as Richard.

He hadn't really said that, had he? But he had. He must have. She couldn't possibly have made up anything quite so dreadful. Her week of bracing herself for the "You're a lovely person and someday you'll find someone who loves you" speech hadn't prepared her for this. This was worse than the "Someday you'll find someone who loves you" speech. This was worse than the "I value your friendship" speech. This was very nearly even worse than no speech at all.

"Hen," Miles finished hoarsely, grabbing both her hands in his, "I just want things to be the way they were."

His larger hands engulfed her small, stiff fingers, sending a tingle of warmth from her palm all the way up her arm. "Palm to palm is holy palmers' kiss." No wonder society compelled the wearing of gloves! The pressure of Miles's hand, palm to palm, bare skin to bare skin, felt like an illicit intimacy as they stood alone in the darkened room.

Henrietta expected Miles to release her hand. He didn't. Around them, the study was entirely quiet; even the crickets in the garden held their breath, and the leaves refused to rustle in the wind. Miles's thumb moved softly over the tender skin of her wrist, soothingly, rhythmically. Almost imperceptibly at first, his hand began to exert a steady pressure on hers, compelling her slowly towards him.

Henrietta's eyes flew to his face in consternation. Miles didn't seem to notice. His gaze was leveled directly at her lips.

If she closed her eyes . . . if she let herself give in to the pressure of their joined hands . . . if she leaned just the slightest bit closer . . .

He could go away and not speak to her again for another seven days.

The thought sluiced through Henrietta's confused haze of emotions as effectively as a bucket of cold water. Oh no, she thought, leaning back, away from the pull of Miles's hand and her own desires. She wasn't going to play this particular game again. He wanted things to be the way they were? Fine. He had set the rules; he could abide by them.

"*No.*"

With just a little more force than necessary, Henrietta yanked her hands out of Miles's grasp.

Miles blinked several times, like a man coming out of a trance, staring at his empty hand as though he had never seen it before.

"No?" he echoed.

"No. It's no good." Miles was still frowning confusedly at his own hand. Henrietta's hands clenched together. Blast it, couldn't he even look at her? She added harshly, more harshly than she had intended, "We can't go back. Ever."

That got his attention. Miles looked sharply up at her. He didn't even bother to dash back the usual lock of hair that fell across his eyes. He just stared at her for a long, startled moment.

"Is that what you really want?"

"It's not a question of want," said Henrietta fiercely. "It's just the way it *is*."

Miles straightened, his face closing over into a nonchalant mask. He put his hands in his pockets, leaned against the desk, and raised both his eyebrows. "I take it that's that, then."

She hadn't realized how much she had been hoping for a negation, an "Actually, this friends thing was a bad idea, and I'm really quite passionately in love with you," until she didn't receive it. How could she have thought Miles was on the verge of succumbing to her dubious charms? She could probably fling off her clothes and dance a minuet around the room, and he would just say, "Hmm?"

Henrietta crossed her arms protectively over her chest and drew in a deep breath. "Yes," she said tightly, every muscle in her body tensed with the effort of trying not to cry. "I suppose it is."

Without waiting for a response, she turned and walked deliberately out the door, executing every step with painstaking precision. She did not look back.

Chapter Twenty-Four

───── ❂ ─────

Charades: *a cunning game of deception waged by an experienced operative*

     —from the Personal Codebook of the Pink Carnation

"Surely, dismemberment is a bit extreme, don't you think, my dear?" Mrs. Cathcart blinked placidly at Amy across the tea table.

"Ah, but can a French agent shoot you if he's missing his arm?" countered Amy. "I thought not. Biscuit?"

The ladies had retired to the Rose Room while the gentlemen partook of their port after dinner. They presented a deceptively charming domestic scene, reflected Henrietta. Amy, her dark curls held back by a bandeau of golden silk, presided over the tea table, pouring steaming amber liquid into dainty rose-painted glasses. Beside her sat Miss Grey, dark hair pulled back with the same severe simplicity as her untrimmed gray dress, placing cups beneath Amy's somewhat erratic spigot with silent efficiency. Across from them, the comfortable form of Mrs. Cathcart spread over a small sofa. In her old-fashioned dress, with its thick, flowered fabric and wide side-panels, her cheeks as rumpled as pressed rose petals, she was the epitome of the country matron, ready to dole out herbal remedies, tie up the bruised knees of clumsy grandchildren, and tote soup to the deserving poor of the parish.

"No, thank you, dear," said Mrs. Cathcart, shaking her white-capped head as Amy offered her a plate of biscuits. From the gentle frown on her face, one would have expected her to be discussing a particularly complicated knitting pattern, or worrying over the fate of a maid who had found herself in the family way. "You're quite right about the difficulty of aiming a weapon without an arm, but wouldn't it be more Christian simply to shoot the man?"

Amy put the teapot down with an emphatic clink of china. "But then how can we question him?"

Mrs. Cathcart considered. "How, indeed?" she murmured, sipping delicately from her cup. "How, indeed."

Amy shifted restlessly in her seat to stare out the window, which reflected back her own impatient face. "I don't understand why Richard won't let us go after him," she expostulated, a wealth of frustration in her voice.

Familial loyalty stirred Henrietta out of her contemplative silence. "We can't risk the school," Henrietta explained for what felt like the thousandth time.

After her encounter with Miles the night before, Henrietta had gathered her scattered wits together, reminded herself of why she had been flitting about the house in the dark in the first place, and betook herself to her brother to announce the appearance of the Phantom Monk. Wars waited for no such trivialities as broken hearts; while it might feel as though the world had shattered into jagged fragments when she wrenched her hand from Miles's in the study, outside, the sun blithely rose and set, the planets circled in their fixed course, and somewhere in Sussex a French spy plotted mayhem.

For a brief moment, Henrietta had basked in the glow of noble self-denial. She could picture herself a veiled figure of mystery, a constant bane to the French, and a source of wonder and speculation at home. "A broken heart, you know," people would whisper. "A heartless rogue—but isn't it always? But her loss is England's gain. Why, the way she captured that Black Tulip . . ." The daydream bubble popped, and Henrietta grimaced wryly at herself. It was quite impossible to imagine Miles as an evil seducer, any more than it was to cast herself as a tragic heroine. Henrietta had always known she ran more to Portia than Juliet. Besides, she never understood how tragic, veiled figures managed to get anything accomplished with their vision permanently obscured like that. Wouldn't they be constantly tripping over small tables? But that, Henrietta considered, was precisely why she would never make a tragic heroine. She had been cursed with a logical mind.

Her sister-in-law, not being cursed with a logical mind, had been delighted at the news of the spy, and had wanted nothing more than to dash off into the gardens, veil in place and pistol in hand.

Richard had not been delighted.

Hauling Amy back from the door, Richard had pointed out that to go haring out after the spy would only confirm anything the spy might suspect, *if*—he added dampeningly—there even was a spy. Running around the grounds at night brandishing a pistol would be guaranteed to convince any clandestine observer that there was something worth investigating at Selwick Hall.

"But," Amy had argued, "don't you see? If we shoot whoever it is, there'll be no one to investigate!"

Richard's lips had clamped shut over a sound that might have been a growl if allowed to grow up. "We don't know that he's alone. There might be others. Are you willing to take that risk?"

Within moments, despite the lack of cape or mask, Richard had transformed back into the Purple Gentian, ordering extra sentries to be placed about the grounds and in the old Norman tower. Preferring to keep the news from the rest of the party as long as possible, Richard had reluctantly agreed to carry on with most of the following day's scheduled activities. Shooting at targets, after all, wasn't so unusual a pastime as to garner undue attention, and a multitude of bizarre behavior could be excused under guise of a picnic. The ropes course had been abandoned, much to Henrietta's relief. It was bad enough combating heartache without being suspended several feet off the ground.

Henrietta pulled her attention back to the present as Amy flourished the teapot in a way that boded ill to the Axminster carpet and Henrietta's new silk slippers. Henrietta hastily scooted her feet farther beneath her chair, and tucked her muslin skirts out of the way of the dripping spigot.

"It would have been so much simpler my way," insisted Amy.

"At least we didn't have to abandon today's activities," put in Mrs. Cathcart peaceably. "It was very clever of your husband to post sentries in the tower."

"Autocratic," grumbled Amy.

"Hideously," concurred Henrietta automatically, but her heart wasn't in it. Through the crack in the door, she could hear the faint clip of booted feet against the marble, the sound of male voices raised in boisterous conversation, coming closer, closer. . . .

Miles.

Henrietta sat very straight, not sure whether to be glad or sorry that she had chosen a chair facing away from the door. Her maid had dressed her hair in the Grecian style, twisted into a topknot with long curls cascading down, and her exposed neck suddenly felt quite vulnerable. Henrietta squirmed irritably in her chair, causing the cascade of curls to brush across the offending area. It wasn't as though Miles hadn't seen her neck before. It wasn't as though Miles would even be *looking* at her neck, more likely than not. After last night's episode in the study, Miles's behavior had been characterized by stunning indifference.

Could it really be called indifference, Henrietta wondered, when there was no interaction to which one could contrive to be indifferent? They had moved across from each other all day, like the planets on an astronomer's orrery, always circling, never meeting. As they shot at targets dressed as Delaroche, Fouché, and Bonaparte, she had caught glimpses of his blond head in the distance, but he had taken care to keep several people between them. They had been separated by the length of the table at dinner, a large candelabra preventing even the most minimal of eye contact. Henrietta suspected Miles of having moved the candelabra, but had no proof.

If he was avoiding her, what of it? Hadn't she practically ordered him to do so? She had no right to cry after what was lost, she told herself fiercely, taking a vast gulp of tepid tea. She was the one who had set the terms and now she had to abide by them.

Why couldn't Miles have *argued* with her when she told him they couldn't go back? If he really cared about her in any way at all, wouldn't he have gone after her? Protested? Done *something*?

The door swung open, and one polished Hessian boot advanced across the threshold. Henrietta hastily yanked her gaze back to the tea tray, feigning great interest in the plate of biscuits. If Miles didn't want anything to do with her, she wouldn't want anything to do with him, either. So there. Muffled by the carpet, the boots strode towards her—Henrietta chomped off a regrettably large bite of biscuit—past her, and stopped by Amy's chair. A hand boasting a gold signet ring on the pinkie descended upon the back of Amy's chair. Mouth full of glutinous goo, Henrietta's head jerked up. It was her brother.

Not Miles.

Henrietta resolutely swallowed her mouthful of biscuit.

Amy tilted her head up at Richard. "Are the sentries all in place?" she hissed in a stage whisper.

Richard nodded. "If they aren't, someone will answer for it," he said grimly, just as the door swung open again.

Henrietta hastily angled her body towards Mrs. Cathcart, started to reach for the biscuit, and thought better of it. She wasn't making that mistake twice. As to other mistakes she had made . . .

Miles sauntered into the room, talking very loudly with the two Tholmondelay twins about something entirely incomprehensible that seemed to involve a great deal of sporting cant. The trio made straight for the fireplace, not so much as glancing in Henrietta's direction.

Placing her teacup on her saucer with a definitive clunk, Henrietta twisted in her seat to face her brother.

"What are we doing tonight?" she asked her brother loudly.

"Playing sitting duck for a French spy," replied Richard sourly.

Richard was clearly not in the best of moods. Henrietta could tell it was killing him to have to pretend to play host to a party of houseguests when all he wanted to do was tug on a pair of black breeches and dash out into the night, rapier at the ready.

"Yes, what *are* we doing tonight?" demanded Ned Tholmondelay, ambling over to the cozy grouping of chairs. "Dorrington over there was telling me the outdoor exercises ain't on. Some mistake, I'm sure."

"Deuced silly notion!" agreed Fred Tholmondelay, strolling over to join his twin.

"Dorrington was right," affirmed Richard.

"You needn't sound like that's such an unusual state of affairs," commented Miles, deserting his casual pose against the fireplace to join them. He positioned himself next to Richard, nodding awkwardly in the general direction of the ladies. Henrietta caught herself trying to catch his eye and made herself stop.

"What's wrong with Miles?" whispered Amy. "He's been behaving oddly all day."

Henrietta shrugged weakly.

Fortunately, Amy had no chance to inquire further.

"You're funning, aren't you, Selwick? Bit of a joke, eh?" urged Fred.

"Richard never jokes about spies," chimed in Amy.

"That's the devil of a shame!" Ned looked crestfallen. "There's a splendid one about a French agent and a Prussian general who go into a tavern, and—"

"Maybe later," broke in Henrietta, as her brother's color went from puce to purple, trying to soften her words with an encouraging smile. Ned beamed back at her. "I don't think this is quite the time."

"May I impress upon everyone that this is a war, not a parlor game?" Richard inquired tightly.

"You can try, but whether you'll succeed is another matter, old chap," muttered Miles, eyeing Ned without favor.

Richard ignored him, clearing his throat with enough force to create a minor gale in Gloucestershire.

"Since we're all here, we might as well get this over with. An operative—"

"We don't know—" began Miles.

"An intruder believed to be an operative," Richard corrected himself, with a pointed look at Miles, "was sighted on the grounds last night. In disguise," he added, before Miles could interrupt again.

"What great luck!" exclaimed Ned Tholmondelay.

"Great luck?" echoed Miss Grey frigidly.

"Who would have thought!" continued Ned eagerly. "Our very own spy! And we didn't even have to go over to France for him. I say, Selwick, this is smashing."

His twin nodded thoughtfully. "Deuced convenient, that's what it is. Like a fox running to the dog!" He paused, much taken by the beauty of his own metaphor.

"By Jove, Fred!" breathed Ned. "You've got it! We'll get up a hunt and run the spy to ground!"

"Blowing a horn, no doubt," said the much put-upon Purple Gentian acidly, "with dogs in full cry."

Ned beamed, delighted at being so well understood. "That's the ticket!"

"We," snapped Richard, "will do nothing of the kind."

"The object is *not* to scare off the spy," Henrietta explained helpfully.

"Thank you, Hen," bit off Richard. "I am sure we are all excessively edified by that statement."

"He really is cranky tonight, isn't he?" hissed Richard's sister to Richard's wife.

"Poor dear, he just wants to be off chasing spies," Amy whispered back.

"Would you two be quiet for a moment?" snapped Richard.

The two women exchanged looks of mutual sympathy and understanding.

Ned, momentarily taken aback, was rapidly recovering. "Ah," he said, "I understand. This is another test, ain't it? And we'll all go off on our own and see who can get the spy back first. We'll use that . . . that sneaking-up-on-people trick you taught us earlier today." He turned to his twin. "Bet you ten guineas I get to the spy first!"

"This is not a test. This is not a game. This is a damned nuisance." Richard took a deep breath, battling for patience.

"Look," broke in Miles, coming to the aid of his beleaguered best friend. "If the spy finds out about the school, that's it for all of us. Old Boney will have our names in the next dispatch."

Fred thought deeply. "But if we catch the spy," he said in the portentous tones of one explicating a complicated theorem, "he won't be able to send our names."

"Ah!" exclaimed Ned admiringly.

"Urgh," said Richard.

Amy came to his rescue, sliding her arm through her husband's.

"I know the loss of tonight's entertainment is a grave disappointment, but we must think of it as merely one more slight to be avenged against that murderous regime," she declaimed earnestly.

Much moved by her words, Ned Tholmondelay burst into a heartfelt round of "Rule Britannia." Miss Grey cut him off just after Britain ruled the waves, but before Britons never, never, never shall be slaves.

"I would not," she said, in her musty voice, "contrive to put myself forward, but it appears to me that inquiries might be made which might minimize the threat posed by this person of inimical tendencies."

"Hunh?" said Ned Tholmondelay.

"I believe she means did he ask anyone about that spy chappy," explained his more perspicacious brother.

Ned nodded, impressed. Fred had always been the brain of the family.

Henrietta stifled a chuckle, and looked automatically at Miles, whose lips were twitching with repressed amusement. Their eyes met in a glint of shared humor before Miles abruptly stiffened and looked away.

Shaken, Henrietta redirected her attention to Miss Grey, who was inexorably listing places at which Richard might have made inquiries—local inns where a stranger might have been noted, neighboring houses that might be hosting house parties, coaching inns for reports of travelers, and on and on and on. Listening to her litany was like fighting an avalanche of treacle; everyone's eyes glazed. Henrietta could only imagine what lessons with her must have been like, and felt relieved for Miss Grey's recently liberated charges.

"I have made inquiries wherever inquiries could be made," snapped Richard, breaking off the relentless assault of words. "There have been no strangers at the nearest inns and no unfamiliar equipages sighted in the vicinity."

"That's the problem with phantoms," commented Miles to no one in particular.

"There is not," replied Richard repressively, "a Phantom Monk."

"That's not what he said when I was five," whispered Henrietta to Amy.

"Have you asked——" began Mrs. Cathcart.

"Yes!" ground out Richard.

"I was going to ask," said Mrs. Cathcart calmly, "whether you had asked for more tea to be brought to us. If we do have a French spy peering through the windowpanes, the tea tray will lend a convincing air of normalcy."

Poised for argument, Richard just gaped at her. Amy squeezed her hand. "Mrs. Cathcart, you are an angel."

"A rather earthbound one," chuckled Mrs. Cathcart comfortably. "What are we to do to pass the time?"

"I," put in Miles hopefully, "could go out and check on the sentries."

"Oh, no, you don't," said Richard darkly. "You're staying right here with the rest of us."

"But——"

"Right here," repeated Richard repressively.

"I have an idea," broke in Henrietta, trying not to refine too much on Miles's eagerness to leave. "What about charades? That way we could give the appearance of a normal party"—she stressed the word "normal" for the benefit of her agitated brother—"while practicing our impersonations."

"Capital idea!" exclaimed Fred Tholmondelay, looking at Henrietta with newfound respect.

"And a French spy won't find this the least bit suspicious?" countered Miles, glowering at Fred.

"Not unless he's in the room with us to hear the characters called out," protested Henrietta. "Surely all he'd see through the window would be a roomful of people playing charades."

"What if . . ." Ned drew a deep breath, gazing around the assemblage in stunned horror. "What if the spy *is* in This Very Room?"

"Trust me," broke in Richard dryly. "I explored that eventuality."

The words cast a pall over the assemblage. Confusion warred with indignation on Ned's freckled face.

"And well you should," put in Mrs. Cathcart peaceably. "You really can't be too careful in such matters, can you, my dear?"

"We have to appear normal," stressed Richard. "Normal. That means no practicing French dialect, no impromptu attempts at wall-climbing, and absolutely no midnight hunts." Richard looked very sharply at Fred Tholmondelay as he said that, failing to realize he was wasting his admonitory looks on the wrong brother.

"One of you young ladies must be musical," put in Mrs. Cathcart with a comfortable smile. "I am sure we could all do with a song to soothe our agitated spirits."

"Perfect!" exclaimed Amy. "Henrietta can sing. What could be more"—she smiled at her husband, who was glancing anxiously out the window at the dark grounds—"normal?"

"I'm not really in voice," Henrietta hedged.

"Don't be silly," chided Amy, who wasn't in the least bit musical. "Your voice sounds just fine to me."

With her usual energy, Amy chivvied everyone from the Rose Room to the music room, herding Miles back to the group when he showed a tendency to veer off towards the gardens.

"But I was just going to—"

"*No,*" said Richard.

"Oh, all right," muttered Miles with no very good grace.

Henrietta sang an experimental scale, voice skipping lightly over the notes.

Miles turned to Richard, who was gazing moodily out the window. "Are you sure—" he began.

"Sit!" snapped Richard.

"Friend, dog, two different concepts," muttered Miles.

But he sat. He chose, noticed Henrietta, the chair farthest away from the pianoforte. Henrietta's eyes narrowed as she shuffled through a pile of sheet music. For goodness' sake, it wasn't as though she had contracted leprosy since last night! Was he afraid she would fling herself at him in a fit of lovelorn excess?

Of course, she reminded herself for the umpteenth time in as many minutes, she was the one who had sent him away. But she hadn't meant *this*. Blast it all, he could at least be civil. Was that too much to ask?

Miss Grey cleared her throat with ominous import.

Flushing, Henrietta grabbed a roll of music half at random and thrust it at Miss Grey. "It's 'Caro Mio Ben,' " she informed her.

"I am familiar with the piece," replied Miss Grey emotionlessly, propping the paper against its bracket, and adjusting a pair of pince-nez on the tip of her nose.

"Right," said Henrietta, taking her pose by the piano. "Let's get started, then, shall we?"

It was not the most receptive of audiences. Richard was gazing moodily out the window, as though expecting a spy to run by, wiggling his ears and thumbing his nose at him, at any moment. Amy had her "I'm pretending to listen, but really I'm thinking of ways to thwart the French" face on. Mrs. Cathcart, of course, was looking warm and supportive, because that was the sort of thing Mrs. Cathcart did; Henrietta knew it was no reflection of her own abilities. The Tholmondelay twins were gazing at her from twin settees with the expectant look of puppies who know they are behaving very, very well at the moment, but might bounce up and start chasing their tails at the least provocation. And then there was Miles. Henrietta tried not to look at Miles.

Miss Grey primly asked if she was ready. Nodding in assent, Henrietta closed her eyes, schooled her breathing as Signor Antonio had taught her, and let the opening bars of the music drift through her. Despite her protests about not being in voice, when she opened her mouth, her E flat was crisp and sure, rolling easily into D, C, and B flat. The aria was one of the first she had learned, and the familiar notes and phrases unrolled easily through her throat.

But the words . . . why had she never noticed the words before? "Thou all my bliss," she sang, "believe but this: When thou art far, my heart is lorn." She had sung that same phrase a dozen, a hundred times, focusing all her attention on notes and diction, timing and dynamics, blithely oblivious to the plaintive recital of heartache. She had sung them, but never understood them.

Lorn. That was one way to describe the ache of Miles's absence, the utter dejection that had seized her every time they had passed each other in awkward silence. Would it be easier if he were far in more than spirit, if she packed her bags and fled back to London tomorrow? But that wouldn't be any use. London was haunted by a thousand memories of Miles. Miles in the park, teaching her to drive. Miles at Almack's, propping up pillars. Miles sprawled out on the sofa in the morning room, scattering biscuit crumbs all over the carpet. Even her bedroom provided no sanctuary, with Bunny propped reproachfully on her pillows like Banquo's ghost.

Determinedly turning her attention back to the music, Henrietta built up slowly through "thy lover true ever doth sigh." She didn't much feel like sighing. She would far rather throw things. Preferably at Miles. She released her ire into the music, singing out the first reprise of "do but forgo such cruel scorn" rather more forcefully than the score required. The music dwelt on scorn, lingering over the word, trilling it, offering it up again and again, flinging it back at Henrietta.

Despite herself, Henrietta's eyes flew past the sprawled forms of the Tholmondelays, over Mrs. Cathcart's lace cap, to Miles's chair at the back of the room.

He wasn't indifferent anymore.

Henrietta's heart rose in her throat, lending force to her voice as her eyes locked with Miles's. He sat bolt upright, no longer sprawled at leisure, his hands locked in a stranglehold on the arms of the chair, pressing the gilded wood so tightly that it was a wonder it didn't splinter in his hands. She read shock and consternation in his face . . . and something more.

Henrietta's third reprise of "cruel scorn" had a depth of feeling that made Mrs. Cathcart blink rapidly, and even Richard, gazing with furrowed brow out the window, paused in his search for Frenchmen to absently reflect that his sister's new voice teacher clearly knew what he was about.

The music gentled, sliding like a caress back into "thou all my bliss, believe but this." Henrietta couldn't take her eyes away from Miles. No one else mattered. No one else was there. She sang only for him, the liquid Italian phrases a plea, a promise, a present.

The thunder of clapping that followed snapped the invisible thread that bound them together. Blinking a few times, Henrietta glanced around the room. Both the Tholmondelays were on their feet, and even Richard had glanced away from the window to gaze at her with the sort of startled admiration bestowed by elder siblings when whacked in the face with a show of extreme excellence.

"Good God, Hen," he said sincerely. "I had no idea you could sing like that."

"Capital performance!" applauded Fred Tholmondelay.

"Smashing!" seconded Ned. "Never knew that Italian whatnot could be quite so, er—"

"Smashing!" supplied his brother for him. Ned beamed in thanks.

Henrietta barely noticed her triumph. Miles was gone. His seat in the back of the room was empty. It sat slightly at an angle on the parquet floor, as though pushed back in haste. Behind it, the thin, gilded doors stood ajar, still quivering with the force of recent passage.

"Would you sing us another air, my dear?" asked Mrs. Cathcart with an encouraging smile. "It is so seldom that one is treated to a performance of such virtuosity."

"I had no idea you could sing like that," repeated Richard bemusedly.

Amy, who was, if not quite tone-deaf, then less than musically inclined, contented herself with beaming in wholehearted delight at her sister-in-law's success.

Indeed, the only one who wasn't beaming wholeheartedly (aside from Miss Grey, for whom beaming would have been an entirely alien action, unsettling facial muscles too long in disuse) was Henrietta. Ordinarily, Henrietta would have basked in their compliments for days, clasping them to her like a bouquet of red roses.

Right now, Henrietta had something else on her mind.

That had not been indifference. She might not be as wise in the ways of the world as Penelope—or at least as wise as Penelope believed Penelope to be—but she knew enough to recognize misery when she saw it. After the past week, she should know.

That did not mean, Henrietta cautioned herself, that Miles necessarily felt anything of a tender nature for her. He might merely regret their rift for the sake of her friendship. Henrietta took a deep breath. And if that was what he wanted, well, friendship was better than nothing; the past day had proved that, if nothing else.

But there had been that *something* in his eyes. . . .

"Another song?" prompted Amy, delighted at the success of her plan for distracting the restless agents-in-training.

Henrietta shook her head, coming to a rapid decision. What was it that Hamlet had said? Something about action sicklied o'er with the pale cast of thought, which Henrietta took to mean that if she was going to sort things out with Miles, she ought to do it right away, before she managed to think herself out of it.

"No," she said to Amy. "No. I need . . . I'll just . . ."

Amy, thinking Henrietta was referring to a need of another kind entirely, nodded understandingly, and turned quickly to Miss Grey, imploring her to play something else.

The Tholmondelay twins shifted restlessly, exchanging martyred glances. Listening to the lovely Lady Henrietta sing was one thing, being subjected to the tuneless strummings of Miss Grey quite another.

"I say, Selwick, what about a more lively form of entertainment?" called out Fred.

Through the window, Henrietta could see a familiar pair of shoulders striding down the garden path, disappearing deep into the carefully contrived wilderness. She knew that walk, she knew that trick of flinging back the head, she knew every least gesture as well as she knew the image in her own glass. Henrietta paused for a moment by the window, watching Miles's dark coat blend with the hedges until there was nothing to be seen. But there was no need to squint into the dark shrubbery; she knew exactly where he was going. Whenever Miles was in disgrace (quite frequently, given his adventurous habits) or needed a place to think deeply (rather less frequently), he always went straight to the same place, the Roman ruin tucked away at the westernmost corner of the gardens. He liked to pitch rocks at the bust of Marcus Aurelius—especially when his classical studies were going poorly. Henrietta bit her lip on a smile at the memory.

How could she have contemplated remaining at odds with Miles? It just couldn't be done.

Unnoticed, Henrietta eased quietly out of the room. She just needed to talk to Miles, and put everything back to rights. When she found him . . .

"Charades, anyone?" demanded Fred Tholmondelay.

Chapter Twenty-Five

———— ♦ ————

Indiscretion: *a fatal miscalculation in judgment by an agent of the War Office; the inevitable prologue to discovery, disgrace, and death*
— from the Personal Code Book of the Pink Carnation

Who ever knew that Hen could sing like that?

A pebble ricocheted off Marcus Aurelius's head, landing with a gurgle in the water below. An affronted goldfish swished his tail reproachfully at Miles and swam off beneath a fallen bit of statuary. The Roman emperor stared superciliously at Miles down his long nose, taunting him to try again.

His aim was off tonight.

Miles gave the gravel at his feet a vicious kick that did more harm to the finish of his boots than it did the ground. Forget aim. It was his judgment that was fatally flawed. Hell, after this past week, Miles rather doubted that he possessed any of that commodity. There was a dangerous French spy on the loose, and what was Miles doing? Nothing useful, that was bloody certain. Quite the contrary, in fact. The history of the past week had been one of blunder after blunder. Were his life a novel, the chapter heading for this latest installment would undoubtedly read, "In which our hero contrives to endanger his valet and alienate his closest friend."

It took Miles a moment to realize he didn't mean Richard.

Miles sank down onto a little marble bench and buried his head in his hands. When had that happened? Of course, Richard was his closest friend, always had been. It was a matter of institutional record, like the method for calling Parliament. Yet, somehow, without Miles even realizing it, Henrietta had wiggled her way in there. Miles forced himself to cast his mind back over the past few years for the source of this decidedly disturbing development. Miles wasn't generally a proponent of retrospection, preferring to let sleeping dogs lie, live in the moment, seize the day, and any other optimistic twaddle that involved turning a blind eye to anything that might involve serious thought, or, even worse, implicate the emotions. However, even a blind man could see that his visits to Uppington House hadn't abated in the slightest despite the fact that his putative best friend had been off in France for the greater part of the past few years, not counting the odd holiday. He could blame it on Cook's superlative ginger biscuits, or humoring Lady Uppington, or any other number of innocuous excuses. But that was all they were, excuses.

When had he started relying on Hen to such a horrifying extent? He had promised Richard, years ago, that he would keep an eye on her (Richard took his protective function as elder brother deuced seriously), but somehow, keeping an eye had turned into hundreds of teas in the morning room, thousands of drives in the park, and more lemonades than Miles cared to count, much of it spilled on his boots in crowded ballrooms. Downey waxed positively vituperative about the effects of lemonade on fine leather. Today . . . Miles couldn't count the number of times he had automatically turned to exchange a quip or comment with Henrietta, before remembering that they weren't supposed to be speaking.

It was sheer misery.

Over the course of the long, miserable day, he had almost managed to convince himself that it would all blow over. Of course, Henrietta was angry—she had every right to be after he had kissed her at Vaughn's ball—but she would come around sooner or later, and they could go back to the way they were. And he hadn't been about to kiss her last night. Really, he hadn't. That had just been an, er, affectionate handclasp. Henrietta would calm down and life could revert to normal.

It had all seemed like such a good idea. Until she started singing.

Her first trill ripped the protective coating of habit from Miles's eyes. By the second, he was in distinct agony. This wasn't just Richard's little sister, anymore. It wasn't even Miles's companion of a thousand dull society balls. At the front of the room stood a woman with a formidable talent, a woman to be reckoned with. As a longtime connoisseur of the opera and its denizens, Miles knew that there were voices, and there were Voices. Henrietta had a Voice. Her clear tones reverberated through Miles's memory like the lingering savor of her lavender perfume, haunting in its purity.

A Voice wasn't all she had. Miles refused to even allow himself to dwell upon the way her bosom had swelled above the bodice of her dress as she drew in a deep breath before she built to the crescendo on the third reprise of *tanto rigor*. Miles groaned in memory, finding his breeches as uncomfortably tight now as they had been then. It wasn't the tailoring.

Looking away hadn't done any good, either. When he glanced down, there were her arms, curving gracefully towards the hands clasped at her waist, like the arms of a Raphael Venus rising from the sea, gently rounded and impossibly fair, ending in pale, delicate hands, with long, tapering fingers and smooth pink nails. Miles had never known there could be such agony in a fingernail before.

Forcing his eyes to her face had been an even bigger mistake. Her cheeks were flushed with the effort of singing, that rare wild tint he had only ever seen on Henrietta's cheeks, like rose petals beneath a fine film of snow; her skin was so translucent one could practically see the blood pounding beneath the surface. Her lips were as flushed as her cheeks, her eyes misty with music. With her lips parted in song, her head tilted slightly back, he could see her arising from a tangle of sheets, eyes dreamy, lips red from his kisses.

Miles contemplated leaping into the fishpond, but it was too shallow to do any good. Besides, he doubted any waters this side of the North Sea would be quite cold enough to dull his ardor, with the image of Hen . . .

Right. Enough was enough. Miles dusted his hands off against his breeches in a determined fashion. He would do what he should have done in the first place, and order his curricle to be brought around first thing tomorrow morning. He would return to London, meet with Wickham at the War Office, wring every last drop of information he could out of his taciturn superior, and then set himself seriously to the task of tracking down Downey's attacker.

Miles glanced wistfully at the lit windows of the hall, visible over the shoulder-high shrubbery. Inside, the members of the house party were filtering back into the Rose Room for tea and coffee; gaily dressed forms moved past the windowpanes singly and in groups. It was too far away to make out individuals, but all Miles could think about was . . .

Shooting Frenchmen, he told himself abruptly, levering himself up off the bench. Shooting lots and lots of Frenchmen.

"Don't even say it," Miles warned Marcus Aurelius.

"Don't say what?"

Miles started, swerved, and nearly toppled over the bench.

It wasn't the Roman emperor come to life. That, Miles could have dealt with. Long-dead historical personages, spies, phantom monks . . . all of those, Miles could have faced with equanimity.

The figure approaching him along the alley of beech trees might easily have been a statue stepped off her pedestal, Pygmalion's mythical lady come to life. Henrietta crossed the final few yards of the path, her white muslin gown luminous in the moonlight. The thin fabric molded itself against her legs as she walked, increasing the resemblance to the statuary of classical antiquity, but no statue had ever had that sort of effect on Miles.

"Shouldn't you be inside?" asked Miles darkly.

Henrietta checked slightly at his inhospitable tone. "I needed to speak to you. About last night—"

"You were right," Miles interrupted tersely. "We can't go back."

Henrietta squinted at him. The moonlight that illuminated the shimmering tails of the fish in the pond and picked out strange patterns in the shrubbery did nothing to illuminate Miles's expression. All she could make out was his stance, leaning against a hedge, hands in his pockets. But there was something about the tense set of his shoulders that belied the casual pose.

"That's just what I wanted to talk to you about," she announced. "I've changed my mind."

Miles's reaction wasn't quite what Henrietta had hoped. Instead of exclaiming with joy, he crossed his arms over his chest. "Well, so have I."

Henrietta frowned at him through the moonlight. "You can't."

"Why not?"

"Because—oh, for heaven's sake, Miles, I'm trying to apologize to you!"

Miles sidled away. "Don't."

"Don't?"

"Don't apologize and don't come any closer."

As if to lend force to his words, Miles resolutely turned away from her, scooped up a handful of pebbles, and began pitching them into the pond with exaggerated attention to aim.

Henrietta's eyes narrowed in sudden comprehension. She plunked her hands on her hips and glowered at Miles. "If you're trying to drive me away so I don't get in your way while you stalk the spy, I don't appreciate it."

"This is not about the bloody spy," bit out Miles. *Plop!* A stone landed with unnecessary force in the murky waters.

Henrietta marched militantly up to him, slippers crunching on the graveled ground, and poked him in the shoulder. Hard. "You were hoping the spy would have to pass through here on the way to the house, weren't you?"

"This." *Splish.* "Is not." *Plop.* "About." *Splash.* "The spy."

Miles brushed his hands off against his breeches. Henrietta grabbed him by the arm before he could sweep up another batch of projectiles, forcing him to face her.

"Am I that repugnant to you that you can't stand the sight of me?"

"Repugnant." Miles eyed her incredulously, his jaw hanging slightly open. "Oh, that's rich. Repugnant!"

Henrietta felt the full force of his mockery, and her face contorted with hurt. "You needn't belabor the point," she snapped.

"Do you know what you've been doing to me?" demanded Miles.

"Me? To you! Ha!" exclaimed Henrietta articulately. As repartee, it wasn't her finest hour, but she was too furious to attempt words of more than one syllable.

"Yes, you! Running around in my dreams, singing like that—I can't think. I can't sleep. I can't look my best friend in the eye. It's been sheer *hell*!"

"Is that my fault?" exclaimed Henrietta. "You're the one who kissed me and then didn't bother to— Wait. Your dreams? You've been dreaming about me?"

Miles backed away, looking horrified. "Never mind. Forget I said that."

Henrietta took a dangerous step forward. "Oh, no. There are no 'never minds.' You're not getting off that easily this time."

"*Damn*," said Miles feelingly. "Fine." He took a step forward. "You want to know the truth? I don't find you repugnant." Another step. "If you must know, I find you the very opposite of repugnant." Another. "It's been all I can do to keep my hands bloody off you the past two days."

One more step and Miles was so close to her that her breath stirred the stiff folds of his cravat. Henrietta cravenly sidled backwards, but the hedge was at her back, pricking her through the thin muslin of her dress, blocking retreat.

"In fact"—Miles's hands closed around her shoulders as his head plummeted towards her—"you have been driving me absolutely bloody *mad*!"

With a desperate sideways movement, Henrietta wrenched herself from his grasp, leaving Miles to stumble headlong into the hedge.

"Oh, no," she panted. "I'm not playing that game again."

Miles's eyes were glazed and his breath rasped in his throat. "Game?" he forced out.

"Yes, game!" snapped Henrietta, tears of rage and frustration gathering in her hazel eyes. "The game where you kiss me and then run off and hide from me for a whole blasted week! It's—I just can't—if you're just looking for a bit of fun, you're going to have to find it somewhere else."

Gathering her skirts in her hand, she whirled in the direction of the house, only to be jerked abruptly short as Miles grabbed her by the elbow.

"That's not what I want!" Miles burst out, swinging her around to face him.

"Then what *do* you want?" demanded Henrietta.

"You, dammit!"

The words hung there in the air between them.

Each stared at the other, Miles's brown eyes locked with Henrietta's hazel, both frozen as still as Lot's wife's peering back into a forbidden land.

Henrietta's heart surged with frenetic joy, before hiccuping to an abrupt stop, and swinging wildly back in the opposite direction. Of all the ambiguous statements! What exactly did he want? And if he wanted her, why on earth had he been hiding from her? An odd sort of wanting that drove the pursuer *away* from the object of desire!

Henrietta waved her hands in the air in frustration. "What exactly is that supposed to mean?"

"Uh . . ." Funny, it had seemed quite clear to him when he uttered it, but when forced to encapsulate the sense of it, Miles couldn't find any appropriate words. Somehow, he didn't think "I want to fling you down among the rosebushes and have my wicked way with you" would necessarily appease Hen's wrath. That was the problem with women; they always insisted on verbalizing everything. "Um . . ."

Fortunately, Henrietta was still in full rant, so Miles was spared replying. "And why," she demanded, "have you been behaving like such an idiot?"

Miles chose not to dispute the appellation, primarily because he agreed to it. In fact, he knew it was the height of idiocy to linger in the garden when what he ought to do was flee straight back to the safety of London, without passing the house, without collecting his belongings. To remain . . . The word "idiot" didn't even begin to encompass it.

As much for himself as for her, Miles said forcefully, "You are my best friend's *sister*."

Henrietta took a very deep breath. Miles struggled nobly to keep his eyes fixed above her bodice. It was a cause doomed to failure from its very inception.

Henrietta's chest heaved to a stop, followed by an expectant silence.

"What?" asked Miles.

"I fail to see what that has to do with anything," repeated Henrietta through gritted teeth. Speaking through gritted teeth involved very little passage of air. Sanity—or some modicum thereof—returned to Miles, along with the capacity for speech.

Miles ran his hands through his hair till it stood up like porcupine quills. "Do you know how many kinds of betrayal that would be? Forget Richard, even. Your parents *raised* me! And how do I repay them? By seducing their daughter."

Henrietta swallowed painfully. "Is that all I am to you? Someone else's sister? Someone else's daughter?"

Of its own volition, Miles's right hand rose to cup her face, gently tilting it back to face him.

"Don't you know better than that, Hen?"

Slowly, she shook her head. "No." Her voice broke, half-laugh, half-sob. "I don't know anything right now."

"Funny," Miles whispered achingly, his warm breath feathering across her lips. "Neither do I."

With infinite gentleness, his lips brushed hers. His hands slid softly into her hair, stroking her temples, easing away aches she hadn't realized she had. Letting her eyes drift closed, Henrietta leaned into the kiss, abandoning herself to the dreamlike unreality of it all. Henrietta's hands slid up to Miles's shoulders, feeling the warmth of his body through the fine wool of his coat as warmth of an entirely different kind spread through her. Around them, the garden was rich with the scent of early June roses, as lush and heavy as an old tapestry. It seemed as though the wind moved more delicately through the trees, and even the cranky old gentleman frog who lived in the pond gentled his croaking complaint. The whole world slowed and drifted in a measureless minuet.

With a movement as soft as a sigh, Miles's lips slid away from hers. They remained suspended in time, Miles's lips a whisper above hers, her hands on his shoulders, his fingers still threaded in her hair. Miles smoothed his thumbs along her cheekbones, tracing the well-beloved contours of her face.

"I missed you," Henrietta whispered.

Miles pulled her tightly against him, rubbing his face in her hair. "Me too."

"Then why did you hide from me all week?" asked Henrietta into his shoulder.

For the life of him, Miles was having a very hard time remembering; the feel of Henrietta's body pressed against his was having a decidedly numbing effect on his brain, even as it brought other bits of his anatomy into acute relief. He dredged up the reason as if from a lifetime ago.

"Because I was afraid I'd do this," he said, nuzzling back her hair, and running his tongue along the rim of her ear. He felt Henrietta shiver in his arms and stilled, giving her a space to protest, to walk away.

Henrietta tilted her chin, leaving her throat bare for Miles's questing lips. "I don't understand," she said softly, "why that was cause for hiding."

"Right now," admitted Miles, "neither can I."

His lips followed the delicate curve of Henrietta's jaw, the rounded chin that looked so demure in repose but could be so stubborn in reality, the elegant line of her throat, pausing to blow gently at the delicate hairs that curled at the base of her neck, where her hair had been swept up and away from her face.

Henrietta didn't gasp; a gasp would have marred the dreamlike quality of the moment, like a leaf floating on a stream on a summer's day, utterly unmoored from responsibility, content to simply drift in the golden heat of the sun. But her fingers curled around Miles's shoulders as she marveled at the amazing sensations to be had from so prosaic an item as a neck. Miles's kisses she had been prepared for— well, as much as one could be prepared for something that made one's head spin like too much claret—there were novels and paintings and whispered discussions in the ladies' retiring room. But no one had ever told her about this. Necks were simply something on which to hang jewelry, to set off with a curl or a flounce; they were not supposed to send quivers of pleasure through one's entire body.

In the spirit of experimentation, Henrietta locked her arms tighter around Miles's neck, stood on her tiptoes, and applied her lips to the underside of his chin—she had been aiming for the spot just at the parting of collar and cravat, but the combination of dizziness and half-closed eyes had a negative impact on her aim. His skin smelled of exotic aftershave, and a fascinating hint of stubble, so fair as to be almost invisible to the eye, grazed her lips.

Miles's reaction was instantaneous, if not quite what Henrietta had hoped for. Recoiling backwards, he blinked several times, shook his head like a wet dog, and held Henrietta away from him.

"Did I do something wrong?" asked Henrietta huskily.

Miles's eyes had a distinctly wild cast, and his hair was even more disarranged than usual. Henrietta gave in to the impulse to smooth a lock back. Miles shied like a nervous horse. "Hell, no—er, I mean, no! That is . . . Oh, blast it, Hen—"

Since he didn't seem to have anything particularly incisive to say, Henrietta decided to put an end to the conversation by the simple expedient of kissing him again. Miles's arms closed around her with enough force to knock any remaining air out of her lungs, but breathing really seemed quite a minor consideration under the circumstances. Who needed to breathe, anyhow? Lips were much more interesting, especially when they were Miles's lips, and they were doing such clever things to the sensitive hollow next to her collarbone. Henrietta hadn't realized before that the hollow was a sensitive one, but she was quite sure she would remember in the future. Miles's lips drifted even lower, following a slow path along her collarbone, down to the hollow between her breasts, and Henrietta stopped thinking in full sentences altogether, or even recognizable words.

Miles was dimly aware that his brain had ceased working in concert with his body several moments since, but the worst of it was that he had ceased to care. Somewhere in the back of his mind, he knew there was a very valid reason that he wasn't supposed to be undressing Henrietta, but whatever insubstantial objection his conscious mind might urge upon him dissipated beside the far-more-compelling reality of Henrietta herself, warm and glowing in his arms, a thousand forbidden dreams made flesh.

And what attractive flesh it was.

Miles made one last effort to restrain his baser desires, one last effort to push Hen away into the little box in his head marked "best friend, sister of." But her hair whispered wantonly against his arm, and her lips were swollen with kisses—his kisses, thought Miles, with a fierce surge of possessiveness. His, his, his. All his, from the long lashes that curved against her cheeks to the hint of a dimple that only appeared when she smiled or frowned very deeply, to the absolutely irresistible expanse of bosom revealed in agonizing detail by her position reclining against his arm.

Even so, Miles might—it wasn't likely, but he might—have set her to her feet, tucked back her hair, and given them both a firm talking-to, if, at that very moment, Henrietta hadn't sighed. It was just a little sigh, hardly louder than the brush of silk against skin, but it carried with it an entire world of amorous innuendo. So might Heloise have sighed in the arms of Abelard or Juliet for her Romeo, begging night to gallop apace and veil their pleasures.

Miles was undone.

So was Henrietta's bodice. One gentle pull drew the fabric down to reveal the rosy areolae, blushing above their fine veil of silk. Miles ran his tongue around first one, then the other, as Henrietta arched in his arms and dug her nails into his back.

He eased the fabric the rest of the way, enjoying the way Henrietta squirmed in his arms as the silk brushed over her nipples. Miles was just lowering his head to replace the fabric with his mouth, when a voice with an edge like cut glass, a voice from very far away, cut through his consciousness.

"What in the hell is going on here?"

Chapter Twenty-Six

I f there were formal gardens at Donwell Abbey, we weren't in them. Clutching my borrowed pashmina around my shoulders, I stumbled along after Colin through a landscape pitted with potholes and littered with killer twigs. The bulk of the house loomed behind us, craggy and featureless in the dark night. Just the equivalent of a city block away, the noises, voices, and lights from the front of the house were completely obliterated, leaving only a landscape that would not have come amiss in a Brontë novel, or one of the wilder creations of Mary Shelley.

We were crossing something that I had no doubt Joan would describe as "the park," conjuring up images of stately oaks and Little Lord Fauntleroy. At the moment, I would have happily traded all the grandeur of the park for the neon grime of Oxford Street, with loud music blasting out of storefronts, chattering pedestrians bustling past, and, most important, firm pavement beneath my feet. My shoes, designed for city wear, did not react well to the ground, softened by yesterday's rain and today's thaw. They sank.

So much for a romantic stroll in the garden by moonlight.

Even the moonlight wasn't obliging. Forget the trope of the moon as chaste goddess. A hopeless flirt, she was too busy playing peekaboo with the clouds to attend to illuminating the landscape. Instead of the scent of flowers, we were surrounded by the forlorn tang of November, compounded of decaying leaves and damp earth. A graveyard sort of smell. I cut that thought off before it could burgeon into the territory of grade-B horror movies, complete with zombie hands poking through the crumbling earth and vampires on the lookout for a midnight snack.

It was all Henrietta's and Miles's fault, I ruminated darkly as I pried my heel out of the mud and hopped after Colin. I had been forced to leave off reading just as Henrietta and Miles kissed in the moon-silvered garden, and had dressed for Joan's party pursued by hopelessly romantic images of trellises and patterned garden paths, the song of the nightingale and the sigh of the gentle summer breeze. If the characters in that perfumed garden tended to assume features other than those of Henrietta and Miles . . . who was to know but me and the mirror in Colin's guest bedroom?

I had neglected to take into account that that had been June and this was November.

And then there was the fact that Miles had been rather madly attracted to Henrietta, while Colin . . . I snuck a glance at the shadowy figure next to me. I don't know why I even bothered with the sneaking; there was no way he could make out my expression any more than I could discern his, even if he were one of those annoying people with a cat's ability to see in the dark. Both his eyes and his flashlight were trained firmly forward, not at me.

He hadn't said anything since that comment about chaperonage.

Of course, neither had I, but that was immaterial.

It wasn't that the silence was uncomfortable. Quite the contrary. It was the peaceful sort of silence that attends long acquaintance, the comfort that comes of knowing you don't need to say anything at all. And that very lack of discomfort made me profoundly uncomfortable.

I pinned down that thought, and followed it, writhing and slippery, to its source. It was the sham of instant coupledom. That was the problem. That indefinable aura of being with someone when you know you're not. It's something that anyone who's been single for a time will recognize, the pretense of intimacy that comes of being the only two singles at a couple-y dinner party, or, in this case, sharing a house for a weekend. It's an intensely seductive illusion—but only an illusion.

I wondered if Colin had picked up on that, too; if he had been as besieged with "So . . . you and that American girl?" as I had with "So . . . you and Colin?" The arriving together; the knowledge that we'd be leaving together; the little checking-up glances across the room, all lending themselves to the fiction of togetherness.

A fiction, I reminded myself, maintained for Joan's benefit.

Was he trying to warn me off, remind me that I was only a guest under sufferance? I cast my mind anxiously back over the day, totting up points on both sides of the ledger. The walk in the garden could just have been to get me away from the tower. In fact, Colin had shown no interest in accompanying me anywhere until I started to lurk around potentially actionable bits of his property. I winced at the memory of that terse note on the kitchen table. "Out." That lent itself so well to other curt phrases, such as "stay out" and "keep away."

As for agreeing to walk with me to the cloisters . . . I grimaced as the obvious explanation hit me. Of course. Joan. It wasn't that he wanted to stroll through the moonlight—or what would have been moonlight if the moon had been a little more cooperative—with me. He just needed a pretext to flee his hostess's predatory grasp, and I had provided him with an ideal excuse. The visiting historian (in my mind's eye, I sprouted tweeds, brogues, and bifocals) needed to be taken to see local objects of historical interest. There was no other type of interest involved.

The white wine I had drunk to keep the vicar company tasted sour on my tongue.

Right. I gathered the tattered shreds of my ego around myself, even though they afforded even less shelter for my lacerated pride than Serena's pashmina did for my frozen arms. Well, I wasn't here to flirt with him, either. So there.

I was beginning to regret the whole ill-conceived adventure. I should have behaved like a good little academic, and stayed back at the house, hunched over a table full of documents in the meager light of the desk lamp, rather than letting myself be drawn in by the echoes of long-dead romances and a strong dose of wishful thinking.

I wasn't turning into one of those desperate singles who fancied that every man she met was flirting with her, was I? The very thought was horrifying. Soon, I'd start reading great meaning into the way the counter guy at the convenience store across the way from my flat counted out my change, or imagine a hungry gleam in my landlord's eye as he descended into my basement bower to empty the electricity meter.

Have I mentioned that my landlord is fifty-something and paunchy?

I twisted to look back at the house, wondering if I should suggest we go back. I could leave Colin to the tender ministrations of Joan, and as for me . . . there was always the bar. And the vicar. Not that I thought the vicar was interested in me, of course. He was just someone to talk to. At the bar.

"You know," commented Colin, grabbing my arm as I stumbled, "you would probably fall less if you walked forward instead of backwards."

I could feel the warmth of Colin's hand through the thin rayon of Serena's dress, seeping through the fabric, combating the November cold.

I removed my elbow from Colin's grasp. "Are these cloisters of yours much farther?" My voice sounded sharp, strained, and stridently American. "I wouldn't want to keep you out here too long."

"I don't mind."

"Someone else might."

"The vicar? You and he did seem to be getting on." Before I could respond to that, Colin's flashlight beam shifted abruptly to the left, catching on an object several yards ahead of us. "There are the cloisters."

"Where?" I said dumbly.

No, it wasn't because I was looking at Colin rather than the tiny circle of light. I was just looking in the wrong place. I had expected . . . well, a building, at least. Stone walls around a courtyard, maybe even a small church of some kind. I didn't expect them to be intact, but some sort of structure was to be expected. Was this all an elaborate practical joke that they played on visiting historians? Perhaps Joan was in on it, too, and the vicar. I dimly remembered some sort of sci-fi movie along those lines, where everyone in town belonged to the same alien race except the unwitting heroine, although I did have to admit that feigning the existence of medieval buildings was quite different from being able to pull off one's skin and transform into a reptile creature.

"There," repeated Colin patiently, lowering the beam a bit, and this time my eyes picked out the lumps in the landscape that were nothing to do with nature.

"This is it?"

"Sad, isn't it?" agreed Colin, flashlight beam drifting across a window that had been rendered redundant by the absence of walls. "Half the buildings nearby were built of Donwell stone."

"I suppose you could look at it as recycling," I said, surveying the depleted ruins, "but it still seems like a waste."

There wasn't much left to the old monastery. I'm sure what there was must have been picturesque in summer, with greenery creeping over the tumbled masonry, but in the autumn dark, the bare, ruined choirs where late the sweet birds sang were more forbidding than quaint. Once, a series of arches must have marked off the peripheries of a courtyard. Now, only half-buried stones and the occasional vestige of a pillar remained. Knee-high walls preserved the memory rather than the reality of rooms, and occasionally, among the wilted weeds, one could see the outline of something that might once have been a paving stone in a past life.

As we grew closer, and the area encompassed by the flashlight expanded, I could see that the walls grew higher as we went on, rising shoulder high in some places, higher than my head in others, peaking and falling again. Only one room, all the way at one end of the cloister, maintained the majority of its original walls. There was even a bit of ceiling remaining, made of heavy stone that sloped inwards like the hull of a ship turned upside down.

It was into that remaining room that I followed Colin, picking my way gingerly across the floor. It was more intact than those farther along the cloister, the majority of the floor stones still in place, but they were weathered and uneven, cracked in unexpected places. In other words, hell on heels.

"Get me to a nunnery," I said lightly, just to say something, and felt like an idiot as soon as the words were out of my mouth. Get me to a nunnery? That was nearly as bad as the "I carried a watermelon" line in *Dirty Dancing*. And it had been a monastery. Not a nunnery. Not the same thing. My medieval history professor would have been having palpitations. I had once confused the Carthusians with the Cistercians and had been afraid we were going to have to rush him to Harvard University Health Services for emergency care.

"Not much of a nunnery these days," replied Colin with amusement, though it was hard to tell whether he was amused with me or at me. The beam of the flashlight swooped in a circle along the floor, picking out signs of recent habitation. An empty Coke can, a discarded packet of cheese-and-onion-flavored crisps. "It's quite popular with the local youth."

"Popular?"

"I came here a time or two myself," he added with a reminiscent grin.

"Ugh," I said, wrinkling my nose at the cold stone floor. "That can't be very comfortable. Or sanitary."

Colin lounged back against one of the remaining walls in a position of supreme masculine smugness. Thinking of conquests past, no doubt. "You'd be surprised. A few blankets, a bottle of wine . . ."

"Spare me the tales of your depraved youth," I said repressively, turning away and tracing a hand along the embrasure of the window, running a finger over the chips and chinks in an elaborate fleur-de-lis.

"Yours wasn't?" His voice was warm, teasing.

I glanced back over my shoulder. "I don't kiss and tell."

"Or just not in cloisters?"

"I don't see the appeal." I dug among my collection of misremembered quotations for ammunition. " 'The grave's a fine and quiet place / But none I think do there embrace.' "

"Ah," said Colin, setting the flashlight down on one of the recessed benches so that the light fanned out against the wall, "but this is a cloister, not a grave."

"It is a sort of a grave, isn't it?" I argued, licking my lips and taking a little step back. It had been so long since I'd flirted with anyone, I'd practically forgotten how. We were flirting, weren't we? "It's a grave of lost hopes and ambitions. You wonder how they must have felt when the monasteries were dissolved, suddenly seeing their whole way of life go the way of . . . well, the grave."

I had no idea what I was saying. I was vaguely aware of my mouth moving, and words coming out, but I couldn't have made any guarantees as to content.

"Besides, it's a *monastery*," I said stubbornly. "Can you think of anyplace less appropriate for romantic dalliance?"

Colin laughed. "Haven't you read your Chaucer?"

"You can't believe everything you read in Chaucer," I protested, but it didn't come out very forcefully, because Colin had ever so casually leaned a hand against the stone wall behind my head.

I made a valiant effort to pull myself together and pay attention to what he was saying, instead of just staring in the general direction of his lips and wondering . . . well, we don't need to go into what I was wondering. History, I reminded myself firmly. That was what I was here for. Spies. Monks. Spies dressed as monks.

Right now, I couldn't have cared less if someone had waltzed across the room in a large flower costume with a sign saying GET YOUR BLACK TULIPS HERE. Every nerve in my body was on man-alert, screaming, "Incoming!" I could feel the warmth radiating from his chest, smell the clean, detergent-y smell that clung to his collar, and my lips prickled with that peculiar sixth sense that only clicks into gear as a man leans too close for plausible rationalization.

My eyes drifted shut.

BRRRRING!

Something emitted a jarring screeching noise, like five fire alarms going off all at once. I froze, eyes still closed and face lifted. I must have looked like a mole caught out of its tunnel by daylight. Above me, I could sense Colin, equally arrested by that dreadful jarring sound. It wasn't an air raid. It wasn't even Joan, come to take her revenge. It was my phone. Bleeping.

Damn.

I kept my eyes closed, in the futile hope that if I stayed very, very still and prayed very, very hard, the sound would go away, and Colin and I could pick up where we'd left off as if nothing else had happened.

BRRRRING! BRRRRING!

My phone bleeped again. Insistently.

The pleasant mix of detergent and aftershave wafted away, to be replaced with cold air. I wrenched open my eyes and peeled myself away from the wall, my pashmina slipping drunkenly down my arms.

"Would you excuse me for a moment?" I asked in an agony of mortification, fishing in my bag for my vibrating mobile. Thanks to its untimely interruption, it was the only thing left vibrating—other than my lacerated nerves. "I mean . . . it's just . . . in case there's an emergency," I finished lamely.

"Certainly," said Colin blandly, so blandly that I had to wonder if I had imagined the whole episode. Like the Cheshire cat, he had managed to rematerialize several feet down the wall. With an elbow resting against the ruined window frame, he looked as unruffled as if he had been standing there the whole time.

Maybe he had been. Maybe I'd imagined the whole thing.

Whatever else I'd imagined, the hideous bleating noise coming from my bag was quite real. The phone was still whining in its Coach cocoon. Scratching my frozen knuckles on the zipper, I wrestled the phone out of the tightly packed bag, squinting at the tiny screen. It glowed an evil neon in the dark cloister.

PAMMY, proclaimed the screen.

I was going to kill her. I was really, truly going to kill her.

I took a deep breath, and repressed the urge to fling the phone to the floor and stomp on it à la Rumplestiltskin. Maybe Pammy was violently ill. Maybe she had been dumped by . . . oh, what was his name? They never lasted long enough for me to remember. Abduction by the Mafia with twenty-four hours to gather a ransom would also be an acceptable excuse for the interruption. Did they even have a Mafia in England? They'd better, I thought grimly.

I clicked the VIEW button, and Pammy's text flashed up on the screen.

HAS HE MADE A MOVE YET?

Abduction by the Mafia was too good for some people.

Casting a furtive glance over my shoulder, I hunched over the phone, and tersely texted back, NO.

Instantly, Pammy's name flashed back up on the screen.

WHY NOT?

My fingers flashed over the tiny buttons with a will of their own.

MAYBE BECAUSE CERTAIN PPL KEEP TEXTING ME!!!

Let her make of that what she would. I jabbed the SEND button, followed by power, shoving the phone back into my bag. The phone died into darkness with a tinny wail. Too late. Why in the hell hadn't I thought to turn the phone off in the first place?

Damn, damn, damn.

"Anyone interesting?" asked Colin.

"Pammy," I replied, striving for rueful amusement and achieving something closer to a grunt, in a "you, Tarzan; me, Cheetah" sort of way.

Colin detached from the wall. And a good thing, too, given the state of the rest of the structure; I didn't have much faith in its stability. On the other hand, binding up his wounded brow would give me a chance to hover tenderly over him. We'll ignore the fact that I failed first aid in high school. Three times.

Maybe it was a good thing he hadn't fallen over.

"What has she done now?" he asked.

"Oh, the usual," I said distractedly, wondering if there was any way to ever so subtly drift in his direction without my heels sounding like cannon salvos on the pitted stone flags. But that would destroy the entire exercise, wouldn't it? The point was to figure out if he had any interest in drifting in my direction, not the other way around. "You know what Pammy's like."

"Yes, I do," he said, so forcefully that I couldn't help but wonder . . .

Colin and Pammy?

Pammy had known Colin's sister ever since she'd moved to London in tenth grade. Serena and Pammy weren't awfully close, but there would still have been ample opportunity for a flirtation with Serena's big brother. No. I just couldn't see it. Besides, Pammy would have told me. Wouldn't she? Hmm. I filed that thought away for later.

"Um, Chaucer." I yanked my borrowed pashmina back up around my shoulders, futilely attempting to effect a return to where we had been pre–Pammy and the Text Message of Doom. "You were saying something about Chaucer?"

In the feeble light of the torch, I saw him shake his head. "It can't have been important."

"It sounded intriguing to me," I said ruefully.

"Did it?" The words were softly spoken, but they were enough to make the skin on my arms prickle in a way that had nothing to do with the November chill. Even the shadows gathered and held their breath, waiting to see what sort of action might follow on the velvet promise beneath those two little words.

"Hullo!"

A cheerful voice echoed through the old cloister, banishing the shadows and sending any romantic tension skittering far, far away.

What next? My fifth-grade homeroom teacher? The St. Patrick's Day Parade? A Fleetwood Mac revival concert? I doubted that Donwell Abbey had been quite this popular even when it was still in possession of all of its masonry and monks.

Somewhere, Cupid was snickering. I hoped he sat on one of his own arrows.

Sally skittered to a stop and rested a hand on the wall to steady herself. If there was anything coloring the atmosphere other than my own wild imaginings, she didn't seem to notice.

"Sorry to keep you! I only just got away. Joan couldn't find the ice." She shook her wild mane of hair in sororal condemnation. "Hopeless. Simply hopeless."

That did about sum it up.

"Has Colin shown you around yet?" Sally asked.

"Not really." Colin strolled casually across the room. "Would you do the honors, Sal?"

"Better than you," she retorted. "I can't believe you've been out here all this time and he's shown you nothing!"

Colin assumed a wounded air. "If you're just going to insult me, I'm off for a drink."

I contemplated saying, "I could do with one of the same," and trailing after him back to the bar, but clamped down on the impulse. I hadn't quite sunk to that level. The operative word being "quite." I remembered my rather blatant attempt at flirtation and was glad for the darkness that hid my sudden grimace.

"Enjoy!" I said instead, with a cheerful little wave. "Better make it a double."

"Double the alcohol?"

"For double the insults," I explained sweetly.

"A hit!" crowed Sally. "Well done!"

"I"—Colin turned and wagged a finger at Sally—"don't like you anymore. And as for you—"

I tried to look as though I weren't holding my breath.

"Yes?"

"Don't worry; I'll think of something." And on that rather enigmatic note, he made his exit.

As a threat, his statement lacked a certain something. Specificity, for example.

As flirtation . . . it fizzed through me like a large gulp of Veuve Clicquot, pure, heady stuff, the grand brut of suggestive remarks. I shouldn't read too much into it. I knew that. Nonetheless . . .

I turned to find Sally regarding me with arms crossed over her chest.

"Just here for the archives?" she said.

Chapter Twenty-Seven

————— ❦ —————

Compromised: *discovered and disgraced; the uncovering of
an agent's identity, followed by enforced retirement. See also
under* Ruin

—from the Personal Codebook of the Pink Carnation

Miles rapidly remembered all the very good reasons he had meant
to keep far away from Henrietta until old age snuffed out baser
desires, or at least the means to accomplish them. But it was too late.
In front of him loomed his best friend—his former best friend—arm
outstretched like a medieval woodcut of a wrathful God. Richard's
very posture crackled with rage.

"Oh, no," breathed Henrietta, hastily yanking her bodice back up
into place.

Amy grabbed Richard by the arm and shoved him behind herself.
Given that Richard stood nearly a foot taller than Amy, the action was
entirely ineffectual. Over Amy's dark head, Richard's face was stiff
with fury and disbelief. Miles swallowed hard, rising slowly to his
feet.

"I don't think we should be here just now," Amy hedged, trying to
herd her husband in the opposite direction.

"Oh, no," said Richard dangerously, placing both hands on his wife's shoulders and moving her to the side. "I think now is exactly the right time to be here. What in the *hell* did you think you were doing, Dorrington?"

Think? Miles didn't recall terribly much thought being involved.

"What do you think he was thinking?" chimed in Amy. "Really, Richard, can't we—"

"There had better be a *bloody* good explanation."

"How did you know we were out here?" Henrietta croaked, hoping to distract Richard from Miles before that "bloody" became bloody in fact. The dangerous glint in Richard's eye gave deadly content to the word.

"One of the sentries reported that there was something unusual occurring in the gardens." Richard emitted a grim bark of laughter. "He didn't know the half of it."

"Richard—" began Miles, moving to stand protectively in front of Henrietta.

"How long has this been going on?" Richard inquired conversationally. "Weeks? Months? *Years?* How long, Dorrington?"

"We didn't—" Henrietta interrupted.

"You stay out of this," warned her brother.

"How can I stay out of this when it's me you're talking about?"

Her brother ignored her. Eyes never leaving Miles, he began stripping off his coat. "We can discuss this at dawn or we can settle this right now."

"Before we do"—yanking off his own coat, Miles sank automatically into a defensive crouch, fists at the ready—"I have something to say."

Richard dropped his coat on the graveled path. "That's just too bad, because I"—with one controlled lunge, he leveled an uppercut straight at Miles's jaw—"don't want to hear it."

With the ease of long practice, Miles ducked the blow and grabbed Richard's arm before he could swing again. They had sparred a thousand times before, in the well-regulated confines of Gentleman Jackson's pugilist establishment, but never in earnest. Miles didn't intend to start now. The two stood locked in a contest of strength, like athletes on a Greek vase, muscles straining against the sleeves of their coats, as Miles strove to restrain his friend.

"Dammit, Richard," yelled Miles, voice ragged with strain, "will you just listen?"

"There's nothing," Richard panted, twisting his right arm free, "to listen to."

"I want"—Miles barely dodged a sharp jab to his stomach—"to marry her!"

"What?" gasped Henrietta.

"What?" roared Richard, stumbling backwards.

"That's an excellent idea!" applauded Amy. "That way, no one is compromised, no one shoots anyone at dawn, and everyone is happy."

The expressions of the other three completely belied the latter part of her statement.

Ignoring the others, Miles looked searchingly at Henrietta. "Hen?"

"You don't have to do this," whispered Henrietta.

"I rather think he does," commented Amy. "It's quite compromising, you know."

"Hen?" repeated Miles urgently.

Henrietta stared at him in mute misery, her mind leaping from one imponderable to the next. She could refuse, and watch her brother either tear Miles to death on the spot, or shoot a hole into him on the field of honor the following morning. While Miles was undoubtedly the more accomplished sportsman, Henrietta knew, the same way she knew that Miles was proposing because it was the only honorable thing to do in the circumstances, that Miles would never, ever lift a hand against her brother. It wouldn't be an equal contest, with one party crippled with guilt. She didn't think that Richard would, once he had time to reflect, really want to hurt Miles, either, but in the mood he was in . . . Henrietta didn't trust her brother to aim wide.

On the one side, death and dishonor. On the other . . .

Or she could marry Miles, existing the remainder of her days with the knowledge that she had forced him into a match on the point of her brother's pistol.

Miles slowly turned to face his former best friend, and Henrietta knew, from the set of his shoulders and the expression of unusual gravity on his face, that if she waited a moment longer, the fatal words would be uttered and the two men who mattered most in her life would be irrevocably committed to a course from which there would be no going back. Ever.

"Yes," Henrietta blurted out. "Yes, I'll marry you."

Richard turned an alarming shade of puce, rounded on his sister, and barked out, "You're not going to marry that . . . that . . ."

"Man?" provided Amy helpfully.

Richard glowered at his wife. "Seducer," he finished angrily.

"Would you rather I married Reggie Fitzhugh?" asked Henrietta acidly, turning on her brother. Anything rather than look at Miles.

"Don't be ridiculous!" snapped Richard.

"Why aren't I allowed to be ridiculous, if you're being ridiculous?" demanded Henrietta, in her best annoying-little-sister mode. Out of the corner of her eye, she could see Miles slowly retrieving his coat. Would he rather have cleansed his conscience at dawn? "That's not fair."

"She does have a point there, you know," commented Amy.

"ARGH!" Richard roared, driven beyond speech. "I am not being—"

"Ridiculous *and* loud."

"Go ahead," Richard clipped. "Marry him. Marry him tomorrow, for all I care. But I don't want to see that"—he jabbed a finger in the direction of Miles—"under my roof ever again."

Miles shrugged into his coat and stepped forward. "Fine," he said quietly, but with an edge of steel beneath his voice that made Henrietta instinctively stiffen. "We'll be married tomorrow. If you'll excuse me, I have a special license to acquire."

With a nod of the head to Amy, and a swift kiss placed somewhere in the vicinity of Henrietta's hand—she could feel the tingle of it all up her arm—Miles turned and strode off towards the stables.

Richard didn't bother to respond. He didn't say anything to his sister. He didn't follow Miles. He turned on his heel and stalked furiously in the direction of the house. Only the crunch of boots on gravel, receding in opposite directions, invaded the uncomfortable silence that followed. Henrietta stared after Miles's retreating back, grappling with the ramifications of what had just passed.

Tomorrow. Henrietta pressed the heels of her hands against her eyes. A special license. Miles hadn't just said they were to be married tomorrow, had he? He couldn't have meant it.

Recovering her powers of speech first, Amy smiled reassuringly at Henrietta. "Richard will come around," she said confidently. "You'll see."

From the house came the ominous sound of a door being slammed. Twice.

Amy swallowed hard. "Eventually?"

BY NOON THE NEXT DAY, the Honorable Miles Dorrington and his new bride were well on their way back to London.

Henrietta glanced surreptitiously down at the ring on her gloved finger. She hadn't asked where Miles had acquired it, or what manner of skulduggery he might have engaged in to procure a special license on such short notice. In fact, they had had no chance to speak at all. By the time Henrietta had awakened that morning, with the vaguely headachy recollection that something of great moment had occurred and it really might have been better to just stay under the covers until the world realigned itself, the household was already bustling with wedding preparations, and Henrietta found herself swept towards matrimony with very little notion of how she had gotten there.

Henrietta had always imagined that she would be attended by Penelope and Charlotte, Charlotte misty-eyed with romance, Penelope grumbling. Instead, Amy helped her to dress, fussing excitedly with flounces and curls, while Mrs. Cathcart calmly rearranged everything as soon as Amy had bustled on to the next task. Amy offered her own wedding dress, but since her sister-in-law was a good four inches shorter than she was, and rather differently proportioned, Henrietta declined with thanks, and donned the evening gown she had worn the night before. There was a fitting irony, considered Henrietta, to being wed in the same gown in which she had been compromised.

Miles had acquired not only a ring and a license, but the bishop of London, who wore his second-best vestments and the irritable expression of a man who has been dragged out of bed at an hour more commonly used for slumber. A makeshift altar had been constructed in the Long Drawing Room, and chairs set out on either side of the room, which Amy had draped with ribbons and flowers with more enthusiasm than grace. In contrast to their gay decorations, the long rows of chairs looked painfully empty. Instead of the friends and family members who should have filled them sat the two Tholmondelays, looking confused but game, and Mrs. Cathcart, single-handedly doing her best to throw a mantle of respectability over the whole hurried affair.

It should have been her father beside her, escorting her down the aisle, not a brother poised for murder rather than matrimony. Her mother should have been at the front of the room, sporting an outrageous hat, beaming proudly, and ordering everyone about. Her parents. Oh, heavens. What would they even think when she told them she was married, and without their presence or consent? Henrietta was quite sure they would have no objections to her marrying Miles, but the manner of her doing so was designed to enrage even the most tolerant of parents. It was something that didn't bear thinking about.

Henrietta didn't have time to dwell on the absent faces. While Miss Grey plucked out the processional with more precision than passion, Henrietta spent most of her walk down the aisle trying to convince her brother not to murder her bridegroom. After several yards of fruitless argument, she finally succeeded in silencing him by pointing out that he was merely lucky that Amy's brother hadn't been the dueling sort. Since Richard's nuptials had been even more irregular than Henrietta's—performed on a Channel packet by a butler turned pirate—she had him there, and he knew it.

"I'd still rather skewer him," muttered Richard.

"Kindly strive to contain your excessive rapture at my nuptials until after the ceremony," Henrietta hissed back, winning a glower from the bishop and an anxious look from Miles.

Was he anxious that she wouldn't go through with the wedding—or that she would? Henrietta filed that thought away as yet another in the steadily mounting list of things that didn't bear thinking on.

After an undignified tussle when the bishop asked, "Who giveth this woman to be married to this man" (resolved only by Amy stamping on Richard's foot), the rest of the ceremony passed with unseemly haste. Henrietta suspected the bishop had deliberately truncated the ritual, but in her distracted state, she couldn't be entirely sure. In fact, she couldn't be sure about anything. The entire ceremony flitted past her with nightmare vagueness, colors blurring, voices melding, everything blending in a horrific carnival of unreality. The pronouncement that Miles was man to her wife took her by surprise, and she received her new husband's fleeting kiss, which bore absolutely no resemblance to the passionate embraces of the night before, with a certain amount of doubt as to whether what had passed could possibly be binding.

If it weren't for the ring on her finger, Henrietta would have been quite convinced that none of it had happened at all.

After the ceremony, she and Miles fled to his curricle, leaving the Tholmondelays to do justice to the hastily prepared wedding breakfast. "Lobster patties, Fred!" she could hear Ned exclaim enthusiastically to his brother, as Miles handed her up into the carriage. At least someone was enjoying it, thought Henrietta philosophically. Richard looked as though he would rather chew his way through a plate of nettles.

As for Miles . . . It was very hard to tell what Miles was thinking. Henrietta snuck a glance at Miles, who was tooling the ribbons as if he had no other concern in the world but to negotiate his horses around a large rut in the middle of the road. Ever since they had departed from Selwick Hall, Miles had been treating her with unfailing courtesy. He had spread a lap rug over her legs, apologized for the necessity of conveying her to London in an open vehicle, offered to stop for refreshment, and even gone so far as to comment on the weather.

Miles was being polite. Too polite. It made Henrietta nervous.

She darted another lightning look at Miles, only to see his eyes hastily scoot back to the road. Henrietta looked away, but couldn't keep her eyes from slowly sliding back in his direction from under the rim of her bonnet. Miles's scooted the other way, like two characters creeping around walls trying to avoid each other in a Mozartian farce.

If only they had been given time to speak before the wedding! Henrietta wasn't entirely sure what she would have said. Was there ever a delicate way to phrase, "You don't have to marry me if you don't want to"? Of course, even if she had found a way to say it, she knew as well as he that it was pure nonsense. He did have to marry her. She was compromised, ruined, fallen, sullied, soiled. Henrietta was running out of adjectives, but any one of them would have served the purpose.

There was an alternative. Henrietta probed the option delicately, like a sufferer of toothache exploring around the rotting tooth. She would only be ruined if the story escaped the confines of Selwick Hall. Richard and Amy surely wouldn't repeat it to anyone, and Mrs. Cathcart could be counted upon to remain discreet, if not for Henrietta's sake, then for her mother's. As for Miss Grey, she never spoke when she could remain silent. The only danger remaining was the Tholmondelays, and while they didn't possess a brain between them, Henrietta had no doubt either Miles or Richard could instill through fear what might be lacking in intelligence.

Annulment. There, she had said it. They could procure an annulment and then Miles would be free, and no one would ever know what had happened except the parties concerned. Miles could drive in the park with dark beauties, flirt with mysterious marchionesses, and acquire opera singers without the unwanted encumbrance of a wife.

Henrietta made a wry face to herself. She had lived in society long enough to know there was no possible way to keep scandal a secret; it traveled mysteriously through the air, like bubonic plague. Besides, Henrietta wasn't quite sure exactly how one went about obtaining an annulment, but she had no doubt that the process would be lengthy, and involve lots of paper, which would invariably come to the notice of someone who would inevitably tell someone else, and before she knew it, respectable women would be sweeping their skirts away from her in the streets.

There was always the nunnery. They were supposed to specialize in fallen women, weren't they?

By the time they stopped in Croydon to change horses, Henrietta was in such a state of miserable tension that she welcomed the diversion. The courtyard of the Greyhound was already teeming with a variety of equipages, from a crested carriage to a green-and-gold accommodation coach, and the Swan was scarcely less busy.

Assessing the mob with an experienced eye, Miles shook his head, and eased his horses along the High Street.

"We'll try the Potted Hare," he announced. "They might be less crowded."

Henrietta couldn't decide whether he was talking to himself or to her, but she decided that some response was probably a good thing.

"That would be nice."

Under the brim of her bonnet, Henrietta grimaced at the stilted words. How, after eighteen years of fluid bantering and bickering with Miles, had she been reduced to this? She had enjoyed more scintillating exchanges with Turnip Fitzhugh—and Turnip, like the vegetable for which he was named, was not chiefly known for his conversational talents.

Miles, noticing the grimace, drew another conclusion entirely, and drew the horses up with unnecessary force as he drove into the courtyard of the Potted Hare. Flinging the reins to an ostler, Miles jumped down to hand Henrietta out of the carriage.

Instead of moving aside to let her precede him, he stood, frowning down at her. A black traveling chaise scraped to a stop behind them, nearly clipping Miles in passing, and disgorging a dandy in the latest cut of coat, who paused to rearrange his already immaculate cravat. A busy coaching inn, Miles admitted to himself, wasn't the best place to conduct a conversation of a private nature. But something had to be said, and soon, because all the uncharacteristic silence was destined to drive him straight to Bedlam. Pygmalion had contrived to turn a statue into a living, breathing female. He, thought Miles glumly, had somehow managed to turn a living, breathing female into a statue.

"Hen—" he began earnestly, taking her by the shoulders.

"I say! Dorrington!" Whatever Miles had been about to say was lost as a familiar voice hailed them. Without waiting for his coachman to bring his carriage to a full stop, Turnip Fitzhugh tumbled out of his chaise. "I say! This is a spot of luck, finding you here. Would have gone on to the Greyhound, but I saw your curricle in the yard, and thought, I'll dine with Dorrington. Can't abide to dine alone, you know."

Clearly, the powers that be took very negative views of a man seducing his best friend's sister, and had wasted no time in exacting punishment. Miles tried to catch Henrietta's eye to share a glance of commiseration, but what little could be seen of her face beneath her bonnet was flung as deeply into shadow as though she had been wearing a veil.

"Fitzhugh," groaned Miles, dropping his hands and turning to face his old schoolmate.

Turnip gave a start as he noticed Henrietta for the first time, a state of affairs not altogether surprising, as Miles's large form had blocked her from his view.

"Lady Henrietta?" He glanced from Henrietta to Miles with a puzzled expression on his good-natured face. "Didn't see you there! Devil of a fine day for a drive, ain't it?"

Miles held out his arm to Hen, wishing the amiable Turnip to perdition. "Shall we see if we can secure a parlor?" he asked resignedly.

"Capital idea!" enthused Turnip. He turned courteously towards Henrietta's bonnet. "What brings you here, Lady Hen?"

"We were just—" began Miles.

"—in Sussex. With Richard," Henrietta broke in, the tone of her voice forbidding further elaboration.

Miles looked sharply down at Henrietta, but received a poke in the eye from an impudent feather for his pains. He could learn to hate that bonnet.

"What are *you* doing here?" he asked Turnip with no good grace, as their small group progressed through the door of the inn. Behind them, a steady stream of vehicles, pausing on the journey from

Brighton to London, continued to crowd into the yard of the coaching inn, in search of fresh horses and a respite from the rigors of the road.

Turnip beamed and waved his carnation-hemmed handkerchief. "Been in Brighton. With Prinny, you know. Devil of a crush at the Pavilion this weekend."

"When isn't there?" asked Miles, gesturing expansively at the innkeeper, in the hopes that the sooner Turnip was fed, the sooner Turnip would leave. Behind them, a queue of cranky travelers was beginning to form, headed by the slender man who had nearly run Miles down in the yard. Judging from the width of his lapels and height of his shirt collar, he was clearly another one of Prinny's hangers-on, fresh from Brighton. That consideration added extra force to Miles's voice as he grumbled, "I don't know why you subject yourself to it."

"You're joking, right, Dorrington? Can't say I care much for the sea, but the prince's entertainments are all up to the crack. Even had an opera singer perform this weekend! Accompanied by some Italian chap, name that sounded like a noodle. Deuced fine—er—" Turnip glanced uneasily at Henrietta and broke off. "Er, singer," he finished with relief. "Deuced fine singer."

Even Turnip looked relieved at the intrusion of the innkeeper.

Wiping his hands on the large white cloth tied about his waist, that worthy waxed exceedingly apologetic, explaining that his private parlor was already spoken for; as they could see, his inn was full to overflowing due to the prince's entertainments that weekend in Brighton; if the lady and gentlemen did not object, there were still places in the coffee room . . . ?

No one objected: Miles, because he didn't care where they sat, so long as they eventually left; Turnip, because he was still talking; and Henrietta, because she wasn't saying anything at all. Miles was very tempted to tap on the top of that confounded bonnet to inquire if anyone was home, but decided that in her present frame of mind, Henrietta was highly unlikely to respond favorably.

The coffee room was swarming with other travelers tucking into pork pie, brace of duck, and large platters of mutton and potatoes, but Turnip, by dint of some cheerful rearranging, secured them a small table in the corner of the room, and dusted off a seat for Henrietta with his handkerchief, all the while expounding volubly on the beauties of Brighton—female and architectural—the dashed fine singer who had entertained them on Friday night, and the wonders of the prince's waistcoats.

"—with real peacock feathers! Seat, Lady Henrietta?" Turnip flourished the recently dusted chair in the direction of Henrietta.

"Pity the peacock," muttered Miles in the direction of Henrietta, but she didn't so much as chuckle.

Henrietta shook her bonnet in the direction of the proffered chair. "If you'll excuse me for a moment, I need to repair the ravages of travel."

At least, thought Miles, she hadn't lost her vocabulary along with her voice. He just wished she'd use it to speak to him.

On a sudden impulse, Miles reached out a hand and grabbed her gloved wrist. Turnip was mercifully distracted, waving his arms in an attempt to attract the attention of a serving maid and acquire a flagon of porter.

"Hen—" he began.

"Yes?" Henrietta's eyes flew to his, suddenly alert.

Miles sat there, mouth half-open, unable to think of a single thing to say. "You aren't planning to climb out a window, are you?" wasn't really an option. "I hate that bonnet" would be honest, but largely unhelpful. And "Why aren't you speaking to me?" wasn't really something that could either be asked in the presence of Turnip, or that could be furnished with a satisfying answer.

"Would you like me to order some lemonade for you?" he finished lamely.

Henrietta's bonnet brim dropped again. "No, thank you," she said politely.

Damn.

Miles subsided into his seat, cursing the vagaries of human communication, Henrietta's milliner, and Turnip and all his descendants unto the end of time.

As Turnip bantered with the serving maid, Miles watched Henrietta edge her way around the man who had driven in behind them, a pink of the *ton* in tan pantaloons, a leviathan of a cravat, and collar points higher than the Tower of Babel. The dandy paused in the door to stare after Henrietta, the stiffened tails of his coat brushing against the wall. Miles scowled openly at the fellow in the doorway. What business did he have staring at Henrietta? She was taken, quite, quite taken, and if that foppish fellow didn't stop ogling her soon (Miles had a fairly firm notion of what "soon" entailed), Miles would have to make sure he knew it. For a moment, the fop looked like he might actually be about to follow Henrietta—Miles's hand went instinctively to where his sword would have been, were he wearing it—but thought better of it, a decision that Miles silently applauded, and instead strolled over to the fire.

Relaxing his vigil, Miles turned back to Turnip, who was engaged in a merry monologue about the wonders of the Prince of Wales's collection of chinoiserie, in which peacocks seemed to figure significantly. Miles wondered if this meant that Turnip was finally going to stop swathing himself in Pink Carnation paraphernalia, and decided that the image of Turnip as a giant peacock was too alarming a concept to contemplate.

"Copied down the name of Prinny's new tailor for you," Turnip said expansively, extracting a small piece of paper from his tightly fitted waistcoat. He beamed fondly at the little scrap. "You wouldn't believe what that man can do with a waistcoat."

Unfortunately, Miles could. Accepting the scrap of paper, he stuffed it absently away in a waistcoat pocket along with other crumpled bits of this and that, some small change, and a bit of string that was there in case it might ever come in useful.

"There was one patterned with emerald green peacocks with real sapphires set into the tails," rhapsodized Turnip, a reminiscent gleam in his eye. "And another—"

"Did you see Geoff there?" asked Miles, in the hopes of getting Turnip off the topic of peacocks and his wardrobe. Over Turnip's shoulder, the dandy in the complicated cravat edged closer to their table, clearly hoping that if he hovered long enough, they would yield their seats. Miles favored him with his best "clear off" glare, before returning his attention to Turnip.

Turnip shook his head. "Not really Pinchingdale's métier, you know. Didn't see Alsworthy there, either. Thought of stopping by Selwick Hall," added Turnip amiably, reaching for his glass of porter, "but a bit out of the way, you know."

"Not really," countered Miles, thanking whatever conjunction of the planets had kept Turnip from pursuing that course. A rampaging French spy running about the premises garbed as a Phantom Monk was bad enough; to have added Turnip to the mix would have been a sure disaster. Turnip would probably have invited the spy in, complimented him on the cut of his habit, asked him how he thought it would look in pink, and offered him a glass of claret.

"It's only an hour from—" Miles broke off abruptly.

"Not by coach, old chap." Mulling over the matter, Turnip didn't seem to notice that Miles's eyes were bulging and his mouth gaping like an unfortunate highwayman at the end of the hangman's noose. "Took me well near two hours last time from Brighton to Selwick's place."

Miles surged across the table and grabbed his former classmate by the sleeve. "Was Lord Vaughn there?"

"At Selwick's? Can't say that he was. Course, that was over a year ago, and—"

"At *Brighton*," interpolated Miles rather more forcefully than he had intended. "Not last year. This weekend."

Damn, he was really no good at the whole subtle questioning game. More than once, Miles had seen Richard at work on a suspect, spinning information out of a suspect as smoothly as a silkworm his thread, spooling it out, question by question, until he knew everything there was to know.

Fortunately, Turnip, not being the brightest vegetable in the garden, didn't seem to notice his gaffe.

"Vaughn?" Turnip tilted his head in contemplation. "Nice chap. Can't say much for his taste in waistcoats—silver is dashed dull, don't you think?—but he does have a nice way with his cravat. What does he call that style of his again? The Serpent in the Garden? A bit like an Oriental, but there's something about that last twist—"

To the devil with subtlety. Miles had always ascribed more to the "thump them on the head" school himself.

"Brighton," Miles repeated. "Lord Vaughn. Was he there?"

Turnip pondered. "Y'know, believe I did see him at the Pavilion. Intimate of the prince, they say—used to go wenching together back in the eighties."

Having no desire to hear any more about the intimacies of the prince's bedchamber, Miles cut Turnip off. "Do you recall which night it was? That you saw Vaughn, I mean?" Miles hastily specified.

Turnip shrugged. "Might have been Friday . . . or Saturday. Pavilion looks much the same from one night to another, you know! I say, why all this interest in Vaughn? Not a friend of yours, is he?"

"Vaughn has some horseflesh I've a mind to acquire," prevaricated Miles, quite proud of himself for having come up with a story Turnip would find completely credible. "I was hoping to look him up in London, but if he's away . . ."

"His grays?" Turnip asked enthusiastically. "They're bang up to the mark. Prime goers! Didn't know Vaughn was looking to sell. May give you a bit of a run for them myself, old chap."

"You do that," said Miles absently.

Now that he knew Vaughn had been in Brighton . . . Turnip's protests to the contrary, for a man with a swift team of horses and a light carriage, it was a mere hour's run from the Marine Parade to Selwick Hall. In fact, Richard had frequently bemoaned his proximity to the Regent's pleasure palace, citing the congestion of the roads and unexpected visits from the likes of Turnip as causes of complaint. Miles winced at the thought of his best friend—his *former* best friend—and forcibly bent his mind back to Vaughn. If that wasn't proof of Vaughn's guilt, Miles wasn't sure what would be—aside from a large placard proclaiming THE BLACK TULIP SLEPT HERE. There would be no use to turning around and thundering off to Brighton; by now, Vaughn must have been well on his way back to London.

In which case, Miles would be waiting for him. He just had to collect Hen, and they could be off. Where *was* Hen?

Miles cut Turnip off in the midst of a tangled exposition about a pair of chestnuts he had seen at Tattersall's last month. "I wonder what can be keeping Hen?"

Turnip frowned into his glass of porter, shifting his shoulders beneath the rich brocade of his coat and fidgeting on the hard wood of his seat.

"I say, Dorrington," began Turnip uneasily. "Didn't want to say anything before, with Lady Hen present, but it ain't at all the thing for you to be here alone with Lady Henrietta. Reputation and all that. Know you're like a brother to her, but——"

"I'm *not* her brother," snapped Miles, watching the coffee room door. How long could it possibly take for one woman to go to the necessary and back? The young fop in the immense cravat was still standing by the fire, so he didn't have to worry about her being abducted by force, but . . . Hen wouldn't have bolted out a window. Would she?

"Just what I was saying," agreed Turnip, looking relieved that Miles had grasped the crux of the problem so readily. "Don't mean to be Mrs. Grundy, you know, but . . ."

"Trust me," said Miles, frowning at the grandfather clock in the corner of the room, "it is a role for which you are singularly unsuited."

"Oh, you mean not being female?" Turnip considered. "Daresay I would look deuced odd in skirts, though some of those sprigged muslin rig-outs ain't half-bad. Little flowers, you know. But what I meant to say"—Turnip abandoned the fascinating subject of haberdashery to drag himself doggedly back to the topic at hand—"is, that is to say . . ."

Miles dragged his attention away from the door and fixed Turnip with a quelling look. "There is nothing havey-cavey going on between me and Henrietta." Miles twisted in his seat to look anxiously at the coffee room door. "But where *is* she?"

Chapter Twenty-Eight

Havey-Cavey (*adj.*): *highly suspect, clandestine, illicit; behavior generally indicative of some nefarious purpose. To be strictly monitored by the conscientious agent*
—from the Personal Codebook of the Pink Carnation

Tucking her shawl more securely around her shoulders, Henrietta started up the narrow flight of stairs to which she had been directed by a busy maidservant. With only the meager illumination to be had from a window on the landing above, the stairwell was dim, and the well-worn treads dipped in the middle. Henrietta picked her way gingerly up the stairs, but her mind was back downstairs in the coffee room, on a pair of anxious brown eyes.

What had Miles really been about to say? No one, not even Miles, could contrive to look that earnest over a beverage. Henrietta mulled through possible endings to that plaintive "Hen—" She didn't like any of them.

Henrietta sighed and shook her head at herself. She was driving herself to distraction with these futile speculations. Playing a game of "What can Miles be thinking?" was not only fruitless—it was absolutely . . .

". . . maddening!" someone exclaimed.

Henrietta paused, one foot on the landing, one on the penultimate step. It wasn't just that the word exactly encapsulated her own sentiments. She knew that voice. The last time she had heard it, it had been employed in a slumberous murmur of seduction rather than an expression of agitation, but the tones were as unmistakable as they were misplaced.

"You must be patient," counseled another voice, a woman's voice with a light foreign accent. Even the wooden barrier of the door couldn't quite detract from the fluid charm of it; although she spoke softly, every tone was as finely hued as a delicately painted piece of porcelain. "You do no good to yourself by this, Sebastian."

Henrietta was so surprised that Lord Vaughn was in possession of a first name that she nearly missed hearing what came next.

"Ten years." Lord Vaughn's cultured voice thrummed with frustration through the chinks in the door. "It has been ten years, Aurelia. What sort of paragon would you have me be, to practice patience for that long?"

Henrietta engaged in rapid mental mathematics. A decade . . . 1793. The little gossip she had managed to glean about Vaughn had been maddeningly imprecise, but the year might coincide with his precipitate departure from England.

It was also, recalled Henrietta, the year the French king had been dragged beneath the blade of the guillotine. Which one was it? Or were they related?

"If so long, why not a little longer?" replied the other.

Lord Vaughn—Henrietta really couldn't think of him as Sebastian, whatever the mysterious woman might call him—drawled something in a low tone that was lost somewhere between the door and Henrietta's ear. Whatever it was, it elicited an intimate chuckle from his companion.

"I do not think"—the accent was very much in the ascendant, as was the affectionate note of laughter—"that a paragon should speak so."

Vaughn's voice again, quick and impatient. "Are you quite certain there was nothing else there?"

Nothing else where? Henrietta frowned at the uninformative

wooden panels of the door, wishing there was some way she could get closer, some way she could see.

There was a swish of fabric, as though someone had just subsided into a chair. "I made the inspection of his belongings with much thoroughness. And most unpleasant it was, too," the woman's voice added tartly.

Richard's belongings, perhaps? Henrietta listened with all her might, willing the conspirators to speak further.

Henrietta heard boots on bare wood as Vaughn strolled across the room, followed by the sound of lips meeting—a hand? Lips? Henrietta couldn't tell. Vaughn spoke, voice heavy with rue and reluctant charm. "Forgive me, Aurelia. I am an ungrateful beast."

Blast. Henrietta scowled at the door. Now he chose to apologize?

"I know," replied the other complacently, and equally uninformatively. "But you have your compensations."

"Most of them measured by guineas," Vaughn replied dryly.

"If I were any other woman," the accented voice chided gently, "I would take offense at that."

"If you were any other woman," countered Vaughn, "I would not have said it." There was a pregnant pause, a rustle of fabric that might have been an embrace, or merely the woman shifting in her chair— Henrietta cursed her sightless state—before Vaughn resumed, his tone brisk. "I leave for Paris on Tuesday."

"Are you sure that is wise, *caro*?"

"I would have an end to this business, Aurelia. The game has been played for long enough." Vaughn's voice rang with grim finality, sending a reluctant shiver through Henrietta's thick shawl. So might Beowulf have sounded outside Grendel's den, girding himself for havoc and death. "The time is come to behead the Hydra."

"You don't know that it is she." The soft soprano voice made one last attempt.

"Everything points to it." Vaughn's tone brooked no argument.

Everything pointed to what? To whom? Henrietta shifted her weight to the top step to press her ear more firmly against the door frame. The elderly step shifted and groaned, protesting her weight.

Booted feet clipped towards the door, clicking ominously against the bare planking.

"Did you hear that?"

Henrietta froze, one hand on the wall.

"What am I meant to be hearing, *caro*?"

"Someone. By the door."

"This old building, it is full of the creaks. You are too imaginative, my friend," the lightly accented voice chided affectionately. "You quarrel with shadows."

"My shadows carry swords."

Vaughn punctuated his words with a staccato flurry of footsteps.

Henrietta didn't wait to hear more. She careened down the stairs in reckless haste, clinging to the banister as she all but fell down the last three steps. She flung herself around the turn of the wall just as, at the top of the stairs, a door creaked open.

Pressed against the wall, panting, Henrietta heard Vaughn's muttered curse, and a warm female voice say, "Did I not tell you it would be so? Come, sit by me, and leave the shadows to their rest for an hour."

He couldn't find them there.

Henrietta's mind raced in tandem with her rapidly beating heart. If Vaughn had been searching Richard's study . . . If the "she" to whom he had referred was somehow, incomprehensibly, Jane . . . If— Henrietta mustered the greatest, most alarming "if " of all—if Vaughn was the Black Tulip, they must get away before he knew they had been there.

Vaughn had said he wasn't leaving till Tuesday. If he were the diabolically clever Black Tulip, he might have been deliberately laying false clues, but Henrietta didn't think his alarm at hearing a footstep outside the door had been feigned. Their best chance was to return to London and inform the War Office of everything that had transpired and allow them to take the appropriate steps.

Tearing into the coffee room, narrowly avoiding a slender man in an immense cravat, wearing a high-crowned black hat pulled low over his ears, Henrietta grabbed Miles by the arm and tugged. "I really think we ought to go now."

Miles looked at her quizzically. "The food only just arrived."

Henrietta cast him a look of urgent appeal. "Please? I'll explain in the carriage."

Miles shrugged, bemused but game. "Righty-ho, then."

Rising, he stretched—Henrietta gave an agitated little hop—snagged his hat and gloves from the chair beside him—*"Come on, come on,"* urged Henrietta under her breath—and tossed a few coins on the table.

"That ought to cover it."

"But—" began Turnip, gesturing inarticulately to the platters and jugs arrayed before them.

"Sorry, Fitzhugh"—Miles paused in the doorway to wave his hat in the direction of his friend—"must be going."

Miles abruptly staggered out of view from the doorframe as Henrietta applied pressure to his arm.

"Havey-cavey," muttered Turnip, shaking his head after them. He speared a piece of mutton and regarded it fiercely. "Deuced havey-cavey!"

Henrietta chivvied Miles out into the yard, glancing anxiously behind them as Miles sent for the curricle. There was no sign of Vaughn in the doorway, or lurking around the sides of the building (Henrietta hadn't discounted the possibility of other exits) or at the windows above their heads. Only the dandy in the absurd cravat had strolled out behind them, yawning in the afternoon sunlight as he waited for his carriage and team to be brought about. There was something vaguely familiar about the man, but Henrietta didn't have time to waste chasing memory to its lair. Undoubtedly one of the many chinless wonders with whom she had stood up at the series of endless events that composed her two and a half Seasons on the marriage market.

"You seem to have acquired an admirer," Miles commented shortly, boosting her into the curricle. He paused to glower at the man in the doorway, who continued to admire his own stickpin, supremely unconcerned.

"Hurry," urged Henrietta. As if to back her up, the horses, a new team, pranced restlessly in their harness as the ostler handed off the reins to Miles.

Miles slapped the horses into motion. "Do you care to explain what's going on?"

Henrietta flapped an agitated hand at him, twisting to stare over the folding back of the curricle at the rapidly receding inn yard. "Later!"

Since it took Miles several moments to get the measure of the new team, and Henrietta seemed more inclined to squirm in her seat and cast anguished glances behind them than speak, it was several moments before Miles broached the topic again.

"Not that I mind being bereft of Turnip's company," said Miles, steering his way expertly around two hens that had decided to cross the road, "but why the sudden desire to leave? Dare I hope it was a passionate desire to be alone with me?" His eyebrows drew together. "Was that man bothering you? If he was, I—"

"No, nothing like that." Henrietta cast a haunted look back over her shoulder. A black post chaise, clearly a private vehicle, although a well-worn one, tooled along the road behind them, but it was far enough away to ensure them a modicum of privacy. Nonetheless, just to be safe, Henrietta hunched towards Miles and lowered her voice for greater secrecy. "There was something suspicious going on back there."

Miles grimaced. "Something about a propitious dancing bear?"

Maybe her voice hadn't needed to be quite *that* low.

Henrietta started again. "When I went upstairs, I overheard Lord Vaughn in the private parlor."

Miles shot up in his seat. "What!"

Since Henrietta had been speaking quite clearly that time, she correctly assumed that Miles's exclamation had more to do with surprise than lack of comprehension. "He was speaking with a woman with a foreign accent—it was a very light accent, but still noticeable."

Miles smacked one gloved hand against the side of the curricle. "Fiorila!"

"Flowers?" said Henrietta, perplexed.

"Poisonous ones." Miles hauled on the reins, preparing to bring the carriage about. "Why didn't you tell me before we left?"

"Shhh!" exclaimed Henrietta, glancing anxiously behind them. The other carriage had also checked.

"I don't think they can hear us." Reluctantly, Miles slapped the reins, signaling the horses to go forward. "It's probably too late to go back," he said, more to himself than to her. "Vaughn and his companion will have flown the coop by now. Damnation! If I'd known—"

"That's exactly why I didn't tell you. It just didn't seem like a good idea." Henrietta struggled to rationalize her impulse. "We don't know who he had with him—"

"Oh, I have a very good idea of that," Miles muttered.

"—or if he was armed," continued Henrietta pointedly. "If he is the Black Tulip, doesn't it make far more sense to apprehend him in London, with all the might of the War Office at your disposal, rather than out in the middle of nowhere? For all we know, the inn might have been swarming with his men! Or he might not even be the Black Tulip," she added as an afterthought. "Something didn't sound quite right."

"Ungh" was what Miles thought of that reservation, but he grudgingly admitted the validity of the former. "I'll go see Wickham tomorrow morning."

"Why not tonight?" asked Henrietta.

"Because tonight"—Miles raised a pair of sandy eyebrows—"is my wedding night."

Henrietta discovered a sudden interest in the scenery.

Wedding night, thought Henrietta, staring unseeingly at Streatham Common. That was what generally followed a wedding. Usually at night. Hence the term "wedding night," which combined the concepts of both wedding and night.

Henrietta bit down hard on her lip, making a concerted effort to rein in her wayward mind before she launched into a long and tangled analysis of wedding customs from the Anglo-Saxons to the present, and what exactly the etymology of the word "night" might be.

The origin of the word "evasion," she thought, glowering at a cow grazing on the Common, would be more to the point.

There were so many thoughts to evade that Henrietta didn't even know where to begin. Did Miles's mention of the wedding night mean that he intended to go through with the marriage? Or was he bringing up the topic in the hopes that she would broach the ridiculousness of their remaining married? His face had been as inscrutable as it was possible for Miles's face to be. He hadn't looked particularly put out at the notion of consummating their marriage—he hadn't sounded bitter or resigned or angry, or any of the other sentiments one might expect of a reluctant bridegroom—but he hadn't seemed particularly enthused, either.

Bleargh.

Miles reined in slightly to allow a farmer's cart to pass. The carriage behind them reined in, too. Henrietta frowned.

"Miles?" Henrietta asked uneasily. "Am I imagining things, or has that carriage been behind us for a very long time?"

Miles shrugged, unconcerned. "It might have been. It wouldn't be surprising if it were. Now, about Vaughn . . ."

Henrietta twisted in her seat to stare back at the carriage. "But don't you find it the least bit odd that they rein in every time you do?"

"What?" Miles twisted sharply in his seat, inadvertently giving a sharp tug on the reins. His horses checked abruptly.

So did the horses of the carriage behind him.

"What the devil!" exclaimed Miles, subsiding back into his seat.

"Exactly." Henrietta drew in a sharp breath between her teeth. "I don't like this."

"Neither do I," said Miles.

He shoved the ribbons into her gloved hands.

"Here, take the reins for a moment. I want to take another look."

Taken aback, Henrietta grappled with the four sets of ribbons Miles had handed her, trying to figure out which was which, as Miles clambered over the back of the seat. Sensing an inexperienced hand on the reins, the horses lurched alarmingly. Miles paused, balanced on the top of the seat, facing backwards.

"Just hold them steady, Hen," he directed, leaping nimbly onto the perch usually reserved for a groom. The curricle rocked dangerously.

"Just hold them steady?!" repeated Henrietta incredulously, struggling to keep the right leader in line. He showed a distressing tendency to try to veer off to the side. It had been a long time since Henrietta had driven anything but Miles's phaeton, and that at the sedate pace mandated by the congestion of the park. She tugged fruitlessly at the reins as the carriage swayed to the right. "Miles! Please try not to overturn us!"

"Damn."

"What?" Every muscle in Henrietta's body tensed, but she didn't dare take her attention from the road. "What is it?"

Miles vaulted back into his seat, taking the reins from her with a practiced hand. "You're not going to like this," he said, urging the team forward and drawing the recalcitrant leader effortlessly back into line.

"What?" Henrietta demanded.

"They," Miles said, cracking the whip with ruthless efficiency, just as a crack of another kind entirely sounded behind them, "have a gun."

Chapter Twenty-Nine

Elopement: *a desperate attempt at flight, usually pursued by one or more members of Bonaparte's secret police. See also under* Parent, Vengeful

—from the Personal Codebook of the Pink Carnation

Another bullet whizzed past, this time driving a long furrow into the polished exterior of the vehicle.

"My curricle!" exclaimed Miles indignantly. "I just had it polished!"

Doubled over at the waist, Henrietta rather thought that was the least of their problems, but she wasn't going to argue about it. She didn't have the breath to argue about it.

"Right." Miles hunched low over the reins, his face a model of steely determination. "That's it. I'm going to give that bounder the ride of his life."

"You mean you weren't already?" gasped Henrietta, clinging to her bonnet with one hand and the seat with the other.

"That was just a little jog!" Miles cracked the reins, a look of unholy glee transforming his face. "Come on, my beauties! You can do it!"

As if seized of the same spirit, the four horses broke into a full-out gallop. Henrietta abandoned her bonnet to devote both hands to clutching the seat. The rebellious piece of haberdashery instantly blew back off her head with a force that betokened imminent strangulation.

"That's the spirit!" Henrietta wasn't sure whether Miles was talking to her or his horses, but she supposed the latter, especially when he jerked his head briefly in her direction and shouted, "You all right, Hen?"

Henrietta mustered a slightly strangled noise of assent, just as the carriage hit a rut, sending the body of the curricle bounding merrily into the air, and landing with a thump that jarred through Henrietta's entire body.

Henrietta was distracted from her mere physical irritation by an ominous rattling noise. Beneath her, the right wheel of the two-wheeled vehicle was shaking in a way that boded no good to the continued stability of the whole. Henrietta's gloved hands went rigid on the side of the curricle as she peered, openmouthed with alarm, at the quivering wheel.

If she were a villain intent on wreaking doom and destruction—and the pistol shots did rather seem to point in that direction—wasn't tampering with the carriage too obvious a source of mayhem to neglect? They had been in the inn with Turnip for such a very long time. There had been so many carriages and people milling about in the courtyard of the inn that none of the harried grooms or ostlers would have paid the least bit of attention to someone paying undue attention to any one vehicle. And Miles's curricle was so distinctive amongst all the plain black carriages and grimy hired post chaises. Henrietta's knowledge of carriage construction was minimal in the extreme, but how hard could it be to loosen a wheel? It would be the work of a moment to kneel by the side of the carriage and slide back the pin. And at speeds like this . . .

The carriage hit another rut, sending Henrietta jouncing into the air, and the wheel shaking in a way that foretold imminent disaster.

"Miles!" Henrietta clutched Miles's arm. "The wheels!"

"Hunh?" Miles glanced rapidly over at her.

"The rattling noise," Henrietta gasped. "Someone must have loosened the wheels!"

"Oh, that!" Miles beamed at her in a way entirely inappropriate for someone courting violent death. "That's just the noise it makes when it's going fast," he explained happily.

They whizzed past the astonished toll keeper at Kennington Turnpike so fast that he had no time to do more than shake his fist at them as they barreled through. "I say! Hen!" shouted Miles over the din of the horses' hooves. "Could you check if he's still behind us?"

Clinging to her place through pure force of will, Henrietta turned an incredulous stare at her husband. Her bonnet whacked her in the face, but Henrietta didn't dare lift a hand to push it back. "If you think I'm letting go and turning around, you're crazy!"

"Don't worry!" yelled Miles. "I'll lose him as soon as we cross Westminster Bridge!"

"If we live that long!"

"What?"

"Never mind!"

"Whaaaat?"

"*I said*—oh, never mind," Henrietta muttered. That was the problem with snide comments; they invariably lost all their punch on repetition. Besides, when facing impending death, what did the odd witticism matter?

Despite her words, Henrietta craned her head around to look behind. Their adversary must have wasted no more time at the toll than they; he was still behind and gaining, black horses covering the ground in long strides.

Westminster Bridge had come into sight, a long arch across the span of the river, crowded with evening traffic. There were pedestrians walking along the balustrades in the twilight, farmers leading their wagons back from market, gentlemen on horseback riding out to nefarious pleasures in the suburbs of the city, and mules laden with yesterday's baking.

Miles and Henrietta barreled into the whole like a cat among pigeons. Henrietta felt the jarring thud beneath them as the carriage sprang from springy turf onto hard stone. Horses shied, bolting for cover. Merchants hurriedly yanked their carts off to the sides of the bridge. Pedestrians flung themselves as far as they could go against the stone railings. Around them, the air was thick with complaints and curses, and behind them, the determined clip of horses plowing straight towards them, thundering along the smooth length of the bridge after them. Henrietta closed her eyes and prayed.

Never entirely steady on its foundations, the bridge swayed alarmingly. Henrietta opened her eyes and wished she hadn't. Below them churned the dark waters of the Thames, dotted with rapidly moving boats like so many water bugs scurrying to and fro. If Miles lost control of the horses, even for a moment, the balustrades would do nothing to check their precipitate descent into the foaming currents.

The horses were still running full out, straight down the center of the bridge; whether Miles was driving them, or they were bolting, Henrietta wasn't entirely sure. Head turned to the side, Henrietta counted arches as they whizzed by. They were past the halfway mark, still going strong straight down the middle of the bridge.

A shout made her jerk her head back to the road. Someone screamed. Henrietta wasn't quite sure, but she thought it might have been she.

Smack in the center of a bridge a cart full of cabbages blocked the way. Its owner, wide-eyed with terror, tugged at the mule's head, futilely entreating him to move. The curricle barreled inexorably closer. Three yards . . . two . . . The wild-eyed farmer dropped the reins and scrambled for cover. The mule didn't budge.

"Oh, my God," breathed Henrietta.

Next to her, Miles drew in an exultant breath. "Just the thing! Hang on, Hen . . ."

Henrietta had heard of driving to an inch, but she had never seen it performed quite so literally before. At the last possible moment, Miles swung the horses to the side in a concerted movement that would have been beautiful in its sheer coordination if Henrietta hadn't been trying quite so hard not to fall out the side of the coach. Moving perfectly in tandem, the horses swept around the side of the cart, passing so neatly through the narrow space that Henrietta could hear the wood of the cart whisper along one side of the curricle and the stone of the balustrade on the other.

Miles muttered something under his breath that sounded like, "My varnish," but Henrietta was too busy ushering up fervent thanks to the Almighty to be quite sure.

And then they were clear again, with an unimpeded path to the edge of the bridge. Miles cracked his whip over his head with an uninhibited shout of triumph.

"Watch this, Hen!" he shouted, as the curricle careened off the bridge and veered sharply to the left—just as the carriage behind them, going too fast to stop, and without enough skill to employ Miles's maneuver, slammed right into the farmer's deserted cart with an explosive crash. Cabbages flew everywhere. A hail of green balls descended upon the passersby and plopped into the greedy mouth of the Thames.

Henrietta caught the merest glimpse of their assailant's carriage, piled high with produce, before Miles flicked the reins again and plunged into a shadowed side street just wide enough to admit the curricle. As it was, the scraped sides brushed against lines of laundry, and the overhangs of the upper stories formed a dark canopy above Henrietta's head. Miles took them down an intricate web of back streets, while Henrietta concentrated on coaching air back into her lungs. As the landscape began to appear more familiar, the streets broader, the houses wider, Miles let the lathered horses slow to an exhausted shuffle.

Henrietta forced her gloved hands to unclench from the sides of the seat, finger by finger.

"Are we . . . safe, do you think?" she asked, blinking unsteadily at their surroundings. She pressed her fingers to her eyes, wondering if it was the twilight that rendered Grosvenor Square so murky and insubstantial, or her vision. The gray-fronted mansions swayed as though they were phantoms composed of fog and might dissolve at any moment, while the trees in the center of the square melded together into an indistinguishable blur of green and brown.

"He won't have followed us here," Miles said, drawing the horses to a stop in front of a wide-fronted mansion, a command the tired horses were only too glad to obey. Miles couldn't stop a satisfied smirk from creeping across his face as he added, "It will take him a while to climb out from under all that cabbage."

"That was quite impressive," said Henrietta shakily. "Especially that bit with the cart."

Miles gave his whip a modest twirl. "There was plenty of room."

"And I hope never to be in a carriage with you when you drive like that ever again." Miles's whip stopped midtwirl. "I thought I was going to be ill. Or dead," she added as an afterthought.

"Didn't you trust my driving?" Miles asked indignantly.

"Oh, I trust you. It was the man with the gun who worried me. Somehow, I didn't think he would be quite so solicitous of my well-being." Starting to shake, Henrietta raised both her hands to her lips. "Someone just shot at us. Do you realize that someone just shot at us?"

Making a muffled noise of concern, Miles dragged Henrietta into his arms. Henrietta went without argument, burying her head in Miles's cravat while a series of nightmare images flashed through her head, faster than the scenery they had charged through on their heedless flight. That dark, faceless carriage pounding after them. The long muzzle of a gun, glinting in the last rays of the sunlight. The sound of bullets, sending up puffs of dust in the road behind them, and chipping at the sides of the curricle. Henrietta's unregenerate imagination presented her with the image of Miles jerking back as a bullet thudded into him, stiffening, and tumbling over the side of the curricle into the wayside dust, his brown eyes open in an unseeing stare. Henrietta realized she was shaking, and couldn't make herself stop. If any one of those bullets had been just a little closer . . .

Henrietta gazed at Miles with anguished eyes. "You could have died!" She thought for a moment, and frowned. "I could have died."

"But we didn't," Miles said soothingly. "See? We're both alive. No bullet holes." He raised an arm to demonstrate, and saw that there was, in fact, a neat round hole in the folded canopy behind him. Miles hastily leaned back against the offending awning, hoping Henrietta hadn't noticed. That had been closer than he'd thought. Whoever it had been in the carriage behind them—and Miles had a damned good idea—was a devil of a shot.

"Oh, goodness," whispered Henrietta, staring at a long furrow along the side of the curricle, right next to Miles's arm.

"Don't." Miles squished her head into his chest. "Don't think about it. Think about"—he was seized by sudden inspiration—"cabbages!"

That won him a startled giggle.

"How many French spies do you think are brought down by vegetables?" he continued, expanding on his theme. "We could make a career of it! Next time onions, then carrots, maybe a few lima beans . . ."

"Don't forget the turnips." Henrietta tipped her head up at him and drew a shaky breath. "Thank you."

"Think nothing of it," said Miles, smoothing a strand of hair off her face.

"I'm all right now," Henrietta said resolutely, pulling away and sitting up straight. "Really, I am. I'm sorry to behave like such a . . ."

"Girl?" Miles grinned.

"That," said Henrietta sternly, "was unnecessary."

For a moment, they smiled at each other in complete accord, wrapped in the comfortable familiarity of old patterns. It was unclear how long they might have sat like that had a groom not appeared, asking Miles if he wished his horses to be led away to the stables.

Henrietta's smile faded, and she looked up at the house and back at Miles with some confusion. The house was virtually indistinguishable from many of the others in the Square, a vast classical pile with a rusticated foundation, and wide pilasters supporting a triangular pediment. Flambeaux blazed on either side of the door, but the windows above stairs were all dark, the dark of a house long shut up. All the drapes were drawn, and the front door had an unused air. The only sign of habitation came from below stairs, where a faint light gleamed from the sunken windows.

It wasn't Uppington House, and it certainly was not Miles's bachelor lodgings in Jermyn Street.

Yet the groom knew Miles, had greeted him by name.

Henrietta's tired mind absolutely refused to grapple with this latest puzzle. She allowed herself to be helped down from the curricle, looking to Miles in bewilderment. "Where are we?"

"Loring House," announced Miles, tossing a coin to the groom, and offering Henrietta his arm.

"Loring House?" echoed Henrietta.

"You know, the ancestral home? Well, not that ancestral. There used to be a house on the Strand, but we lost that one in the Civil War."

"But . . ." Henrietta fumbled for words, fearing that being jounced around in the carriage had done permanent damage to her mental capacities, because she was having a great deal of trouble making sense of the situation. She stopped just before the front steps. "Aren't we going to your lodgings?"

"I thought about it"—Miles stuck his hands in his pockets—"but I couldn't take you there."

Henrietta's heart sank.

"You couldn't?" she said neutrally, wondering if it might not have been better just to have been shot back at Streatham Common and have done with it. At least then, Miles could have borne her broken body in his manly arms. Hmph. Henrietta abandoned the image. Knowing her, she would probably have contrived only to be wounded, and would have been cranky and in pain, and there would have been nothing the least bit romantic about it.

Miles squared his shoulders, which, given the breadth of his shoulders, was an impressive sight to behold, and one to which Henrietta, even in her state of confusion, could not be completely immune.

"They're not bad as bachelor lodgings go, and Downey keeps things tip-top, but—you would be out of place. They're not what you're used to."

"But—" began Henrietta, and then checked herself, biting down on the impulse to protest that wherever he was would be a home to her. If he was looking for excuses, reasons to be rid of her, it would be far more graceful just to accede and let him take her home. But why hadn't he taken her to Uppington House?

Some of the strain evident in Miles's face eased as he grinned unwillingly at her. "Hear me out before you argue with me, all right?"

Henrietta's heart clenched at the affectionate tone, and she nodded mutely, not trusting herself to speak.

"I couldn't take you to Jermyn Street, because Turnip would be right. It would be havey-cavey. It would smack of . . ." Miles waved a hand helplessly in the air.

"Elopement?" supplied Henrietta numbly.

"Exactly. Hiding out in hired rooms . . . it would just be all wrong. You deserve a real home, not shoddy hired rooms."

"But why here?" she asked. Was he planning to put her up in Loring House for the night before conveying her back to her family for the inevitable conflagration? She supposed she could always go to Europe for a bit until the resulting scandal died down. . . . The nunnery was beginning to look very attractive again.

"Well"—Miles stuck his hands in his pockets and leaned back against the railing in his favorite pose, looking painfully boyish—"I couldn't very well take you back to Uppington House, and it might have taken a while to find a suitable townhouse to let. And my parents are never here to use this old pile, so . . . welcome home."

"Home?"

Miles began to look a little worried. "The furnishings are probably a bit out-of-date, but the house itself isn't that bad. It will need some cleaning up, but at least there's plenty of room, and—"

"You mean you don't want an annulment?" Henrietta blurted out.

"What?" exclaimed Miles, staring at her with evident confusion. "What are you talking about?"

"Oh," said Henrietta, feeling about two inches tall and wishing there were a convenient toadstool she could crawl under. "Never mind, then."

"Hen." Miles put a hand beneath her chin and tipped her face up towards his, looking earnestly down at her. Henrietta didn't even want to think what she must look like, her face streaked with dust and grime from the road, her hair a snarled mess. "I have a proposition to put to you."

"Yes?" she said hesitantly, wishing she didn't look quite so much like Medusa after a particularly violent rampage.

"A sort of favor," Miles continued. "Not just for me, but for both of us."

Henrietta waited in silence, nerves stretched to the breaking point. She wasn't even going to venture to guess. Bad things happened when she did that. Like annulments and toadstools and cabbages.

"I know this hasn't been the most"—Miles cast about for words— "regular of courtships. But, if you think you can manage it, I'd like to put the manner of our marriage behind us. After all, we have more of a chance than most couples. We rub along fairly well together. And we like each other. That's more than most marriages have to start out with." Miles's hands dropped from her face to her shoulders, holding her just far enough away so he could see her face. "What do you say?"

What Henrietta wanted to say wasn't easily translated into words. Part of her was basking in sheer relief. Having braced herself all day for the moment when Miles would present all sorts of excellent arguments for the dissolution of their marriage, having him entreat for the contrary took her completely by surprise.

And yet . . . yet . . . there was a sting to it. It was kind, and it was sensible, but how meager kind and sensible felt. Henrietta certainly had no hopes for effusive declarations, but, in an inexplicable way, the luke-warm affections Miles had invoked were almost more hurtful than an outright repudiation. A line from an old poem flitted through her head: "Give me more love or more disdain, the torrid or the frozen zone." She had never understood it then, but now she did; love or disdain, at least either stirred the passions. But, oh, to be treated by the object of one's adoration with temperate fondness! It blighted any romantic illusions more surely than an outright rejection.

Gazing wordlessly into Miles's earnest brown eyes, Henrietta felt very small and very vulnerable. But it was, after all, not his fault if she didn't inspire him with burning passion, and he was doing his utmost to make the best of an awkward situation—which was more than she was doing. Henrietta gathered her scattered wits together. What Miles proposed was eminently sensible. And she was, she thought to herself wryly, always sensible. It wasn't ideal, but it was better than nothing. And maybe . . . in time . . . Henrietta squelched that thought before it could grow up. She was letting herself in for enough heartbreak as it was.

"Yes," she said tentatively. "Yes. I'd like that."

Miles let out a gusty sigh of relief. "You won't regret it, Hen." With one exuberant movement, he swooped down and whisked Henrietta into his arms.

"What"—Henrietta clung to his neck for dear life as he bounded up the front steps two at a time—"on earth do you think you're doing?"

Miles grinned rakishly. "Carrying my wife over the threshold, what else?"

Chapter Thirty

——— ◊ ———

Nuptials: *an alliance between interested parties for the furtherance of a mutual goal*
          —from the Personal Codebook of the Pink Carnation

"The threshold appears to be closed," pointed out Henrietta.

"So little faith," complained Miles. "Watch and learn."

"If you even *think* of using me as a battering ram . . . ," warned Henrietta, as Miles lifted a booted foot and rammed it hard against the door.

On the third kick, the door flew open, propelled by an indignant individual with white hair growing in tufts from either side of his forehead like the horns of an untidy devil.

"In *civilized* establishments . . . ," he began strongly, chest puffing out to alarming proportions, before he registered the identity of the heedless hoodlum who had been battering at the hallowed portals of Loring House. Henrietta, held horizontal at just that level, watched with fascination as the irate personage's chest abruptly deflated. "Master Miles! Master Miles?"

The butler's eyes flew from Miles to Henrietta and back to Miles in a state of evident alarm. *The Loyal Retainer's Guide to Better Buttling*, while excellent with regard to tips for polishing silver and removing the cloaks of foreign dignitaries, was highly unclear as to the proper protocol for receiving prodigal sons and prone women.

"Hullo, Stwyth," said Miles exuberantly, not in the least bit daunted. Henrietta resisted the urge to hide under his cravat. "This is your new mistress, Lady Henrietta."

Henrietta gave a sheepish little wave as Miles bore her triumphantly across the threshold beneath the nose of the flabbergasted butler.

"Stwyth?" she whispered to Miles.

"He's from Wales," Miles whispered back. "They haven't discovered vowels yet."

"My lady," stuttered Stwyth. "Sir. We weren't informed of your arrival. Your rooms . . . the house . . . we didn't know . . ."

"That's all right, Stwyth. Neither did I," Miles tossed back nonchalantly over his shoulder as he strode towards the stairs. "But we'll be staying here from now on."

The butler hastily gathered the tattered shreds of his composure, drawing himself up to his full height, which was somewhat shorter than Henrietta's, or what Henrietta's would have been, had she not been dangling several feet off the ground. Henrietta tried to remedy that fact by dint of rolling sideways, but Miles held firm.

"May I say, sir, on behalf of the entire staff," announced Stwyth, trotting along behind, "how delighted we are that you have finally decided to make your home at Loring House."

"You may," acceded Miles, starting up the stairs, Henrietta squished firmly against his chest, "but preferably some other time. You can go, Stwyth. Go . . ." What did butlers do when they weren't opening doors? "Go buttle."

Under the crook of Miles's arm, Henrietta saw Stwyth's rigid features curve into what, in a lesser mortal, would have been a grin.

"Indeed, sir," he intoned, and bowed himself hastily out of the hall.

Henrietta turned bright red and banged her head against Miles's cravat. "Oh dear," she moaned. "He knows."

"Hen?" Miles jiggled her to make her look up. "We're married. It's allowed."

"I still don't really feel married," admitted Henrietta.

"We can work on that," said Miles, kicking open a door at the head of the stairs. "In fact, we will definitely work on that."

The door opened onto a small room furnished with a writing desk and several delicate chairs. It was hard to tell what else the room might contain, because the drapes were drawn, and most of the furniture shrouded in Holland covers to protect against dust and the ravages of time.

Miles backed out again. "Damn. Wrong room."

"Shouldn't you put me down?" asked Henrietta plaintively, as her dangling feet narrowly escaped amputation on the doorframe.

"Only"—Miles leered dramatically down at her—"once I've found a bed."

Just in case she had any ideas of escaping, Miles boosted her higher into the air. Henrietta let out a squeal of protest and clasped her arms more firmly around his neck. "Don't drop me!" she demanded, laughing.

"That's more like it," said Miles with great satisfaction, hefting her happily in his arms. His voice softened. "I like it when you laugh."

Something in his expression made Henrietta's throat tighten. "With you, or at you?" she quipped uneasily.

"Near me," Miles said, tightening his hold on her. He rubbed his cheek against her hair. "Definitely near me."

"I think that could be arranged," Henrietta managed, doing her utmost to refrain from blurting out embarrassing declarations of love that could only alarm Miles and put an end to their precarious entente.

"I think it already has been," Miles countered, striding down the hall. "Or didn't you hear that bit this morning?"

"I was a bit distracted."

Miles sobered. "I noticed. But," he said firmly, stopping in front of a door at the end of the hall, "we are not going to think about any of that tonight. Tonight, there is just us. No French spies, no angry relatives. Agreed?"

Henrietta was quite sure there was a flaw in that plan somewhere, a rather large flaw, having to do with someone chasing them while hurling bullets in their direction, but it was very hard to think logically when Miles looked at her like that, his brown eyes intent on hers. He was so close that she could see the little crinkle at the sides of his eyes, crinkles caused by a lifetime of smiles, and the darker hue of his hair near the brow where the sun hadn't touched it.

"Do I have any choice in the matter?" asked Henrietta with mock solemnity, wishing her voice didn't sound quite so breathless.

"You did promise to obey." Miles tipped her towards the doorknob. "Would you mind getting that, please? My hands are full."

"I'm not sure I would exactly call that a promise," Henrietta hedged, obediently leaning over and turning the doorknob. "It was really more of a . . . um . . ."

"Promise," reiterated Miles smugly, shouldering open the door and edging sideways into the room. It smelled of dust and disuse, but in the light from the hallway, he could see that it contained the crucial item: a bed.

"Strongly worded suggestion," Henrietta finished triumphantly, tipping her face up towards his with an expression that dared him to try to top that.

"So what you're saying," said Miles, with a mischievous glint in his eye that Henrietta knew of old, combined with something new and infinitely more unsettling, "is that I have to find other ways of making you cooperate."

"Ye-es," said Henrietta, noticing slightly uneasily that they were rapidly approaching the bed. Beds and wedding nights did tend to go together. She tried to look as though being borne off to a very large bed were a commonplace occurrence.

Which, she thought with a slight pang of jealousy, for the marquise it probably was. Whether the marquise had been borne off by Miles was too distressing a question for Henrietta to consider.

"What did you have in mind?" she asked instead.

"This," said Miles, and kissed her before she could say anything else, kicking the door closed behind them.

As a technique for inducing cooperation, it had much to recommend it. By the time Miles lifted his mouth from hers, Henrietta was having a very hard time remembering what they had been sparring about in the first place. She wasn't even entirely sure about her own name.

"But . . . ," she began dazedly, since Miles couldn't be allowed to have the last word—or the last kiss.

Miles grinned roguishly. "Not convinced yet?" he asked rhetorically, and kissed her again, a kiss that made its predecessor feel like a discreet peck in a drawing room. His arms were warm and tight around her, pressing her so closely that Henrietta lost all sense of where her body left off and his began. The rising heat between them burned layers of clothes into nothingness. Henrietta's senses were filled with Miles; the scent of his hair and his skin, the sensation of his tongue filling her mouth, sealing her lips to his, the press of his waistcoat buttons against her side, and the prickle of his hair beneath her fingers, all melded into a complete cosmos, a world where nothing existed but the unit formed by their joined lips, hands, bodies. The room tilted and swayed, like a planet spinning on an astronomer's model.

Henrietta made a muffled noise as her back connected forcefully with something soft and springy, followed by something large and heavy landing on top of her. It abruptly dawned on her that the falling sensation had been more than the effect of Miles's kisses.

"Mmmph!" protested Henrietta, poking at the large lump on top of her. Not being able to breathe while Miles was kissing her was one thing, having all the air forcibly squashed out of her quite another.

The large lump rolled onto his side, taking her with him. "Sorry," he whispered into her ear, his breath reawakening all the nerves that had been squashed into silence with her precipitous descent to the bed. "I tripped."

"I noticed," replied Henrietta, although she was having trouble noticing much of anything at all as Miles pressed his lips to the hollow of her throat.

"Did you?" It was clear Miles's mind was not on the conversation either, as his lips trailed down her collarbone, to the bodice of her dress, which was obligingly drooping far below where it ought to be. His teeth nipped at the edge of her bodice, which obediently slipped another crucial inch. Momentarily distracted, Henrietta realized that the shivers down her spine were caused by more than the sensation of Miles's breath against bare skin. At some point, the long row of buttons that had fastened her twill traveling dress had been deftly undone.

Henrietta's chin dropped sharply down, nearly banging Miles on the head.

"How did you do that?" she asked incredulously. "I never even noticed."

Miles freed her arms from the dress with an expert tug. Henrietta made an automatic grab for the fabric as her bodice plunged to her waist, but Miles grabbed her hands, lifting them one by one to his lips. "I have many talents of which you know nothing—yet," he added meaningfully.

"Evidently," said Henrietta bemusedly, as the rest of her dress followed her bodice.

"Absolutely." The pile of fabric landed with a dusty thump by the side of the bed.

Henrietta propped herself up on an elbow, resisting the urge to dive under the covers. Clad only in her chemise, she felt her arms were very bare. "Have you ever considered a career as a lady's maid?"

"I'm better at the undressing bit"—Miles yanked his shirt over his head, revealing a very impressive expanse of chest—"than the dressing."

"Hmm," said Henrietta, watching the ripple of muscles along Miles's chest as he tugged the sleeves from his arms. She wasn't going to think about the women he had undressed in the past. They were in the past. Gone. Finished.

And Henrietta was seized with a determination to make quite sure there was never another. He was hers now, all hers, and even if he hadn't married her for love, well, there was nothing that said she couldn't do her best to seduce him, was there? Even if she had no idea how to go about it. Even Cleopatra had had to start somewhere.

Tentatively, Henrietta placed a hand on Miles's chest, fascinated by the way the muscles contracted in response. She ran her hands up to his shoulders, tilting her head back so that her hair flowed over her shoulders. It felt oddly sensual against her almost bare back, and she swished it back and forth.

"Hen," whispered Miles, staring at her transfixed, in a way that made Henrietta feel lithe and beautiful and bold.

"Hello," she said softly, tracing the line of hair on his chest down until she encountered the waistband of his breeches.

"Hello to you, too," gasped Miles, grabbing her hands before she could go farther. Lifting them over her head, he leaned in for a long kiss, trying to bring his raging passions under control. His body, unfortunately, had other ideas.

He wanted to jump up and down and shout, "Mine, mine, mine, mine, mine!" but since he had the sense to realize that might alarm Henrietta—and overset the ancient bedstead—he rendered his message in a more subtle way, running a finger down the strap of her chemise until it slid down her shoulder. She shivered, looking up at him with wide, unfocused eyes.

Miles decided subtlety was highly overrated.

"You," pronounced Miles, "are wearing too many clothes." Grabbing the thin fabric in both hands, he tugged. *Riiiiiip.* The chemise parted jaggedly down the middle.

"Miles!" gasped Henrietta.

"I'll buy you another," said Miles thickly, cupping her breasts in his hands. "Just not now," he added, as his head lowered to her chest. "Maybe next week."

For once, Henrietta was in no condition to argue. The sensation of Miles's tongue teasing her nipple wiped out coherent thought, and what would undoubtedly have been a highly witty rejoinder turned instead into an inarticulate gasp, as her fingers threaded through his hair, instinctively drawing his head closer. His lips tightened, tugged, sending shivers of sensation rolling straight down to Henrietta's toes.

Together, they sank back into the ancient mattress, arms locked around each other, bodies fitting perfectly together. Feeling wonderfully wanton, Henrietta pressed closer to him, sensing more than hearing him groan as she brushed against the bulge in his breeches.

Emboldened, she wiggled against him, enjoying the way his breath speeded in her ear, and his hands tightened on her back.

Desperately trying to school himself to go slowly, Miles wrenched his mouth from Henrietta's, trailing kisses along her neck, her ear, as his hands explored the tantalizing arch of her waist, the generous curve of her hip. Her skin felt like silk beneath his fingers as they slid up the inside of her thigh. Somewhere between her knee and the tangle of curls between her legs, Miles had stopped breathing. He didn't notice. What remained of his mind was concentrated on far more pressing matters.

Spitting out a mouthful of hair he had accidentally ingested, Miles scrambled with the fastenings of his breeches, yanking them hastily over his hips. Clumsily, Henrietta tried to help, laughing breathlessly as Miles tried to kick the breeches off his legs, cursing as the fabric clung to his foot.

"Laugh, will you?" he demanded, triumphantly sending the breeches flying, and pouncing on his wife. "We'll see about that."

Henrietta's laugh turned into a squeal of surprise as Miles pressed a kiss to the inside of her thigh. His tongue moved higher, flicking between her legs, sending quivers of sensation jilting through her. Her skin felt too tight for her body, tension building in the core of her being. She suddenly desperately needed Miles's arms around her, his lips on hers.

She tugged on his hair, and he surged up along the mattress to join her, his hand moving to replace her mouth. Henrietta knew she was making little mewing noises, but she couldn't find it in her to care; she pressed herself against Miles's fingers.

"I don't think," Miles's voice came as though from a long way away, even though his mouth was right next to her ear, "I can wait any longer."

"Mmm," said Henrietta, which Miles correctly interpreted as license to proceed.

Slowly, he began to enter her. At least, he intended to go slowly, with proper deference to her virginal state. Instead, Henrietta twined her arms around his neck, making little panting noises as she moved anxiously against him, driven by the restless pressure building inside her. Murmuring her name, Miles plunged deeply into her, ripping through the thin barrier that barred his passage.

Henrietta let out an indignant gasp. Miles froze, suspended above her.

"Hen?" he rasped. "Are you all right?"

Henrietta considered. Miles's heart wrenched in a way that almost distracted him from the clamorous demands of certain parts of his anatomy as Henrietta's nose squinched and her lips quirked in a heart-stoppingly familiar expression. After an endless moment—as Miles's arms began to quiver with the agony of holding still—she gave a little nod.

She moved experimentally against him, arching her hips the tiniest bit.

"I think so."

"Are you *sure*?" gasped Miles, even though he wasn't at all sure what he would do if the answer were no. Jump out the window, most likely. He was spared that fate by Henrietta tightening her legs around him in a way that left no doubt as to her intentions. She strained against him, nodding as emphatically as she could, because little jolts of pleasure made speech a perilous prospect at best. She could feel him beginning to move, filling her, his shoulders warm and familiar beneath her hands, the fine hairs on his chest teasing her already sensitive nipples.

Henrietta clung to sanity, fighting the waves of sensation threatening to sweep over her.

"Miles?" she said uneasily.

"Still here," he murmured into her ear, his hands moving tenderly over her waist, her hips, stroking, coaxing. Using his hands to gather her closer, he drove deeper and deeper into her, pressing to the very core of her being. "Always."

Henrietta cried out in surprise as pleasure scintillated through her, like a thousand champagne bubbles glistening by candlelight, oscillating and bursting in a golden glow. As she convulsed around him, Miles groaned and surrendered to his own release. Together, they collapsed back against the dusty counterpane in a state of satiated somnolence.

Miles rolled to his side, taking Henrietta with him. She sighed contentedly, fitting herself against his side, one leg thrown over his, and her head tucked in the crook of his neck. Miles rubbed his cheek against the top of her head, enjoying the scent of her hair, the feel of her sweaty skin against his, the pressure of her breast against his side. He ran one hand down the tangled length of her hair, enjoying the silky feel of it beneath his palm. Henrietta gave an irritated wriggle as his finger snagged on a knot, but didn't say anything.

"Hen?" Miles poked her. "Are you alive?"

"Mmm," murmured Henrietta.

"That's all you have to say?" protested Miles.

"Mmm," repeated Henrietta, and nestled deeper into the crook of Miles's shoulder.

Miles grinned. "Eighteen years, and I've finally rendered you speechless."

Henrietta shifted slightly. "Mrr-grr-grr," she mumbled into Miles's shoulder.

"What was that?"

Henrietta tilted her head back. "Wonderful," she sighed. "Splendid. Superlative. Superb."

"Couldn't resist, could you?"

"Blissful, ecstatic, euphoric, brilliant . . ."

"Enough!" exclaimed Miles, rolling her over onto her back.

Henrietta had a decidedly wicked glint in her eye. "Marvelous," she said deliberately, "magnificent, glorious . . ."

"Right," said Miles. "You leave me no choice."

By the time the first rays of dawn began to peek through the bed curtains, Henrietta was forced to agree that there were moments for which even adjectives were entirely inadequate.

had, all of them, been looking in entirely the wrong direction. In the meantime, the deadliest spy in London, the one person who above all ought to have been observed and curtailed, roamed free.

Henrietta must be warned. At once.

Jane smiled sweetly at Captain Desmoreau, who showed a stubborn refusal to leave her side, and told him she was really quite perishing of thirst. Would he be so kind . . . ?

He would. Desmoreau set off into the throng. Rising, Jane wended her way past a cluster of dowagers merrily ripping apart reputations like so much disorderly tatting, past the gloomy Louis Bonaparte, complaining about his myriad phantom illnesses, past the admiring circle who thronged Bonaparte's wife, Josephine, her step steady, her expression serene, a Galatea with no other purpose but to adorn a pedestal at the Bonapartes' court.

The door was in sight. Four more paces, and she could escape into the hallways, and thence to her cousin's house, to pack for a hasty journey for England. This was not a task Jane cared to entrust to another. Couriers had an unfortunate habit of disappearing en route. Three paces. Jane's mind was already leaping ahead. She would ride dressed in male clothes; it would be faster than taking the coach and cause less comment. She would have Miss Gwen put it about that she had taken sick and was keeping to her bed. Something nasty, something contagious, something that would ward off well-wishers. Two paces. She would cross at Honfleur rather than Calais; the port was less closely watched, and she had a fisherman in her pay, on the condition that his boat be at her disposal whenever she should need it. One pace left . . .

"My goddess!" A white-shirted figure lolled dramatically in her path, waistcoat open and sleeves billowing. Augustus Whittlesby, English expatriate and author of the most execrable effusions of verse ever to assault the ear, flung himself at Jane's feet in an aspect of adoration. "My muse! My peerless patroness of sesquipedality!"

"Good evening, sir," Jane replied for the benefit of any listeners, adding softly, "Not now, Mr. Whittlesby!"

He pressed a languid hand to his forehead, ruffles billowing about his face. "I swoon, I perish, I expire at your feet, if you will not do your humble servant the inestimable honor of giving ear to my latest ode in praise of your prodigious pulchritude." For her ear alone, he muttered, mouth hidden from the company beneath the flowing muslin of his sleeve, "You really must hear this, Miss Wooliston."

Jane's face tightened, but she knew better than to object when her fellow agent spoke in such a tone. Having perfected his role years ago, Whittlesby almost never broke character, and would certainly not do so in the heart of the enemy's lair, Bonaparte's palace, for any but the most pressing reasons. Placing a hand on Whittlesby's arm, she said sternly, "One moment only, Mr. Whittlesby. My cousin grows alarmed if I stay out too late."

Whittlesby flourished a bow that ended somewhere in the vicinity of Jane's silk slippers. Taking her arm and leading her through the door, into a small anteroom, he said loudly, for the benefit of those behind them, "I assure you, my ardent angel, you shall not regret this small mercy." In a harsh whisper, he added, "Orders. From England."

"Mr. Whittlesby, you do me too much honor with these effusions. What are they?"

"Honor itself pales before such divinity," declaimed Whittlesby. He bowed over Jane's hand. Jane leaned forward slightly. "Trouble," he muttered. "In Ireland. Wickham wants you there."

"Honor may pale, but you put me to the blush, sir," protested Jane, making a show of retrieving her hand. "I can't. I return to England tonight."

"Oh, the beauty of your blush! Blessed, blithe, bounteous blush! Like the dew-touched petals of the fairest rose, spreading their bounty to the awestruck sun." Whittlesby flung himself to his knees before her, lifting his face in exaggerated awe. "My orders were clear and urgent. Tonight. A carriage will be waiting. Bring your chaperone."

A shadow of a frown passed along Jane's serene face as she extended a gracious hand to the prostrate poet. "Only a heart of stone could resist such a plea, Mr. Whittlesby, and mine, alas, is of far more malleable matter."

Whittlesby pressed his forehead to her hand in humble obeisance, and extracted a roll of parchment tied with pink ribbons from the billowing muslin folds of his shirt. Flourishing it in the air to make sure that anyone in the salon watching might have a good view, he pressed the roll into Jane's hand.

"Every third word of every third line," he muttered. While Whittlesby's verse always served as vehicle, the code changed each time. The Ministry of Police knew Whittlesby only as a writer of bad poetry—it was a measure of Whittlesby's devotion to the cause that he was, in fact, quite a proficient poet, and had, before the war, entertained genuine ambitions in that direction—but the agents of the English Crown were taking no chances.

"I assure you, Mr. Whittlesby, I shall read it with the utmost care," replied Jane, making a great show of unrolling the paper so that anyone could see the irregular lines of verse scrolled across page. "I need a message sent."

Whittlesby staggered, and dropped to the ground, overcome with rapture at her acquiescence. "Done. To whom?"

"Come, come, sir! Steady yourself! How can I enjoy your ode with your collapse upon my conscience?" Bending over him in feigned concern, Jane outlined her wishes in a rapid whisper.

Whittlesby's eyes widened. "Good God! Who would have—"

"No, no, Mr. Whittlesby, say no more. I am quite overcome by your compliments." Jane extended a hand to help him up, her back to the salon. Her face was pale and serious as she said softly, "You must not fail."

Whittesby lifted Jane's gloved hand to his lips. "Fail my muse?" he said, with a twinkle of humor as his eyes flicked up at Jane. "Never."

Jane's eyes lacked an answering twinkle. "Some things, Mr. Whittlesby, are too serious for poetry."

"I will do my utmost," promised Whittlesby.

"I never expected less," said Jane austerely. Her fine lawn skirts flicked around the turn of the doorway, and were gone.

Within five minutes, the word had passed around Mme. Bonaparte's salon. That tedious English poet had so distracted poor Miss Wooliston that she had departed for home under pretext of a headache—and who wouldn't, my dear? Really, the man was a pest, and his verse! The less said about his verse, the better. As for Whittlesby, at least one should be spared his effusions for the remainder of the evening. He had departed mere moments after to Miss Wooliston, to succor flagging inspiration, he said. The dowagers knew what that meant. Inspiration, indeed! More like the bottom of a bottle. Disgraceful, quite disgraceful. But what could one expect of an Englishman and a poet?

While the dowagers gossiped on, in the Hotel de Balcourt, two women rapidly packed by candlelight. In a stable not far from the Tuileries, a man in a flowing shirt smacked his hand sharply against the rump of a horse. "No delay!" he called after the caped and hooded courier. The courier, one of three in possession of the identity of the Black Tulip, waved a hand in enthusiastic assent. With clear roads and favorable winds, he might even be in London by evening of the following day.

And in London, the deadliest of all spies plotted one final move. By the following evening, it would all be over. . . .

Chapter Thirty-Two

Fool's Paradise: *the illusion of calm, designed to lull one's adversary into incautious behavior; the invariable prelude to concerted enemy activity. See also under* Path, Primrose
—from the Personal Codebook of the Pink Carnation

Miles strode jauntily past the guards on duty at 10 Crown Street, a posy of primroses in his hand and a beatific smile on his face.

One of the guards nudged the other. "Who's he come courting?" he asked sarcastically, eliciting an appreciative snicker from his fellow.

Miles didn't notice. Miles was too happy to notice. In fact, he rather doubted that all of Bonaparte's artillery, ranged along the breadth of Pall Mall, could fright him out of his good humor just now. Miles shook his head in bemusement as he wove through the press of busy people in the corridor. What, after all, had changed? His best friend still hated him. A dangerous French spy was still on the loose in the streets of London. He had to somehow explain to Lord and Lady Uppington that he had . . . well, if not exactly eloped with their daughter, at least entered into a marriage so precipitate as to cause heads to wag until some greater scandal diverted the attention of the *ton*. That thought alone ought to have been enough to dampen even Miles's buoyant spirits.

Yet, even the prospect of confronting the Uppingtons—Lady Uppington expostulating, Lord Uppington grim—faded back into a dim backdrop when considered next to the image of Henrietta as he had left her, one pale arm flung over her head, hair any which way on the pillow, and mouth open as if she were about to say something, even while she slept. Miles grinned, remembering last night's spate of adjectives. One thing was for certain: Life with Henrietta would never want for words.

Miles announced himself to Wickham's harried subordinate, who advised him to take a seat, and disappeared back into the inner sanctum.

Miles sat, and, despite telling himself he really ought to be thinking about useful topics, like spies, the catching of, went back to grinning besottedly. The person sitting next to him shuffled his chair discreetly in the opposite direction.

Amazing how three little words could cause such bother.

There were so many treacherous verbal trinities, mused Miles. *I owe you. Pass the decanter*. And, of course, *Out that window!* which, in Miles's experience, had caused more pain and ruined clothing than any other three words. Miles dragged in a deep breath. No matter how many trilogies he dredged up, there was no avoiding it. Those were not the three words at issue.

Somewhere along the line, he had fallen in love with Henrietta.

How in the hell had that happened? It didn't seem quite fair. He had just been going along his ordinary business; he hadn't gone mooning about like Geoff, or trysting with women under a secret identity like Richard, both of which could be reasonably assumed to end in uncomfortable romantic attachments while Cupid clutched his bow and doubled over with derisive laughter. But, yet, there he was, grinning like a madman despite having been threatened with castration by his best friend and shot at by French agents; concocting romantic dinners instead of cunning plans; and, in his weaker moments, actually contemplating poetry. Fortunately for him, Henrietta, and the Western poetic tradition, the result of his contemplation was brief and decisive. He couldn't write it.

But he *could* make Henrietta happy, Miles assured himself. On the walk over to the War Office, he had given deep and serious thought to this weighty topic. There was, of course, always jewelry. It had been Miles's past experience that nothing said, "Thank you for a splendid night of passion," quite like a strand of emeralds. There were only two slight drawbacks to that plan. First, Henrietta already had a strand of emeralds, complete with matching bracelet and earrings. And, even if she hadn't . . . well, Miles couldn't quite put it into words, but the techniques one used to placate a mistress were perhaps not best suited to wooing a wife. He needed something more personal, more tender, more . . . damn. He couldn't even come up with appropriate adjectives, much less a dashing gesture that would sweep Henrietta off her feet. Aside from picking her up. He quite liked picking her up.

But this, he reminded himself selflessly, was supposed to be about Henrietta and what *she* would like, which also unfortunately ruled out boxing matches, trips to Tattersall's, and—Miles's personal favorite—the removal of clothing. From what he knew of females, they were generally more intrigued by the acquisition of clothing than the removal of it. Miles shook his head at the waste of time and fabric. Fig leaves. Now, there was a form of fashion he could support. Of course, some of those dresses of Henrietta's weren't half bad, the ones with the filmy skirts that outlined the length of her legs as she walked, and the scooped bodices that— Ergh. Miles cast a guilty glance around the room and placed his hat on his lap with exaggerated nonchalance, wishing that current fashion didn't mandate breeches that were quite so damnably formfitting.

Miles resolutely turned his mind to safer topics. He did vaguely remember hearing someone going on at a ball once about flowers speaking the language of love. Miles dubiously regarded the squished posy of primroses, already turning slightly brownish around the edges. They didn't say anything to him other than "Water me!" He supposed there might be a metaphor in there somewhere—love needing nourishment, and all that sort of drivel, but from what he knew about gardening, nourishing flowers involved a great deal of compost, which even Miles was quite sure was about as far from romance as one could get. "Oh my love is like a dung heap" was far more likely to get a chamber pot flung at his head than cries of rapture.

Miles shook his head. He briefly considered nipping out of the War Office and running over to Hatchards for one of those romantic novels Henrietta seemed to find so engrossing, but rapidly rejected the idea. After all, even if he managed to find an appropriate book, how would he know where to look? He doubted they had an appropriate index, with entries like "Wives, for the wooing of," or convenient chapter headings, such as "How to Deliver a Declaration of Love in Ten Easy Lessons." Miles cringed, imagining the derisive laughter sure to follow his possession of such a publication.

A dinner *à deux*, Miles decided. That was the ticket. There would be champagne, and oysters, and chocolate—not all at once, he concluded, after some consideration. Miles adjusted his mental image slightly and added some grapes, for the peeling. He could feed them to Henrietta one by one, and if one, or two, or ten just happened to slip into her bodice and need retrieving, well, they were slippery things, peeled grapes. Those Romans certainly knew what they were doing, thought Miles happily. Peeled grapes . . . a couch big enough for two . . . maybe some custard . . .

Wickham's aide reappeared, loudly clearing his throat. Miles rose with a start, spilling an entire bucket of mental grapes, none of them, unfortunately, anywhere near Henrietta's bodice.

"He'll see you now," the aide said in harried tones, chivvying Miles towards the office. "But make it quick."

Miles nodded in acknowledgment and bounded through the door into Wickham's office. Someone had replaced the map on the wall since his last visit, evidently employing a stronger pin. The map quivered a bit as the door slammed shut behind him, but remained in its place.

Miles dragged his accustomed chair in front of Wickham's desk. "Good morning, sir!"

Wickham's shrewd eyes traveled from Miles's beaming countenance to the somewhat wilted primroses. "I can see that you think it is," he replied, adding, "For me, are they?"

Confused, Miles looked down at his hand, started, flushed, opened his mouth, closed it again, and looked as flustered as a strapping man of sporting tendencies can contrive to look.

"Er, no," he said, shifting the primroses hastily behind his back. "I've just been married!"

"Congratulations," said Wickham dryly. "I wish you both very happy. I take it you did not come to see me simply to inform me of your recent nuptials?"

"No." Miles's expression took on a more serious cast as he scooted his chair closer to Wickham's desk. "I have reason to believe the Black Tulip is Lord Vaughn."

The spymaster eyed him dispassionately. "Do you?"

Miles nodded grimly, and proceeded to start at the beginning. "Someone crept into Selwick Hall this weekend disguised as the Phantom Monk of Donwell Abbey."

Wickham cast Miles a faintly quizzical glance.

Miles waved his hand dismissively, realized he was still holding the despised posy, and hastily stuck it under his chair. "A local tale. It doesn't signify, sir." He leaned forward in his chair. "At first, I thought our phantom was only after Selwick's papers—"

"A reasonable assumption," murmured Wickham.

"Thank you, sir. The evidence appeared to bear that out. We found the papers in Selwick's desk disarranged, but nothing else in the house had been disturbed, and there were no signs of activity anywhere on the grounds." Miles paused slightly, remembering exactly what sort of activities had been occurring on the grounds.

Wickham's keen eyes narrowed. "And in Selwick's desk?"

"Only estate papers, sir. Selwick has always been quite careful not to leave sensitive documents lying about."

"I assume that isn't the extent of your tale." Wickham glanced at the clock on his desk, Atlas supporting not the world, but the time.

"Right." Miles took the hint and hurried rapidly through the rest. "We stopped at an inn, where my companion overheard Lord Vaughn in conversation with the opera singer Mme. Fiorila—at least, I'm fairly certain it was Mme. Fiorila," Miles corrected himself. "Upon leaving the inn, we noticed we were being followed. Since the London-to-Brighton road is a popular one, I initially thought nothing of it, until their coachman drew a gun. We evaded pursuit and returned to London. So you see"—Miles thumped enthusiastically on the desk, making Atlas jump—"it must have been Vaughn! Who else would have known to follow us from the inn?"

"One point requires clarification, Mr. Dorrington. Who is 'we'?" inquired Wickham. "Were you with Selwick at the time?"

Miles flushed. "Er, no. At least, not with that Selwick. I was with his sister, Lady Henrietta."

Wickham responded to that extraneous detail with an attention he had failed to display to anything else Miles had said thus far. He sat bolt-upright in his chair, fixing Miles with the stare that had been known to make French agents leap out third-story windows and hardened English operatives slink beneath their capes.

"Lady Henrietta Selwick?" he repeated sharply.

"Ye-es," affirmed Miles, regarding his superior with some confusion. "You know, Selwick's younger sister?" It didn't seem quite the time to impart the news that she now bore another title; Wickham's expression was more funereal than bridal.

"That, Mr. Dorrington," said Wickham harshly, "is bad news. Very bad news, indeed."

"Bad news?" Miles was half out of his chair, grasping the edge of Wickham's desk.

Wickham had already levered himself out of his desk chair and was striding towards the door. "It means," he explained, reaching for the door handle, "that Lady Henrietta is in grave danger."

SOMETHING SHARP was poking Henrietta in the arm.

Making sleepy noises of protest, Henrietta rolled over and buried her face into the fluffy depths of the feather pillow. She flung out an arm and wiggled deeper into the sheets. But there was an odd, musty smell to the pillow, not like her own lavender-scented linen, and the sheets felt strange against her bare skin.

Henrietta's eyelids flew all the way open, and she sat abruptly up in the bed, clutching at the coverlet as it threatened to fall to her waist. Last night. Her wedding. Miles . . . It had all really happened, hadn't it? Yes, of course it had, she assured herself. Or else, why would she be unclothed in a strange bed? As to what had transpired in that strange bed . . . Henrietta turned redder than the opulent crimson counterpane.

The cause for her blush was absent, but in his place perched a hastily folded note. Reaching out, Henrietta unfolded the scrap of paper, and leaned groggily back against the pillows. In Miles's large, untidy handwriting, the note stated, "Went to War Office. Back by noon." It was signed with an exuberant squiggle that might have been an M, a D, or an amateur portrait of Queen Charlotte.

Not precisely an ode to her charm and beauty.

Henrietta shook her head and chuckled. How like Miles it was! There was a postscript, however, that brought more of a sparkle to her eye than any of the effusions, verse and prose, of her past admirers. At the bottom of the page, Miles had scrawled just one word: "Magnificent."

Henrietta clutched the note to her chest, beaming besottedly. It really had been quite magnificent, hadn't it? Lifting the note, Henrietta read the word again. Magnificent. That did say "magnificent," didn't it, not "maleficent" or "malodorous" or "magnificat"? Henrietta peeked again, just to make sure. Yes, it quite definitely said "magnificent." Happily crinkling the edges of the paper, Henrietta read the postscript over four more times, until the letters began to unfold into little black squiggles and the word "magnificent" began to disintegrate on her tongue, and she had to remind herself of what it meant.

Resolutely refolding the note (after just one last peek to make sure the word was still there, and not just another iteration of "Miles" that had happened to sprawl over into extra letters), Henrietta settled back against the pillows, the little square of paper balanced on her chest, tucking her chin down along her collarbone to squint at it. It wasn't exactly a love letter, she reasoned, nobly resisting the urge to snatch it open again, but it was a token that Miles intended to go along with his end of the bargain, and do his best to make things work. Bargain. Henrietta struggled up onto her elbows, dislodging the piece of paper. That did take some of the glow out of it. She didn't much relish being a romantic charity case, tossed alms in the form of a spare word.

He was also kind to small children and animals. Ah, but would he write a love letter—oh, fine, a love word—to a discontented puppy? No, Henrietta slowly concluded, but, then, puppies couldn't read, so, to a puppy, a spare bone really might be quite the same thing. And one word was such a little bone. . . .

Henrietta flopped over, whapping her face into the pillow. Hard.

Such thoughts were entirely, *whap*, entirely, *whap*, counterproductive. A flushed but resolute Henrietta emerged from the feathers. Pushing her hair back out of her face, and brushing aside a stray feather that had gotten caught in the tangles, she clambered out of bed, winding the bedsheet around her as she went. Enough tormenting herself with silly speculations that couldn't possibly be resolved. She had a house to be organized (Henrietta scrunched her nose, remembering the musty smell of the pillow; airing the linens was definitely in order), servants to be reviewed (Henrietta turned another color entirely, remembering her first meeting with the staff the night before, while not on her own feet), and a letter to be written to her parents.

Henrietta's hands stilled on the edges of the sheet at the thought of her parents. Servants first, she decided. She could work her way gradually up to dealing with her parents over the course of the afternoon. She would be willing to wager that Richard had already written them, had probably written to them before the thrum of Miles's carriage wheels had echoed away down the drive. Whatever Richard had written was bound to portray the weekend's events—and the morals of the characters concerned—in a less-than-flattering light. Henrietta wasn't sure if what had happened was amenable to flattering lights, but if there was one, she intended to find it. Estrangement from her parents . . . it just wasn't to be thought of. It would be as dreadful for Miles as it would be for her.

Henrietta reached out her hand to ring for her maid to help her dress. There was one slight flaw to that plan. She didn't have a maid. Nor, for that matter, did she have any clothes.

She eyed yesterday's travel-stained dress with disfavor, picking it up with two fingers. The skirt was liberally streaked with dirt; there were splatters of goodness knew what (Henrietta certainly didn't want to know) on the hem, a tear in the bodice, and—merciful heavens, was that a leaf of cabbage stuck to the sleeve?

"I just don't want to know," muttered Henrietta, shaking the dress by the other arm until the offending vegetation fell off onto the red-and-blue-figured carpet.

Henrietta contemplated raiding the wardrobes of Loring House, but couldn't help but suspect that she and Miles's mother would have radically different tastes in clothes. And while the classical mode was still in style, going about draped in a sheet struck her as not only risqué, but drafty. Yesterday's clothes would have to do, until she could go to Uppington House to fetch more.

Grimacing, Henrietta wiggled into the begrimed garments, managing to reach just enough buttons to prevent the dress from plummeting precipitously. There was a tarnished silver brush on the dressing table, and Henrietta used it to attack the knots and snarls that had sprung up all over her head. Henrietta blushed at the recollection of how some of those tangles had developed. She could feel Miles's hands running through her hair, his lips on hers, his . . . er. Henrietta glanced guiltily around.

"Silly," she muttered to herself.

At any rate, she thought, moving onto safer ground, a good number of those tangles dated back to their precipitate flight from the inn. The memory of the faceless black coach behind them was enough to make Henrietta's happy pink glow fade away entirely.

Miles seemed so sure that it was Vaughn.

Frowning, Henrietta pulled the brush slowly through her hair, working her way through the tangles.

Everything pointed to Vaughn. That undue attention he had only displayed upon hearing she was the sister of the Purple Gentian, that strange episode in the Chinese chamber, and his habit of cryptic conversation. He had told her he hadn't been to France for many years. Yet, yesterday, he had spoken of returning to France as if after a brief absence. He was on the trail of a mysterious female, and, most damning of all, he was in a position to have followed her and Miles out of the inn.

And yet . . . something rang a false note, like a song sung slightly flat. Henrietta frowned into the mirror, trying to isolate the source of her discontent, drawing her mind back to the narrow stairwell, the muffled voices heard through the chinks of the doorframe.

With her faculty of sight obstructed by the door, Henrietta had been entirely concentrated upon Vaughn's voice, every last timbre and hint of emotion. Voices were something of which Henrietta had made rather a study. Vaughn had been frustrated, he had been irate, but there was no tang of malice in it. Instead, she had heard an ineffable weariness that inspired the sort of sympathy one felt for Lear tossed out upon the heath, a strong and stubborn man brought to the end of his endurance. Henrietta wrinkled her nose, giving her hair an unnecessarily vigorous stroke with the brush. Such flights of fancy were entirely extraneous to a properly ordered investigation.

A man could smile and smile and still be a villain; he could have a voice resonant with sorrow and still be plotting to murder Jane and overthrow the English throne. But Henrietta was quite convinced that Vaughn was not. Henrietta grimaced; she could imagine what Miles would make of that argument.

If not Vaughn, who? After all, who else had been at the inn to know of their presence? Turnip? The notion was as laughable as Turnip's infamous collection of carnation-colored waistcoats.

But the thought of Turnip reminded her of something else. Or rather, of somebody else.

Henrietta paused with the brush suspended in midair and stared unseeing into the mirror, hazel eyes crinkling around the corners in concentration as the elusive memory that had been teasing her snapped into place. A man in dandified clothes with a thin black mustache, stepping aside to allow her to pass. He had been there, hovering close by their table, when she barreled down the stairs, standing ever so casually by the fireplace. Watching.

Despite the overshadowing hat and the immense folds of the cravat, there had been something familiar about him. Of course, she cautioned herself, she had been quite overset and distracted at the time, first by the tension with Miles, and then by the encounter with Vaughn. None of her senses had been at their sharpest.

And yet . . . Henrietta put the brush down with a definitive click on the dressing table. It was certainly worth investigating. And if her hunch was mistaken, Miles need never know. She had no grand plans for swooping in and making grand accusations, no aspirations towards daring escapades. Those were more in Amy's style than hers. As Henrietta had learned the previous day, she really had no taste for danger.

But she wouldn't be in any danger, decided Henrietta, sweeping back her hair. She would just snoop about a bit, and return home. What could be safer?

And she knew just how to go about it. . . .

MILES BOUNDED OUT OF HIS CHAIR and grabbed Wickham by the elbow before he could open the door. "Grave danger?"

"Danger to Lady Henrietta, to the Pink Carnation, and to the whole of our enterprises in France," Wickham said gravely. Removing his elbow from Miles's limp grasp, he opened the door and shouted, "Thomas!"

Miles stared in frozen horror at his superior. "Why?" he demanded. "What danger?"

Wickham frowned at him. "All in good time. Ah, Thomas, arrange for a detail of soldiers to be sent to Uppington House—"

"Loring House," corrected Miles tersely.

That momentarily achieved Wickham's attention. "Loring House?"

"Married," Miles said briefly.

Wickham assimilated that information with a brief flicker of his eyelids. "Indeed." He turned back to his secretary, whose eyes were darting nervously from one man to the other. "Send a detail of soldiers to Loring House—"

"Wait," Miles interrupted again.

"Yes?" snapped Wickham.

"Lady Henrietta. No one knows she's at Loring House. Isn't she safer without a troop of soldiers announcing her presence? If I can keep her there quietly, make sure she doesn't leave the house—"

"Thomas!" The secretary snapped to attention. "I want two men guarding Loring House. They are to be dressed as gardeners." Wickham turned to Miles. "Loring House does have a garden, I take it?"

Miles nodded meekly.

"If Lady Henrietta makes any attempt to leave the house, she is to be returned to it. If someone other than Mr. Dorrington, Lady Henrietta, or their staff attempts to enter the house, they are to be prevented. Any suspicious behavior is to be reported to me at once. *At once*. The safety of the realm depends upon it. Is that understood?"

It was understood.

Wickham's secretary scurried off. Miles intercepted Wickham before he could return to his desk, implicitly dismissing Miles.

"What happened?" Miles demanded.

Wickham freed his arm from Miles's hand, proceeding to his desk at a measured pace that did nothing for Miles's nerves. "Lady Henrietta's contact—"

"Hen has a *contact*?" muttered Miles.

"Lady Henrietta's contact," Wickham continued, glaring pointedly at Miles to show he would brook no further interruptions, "disappeared late last week from her shop in Bond Street. We found her yesterday. In the Thames."

Miles swallowed hard.

"What has this to do with . . . ," he began, knowing full well what the answer must be, but hoping against hope that there might be some other explanation. An innocuous explanation. An explanation that wouldn't place Henrietta in peril.

"If you do not know the answer to that, Mr. Dorrington, I cannot imagine why we continue to employ you here!" Catching sight of Miles's stricken face, Wickham took a deep breath and modulated his tone as he explained, "We found her yesterday. It took us until this morning to identify her."

Miles blanched. "Torture?" he asked unevenly.

"Undoubtedly."

"Do you think—"

Wickham spread his hands in a gesture of frustration. "We cannot know for certain. But the methods employed were"—Wickham paused, the furrow between his brows deepening—"extreme."

Miles cursed violently.

"Your story," Wickham said wearily, "is distressing, but not surprising. It confirms what we expected."

"Your agent cracked," Miles said bluntly.

Wickham didn't bother to argue with the implied aspersion to his minions.

"Precisely. The Black Tulip knows your wife can lead him to the Pink Carnation."

Chapter Thirty-Three

Magnificent: *intensely dangerous, even deadly. See also under*
Splendid, Superb, *and* Superlative
— from the Personal Codebook of the Pink Carnation

It had all seemed like such a good idea back at Loring House.

Henrietta hunched over a grate in the sitting room of a modest townhouse, pretending to rake ashes while her eyes busily searched the interior of the chimney for any suspicious rough patches that might denote a hidden cache of some kind, or the entrance to a priests' hole. Henrietta didn't think the townhouse, a narrow construction in a genteel but hardly fashionable area of town, was of an age to possess a priests' hole, but who was to say that one hadn't been added later for purposes other than priests? There might be a smugglers' hole, or a guilty lovers' hole, or any other manner of hidey-hole tucked away in the bricks of the chimney.

It would have been an inspired course of action, if only the interior of the chimney had not been entirely composed of suspicious rough patches. The soot-caked bricks jutted out at all sorts of angles, any one of which could be the lever that released a hidden door—or simply a soot-caked brick. A subtle peek under the carpet in the guise of sweeping had proved equally fruitless. The panels of the floor marched in faultless order, not a trapdoor among the lot. The walls were lamentably plain, free of ornately carved paneling or gilded moldings that might double as secret mechanisms. In short, Henrietta was feeling quite, quite thwarted.

Back at Loring House, Henrietta had finally chased down the elusive memory that was taunting her to its own hidey-hole, deep in the recesses of her brain. Henrietta would have liked to have claimed it was that mumbled "Pardon me, madam" that had awakened her suspicions, that her trained ear had caught the familiar lilt in that light tenor voice, even through the muffling layers of cravat. It wasn't. The voice had been excellently done, not gruff enough to arouse suspicion, but not high enough to set one thinking about castrati and the breeches roles in Shakespearean comedies. It hadn't even been the breeches themselves; they had been ingeniously padded with buckram, and so many young bucks were eking out their own minor endowments with a little aid from art and padding that, even had the padding been obviously ill-done, no one would have suspected. The fashionable clothes provided an excellent screen. The high points of the collar shaded cheeks too smooth to be masculine, and lent through shadow the specious appearance of reality to the glued-on hairs of a fake mustache. The monstrous cravat shielded a chin too delicately pointed to be male and a throat that was more Eve than Adam. Elaborate waistcoats and stiffened coattails provided better means than binding one's breasts for hiding a female form.

In the end, it was those same clothes that had set Henrietta wondering.

Why would someone so obviously all up to the crack wear his hair in an old-fashioned queue? A young pink of the *ton,* like Turnip, would have his hair cut short, fashionably tousled in a Brutus crop, or whichever other classical figure was the model of the moment. Queues were the province of the old, the unaware, or the resolutely stodgy, distinctly at odds with boots by Hoby, and a cravat tortured into the complicated folds of the Frenchman at the Waterfall. A nice touch, that, thought Henrietta, sifting ash into her bucket from the side of the shovel, watching the fine fall of not-quite-dead embers.

Once Henrietta had recognized the incongruity of the queue, the rest followed. She had only seen that shade of black hair on two people. It wasn't the rare blue-black of Spain, or the coarse brown-black that so often passed for the color among the dusty blondes and muddy brunettes who dotted the British Isles, but true, deep black that shimmered silver when the light struck it.

One was Mary Alsworthy. Her hair was the sort of shining black curtain that poets blunted their pens on, but Henrietta couldn't see her cavorting about unpopular inns in breeches, even if they were fashionable breeches. Mary Alsworthy might elope in the dead of night, but she would do it in full rig, velvet cloak, and a yippy lapdog on her knee, just to make it easier for her pursuers to follow and stage a grand scene.

The other was the marquise.

What vanity, Henrietta wondered, had led her to leave her hair down? Perhaps not vanity, but practicality, Henrietta concluded generously, shoveling ash. To cut off her hair would have undoubtedly occasioned notice—although so many were doing that nowadays, in token of those whose heads had been lopped off in the Terror—and the lush mass was too much to bundle beneath a hat without the shift being immediately obvious.

The voice, the hair, the height, the form, it all fit—but nothing else did. Henrietta would have been willing to stake her best pearls that the man in the inn had indeed been the marquise, but to what end? The marquise's motives all ran in the opposite direction. Estates, title, riches, consequence, husband, all had been stripped from her by the Revolution. Henrietta rather doubted she regretted the loss of that last, for all her pious utterances to the contrary, but consequences and riches were quite another matter. Hadn't the dowager said little Theresa Ballinger had an eye for the main chance?

The main chance might have led her to throw in her lot with the new power brokers in Paris, but if so, it hadn't gained her much. Her townhouse was in an area that was respectable, but not grand, sparsely furnished rather than the silvered opulence one would have expected of the marquise. The rugs were worn, the walls were bare, and the furnishings badly in need of being recovered.

None of it added up.

And she knew, with grim certainty, that if she broached the theory to Miles, he would unerringly poke his finger into each of those logical holes, one by one. And then—Henrietta winced in a way that had nothing to do with the bit of ember that was gnawing a hole in the rough fabric of her skirt and finding it tough going—and then Miles's face would curve into a great, big smug grin, and he would hoot, "You're jealous!" He might have the restraint not to hoot; he might manage to force the words out in reasonably nonhooting tones, but the hoot would be there, taunting her. Henrietta's cheeks burned at the very thought. And what proof did she have other than one black queue, seen in passing in a crowded coffee room? Certainly nothing that would convince a court of law. *M'lud, the girl is obviously love-struck. Makes them unreasonable, you know.*

Henrietta had no idea why the opposing counsel in her head sounded quite so much like Turnip Fitzhugh, but, then, Turnip was always popping up where one least expected him.

Banishing Turnip, Henrietta rested her shovel against the grate and stretched her tired arms, where muscles she hadn't realized she possessed were engaged in vociferous protest. A hot bath, that was what she wanted, with lots of lavender-scented bath salts and enough steam to make the room go hazy.

Hands on her hips, Henrietta took one last look around the sparsely furnished room. She might as well have that bath sooner rather than later. So far, her mission had been fruitless in the extreme, unless one counted finding half a dried apple under one of the settees. It showed no sign of being poisoned, or being anything else of interest, other than old, withered, and thoroughly disgusting.

Taking one of Amy's suggestions, Henrietta had garbed herself as a maidservant, borrowing a coarse brown wool dress from one of the baffled underservants at Loring House. Henrietta had gabbled a hastily contrived story about a fancy dress party (the maidservant had appeared entirely unconvinced) and slunk sheepishly back up to the upper reaches to don her prize, which, for all its plainness, had the advantage of being far cleaner than Henrietta's own clothes from the day before, and entirely cabbage-free. Henrietta resolved to give all the servants at Loring House a respectable raise in the very near future. They might think her a madwoman, but she would rather they think her a generous madwoman.

Thus attired, Henrietta had slipped out of the house. Amy had been entirely right; with her plain dress on, and a simple white cap over neatly braided hair, no one gave her a second glance. Her entrance through the kitchen of the marquise's townhouse occasioned no comment; the cook was bent over the fire, and a kitchen maid was too busy chopping and telling the cook about that girl what had been done wrong by the groom's second cousin once removed to pay any notice.

Once inside, Henrietta had first gone upstairs, making for the marquise's boudoir. She wasn't entirely sure what she was looking for—a series of signed instructions from Paris would have been most helpful—but anything of a suspicious nature would do to get the attention of the War Office, and wipe the hoot out of Miles's voice. The clothing worn by the mysterious gentleman at the inn, wigs, false mustaches, a cache of correspondence in code. Any of those would provide assurance that she wasn't just—Henrietta grimaced at the possibility—acting out of pure, rank, baseless jealousy.

Unfortunately—Henrietta plunged her shovel back into the fireplace—so far, jealousy was looking more and more like the only explanation. She had only moments in the marquise's boudoir before the click of heels heralded the arrival of the marquise's lady's maid, but there was nothing there that wouldn't be found in Henrietta's own. Even the little pots of face paint seemed no more than one would expect to find on the dressing table of a sophisticated lady of the world. Henrietta toyed with the notion of notes slipped into the base of the hares'-foot brushes used to apply cosmetics, but the idea seemed too wild, and certainly nothing to be heeded by the War Office. Besides, they hadn't made a crinkling noise when she squeezed them.

Bucket and shovel serving as a screen, Henrietta had made her way through the other bedrooms, but they were all clearly untenanted. The rooms were painfully bare, carpeted only with dust, the feather ticks sagging dispiritedly on their elderly frames. Henrietta had peeked into one armoire, for form's sake, and found it entirely empty, except for an adventurous spider that mistook Henrietta's shoulder for a tuffet. Remembering her position as an emissary of the War Office, Henrietta didn't scream. She squished it instead, rather more vindictively than necessary.

The barrenness in itself, Henrietta mused, was more interesting than otherwise. Even the marquise's bedchamber, with hangings on the bedposts and gowns in the clothes press, had a starkly temporary air, like the room of a wayside inn. The marquise's belongings formed a fine film over the furniture, hastily unpacked and as easily swept away again.

Of course, Henrietta reminded herself, that could have more to do with poverty than nefarious circumstances.

The sitting room, with the weary air inherent to hired lodgings, had been Henrietta's last hope. It, like the bedroom, seemed at least to be somewhat lived in. There were the remains of a fire in the grate— which Henrietta quickly set about demolishing to justify her presence in the room—and a scattering of books on a spindly-legged table by the settee. Henrietta had flipped through them, but found no secret caches containing pistols or vials of poison, no faint marks over letters indicating a code, no filmy sheets of paper wedged between the pages, bearing messages beginning with "Meet me at midnight under the old oak in Belliston Square. . . ." The books themselves clearly belonged to a former tenant. *La Nouvelle Héloïse* might be in the marquise's style—Rousseau's sentimental novels had enjoyed a great vogue in France a few years back—but his *Discourse on the Origin of Inequality* was decidedly not light reading, nor was the *Vindiciae Contra Tyrannos*. It was in French, rather than the original Latin, but still not the sort of work Henrietta imagined the marquise leafing through for pleasure.

In short, Henrietta's mission had been an utter waste. All she had learned was that the previous owner of the house had serious-minded taste in reading material and that housework was harder than it looked. Miles, she thought grimly, *would* hoot if he knew.

Well, there was no reason for him to know. Henrietta dropped the despised shovel into the bucket with a little puff of ashes. With any luck, he would have stopped off at White's for a round of darts with Geoff before returning to Loring House, and she could slip back and into normal clothes before he even realized she had been gone. In fact, she could stop by Uppington House on the way home and change into fresh clothes, and if Miles inquired, she had spent the whole morning arranging for her clothes and books—and Bunny, of course—to be sent over to Loring House. It was, she decided airily, straightening and brushing her grimy hands off against an already blotchy apron, an entirely plausible course of action.

Or it would have been, had not a footstep in the hall sent Henrietta flying back into place over the fireplace. As the door to the sitting room opened, Henrietta realized she was holding the shovel by the pointy bit, and rapidly reversed it, hoping the marquise hadn't noticed.

The marquise's attire was at distinct odds with the hopeless shabbiness of her hired house. She wore a diaphanous gown of lilac muslin that floated around her in a fine film, more like mist than fabric, and her black hair, that lush, silver-black hair, had been twined into a complicated arrangement of curls, threaded with shimmering lilac ribbon, and winking with diamond-headed pins. There was nothing stark about her attire, but Henrietta was put irresistibly in mind of the warrior goddesses so beloved of the Romans, Minerva in her chariot, or Diana in her glade, both entirely devoid of human weakness.

Crossing to the window that overlooked the street, the marquise flicked an impatient hand at Henrietta, and said in a voice as flat and hard as Minerva's breastplate, "You may go."

Keeping her head down, Henrietta bobbed a clumsy curtsy, and began to gather the accoutrements of her disguise. She was just hefting the bucket of ashes, mentally rehearsing the tale she intended to tell Miles, when the marquise looked at her again, sharply. Henrietta's shovel handle rattled against the side of the bucket.

"You. Girl."

Henrietta stilled, shoulders hunched, head bowed, her cessation of movement, she hoped, answer enough.

The marquise spoke again, her voice sharp with impatience, and something else. "Yes, you. Come here."

Bucket in hand, Henrietta shuffled slowly forward.

"Where do you have her?"

The door of Lord Vaughn's breakfast parlor slammed into the silk-hung wall, driving a long snag into the fragile hangings. The door itself held to its hinges, but only just.

After Wickham's revelation, Miles had covered the space between the War Office and Grosvenor Square in record time, heedlessly upsetting applecarts, shouldering aside innocent passersby, and stepping on small animals, all the while assuring himself that Henrietta was a notoriously late sleeper, that she would never have left the house, that the Black Tulip couldn't have possibly traced them to Loring House yet. He had held the image of Henrietta, brown hair fanned across the crimson counterpane, peacefully slumbering, to him like a talisman.

Seeing that empty bed had been one of the worst moments of his life. The worst. Worse than the scene in the garden, worse than the loss of Richard's friendship. Wild with disbelief, Miles had tossed aside the bedcovers, crawled under the bed, even thrown open the doors of the armoire as if, for some arcane reason, Henrietta might have crawled in there and gotten stuck. It wasn't until after he had charged through both dressing rooms, turned the old wooden bathtub upside down, and yanked down the bed hangings that he'd seen the note lying there among the discarded bedclothes. He'd snatched it up, hoping—well, he wasn't even sure what he was hoping for. His mind hadn't been working along orderly lines.

Beneath his message, in Henrietta's graceful, looping letters, it said only, "Gone out, too. Should be back by noon. H." And beneath that, a postscript, in mirror to his own. "Splendid."

Miles had crushed the note in his hand, making promises to any minor deity he could think of, anyone, anything, just so long as he could get Henrietta back, unharmed.

She hadn't been at Uppington House. Penelope hadn't seen her. Nor had Charlotte. Geoff couldn't be found to be questioned, so Miles left a note, marked urgent. One last stop at Loring House, where Henrietta hadn't reappeared—Stwyth didn't know where she had gone—and her very absence screamed out a reproach, announced the worst. She must have been taken. And Miles knew bloody well where to go to get her back.

Fueled by anxiety and rage, cravat askew and jacket begrimed from having spent the day sprinting through the malodorous streets of London, Miles wasted no time in heading straight for the dragon's lair, Lord Vaughn's London residence. And if he didn't have Henrietta . . .

But he would. There was no point in admitting other possibilities. He would bloody well give her back, and then Miles would make equally bloody sure he would swing for it. Slowly and painfully, until his face turned as black as that thrice-damned tulip he employed as his insignia.

"What have you done with her?" Miles demanded, breath rasping in his throat, as the door creaked and swayed behind him.

Attired in a dressing gown patterned with Oriental dragons, Lord Vaughn sat at his ease at one end of a round table made of satiny cherry wood, circumscribed with an inlay of pale woods in a geometrical pattern. At one elbow stood a fluted coffeepot, and he sipped from a cup of the same beverage as he flipped idly through the pages of the morning's paper. He was the very image of a gentleman at leisure.

Waving back the footman, who drew up stiffly to attention as if to ward off the intruder, Vaughn treated Miles's precipitate entrance with as little attention as though such scenes were a commonplace of his breakfast routine. Or, thought Miles darkly, as though he had been expecting him.

"With whom, my dear fellow?" Vaughn asked idly, turning over another page of the paper.

"Who?" Miles demanded incredulously, clamping down on the

urge to strangle the bounder with the sash of his own robe. Only the recollection that Vaughn could tell him more alive than asphyxiated held him back. *"Who?"*

Summoning up coherent phrases was a matter of another order of effort entirely.

Vaughn looked lazily up from his copy of *The Morning Times*. "As edifying as I find your owl impression, I believe a name might be more to the point."

"Right." Miles flexed his hands, grappling with his temper. "If that's the way you want to play it."

"It might be helpful if you apprised me of the rules of the game I'm meant to be playing," remarked Vaughn mildly. "It would be vastly unsporting of you to do otherwise."

"No more unsporting than you sitting there, pretending you haven't any idea of what I'm talking about," countered Miles heatedly.

Vaughn raised an eyebrow.

Miles planted both hands on the table, leaned forward, and lowered his voice to a dangerous undertone.

"What have you done with Lady Henrietta?"

Vaughn presented an excellent facsimile of surprise. His jaded eyes lifted momentarily from his coffee cup in an expression of mild interest. "Lady Henrietta? Gone missing then, has she?"

"She hasn't *gone missing*. She's been abducted, and you damn well know it. Where have your henchmen taken her, Vaughn?"

"Henchmen," repeated Vaughn flatly. He placed his cup carelessly in its saucer, the very picture of amused urbanity. "As much as I admire and—dare I say?—esteem Lady Henrietta, I do draw the line at abduction. So common."

Vaughn signaled for a footman to pour him another cup of coffee.

Miles fumed. He hadn't expected Vaughn to crack instantly— after all, the man was a deadly spy, and they were adept at this sort of thing—but he had hoped for some sort of reaction, a shifty flicker of the eyes towards a hidden door, a mysterious motion to a footman. He could threaten to search the premises, but he doubted it would avail him anything. Vaughn was too sensible to have hidden Henrietta in his own house. He must have a hidey-hole somewhere, a cottage in the country, or a dodgy flat in one of the seedier parts of town, where he could question his victims at his leisure.

Victims. Miles remembered Henrietta's unfortunate contact and wished he hadn't.

He took some slight comfort from Vaughn's presence at the break-fast table. The identity of the Pink Carnation was important enough that Vaughn would want to question her himself. Damn. Miles could have thumped himself over the head with the heavy silver tray on the sideboard if it wouldn't have impeded his ability to rescue Henrietta. Why hadn't he thought of that before? The thing to do was to lie in wait until Vaughn left the house and then follow him to his hidden lair. Damn, damn, damn. Why hadn't he thought of that before he came haring over here?

"Why am I meant to have abducted Lady Henrietta?" Vaughn in-quired with deceptive mildness. "Let me see." Vaughn drummed his fingers against the polished wood of the table in a practiced gesture that set Miles's teeth on edge. "Overcome with passion, I spirited her away in my carriage to Gretna Green—no, that won't do, will it, as I'm still here? Come, Mr. Dorrington, this is the stuff of Covent Gar-den, not civilized people."

"I'll duel you for her." Miles knew that the more valorous course would be to feign embarrassment, apologize, and back out, but worry spurred him on. Who knew how long it would be before Vaughn went to see Henrietta? Or what his minions might be doing to her now? He wanted this settled now.

And he wanted to do bodily violence to Vaughn.

The latter, Miles assured himself, was a purely secondary consid-eration, but if poking holes in Vaughn could make him reveal Henri-etta's whereabouts, Miles wouldn't sneer at the opportunity.

"A duel?" Vaughn sounded more amused than otherwise. "I haven't been challenged to one of those in years."

If looks could wound, Vaughn would already have been spread out on the turf of Hounslow Heath. "Consider this your opportunity to make up for lost time."

"Much as I relish the prospect"—Vaughn cocked an eyebrow at Miles—"I really cannot do so under false pretenses. You see," he said apologetically, "I don't have Lady Henrietta."

Miles was rather surprised that Vaughn persisted in maintaining his charade. He didn't think it was fear of the field of honor—Vaughn had a reputation as a fierce and practiced swordsman, whatever he might say about a recent dearth of duels—but it was deuced annoying.

"Do you expect me to believe that?" demanded Miles.

Vaughn spread his arms in an expansive gesture. "Would you care to search the premises?"

"Oh, no." Miles narrowed his eyes. "I'm not falling for that. You wouldn't have her here; that would be too obvious. A flat somewhere . . . or a cottage in the country . . ." He watched Vaughn closely for a flicker of recognition or fear, but the man's face betrayed nothing more than well-bred incredulity.

"All the same," Vaughn said politely, "my house is at your disposal, as are my staff, should you care to question them." His tone suggested that he thought Miles would be a fool to do anything of the kind. But that, reasoned Miles, was just what Vaughn would want him to think.

Miles played his last card. "Do the words 'Black Tulip' mean anything to you, Vaughn?"

"As a flower"—Vaughn shook out his paper with a nonchalant gesture—"they leave something to be desired. If you hope to win Lady Henrietta back with bouquets, you would do better to buy her roses. Red ones."

Before Miles could tell Vaughn exactly what he should do with his roses, in horticultural detail, the quiet of the breakfast parlor was breached by the sound of a large object plummeting to the floor just outside the door. China crashed; spurs scraped against the parquet floor; a male voice rose in remonstration. Miles whirled towards the door, filled with formless hope. Henrietta might have freed herself from Vaughn's henchmen and fought her way downstairs. That was his Hen!

The happy image shattered as the door once again rebounded

against the wall. A slender man in brown barreled through, followed by the huffing form of an agitated servant.

"Sir!" The latter flung himself upon his employer's mercy, his wig askew and his stock untied. "I tried to stop him. I tried—"

"Mr. Dorrington?" the other man elbowed past, halting abruptly in front of Miles. Any hopes Miles might have had of his being Henrietta in disguise were firmly dashed. It was hard to make out the man's features, since they were caked in a thick mask of grime, but they weren't Henrietta's, and that was all Miles cared about.

"Yes," said Miles warily.

He glanced to Vaughn, still seated in state at the head of the table, but Vaughn looked, for once, quite as baffled as Miles felt.

"Followed you here," the man in brown explained, still fighting for air. His garments, on closer inspection, might have once been some color other than brown, but looked as though they had been washed in mud, allowed to dry, and muddied again. "I've been looking for you all day."

"For me," said Miles flatly.

"For you or for Lady Henrietta." At the mention of Henrietta's name, the denizens of the room snapped to attention, with the exception of the footman, who had lowered himself to his knees, and was mournfully examining the scratches in the elaborate inlay of the floor, occasionally emitting small whimpering noises at a particularly jagged gash. "I'm to give you this."

Miles snatched up the note the courier proffered, as grimed as the man himself, immediately recognizing the hand. Jane had wasted no time on explanations. There were only three words written on the little piece of paper, and Miles exclaimed them aloud without even realizing he had done so.

"The Marquise de Montval?"

Crumpling the note in one large hand, Miles shoved it into a pocket. He pointed a finger at Vaughn. "I *will* be back," he warned, and slammed out of the room.

The fine lines around his eyes more pronounced than usual,

Vaughn watched him go, directed a footman to take the courier to the kitchens to be fed, and thoughtfully drained the last of his coffee.

Folding his paper, Lord Vaughn flicked a finger in the direction of the silent footman who stood by the sideboard.

"Tell Hutchins to attend me in my dressing room. And see that my carriage is brought around. At once."

"My lord." The footman bowed his white-powdered head and departed.

"I," commented Vaughn to the empty air above the sideboard, cinching the waist of his dressing gown, "have an assignation to keep."

His lips twisted into a sardonic smile.

"With Lady Henrietta."

Chapter Thirty-Four

———— ❦ ————

Assignation: *an ambush, generally set in motion by the agents of the enemy. See also under* Tête-à-Tête *and* Rendezvous

—from the Personal Codebook of the Pink Carnation

"Did you really think I wouldn't recognize you, Lady Henrietta?"

"Lydee 'Enree-ayta?" gabbled Henrietta hastily in a foreign accent that might have been Italian or Spanish or just gobbledygook; Henrietta didn't have time to think through her putative nationality, only that wherever it was, it was heavy on the vowels. "'Ooo eees dees Lydee 'Enree-ayta?"

The marquise pursed her lips in a gesture of extreme exasperation, and rolled her eyes briefly heavenward.

"Your disguise is clever," she said in a tone heavy with sarcasm, and entirely free of the purring note that had distinguished her public persona. "I grant you that. But your accent leaves much to be desired."

"I no unnerstan'. Eet eez, 'ow you say? Dee way I speak."

"Enough, Lady Henrietta. Enough. I haven't the time. And neither"—the marquise's black eyes narrowed in a decidedly inimical way—"have you."

"I have plenty of time," said Henrietta, dropping both her bucket and her role, and backing away a bit under that basilisk stare. "But clearly you don't. I'll just be getting along then, shall I? I don't want to keep you if you're busy."

The marquise ignored that. "Were you looking for your little friend?" she asked, watching Henrietta's face like a tailor sizing up a bolt of cloth.

"My little friend?" Henrietta didn't have to feign her confusion. The last time she had possessed anything she might have referred to as a little friend, she had been five years old. The little friend in question had been an imaginary dwarf named Tobias, who lived in a tree in the gardens of Uppington Hall.

The marquise's face took on an expression of extreme satisfaction as she glanced towards the window. "He's not here yet, but he will be. Oh, yes, he will be."

Henrietta took in the vast expanse of bosom and long line of leg revealed by a creation that could scarcely be called a dress. The marquise didn't look like a vindictive agent of the French Republic. She looked like a woman awaiting a lover. Henrietta's lover, to be precise.

Henrietta remembered that ride in the park. Miles wouldn't have . . . No, she reassured herself. He wouldn't have. He had gone to the War Office.

But if the marquise had sent him an invitation . . . The entire scenario unfolded in Henrietta's head. Miles, guilty at raising expectations he was no longer capable of filling (the word "adultery" came to mind—but adultery with whom? Did it count as adultery if one was an unwanted wife, and the other the woman of one's choice?), tucking the note into his pocket, resolving to stop by after his morning's meeting, just to explain. The marquise greeting him, all misty draperies, inflated bosom, and expensive perfume.

The barren townhouse was not the center of a spy ring, then, but a setting for seduction. The seduction of *her* husband.

Henrietta didn't know whether to stick her head into the bucket of ashes or go for the marquise's eyes. The latter struck her as a decidedly more attractive option.

"Do you mean Miles?" Henrietta asked sharply.

"Miles?" the marquise turned in a swirl of filmy fabric, like a rainstorm seeking a heath. "You mean Dorrington?"

Henrietta scowled. "In my experience, those names generally tend to go together."

"Why, you poor little dear." Henrietta would rather a hundred women's scorn than the marquise's pity; it ate like acid at the edges of her self-composure. The marquise laughed delightedly. "I do believe you're jealous."

Henrietta didn't say anything. How could one refute something so palpably true?

Before Henrietta could attempt to construct a dignified answer, the marquise's attention was mercifully arrested by the sound of carriage wheels grating against the uneven cobbles of the quiet street. The marquise drew in a silent breath of exultation that swelled her bosom to new and even more alarming proportions, face alight with a wild triumph.

"We'll have time enough for that later," she said, grabbing Henrietta by the elbow. "But right now, you, my dear, are decidedly *de trop*."

The wheels slowed to a stop. Somewhere outside the window a horse whinnied, and a pair of booted feet hopped to the ground. Henrietta caught the merest glimpse of a brightly painted curricle before the marquise marched her away from the window, her arms surprisingly strong beneath their translucent draperies. Henrietta would have thought she would have been shoved summarily out the door, but the marquise had other ideas. Wrenching open the door of a large cupboard, as empty as the rest of the cupboards throughout the house, she gave Henrietta a stiff shove.

Caught by surprise, Henrietta clipped her shins on the edge of the wardrobe, and tumbled headlong into the dusty interior, banging an elbow painfully against the floor, and grazing her forehead on the back wall. The marquise scooped up Henrietta's legs and shoved them the rest of the way in, slamming the doors shut. Scrambling on her hands and knees to right herself in the cramped space, Henrietta heard a click like a latch being drawn.

"Not ideal," commented the marquise, from just outside the cupboard, "but it will do for the moment."

Henrietta would have chosen a stronger term than "not ideal." Her face was jammed up against the right angle where the side joined the back, and her legs were twisted behind her in a position reminiscent of a mermaid's tail. Henrietta was quite sure of one thing: Legs weren't meant to bend in that direction. Sneezing miserably, Henrietta began to painstakingly wiggle her way upright, easing her legs sideways.

The marquise banged on the side of the cupboard with an imperious fist.

"Quiet in there!"

Eyes streaming, Henrietta twisted her head to glower in the general direction of the sound, but she had no breath to retort. She was too busy sneezing.

With abraded palms, broken nails, and snagged hair, Henrietta managed to claw her way roughly upright within the tight confines of the cupboard, legs curled beneath her. The cupboard was perhaps two feet deep and three feet wide, leaving little room to maneuver. By tilting her head sideways, Henrietta could see through a knothole in the warped wood of the cupboard door (quality in furnishing had clearly not been a priority of the original owner). Through her knothole, Henrietta watched the marquise disposing herself elegantly on the couch in the style of the famous portrait of Mme. Récamier. The fine folds of her skirt draped gently over the length of her legs, outlining more than they concealed. Her head was tilted to show the fine line of her throat, glossy pale against the one dark curl that twined its way in artful wantonness towards the scoop of her bodice. Henrietta wrenched her eye from the knothole and pressed her aching forehead against the rough wood of the inside of the door.

Through her pine prison, Henrietta could hear the door of the sitting room opening, the murmur of a servant's voice, too soft to catch a name, and then the entrance of a pair of booted feet.

With resigned fatalism, Henrietta reapplied her eye to the knothole. It was, unfortunately, only about four feet off the ground, providing her with an excellent view of the marquise, as she elegantly unfolded herself from the couch, slowly stretching yards of leg in a way designed to show them off to their best effect. It was, thought Henrietta, spine as stiff as the Dowager Duchess of Dovedale's, positively indecent. And why couldn't she look like that?

The marquise held out a jewel-laden hand to the possessor of the heavy footsteps in a gesture so effortlessly graceful that Henrietta nearly applauded at the sheer virtuosity of it.

Her gentleman caller, no doubt equally enthralled, came forward to bow over the hand, moving directly across Henrietta's knothole. Back to Henrietta, he bowed over the marquise's hand. It was a broad enough back, encased in a skintight coat, as the fashion demanded. But it wasn't Miles's back.

Henrietta sagged against the side of the cupboard, overcome with such blinding, overwhelming relief, that for a moment it seemed entirely immaterial that she was crouched in someone else's empty furniture. It wasn't Miles. Of course it wasn't Miles. How could she ever have doubted him?

But if it wasn't Miles, who was it? And why would the marquise have assumed that the mystery caller was of any particular significance to Henrietta? If Henrietta remembered correctly, "little friend" took on an altogether more suggestive meaning in French than it did in English.

The gentleman was still standing, leaving Henrietta with only a swath of torso visible through her knothole. But he had been considerate enough to turn slightly, displaying an expanse of embroidered waistcoat, a waistcoat adorned with a veritable garden of tiny pink carnations. Only one man in London—or, at any rate, only one man in London of Henrietta's acquaintance—would wear such an execrably ugly waistcoat, and compound the sartorial solecism by combining it with a carnation pink jacket.

What on earth had Turnip Fitzhugh to do with the marquise?

"I cannot say how delighted I am to see you again, Mr. Fitzhugh." The purr was back in the marquise's voice.

Again?

"Delight's all mine," Turnip reassured her, brandishing a large bouquet. "Lots and lots of delight."

A dozen types of wild surmise began to skitter about Henrietta's head.

Turnip and the marquise had both been at the inn; the unknown gallant (otherwise known as the marquise) had hovered by their table, had cast several long glances in their direction. Could Turnip and the marquise be lovers? It was difficult to imagine the fastidious marquise in the arms of Turnip, who combined one of the best natures in the world with an utter lack of sense or taste. Henrietta doubted that the marquise would have any appreciation for the former. On the other hand, Turnip also possessed a veritable pirate's trove of golden guineas; the Fitzhugh fortune was managed by very responsible bankers in the City, and not all of Turnip's waistcoat purchases had so much as dimpled the principal. The marquise might not prize an earnest heart, but she would no doubt cherish, honor, and obey fifty thousand pounds a year, a townhouse in Mayfair, and three country estates, one with a rather nice collection of Raphael's lesser-known Madonnas.

It did make a certain amount of sense. Even the "little friend" comment fell neatly into the pattern. As an old schoolmate of Richard's, Turnip frequently did his duty to the demands of long acquaintance by leading Henrietta out for the odd quadrille, or fetching lemonade on those occasions when Miles was not to be found. Having seen them together at the inn, the marquise must have marked Henrietta out as a rival for access to the Fitzhugh coffers. It was an explanation that fit very well with the dowager's description of the marquise's character, and entirely removed any possibility of branding her a dangerous French spy. Henrietta couldn't help but feel some slight disappointment at the latter.

The marquise motioned to someone outside of Henrietta's very limited line of vision. "Jean-Luc, would you be so kind as to fetch the coffee?"

In the marquise's throaty voice, even a prosaic term like "coffee" managed to smolder with significance.

"I can't say I'm much one for coffee myself," confided Turnip, disposing himself on the settee, and comfortably stretching his long legs out in front of him.

The marquise joined him in a filmy swirl of draperies. "Why, Mr. Fitzhugh, I intend to make you a coffee you cannot refuse."

"Devilish good coffee, then?" inquired Turnip.

"The very strongest," assured the marquise, laying a manicured hand lightly on his thigh.

Henrietta rolled her eyes at the inside of the cupboard door. This was getting ridiculous! She had plunged from the heights of espionage into the depths of French farce. It was time to go home and confess all to Miles—or maybe not all. Henrietta's shoulders would have sagged had there been room for them to do so. It would be very hard to explain away wild fits of jealousy without revealing the existence of an emotion that would undoubtedly send Miles fleeing to the nearest opera house. There had been no allowance in their bargain for anything stronger than fondness, and certainly not for those three dangerous little words. Suddenly, remaining in the marquise's cupboard indefinitely began to seem like a very attractive way to spend the rest of the afternoon.

There was nothing, reflected Henrietta, shifting uncomfortably on numb legs, like crouching in servant's clothing in someone else's closet to make one realize how low one had sunk. She used to have an orderly life, a sensible life. Her friends came to her for advice. Everyone liked her. And where was she now? Contemplating becoming a closet gnome.

Henrietta experimentally rattled the cupboard door. The latch held, but, like everything else in the house, it didn't feel terribly sturdy. Henrietta tried again.

"I say," said Turnip, looking quizzically at the suddenly shaking piece of furniture. "I do believe your armoire is trying to move."

For a moment, the marquise's seductive mask dropped, to be replaced by an expression of pure annoyance. Henrietta gathered that when the marquise put people places, she expected them to stay put. That thought was enough to make Henrietta rattle the latch again.

"It's nothing but a draft," explained the marquise through

clenched teeth. "Old houses like this are full of drafts. They whistle through the walls like rumor. And we all know how rumor can spread, don't we, Mr. Fitzhugh?"

"Soul of discretion, myself," Turnip strove to reassure her. "Mummer than the tomb. Quieter than a corpse. Closer-lipped than a—"

"But who knows," the marquise broke into Turnip's spate of similes, "what a mere moment's indiscretion may do?"

Henrietta knew, but declined to volunteer her expertise. The marquise's question had sounded more rhetorical than otherwise.

"One must be so careful in these trying, trying days. One little word, one little slip, can be someone's undoing. Ah, thank you, Jean-Luc."

A heavy silver tray was set down in front of the marquise, its baroque opulence at odds with the faded and snagged upholstery of the settee. Henrietta wondered if she had smuggled it out of France with her; it wasn't the sort of item one could sew discreetly into the hem of one's cloak.

"Coffee, Mr. Fitzhugh?" The marquise gestured towards the tray with a graceful hand. Her voice hardened, stiffer than the heavy silver handle of the coffeepot. "Or should I call you by your real name?"

"The mater and pater call me Reginald," supplied Turnip doubtfully. His voice changed. "I say, what was that doing in the coffeepot?"

"I promised you a coffee you wouldn't be able to refuse," replied the marquise. Her voice was no longer seductive, but so flatly matter-of-fact as to be almost entirely devoid of inflection. Henrietta, who had been massaging the feeling back into a leg gone numb, reapplied herself to the knothole.

In one fine-boned hand, the marquise held a thin pistol with a mother-of-pearl handle. She leveled the pistol at Turnip. "And I always keep my promises."

Henrietta closed her gaping mouth before she could get a splinter on her tongue. She had heard of weddings at gunpoint, but never at the hand of the prospective bride. Potential explanations flashed through Henrietta's mind. A woman scorned? Perhaps the marquise, mad with wounded pride at seeing Henrietta and Turnip together, had decided to emulate Medea and exact her revenge? Turnip had been abroad, and fairly recently, too. He might have conducted a passionate romance with the marquise prior to her return to England and then flung her aside. Turnip, however, wasn't really the flinging type. He was far more likely to be flung.

Far less alarmed than Henrietta, Turnip examined the pistol with a professional eye. "That's a deuced fine piece, but not at all the thing to go waving about. Could go off, you know."

"That," said the marquise dryly, "is generally the idea."

Turnip looked perplexed.

"No more games, Mr. Fitzhugh." The marquise looked Turnip straight in the eye. "I know who you are."

"Deuced odd if you didn't," replied Turnip cheerfully, peering into the coffeepot to see if there might be any liquid in there now that the pistol was gone, "considering you invited me."

There was one last possibility. One incredibly attractive possibility. But why would the Black Tulip waste her time on Turnip Fitzhugh?

Jean-Luc had moved to stand behind Turnip. At least, Henrietta assumed it must be Jean-Luc. All she could see of him was livery heavy with silver buttons and a pair of viciously flexing hands. The marquise forestalled Jean-Luc with an infinitesimal flick of her wrist. Henrietta slid her hand along the crack of the doors, digging her fingernails into the wood, trying to find a way to lift the latch. She wasn't sure just how much use she would be against a burly man and a primed pistol, but if she could divert their attention, even for a moment . . .

Leaning back against the arm of the settee, the marquise raised an admiring eyebrow. "You are bold, Mr. Fitzhugh. Very bold."

"Faint heart never won fair lady, and all that." Turnip beamed, lifting his chin and doing his best to look bold. "Pride myself on that *je ne sais* . . . er . . ."

"*Quoi?*" demanded Jean-Luc.

Turnip looked appreciatively back over his shoulder. "Righty-ho! That's the word! Don't know how it came to slip my mind."

"Your mind, Mr. Fitzhugh," gritted out the marquise, rapidly losing patience, "is not all that is going to slip if you persist in this folly."

"Don't know if I'd call it folly," cogitated Turnip. "Foolishness, maybe."

"Jean-Luc," snapped the marquise, out of patience, "bring the chains to bind our stubborn friend."

"But I am in chains, dear lady! Chains of love! Not real chains, of course," Turnip clarified confidingly, "but it's what you'd call a . . ."

"Argh!"

A hearty masculine yelp echoed through the room. It had not come from Turnip, but from the street outside.

Inside the cupboard, Henrietta went cold with alarm.

"No, not that," said Turnip. "Believe it begins with M. Matador?"

It was the right initial, even if the wrong name. Henrietta knew that yelp, a hearty bellow compounded of annoyance and indignation. Henrietta whammed her shoulder against the doors. Through the wooden walls of her prison, she could hear the sounds of a struggle. Something shattered a long way off. A series of curses and crashes followed, most of the former in French, attesting to the fact that Miles was more than holding his own. Closer by, the marquise had risen to her feet, face rigid with alarm and displeasure. Turnip, too, stood up, his broad brow wrinkled with confusion.

"I say," he began, "that sounds like—"

An explosion sounded somewhere in the distance, followed by a loud curse and a heavy thud.

"Dorrington," finished Turnip, in the sudden silence.

Henrietta flung herself desperately against the doors of the cupboard. The beleaguered latch at long last gave way. The doors burst open, sending Henrietta sprawling untidily onto the sitting room carpet.

"Miles!" screamed Henrietta.

"Lady Henrietta?" exclaimed Turnip.

"Guards!" called the marquise.

Stunned by her fall, Henrietta twisted sharply towards the door. In the hallway outside, she heard a familiar voice saying something exceedingly impolite; deep inside her chest, her heart resumed its proper business. Miles was alive. And—glass shattered against plaster—still fighting. Whoever had fallen, it hadn't been he.

But what on earth was he doing here?

"Didn't know you were here, Lady Hen," commented Turnip affably. "Have some coffee."

"Yes," said the marquise, leveling the pistol at Henrietta. "Do."

"I say"—Turnip tapped the marquise on the arm—"don't know what the custom is in France, but not at all the done thing to point firearms at guests."

The marquise ignored him, continuing to point the mother-of-pearl pistol at Henrietta.

"Kindly hand me the pistol in your belt and the knife strapped to your calf," instructed the marquise.

Henrietta looked at her quizzically. "What makes you think I have either of those things?"

"All amateur spies have pistols in their belts and knives strapped to their calves," replied the marquise acidly. "It is a tedious commonplace of the profession."

Both had been listed in Amy's helpful pamphlet, *So You Want to Be a Spy*, but Miles's dueling pistols were back in his old lodgings, and the staff of Loring House already thought she was crazy enough without her waltzing into the kitchen and asking to view their knife collection. There had been a dusty old pair of fencing foils propped above the mantelpiece in what might once have been Miles's father's study, but neither was the sort of piece a girl could inconspicuously pop down her bodice.

"Ah," said Henrietta, in the hopes that the marquise might be distracted until Miles could subdue her henchmen in the hallway. "But I am not an amateur spy."

She wasn't, really, she assured herself. She was more of a liaison.

"You begin to bore me, Lady Henrietta." In the sort of casual gesture with which she might have applied rouge or flipped through a program at the opera, the marquise flicked the lever that cocked the pistol.

"I don't think you want to do that," said Henrietta, slowly raising herself up on her elbows, and wishing she had had the forethought to bring a pistol of her own.

"Why not?" asked the marquise, sounding thoroughly bored.

"Because," ventured Henrietta, cautiously pushing herself up onto her knees and trying to look mysterious, "I'm more use to you alive than dead."

"Whatever might have given you that idea?" inquired the marquise, her voice as level as her gun.

Down the hall, assorted thuds and grunts suggested that Miles was still keeping the marquise's guards busy. How long would he be able to hold them off if the marquise added her pistol to the fray? Henrietta made a desperate shooing motion at Turnip. Turnip, misinterpreting, started trying to fill one of the cups from the empty coffeepot.

Seeing no aid from that quarter, she made a desperate bid to hold both the marquise's attention and her pistol point.

"I," said Henrietta very slowly, "have information for which your government"—she looked closely at the marquise, but the marquise's face revealed nothing but thinly veiled boredom—"would pay dearly."

"Do you?" The marquise's smile was dry, uninterested.

"Dead women tell no tales, you know." Henrietta warmed to her theme.

"But you, Lady Henrietta," said the marquise, "have already revealed everything I needed to know."

"I have?" Henrietta cast her mind anxiously back over the past few days. She couldn't have led the marquise to Jane—could she?

"Are you quite sure about that?" she asked desperately. "I mean, you really wouldn't want to go back to your superiors with possibly incomplete information. Think how angry they would be if you could have found out more. And what if you're mistaken? Just think about that. Are you sure? Are you quite, quite sure?"

The marquise sighed in a manner indicating the extreme ennui of one who had heard prisoners pleading for their lives before, and found it a tedious, if necessary, corollary of her chosen profession.

"Quite"—the marquise's finger tightened on the trigger—"sure."

Chapter Thirty-Five

Coffee, the taking of: *a situation of extreme peril, frequently requiring urgent assistance. See also under* Milk, Addition of
—from the Personal Codebook of the Pink Carnation

"Hen!"

The marquise's head swiveled to the left as Miles burst into the room, trailing four ruffians dressed as footmen. Two clung to his arms, one trailed from Miles's legs, and the fourth was ineffectually trying to leap onto his back.

Miles disposed of the last with a hearty butt of his head, whacked the man hanging onto his right arm out of the way by dint of flinging up a stiff arm to knock him backwards into the wall, used his newly freed hand to punch the guard on his left in the stomach, and dispatched the one clinging to his legs with a single well-placed kick to the head.

Four groaning Frenchmen clutched various parts of their anatomy as Miles rushed precipitously towards Henrietta, eyes for no one but her. "Dammit, Hen, are you all right?"

The marquise recovered before her minions. In one fluid movement, she hauled Henrietta up off the floor, pulled the smaller woman back against her, and shoved the point of her pistol against Henrietta's temple.

"Not so fast, Mr. Dorrington."

Miles skidded to a stop, nearly overbalancing in his haste. He had, he realized, missed a minor detail. The gun that the marquise was in the process of pointing at Henrietta. Damn.

The marquise dragged Henrietta back a step, black eyes flashing from Miles to Turnip and back again. "Neither of you gentlemen move. If you do, the lovely Lady Henrietta will no longer be quite so lovely. Do I make myself understood?"

"Perfectly," said Miles tersely, holding himself absolutely still. Henrietta's face was grimed with dust, and he could see what looked like a nasty scrape on one cheek, but there didn't seem to be any bullet holes, open gashes, or other serious wounds anywhere on her person. Yet. Miles looked directly at the marquise. "What do you want?"

The marquise tilted her dark head, drawing out the moment. "You, Mr. Dorrington, are not in any position to bargain."

"Let her go, and we'll see you safely out of the country," Miles offered recklessly, squelching any thought of what his superiors at the War Office might say to such an offer. He made an effort to keep his posture relaxed, but his eyes were intent as he scanned the marquise for the slightest sign of an opening. If her hand wavered, even for a second . . .

Henrietta shook her head at him, causing the marquise's hand to tighten on the trigger.

Miles stiffened in alarm. "Don't move, Hen," he begged. "Just don't move." He turned back to the marquise. "Well?"

"What are you willing to do to have her back unharmed?"

"Miles, don't!" burst out Henrietta. "You can't let her escape. And I"—her voice faltered, but she went resolutely on, chin set in a stubborn line—"I'm expendable."

"Not to me," Miles said harshly.

"How sweet," said the marquise, in a tone that implied she thought it anything but. "Are you quite finished?"

The marquise jammed the muzzle of the pistol harder against Henrietta's cheek. Henrietta squeaked. Miles tensed.

"Do go on," continued the marquise sarcastically. "Don't allow me to interrupt your little interlude. After all, it may be the last one you have."

"Havey-cavey," muttered Turnip, shaking his head. "Deuced havey-cavey."

Henrietta looked at him in exasperation, stubbing her nose against the pistol for her pains. "*Now* you find the situation havey-cavey?"

"I would remain quiet, if I were you, Lady Henrietta," cautioned the marquise. "And if you think I can be induced to display mercy upon a plea of true love"—on the marquise's lips, the words plummeted to something lower than myth—"you are distinctly mistaken."

"Not mercy," Miles swiftly interpolated, "but common sense. As you can see, Henrietta and I have other things to occupy ourselves, and Turnip is no harm to anyone but his horseflesh. We'll turn our backs and count to ten, and you can just go."

"Not without what I came for."

The marquise looked pointedly at Turnip Fitzhugh.

So did everyone else.

Turnip toyed with the edge of his cravat and looked bashful. "Flattered, I'm sure."

"You can drop the act now, Mr. Fitzhugh," said the marquise, digging her fingers cruelly into the flesh of Henrietta's left arm. "I've been waiting a long time for this moment."

"It can't have been that long," put in Turnip. "I've only known you this past fortnight."

"Perhaps," commented the marquise. "But I have known of you much longer, Mr. Fitzhugh. Or should I say . . . the Pink Carnation?"

"Oh, you shouldn't," muttered Miles. "You really shouldn't."

Henrietta frowned fiercely at him, or as fiercely as she could frown with a pistol indenting one cheek. Miles nodded slightly, to show he understood. If the marquise thought that Turnip was the Pink Carnation, it was safer to let her go on thinking that for the present. Turnip was obdurately dense enough to baffle even the most accomplished of spies. Eyes still locked with Henrietta's, Miles tilted his head slightly to the side. Henrietta narrowed her eyes at him, indicating lack of comprehension. Miles took a deep breath. Trying not to look at the deadly muzzle boring into Henrietta's face, Miles let his eyes shift sideways, his head tilt, and his shoulders sag. Lifting his head, he peered anxiously at her, silently asking if she had understood. Henrietta's eyes widened with understanding; it was all the reassurance Miles needed. He held a finger to his nose to indicate silence. Henrietta compressed her lips in an expression that said, clear as words, "I know, I know." Despite himself, Miles felt his own lips quirk into a crooked grin.

Intent on her prize, the marquise missed the entire exchange. Turnip's face went through the muscle contractions that substituted for cogitation in the Fitzhugh family. After much painstaking thought, his wrinkled brow smoothed and his face lit with comprehension.

"You think I'm—oh, I say! That *is* deuced flattering. Wish I could oblige, but haven't the brains for it, you see, just the waistcoats." Turnip indicated his flower-embroidered clothes, looking up at the marquise like a dog who had just fetched a particularly charming bone for the delectation of his master.

His eager face fell slightly at the lack of answering amusement. Nothing if not eager to please, Turnip tried again. "D'you see?" he urged, gesturing again at his torso. "The waistcoats?"

The marquise didn't see. But Miles saw his moment. Distracted by Turnip, the marquise had loosened her grip on Henrietta; the marquise's fingers barely creased the fabric of Henrietta's sleeve, and the gun hovered an inch from Henrietta's face. A better moment might arise, but they couldn't count on it.

Miles inclined his head sharply at Henrietta. Henrietta bit her lip and gave an infinitesimal nod.

Pressing her eyes briefly closed, Henrietta flung herself sharply to the side, just as Miles lunged at the marquise. The weight of Henrietta's body threw the marquise off balance, causing her to stagger wildly as Henrietta plummeted towards the floor. Miles grabbed the arm in which the marquise held the gun, wrenching it upwards into the air. The pistol went off, the shot nicking chips of plaster from the ceiling. Henrietta instinctively ducked, rolling out of the way of a large chunk of falling plaster.

"You won't," Miles panted, twisting the marquise's wrist as he struggled with her for the gun, "be needing that anymore."

Too breathless for words, the marquise merely snarled. An inadvertent gasp of pain hissed through her lips as Miles applied extra pressure. At the back of the room, the marquise's minions staggered and stumbled back into action, lumbering to the aid of their mistress. The emptied gun popped out of the marquise's hand and into Miles's.

Turning, Miles tossed the gun to Turnip. "Hold this!" he demanded, bracing himself to face the marquise's henchmen, their battered faces incongruous under their formal white wigs, livery torn and stained from their prior brawl.

Catching the gun, Turnip regarded it with bewilderment for a moment, as if unsure what to do with it, and then turned and tossed it to Jean-Luc, just as Miles repelled the first of his attackers with a stiff fist to the jaw.

"The idea is *not* to give the weapons to the other side!" exclaimed Miles in exasperation, jabbing at another attacker with his left fist.

"Oh, right." Turnip shook his head self-deprecatingly and advanced on Jean-Luc, who responded by muttering something very uncomplimentary in French and ramming a ball into the pistol. "I say, would you mind handing that back? Wasn't supposed to give it to you."

Miles muttered something equally uncomplimentary in English, and lunged at Jean-Luc. Behind him, the marquise reached up and yanked one of the glittering pins from her hair, revealing a slim but lethal blade. Her shining dark hair tumbled down behind her as she levered the stiletto at Miles's back.

"Oh, no, you don't!"

Henrietta flung herself at the marquise's back, grabbing at the arm with the stiletto, only to be sent staggering back as the marquise deftly elbowed her in the stomach. Gasping for air, Henrietta stumbled backwards in a half-crouch as the marquise swirled to face her in a swish of filmy fabric, brandishing the stiletto like a sword.

The marquise advanced on Henrietta, blade extended. Holding her skirts with one trembling hand, Henrietta took a corresponding step back, feeling her way blindly backwards.

The marquise's black eyes narrowed, focused on Henrietta like a snake marking out a mouse. "You, my dear, have outlived your usefulness. Just like your friend at the ribbon shop."

"My friend at the ribbon shop?" Henrietta refused to allow her attention to be diverted from the glittering blade in the marquise's hand as she picked her careful way backwards.

"Would you like to know what I did to her?"

"No," broke in Miles, sending the fallen gun ricocheting across the uncarpeted floor with one swift sideways kick. Jean-Luc and Turnip both dove for it, like two dogs after the same bone. "She wouldn't." Miles delivered a sharp uppercut to one attacker's jaw, before ducking a punch from the other.

"Your friend didn't want to talk at first, either, but," purred the marquise, "I convinced her. With this." Striking out with the stiletto, she raised a stinging welt on Henrietta's hand. Henrietta gasped with pain.

Miles angled instinctively towards Henrietta, and his next punch went wide. With an irritated grunt, he disappeared under four flailing Frenchmen.

"What did you do to her?" demanded Henrietta.

"She told me"—the marquise jabbed again, but this time Henrietta was prepared, and jerked out of the way in time to avoid the narrow point—"some very interesting things about you, Lady Henrietta."

The first slash had been meant to admonish; the second had been aimed straight for the heart. Henrietta would have shivered if all her energies hadn't been focused so narrowly elsewhere.

"Did she?" The marquise seemed less dangerous speaking than silent, with part of her energies directed away from her prey. If only she could get close enough to trip the marquise without exposing herself to that deadly blade! Henrietta scooted herself behind a small table, but the marquise slid gracefully around it, her draperies providing no more impediment than the mist that they resembled.

"She told me"—the marquise stalked Henrietta inexorably backwards, but Henrietta didn't dare take her eyes off the blade in her hand long enough to see where she was driving her—"that you were in communication with the Pink Carnation. All I had to do"—the marquise snagged a hole in Henrietta's borrowed bodice, but the thick cloth foiled incursions as effectively as chain mail—"was follow you."

"Not far enough," muttered Henrietta, just as her foot struck something, sending her reeling backwards just in time to evade another thrust to the heart. Flailing, her back slammed into the wall, stunning her.

"So clumsy," tsked the marquise, moving in for the kill.

The best swordsman fears the worst, Henrietta reminded herself, letting herself slide down the wall as the marquise drove her weapon into the ancient wallpaper where Henrietta had been leaning a moment before. The blade bent with the force of the thrust.

Scuttling on hands and knees, Henrietta ducked around the marquise's legs as the marquise flung aside the blunted blade and reached up with a swift, vicious movement to draw another from the dark mass of her hair. Another section of hair came unmoored, slithering down the marquise's back like snakes crawling from their basket.

As if from a long way away, Henrietta could hear the thuds and grunts that betokened men in the thick of a fray. There would be no help from that quarter.

"Hen!" shouted Miles, blond head popping up momentarily from the confused mass of bodies. "You"—*wham!*—"all right?"

Henrietta rolled as the marquise stabbed downwards, spitting her own hair out of her mouth as she careened sideways. Through the screen of brown strands she could see the blade descending again and desperately propelled herself back in the other direction, rolling once, twice, three times, until her movement was arrested with a jarring thud, as she whammed hip-first into something hard and unstable. It rocked slightly, before settling back into place, ashes shifting and settling.

She had been tripped by her own blasted disguise. Next time, if there was a next time, she was bloody well disguising herself as a duelist. Breeches, a sword, pistols. Not a bloody, inconvenient, underfoot, why-don't-you-just-help-the-enemy metal bucket and shovel, thought Henrietta hysterically as the marquise's new and, if possible, even pointier stiletto descended in a deadly arc.

A shovel. It wasn't a pistol, or even a sword, but it was *there*, which counted for far more.

Grabbing the shovel out of the bucket, rocking backwards with the force of the movement, Henrietta swung it wildly upwards, knocking aside the marquise's blade, the heavy iron of the fire tool sending the slim silver blade cartwheeling through the air. From the amorphous mob of men on the other end of the room, she heard a shocked yelp of pain and a truly filthy French curse.

"Sorry!" she called out automatically.

"You, Lady Henrietta," announced the marquise, breathing heavily and looking decidedly miffed, "are proving something of a problem."

"I try," croaked Henrietta, trying to scuttle backwards and stand up all at once, a course of action that made up in desperation what it lacked in coordination.

Above her, the marquise was reaching into her hair with a practiced movement, drawing forth yet another diamond-headed implement of destruction. How many of those did the woman have? Henrietta wondered desperately. Her memory conjured an image of the marquise's elaborate coiffure, studded with diamond-headed pins. If each pin contained a stiletto—she could pin Henrietta to the wall like a butterfly on a naturalist's worktable and still have enough left to adorn her coiffure.

Unless she got close enough to the marquise to whack her over the head with the shovel, the deadly onslaught would continue unabated. She needed something else, something that would put the marquise out of commission long enough for her to do something terribly brave, like run to the other side of the room and hide behind Miles.

"By Jove!" shouted Turnip gleefully from the other side of the room. "I've finally got it!"

The marquise's head shifted sharply to the side. Her face contorted with annoyance as she saw the mob of men exchanging fisticuffs with Miles, while Turnip sat triumphantly on top of Jean-Luc, waving the retrieved pistol in the air.

"Idiots!" cried the marquise in tones that could have shattered glass, flinging her arms in the air in a magisterial gesture reminiscent of Morgan le Fay's calling down demons. "Secure the Pink Carnation!"

Two of Miles's assailants abruptly switched course and rushed at Turnip. Turnip looked alarmed and dove for the floor, trying to crawl underneath the settee. The settee bucked and shook alarmingly. Left with only two attackers, Miles took care of the problem by slamming their heads together with a truly unpleasant cracking noise.

That moment's hesitation was all Henrietta needed.

With strength fueled by desperation, Henrietta grabbed up the bucket of ashes and flung its contents flush into the marquise's face. At least, that was what she intended to do. As she staggered under the weight of the heavy bucket, Henrietta's aim was anything but controlled. Propelled by its own weight, the bucket tore out of Henrietta's hands. Instead of the ashes flying upwards into the marquise's eyes, the whole bucket slammed into the marquise's elegantly garbed stomach. With a satisfying oomph, the marquise toppled backwards. Having dealt with his own attackers, Miles bounded across the room, staggered back a step, and caught the marquise before she hit the ground.

"Got her!" he exclaimed triumphantly, twisting the marquise's arms behind her back.

Shaking a floppy lock of blond hair out of his eyes, Miles looked over the marquise's head (a wise decision, since the marquise's face, had he chosen to look at it, was contorted into a Medusa's mask of pure rage) at Henrietta.

Dried blood streaked his face, much of it his own; one eye was already dangerously swollen; and a long scratch marred one cheek. Henrietta thought he looked wonderful.

Their eyes met over the kicking, spitting form of the marquise.

"Sorry I took so long," said Miles, the expression on his face belying the banality of his words.

"Well, four men," said Henrietta in much the same tone, but her cheeks were glowing and her eyes bright. "It's understandable."

The marquise glowered, and tried to kick Miles in the shin. Miles instinctively sidestepped and retaliated with a swift stomp to the marquise's foot without ever taking his eyes from Henrietta.

"I wanted to rescue you," he said softly.

"You did," Henrietta reassured him. She considered, her lips curving into a smile. "It just took you a while."

The marquise went limp.

Tugging the marquise upright by dint of pulling on her arms, Miles drank in the sight of Henrietta, eyes roving over every tangled snarl of hair, every scratch, every bruise. "I tore the house apart when I got home, and you weren't there."

The marquise rolled her eyes. "If I had wanted to hear romantic drivel, I would have gone to Drury Lane," she snapped.

Henrietta cast her a quelling look. "Nobody asked you." She turned back to Miles, lifting eager eyes to his battered face. "Go on. You were worried?" Henrietta knew it was petty and immature to fish for crumbs of affection, but she was past caring.

"Frantic," Miles admitted.

Henrietta beamed.

"Don't get any ideas," Miles warned. "If I have to go through another afternoon like that one, I'm locking you in a tower for life."

"Will you share it with me?" asked Henrietta softly, trying not to sound as though every fiber of her being was concentrated into those seemingly banal words.

Miles's battered lips quirked into a cocky grin that made his cut lip crack open again. Miles didn't seem to notice. He was just opening his mouth to speak, when a loud voice bleated from the other side of the room.

"I say!" called Turnip. "Hate to interrupt, but I'm having a spot of bother over here."

With an expression of intense annoyance, Miles broke off, turning to survey the wreckage.

Henrietta did likewise, contemplating Turnipicide. Blast, blast, blast. What had Miles been about to say? He might have missed the point entirely. He might have been about to have made a snide remark about incarcerated princesses or her inability to share or any number of things. Or not. It was very hard to interpret the expression of someone whose eye was swelling up and whose lip was trickling blood like a vampire with a drinking problem.

On the other side of the room, Jean-Luc sprawled on the carpet, a dented silver coffeepot lying beside him. Jean-Luc's skull might have been thick, but old silver was thicker. The two footmen whose heads Miles had banged together were also lying on the floor. One twitched groggily, opened an eye, saw Miles, and hastily went limp again, which Henrietta thought an entirely sensible reaction, given the circumstance.

Of the two remaining, one was leaning against the wall, holding his arm at an odd angle and emitting occasional groaning noises. The final ruffian had Turnip pinned beneath the settee, and was making forays with a poker, like a cat swiping at a mouse.

Henrietta and Miles exchanged one look and both burst out laughing.

"I say," came Turnip's aggrieved voice from beneath the settee. "It's not funny!"

Henrietta laughed harder, clutching her stomach as all the tension of the long, awful day rolled out of her in peal after peal of helpless laughter.

"Steady there, old girl," said Miles, but there was enough warmth in his voice to make the laughter catch in Henrietta's throat. "Toss me a bit of rope to tie her up, will you?"

Henrietta swiped tears out of her streaming eyes, and unlooped one of the tasseled cords that held back the threadbare drapes. The curtain fell, plunging the room half into shadow.

"Will this do?" she asked.

"Brilliantly," said Miles.

"Hmph," said the marquise.

"Well, well," said an entirely different voice altogether.

In the open sitting room door, a new shadow fell across the threshold. Miles swiveled towards the door, the marquise still pinioned in his grasp. Henrietta froze, rope still dangling from her hand.

Across the threshold strolled a pair of gleaming black boots. The new visitor wore a black brocade frock coat shot through with silver. A shining quizzing glass framed in the shape of a snake swallowing its own tail dangled just below the immaculate folds of his cravat. In one hand, he carried hat and gloves, with the casual air of a gentleman paying a morning call. A sword swung jauntily from his side.

One elegant hand went to the sword at his hip with the air of a man who well knew how to use it. The light winked off the rings adorning his hand as his fingers closed around the silver hilt.

"Is this a private party, or may anyone join in?" drawled Lord Vaughn.

Chapter Thirty-Six

———— ❧ ————

Deus ex Machina: *1) an interfering interloper of unascer-
tainable intentions; 2) a weak plot device. Note: Neither is to
be desired*
—from the Personal Codebook of the Pink Carnation

"Sebastian," said the marquise flatly, so flatly that Henrietta
couldn't tell if she was pleased or distressed or even the least bit
surprised.

The marquise's use of Lord Vaughn's first name did not bode well.
The marquise had never admitted straight out to being the Black
Tulip. What if she were only a lieutenant, a second in command act-
ing on the orders of someone altogether deadlier and more devious?

Miles's reaction was decidedly less ambiguous.

"Vaughn," he gritted out, tightening his grip on the marquise, who
was showing a distressing inclination to use the distraction as an excuse to escape. "What in the hell are you doing here?"

"I succumbed to a gallant impulse. I perceive"—Vaughn's lazy
eyes took in the dazed French operatives, the shaking settee, and the
marquise, her arms pinioned by Miles—"that it was unnecessary."

Miles was in no mood for circumlocutions. "Whose side are you
on?" he asked bluntly.

Vaughn extracted an enameled snuffbox from his pocket and flipped open the lid. With an elegant gesture, he dropped a pinch of snuff upon his sleeve and sniffed delicately. "I must say, I wonder that myself sometimes."

"His own," responded the marquise, trying to yank her wrists out of Miles's grasp. "Isn't that right, Sebastian?"

"Not this time," replied Lord Vaughn, lazily surveying the room. "I find myself inexplicably drawn to altruism in my old age."

"Is that altruism on behalf of the French?" asked Henrietta, hovering protectively next to Miles.

Vaughn looked blank. "Wherever did you acquire that absurd idea?"

"Secret meetings," put in Miles, holding both the marquise's wrists in one hand and hastily yanking the cord around them with the other. If Vaughn was planning to employ his sword for pernicious purposes, Miles wanted the marquise safely trussed. The thought of her looming over Henrietta, stiletto poised to strike, sent black bile bubbling through his chest like the contents of a witch's cauldron.

The marquise flinched as Miles tugged the knot closed with unnecessary force. "Mysterious documents. Clandestine conversations. And"—Miles gave the rope an extra yank—"your obvious acquaintance with *her*." He indicated the marquise with a curt nod of his head. Rising without ever taking his eyes off Vaughn, Miles moved to stand protectively in front of Henrietta.

Henrietta immediately popped back around.

"Who is the 'she' you were looking for?" asked Henrietta, eyeing Vaughn's sword askance. "And why did you lie about having been in Paris?"

"That," said Vaughn, "is no one's business but my own, even to you."

Henrietta wasn't quite sure what to make of that "even." Miles was. His shoulders squared in a way that boded ill for Vaughn's preference for privacy. "Not when the safety of the realm is at issue."

"I assure you, Mr. Dorrington," drawled Vaughn, in a tone calculated to annoy, "the realm has little to do with it."

"Then what does?" Miles asked sharply.

"My wife."

"Your wife?" echoed Henrietta.

Vaughn's lips twisted in a mockery of a smile. "I admit, after all this time, the phrase does not dance trippingly off the tongue. Yes, my wife."

"Your dead wife?" repeated Miles with heavy sarcasm.

"His not-so-dead wife," interjected the marquise, a slight smile playing about her lips.

Vaughn twisted sharply to look down at her. "You knew?"

"It came to my attention," replied the marquise calmly.

"Would someone care to explain?" growled Miles. "Not you," he added, as the marquise opened her mouth.

"It's quite simple, really," said Vaughn blandly, in a tone that suggested it was anything but. "Ten years ago, my wife . . . chose to depart. The details are unimportant. Suffice it to say that she left, and in such a way as to make the tale of illness the best way of warding off scandal."

"So you knew she was alive?" ventured Henrietta.

"No. The carriage in which she had departed had an unfortunate encounter with a cliff. I assumed she was in it. I labored under this happy misapprehension until three months ago, when the first of several letters arrived, advising me of her continued existence, and offering up certain of her correspondence as proof."

"Ah!" said Miles. He still had that note floating around somewhere, most likely in his waistcoat pocket, along with the name of Turnip's tailor.

"Ah?" Henrietta looked at him quizzically.

"Later," muttered Miles.

Vaughn, however, had reached his own conclusions regarding missing correspondence and rifled rooms.

"Were you the ruffian who attacked my poor valet? Hutchins has been limping for this past fortnight." Using his quizzing glass, Vaughn gestured languidly at one of the perfectly starched ruffles of his cravat. "It has quite affected his treatment of my linen. Nervous temperament, you understand."

"At least I didn't have your valet stabbed," glowered Miles.

"Stabbed?" asked Vaughn, eyebrows ascending.

"Don't claim you don't know about it."

"He doesn't," put in the marquise, working at the bonds on her wrists.

"Your credibility," Miles informed her, swooping down and yanking the rope into a third knot, just in case, "is not exactly the highest just now."

The marquise straightened her back and looked down her nose, no easy feat for one sprawled on the ground, encompassed by a curtain cord.

"Would the Republic employ such a warped tool?"

"From what I've seen"—Henrietta removed a hidden stiletto from the marquise's hair, eyeing both it and its owner with distaste—"yes."

"I cannot tell you how flattered I am by the universally high assessment of my character," commented Lord Vaughn. "Remind me of that the next time I contemplate a spot of knight-errantry."

Henrietta flushed guiltily. "I am sorry."

"I'm not," said Miles. "Madame Fiorila?"

"An old friend, nothing more. She was kind enough to offer her services in pursuit of my errant spouse. My valet?"

Miles had the grace to look sheepish. "A mistake on my part. One last question. Why all the interest in Henrietta?"

Vaughn directed a shallow bow in the direction of Henrietta, who was mining the marquise's coiffure for instruments of destruction. A small pile had developed next to her, safely out of the reach of the marquise. "You, of all people, should be able to discern the reason for that, Mr. Dorrington."

"Right," mumbled Miles.

Damn. He had liked it better when he thought Vaughn was a spy. But Henrietta wouldn't have been interested in an attenuated rake. Would she? Women did tend to be drawn to the sardonic, brooding type—look at all those romances Henrietta was constantly trading back and forth with Charlotte. The thought was enough to turn Miles's blood icier than the Thames in January. He glanced towards Henrietta, but the blush that heated her cheeks as she steadily met Vaughn's gaze did nothing to allay Miles's fears or improve his temper.

The marquise emitted a husky laugh with an undertone harsh as sandpaper. "So that explains it! I wondered what might move you to interfere in my affairs at this late date, Sebastian. I hadn't thought it would be anything so"—her derisory glance flicked over Henrietta's begrimed face and tousled hair—"common."

Vaughn regarded her with grim amusement. "You always had all the sensibility of a rhinoceros, didn't you, Theresa?"

"There was a time when you thought otherwise."

"There was a time," Vaughn returned, with a fastidious flick of his handkerchief, "when I had very poor taste."

The marquise's lips went white around the edges.

Henrietta felt rather as though she had arrived late to the theater and entered a play in the third act. "Do forgive me for interrupting," she said, with what she thought was eminently pardonable asperity, "but what are you talking about?"

"Has Theresa"—the way Vaughn drawled the name, drawing out the central vowel, resonated with insult—"told you about her activities in Paris? Marat, Danton, Robespierre, all friends of our fair Theresa. Of course, that was many years ago, when it was still fashionable to court the extreme. But you didn't stop there, did you?"

"You knew them, too."

"It was an intellectual exercise for me. But not for you, was it?" Vaughn tapped a finger thoughtfully against the enameled lid of his snuffbox. "I must say, you have surprised me. I shouldn't have thought you would like your new masters any better than your old ones."

"You never understood," the marquise replied scornfully.

"Far better than you, I believe," countered Vaughn. "With your brave new Republic baptized in blood. Was it worth it, Theresa?"

"Can you ask?"

"Can you answer?"

"Can you save the Platonic dialogue for some other occasion?" demanded Miles, stomping over towards the marquise. "As fascinating as I'm sure we all find this little window into your past, Vaughn, I, for one, will feel better when our flowery friend here is safely in the custody of the War Office."

"I second that," said Henrietta, rubbing her bruised arm. Little welts were already beginning to form where the marquise's fingernails had bitten into her skin, complementing the graze on Henrietta's forehead, the scratches on her knees, and more contusions than she cared to think about.

Vaughn's sword rang free of its scabbard.

Miles whirled into a defensive crouch, casting about for something with which to fight him. Catching sight of a large metal object on the floor, he grabbed for Henrietta's discarded shovel and raised it to the ready. Vaughn ignored him. Instead of turning his sword on Henrietta or Miles, Vaughn put the gleaming tip to the marquise's throat. In a movement so delicate that it didn't even raise a line on her pale skin, he drew out a gleaming silver chain.

"You might want to show this little bagatelle to your superiors when you deliver our charming Theresa to them," Vaughn said mildly.

Miles let the shovel drop, looking rather disappointed at being balked of the chance to bludgeon Vaughn.

Henrietta let out all her pent-up breath. She hadn't thought she was that terribly obvious, but Vaughn quirked a jaded eye in her direction. As Miles bent to examine the marquise's necklace, Vaughn sheathed his sword and took a step towards Henrietta.

"Did you really think I was going to use that on you?"

Henrietta made an apologetic face. "The evidence really was quite damning."

Vaughn's voice was rich with shared memory, smoky and evocative as incense. "So I remain doomed to be dammed, Lady Henrietta?"

As always with Vaughn, Henrietta felt her way uncertainly through a verbal maze. This time, however, she was quite sure there were no dragons lurking in its depths.

"Not in that particular circle of inferno," she said firmly, tilting her head towards the marquise. Miles was examining the marquise's necklace, which happened to be resting just above a very impressive display of cleavage. Quashing that line of thought, Henrietta forcibly dragged her attention back to Vaughn. "Whether you linger in other nether regions is, as I told you before, entirely your own affair."

"Dante," commented Vaughn lightly, "had Beatrice to lead him from the depths."

Henrietta resisted the urge to crane her neck around to monitor Miles, and forced herself to smile pleasantly at Vaughn. It was always quite flattering to be compared to literary heroines, even of the more milk-and-water variety. And it was even more flattering to have attached a man of wit and cultivation, even if, like Shakespeare's Beatrice (not to be compared with Dante's), Henrietta found him too costly for workaday use. It would, Henrietta imagined, grow irksome to be perpetually marching through a maze of someone else's devising, to be forever fencing and weighing meanings over the breakfast table and in the bedchamber.

There was nothing subtle about Miles. Henrietta lost the battle with herself and peeked. Miles, gratifyingly, was paying very little attention to the marquise's more obvious attributes. Instead, his gaze was fixed upon Henrietta and Vaughn with a scowl that needed very little interpretation.

Henrietta turned back to Vaughn feeling immeasurably cheered.

"I think that you'd be rather bored by a Beatrice," she advised firmly. "What you need is a Boadicea."

"I'll bear that in mind the next time I come upon a band of marauding Britons," said Vaughn dryly. "I've always liked women in blue."

Miles's scowl erupted into a loud growling noise. "If I might interrupt?"

Henrietta hurried the few paces to his side and peered over his shoulder. "What did you find?"

From the central panel of the large diamond-studded cross that hung about the marquise's neck, Miles had extracted a thin roll of paper. The writing was small, and in French, bits of it reduced to numbers, but the import was still clear.

"My goodness," echoed Henrietta.

"She used to keep love letters in there," said Vaughn, coming up behind them.

"Yours?" asked Miles.

"Among others," said Vaughn. He shrugged. "I consider it a passing phase, like the measles—only sooner cured and with fewer lingering effects."

"The sides also open," Miles told Henrietta, ignoring Vaughn. He opened his fist to reveal a small silver seal. Henrietta plucked it from his palm, turning it over. Incised into the surface, dulled with years of wax, but still legible, was the rounded outline of a small but distinctive flower. A tulip.

"And this," said Miles grimly, opening his other palm to reveal a small vial, fashioned out of glass, and filled with a grainy substance that shifted with the movement of Miles's hand.

"What is it?" asked Henrietta.

"Enough poison to put half of London off their dinners— permanently," supplied Vaughn, assessing the white powder with a practiced eye.

"Enough to see her swing, that's for certain," said Miles, favoring Vaughn with a curl of his lip that strongly suggested just which Londoner Miles would like to see put permanently off his dinner.

Vaughn turned to Henrietta and executed a practiced obeisance. "Leaving London," he said, face and voice perfectly bland, "free for the fair to reign unhindered."

Henrietta, face streaked with grime and hair in a snarl, rolled her eyes.

Miles reacted somewhat more strongly. He dropped the marquise's necklace and rounded on Vaughn.

"She's taken," gritted out Miles. "So you can just stop looking at her like that."

"Like what?" asked Vaughn, enjoying himself hugely.

"Like you want to take her home and add her to your harem!"

Vaughn considered. "Last I looked, I wasn't in possession of one, but you know, Dorrington, it really is an excellent idea. I shall have to see to it at once."

Henrietta, who had been watching the exchange with hands on hips and mounting incredulity, marched in between the two men.

"In case you forgot, I'm standing right here. Hello!" She executed a sarcastic little wave. "And I'm not," she said with a repressive glower at Vaughn, "being carted off to anyone's harem."

"I can see that," replied Vaughn, the laugh lines at the corners of his eyes deepening. "You would be dreadful for morale. Even if pleasing to the eye. No." He shook his head. "The Chief Eunuch would never agree."

"It's not the eunuch I'm worried about. He"—Miles jabbed a finger at Vaughn, looking fiercely at Henrietta as he did so—"is just a rake."

"Just?" murmured Vaughn. "I prefer to regard it as a way of life."

Miles ignored him. "He may be able to turn a clever phrase, and do that . . . thing with his cravat—"

"A design of my own devising," interjected Vaughn blandly. He subsided with a slight gurgling noise as Henrietta's foot descended heavily on his.

Miles saw the interplay but misread the significance.

"Dammit, Hen, how can you let yourself be so taken in? All those flowery compliments—they're just what rakes do. It's pure flummery. It's not real. No matter what he says, he doesn't love you like—er—" Miles broke off, face frozen in an expression of hopeless horror.

A shocked silence descended over the room. Turnip's head poked curiously out from under the settee.

"Like?" prompted Henrietta in a voice that didn't sound like her own.

Miles blinked rapidly, mouth opening and closing in soundless alarm, looking like a condemned man brought face-to-face with the headsman's ax for the first time. Concluding there was no escape, Miles climbed the scaffold with dignity.

"Like I do," he said heavily.

"Love? Me? You?" squeaked Henrietta, both vocabulary and vocal range deserting her. She thought a moment, and added, "Really?"

"That wasn't how I was going to say it," burst out Miles, looking at her entreatingly. "I had it all planned out."

Henrietta's face dissolved into a dizzying smile. Shaking back her hair, she announced giddily, "I don't care how you said it as long as you don't take it back."

Miles was still mourning the loss of his Romantic Plan. "There was going to be champagne, and oysters, and you"—he held out both hands as though shifting a piece of furniture—"were going to be sitting there, and I was going to get down on one knee, and . . . and . . ."

Words failed Miles. He waved his arms about in mute distress.

Words seldom failed Henrietta.

"You great idiot," she said in such loving tones that Vaughn discreetly removed himself several paces, and Turnip climbed all the way out from under the settee to attain a better view.

Holding out both hands to Miles, Henrietta lifted shining eyes to his battered face. "I never expected grand declarations of love or romantic gestures."

"But you deserved them," Miles said stubbornly. "You deserved flowers and chocolates and . . ." He paused, scrabbling around in his memory. He didn't think it was precisely the moment to bring up the peeled grapes. "Poetry," he finished with grim triumph.

"I think we can contrive to muddle by without it," Henrietta said with mock solemnity. "Of course, if you could see your way to the occasional ode . . ."

"You deserved better," Miles insisted. "Not a hurried marriage, and a hurried wedding night and—"

Henrietta dimpled. "I have no complaints on that score. Do you?"

"Don't be absurd," he said gruffly.

"There you have it, then," she said firmly.

Miles opened his mouth to argue. Henrietta stopped him by the simple expedient of placing a finger on his lips. The gentle touch silenced Miles more abruptly than being tackled by a horde of rampaging Frenchmen. Henrietta resolved to remember that for future arguments. She just hoped the French never figured it out.

"I don't want better," she said simply, eyes eloquent on his. "I want *you.*"

Miles made a strange choking noise that sounded like it wanted to be a laugh when it grew up. "Thanks, Hen," he said tenderly.

"You know what I mean."

"Yes." Miles lifted the hand she had held to his lips and kissed the palm in a gesture of such reverence it made Henrietta's throat tight. "I do."

"I love you, you know," she said, around the strange obstruction in her throat.

"I didn't know, actually," Miles said, looking at her wonderingly, like a voyager viewing his home after a long journey, putting together all the old familiar places again in a new and beloved way.

"How could you not?" demanded Henrietta, "with me following after you like a lovesick duck?"

"A duck?" echoed Miles, face creasing into an incredulous grin. His shoulders shook with suppressed laughter. "Trust me, Hen, you never looked like a duck. A *hen*, maybe." Miles wiggled his eyebrows. Henrietta groaned. "But never a duck."

Henrietta whacked him on the chest. "It's not funny. It was dreadful. And then when you were forced to marry me . . ."

Miles coughed, his amusement fading. "I'm not sure 'forced' is exactly the right word."

"What else would you call it when someone threatens to call you out?"

"There's one slight problem with that logic." Miles paused, looking slightly sheepish. "In case you didn't notice, Richard didn't exactly want us to marry."

Henrietta's eyes narrowed as she digested this information. She looked closely at Miles. "You mean . . ."

"Mm-hmm." Miles scrubbed his hand through his hair. "I was afraid that if I gave you time to think it through, you would recover your senses and agree with him. It could have been hushed up, you know. Richard's staff is inhumanly discreet, and as for the Tholmondelays . . ." Miles shrugged.

"That," said Henrietta meltingly, looking like someone who had just been handed a decade's worth of Christmas presents all at once, "is better than poetry."

"Good," said Miles, taking her into his arms. "Because," he added, his lips a whisper away from hers, "I'm not writing you any."

Their lips met with a purity of emotion that was ode, sonnet, and sestina all in one. No rhymes had ever been smoother, no meter more perfect, no metaphors more harmonious than the melding of mouths and arms, the press of her body against his, as they leaned against each other in an enchanted golden circle where there were no French spies, no sardonic ex-suitors, no importunate schoolmates, nothing but the two of them meandering languorously through their own personal pastoral idyll.

"Devil take it, I knew there was something havey-cavey going on," said Turnip, who had climbed entirely out from under the settee and was looking as censorious as someone in a carnation pink coat could contrive to look.

"It's not havey-cavey," tossed back Miles, eyes never leaving Henrietta, who looked delightfully flushed and even more delightfully befuddled. "We're married."

Turnip considered. "Don't know if that makes it better or worse. Secret marriages, not at all the thing, you know."

"They will be now," prophesied Miles. "So why don't you just go find yourself one, before everyone else starts contracting them, too."

Vaughn coughed discreetly. That eliciting no reaction, he coughed somewhat less discreetly.

"As charming as this is," he said in a tone that caused a flush to rise to Miles's cheeks, "I suggest you postpone your raptures until the Black Tulip is in the possession of the proper authorities. I assume you do know those proper authorities, Dorrington?"

Miles reluctantly relinquished his grasp on Henrietta's shoulders and turned to face Vaughn, keeping one hand protectively on her waist, just in case Vaughn still cherished any notions about harem girls.

"I do," he said, adding, with just a hint of malicious satisfaction, "They're the ones who set me on to you."

Vaughn sighed, brushing an imaginary speck of dust from the ruffles of his sleeve. "I don't understand. I lead such a quiet life."

"Like Covent Garden at sunset," muttered Miles. "Ow!"

"That's what shins are for," explained Henrietta benignly.

"If that's what you think, remind me to wear thicker pantaloons," said Miles, rubbing his aching appendage. "Potentially armored ones."

"I'll make them for you myself," said Henrietta.

"I'd rather you remove them yourself," Miles whispered in her ear.

The two exchanged a look of such smoldering intimacy that Vaughn found it necessary to cough again, and Turnip burst out with, "Discussing a gentleman's nether garments—not at all the thing in mixed company, you know!"

"We're married," chorused Henrietta and Miles.

"Sickening, isn't it?" commented Vaughn to no one in particular. "Remind me never to be a newlywed. It is an insufferable state."

A sarcastic voice rose from the floor. "Could you please get on with deciding my fate? This floor is exceedingly uncomfortable, and the conversation even worse."

Henrietta glanced down. "You don't seem unduly perturbed."

"Why should I be?" said the marquise, in tones that suggested she saw this as merely a temporary setback. "You have a most amateur organization."

"Who managed," pointed out Henrietta, "to catch you."

"A mere technicality," snapped the marquise.

"We'll have to take her to the War Office," Miles interrupted. "And then"—he exchanged another look with Henrietta that made her go pink to the tips of her ears—"we are going home."

Home. It was such a lovely word.

"I find myself again moved to gallantry," said Vaughn in tones of intense weariness. "If you wish, I will undertake to deliver our mutual friend to—the War Office, you said?"

Miles visibly hesitated.

"Or," said Vaughn smoothly, angling his head towards Turnip, "you could have him do it."

Miles handed Vaughn the ends of the rope. "You're a good chap, Vaughn. And if she escapes, I know where to look."

"You have a rare jewel, Dorrington. See that you take good care of her."

Miles had no difficulty whatsoever in promising to do so.

As dusk settled on the city, Miles and Henrietta wandered hand in hand through the tangled streets of London to Loring House. Strains of red and gold flared in the sky like heraldic banners signaling triumph. Henrietta and Miles didn't even notice. They meandered through the gloaming in their own rosy glow, eyes for no one but each other. The special providence that looked out for fools and lovers guarded their path. If refuse grimed the ground underfoot, neither noticed; if footpads plied their sinister trade, they did it elsewhere. And if, from time to time, the couple took advantage of the lengthening shadows to exchange something more than whispers, spying eyes and wagging tongues held no fear for them.

Given the profusion of long shadows and convenient cul-de-sacs, it was a very long walk home, indeed. It was full dark by the time Grosvenor Square came into view, and they had worked out to their satisfaction a program of events for the evening, which included a bath (a suggestion to which Miles acceded with an alarming alacrity that boded ill for the elderly bathtub), bed (Miles), supper (Henrietta), and bed (Miles).

"You already said that," protested Henrietta.

"Some things bear repeating," Miles said smugly. He leaned closer, his lips brushing her ear as they walked up the stairs to the front door, in the uneven light of the torchères. "Again, and again, and again."

"Incorrigible," sighed Henrietta, with a look of mock despair.

"Indubitably," agreed Miles, just as the front door swung open in front of them.

Miles opened his mouth to inform his butler that they would be not at home to callers. Not today, not tomorrow, preferably not even next week.

"Ah, Stwyth," began Miles, and stopped short, careening into Henrietta, who was doing her best to imitate a pillar of salt.

.It wasn't Stwyth at the door. Nor was it the underhousemaid from whom Henrietta had borrowed her current costume.

In the doorway of Loring House stood a petite woman dressed in rich traveling clothes. Lady Uppington's gloved hands were on her hips, and one booted foot beat an ominous tattoo against the marble floor. Behind her, Henrietta could see her father, also dressed in traveling attire, arms folded across his chest. Neither looked happy.

"Oh, dear," said Henrietta.

Chapter Thirty-Seven

Ever after, happily: *1) the incarceration of England's ene-*
mies; 2) the felicitous result of the transcendent power of re-
ciprocated affection; 3) all of the above
          —from the Personal Codebook of the Pink Carnation

"In," said Lady Uppington in a tone that boded no good. "Both of you. Now."

Henrietta went with all the enthusiasm of an aristocrat mounting the steps to the guillotine. Miles followed meekly behind.

"Hello, Mama, Papa," said Henrietta in a slightly strangled voice. "Did you have a nice time in Kent?"

Her father raised a silvered eyebrow in a look that managed to convey incredulity, disappointment, and anger all at the same time. Quite impressive for one eyebrow. Henrietta clamped down on a surge of nervous giggles that she feared would do little to improve her position in the eyes of her parents.

Lady Uppington didn't rely on facial expressions to convey her feelings. Slamming the door with a vehemence that left no one in any doubt as to her emotions, she whirled to face her errant offspring.

"*What* were you thinking?" she demanded, pacing in furious circles around Henrietta and Miles. "Just answer me that! What *were* you thinking?"

"We caught a French spy," interjected Miles hopefully, distraction having worked upon Lady Uppington in the past.

It failed miserably.

"Don't even *try* to change the subject!" snapped Lady Uppington, looking, if anything, even angrier than before. "I can't go away for one weekend! *One weekend!* I am rendered speechless, *speechless*"—Lady Uppington flung both arms into the air—"by the sheer imprudence of your actions, by the complete lack of respect you have shown for your reputation, your family, and the solemn nature of matrimony."

"It was all my fault," interrupted Miles gallantly, placing a protective hand on Henrietta's shoulder.

Lady Uppington jabbed a finger at him. "Don't worry. I'll get to you in a minute." She turned the admonishing appendage back on Henrietta. "Did I raise you to behave like this?"

"No, Mama," protested Henrietta. "But what happened was . . ."

"We know what happened," said her father grimly. "Richard sent to us."

"Bleargh," said Henrietta.

"Clearly, I have failed," announced Lady Uppington. "I have failed as a mother."

Henrietta cast a desperate glance over her shoulder at Miles, who looked about as ready as she was to dissolve into a guilty puddle of remorse on the dingy marble floor.

Lord Uppington stepped in, looking at them both with an expression of resigned irritation.

"It's not the match itself that we mind," Lord Uppington said mildly. "We're very happy to have you officially join the family, Miles. There is no one we would have preferred for Henrietta."

Miles perked up slightly.

His face fell again as Lord Uppington went on in the same measured, wearied tones. "However, we cannot understand what would induce you to behave in so precipitate, and"—Lord Uppington looked hard at both his daughter and his son-in-law, pronouncing the next word with painful clarity—"*unintelligent* a fashion. I had thought you both had better sense than that. We are painfully disappointed in you both."

"Unless," cut in Lady Uppington, looking closely at her daughter, "there was a reason for your unseemly haste?"

Henrietta's head shot up again—in indignation. "Mother!"

Lady Uppington assessed her daughter's flushed cheeks with an expert maternal eye and arrived at her own conclusions. "Don't fly into a snit with me, young lady. What did you expect people would think?"

"Er," said Henrietta intelligently.

"And your brother!" Lady Uppington shook her head in a way that boded no good to Richard once she got her hands on him. "I don't know what he was thinking to let you rush into matrimony like that. I have raised a brood of children without an ounce of sense between them." She emitted one of her infamous harrumphs, the sound that had cast countesses out of countenance, and frightened royal dukes from the room.

Henrietta winced. "Sorry?" she ventured.

Lady Uppington noted the wince, and pressed her advantage. "Didn't any of you stop to think that so hurried a marriage would spark scandal rather than stem it? Hmm?"

Henrietta felt Miles's hands tighten on her shoulders, and his breath ruffle her snarled hair as he said resolutely, "But we *are* married."

"Yes, yes," said Lady Uppington irritably. "We'll have to think of some sort of story. A secret engagement, perhaps," she muttered to herself, waving a hand in the air, "or a strange wasting disease . . . Hmm. Miles thought he only had three days to live."

Henrietta glanced up at Miles, a bit battered, but otherwise a strapping specimen of manhood. Just how strapping a specimen was something that did not bear thinking of in the presence of her parents. Henrietta's cheeks turned pink.

"I don't think anyone will believe that," she said.

"You can criticize," said Lady Uppington sternly, "when you come up with a better idea."

"Why not," suggested Miles, thinking hard, "tell everyone that it was a private ceremony? Which it was," he added as an afterthought. "It wasn't as though we went to Gretna Green. The bishop of London was there."

"And what he was thinking, I don't know, either," said Lady Uppington in a way that suggested trouble for the diocese.

"Miles might have something there," commented Lord Uppington, eyes meeting his wife's. "If we can play on people's snobbery . . ." He raised an eyebrow.

Lady Uppington snapped to attention like a Renaissance explorer sighting land after a long and perilous voyage plagued by scurvy and sea serpents. "That's it! If we say it was very small, very select . . . only the best people, of course . . ."

Henrietta caught on, and she gave an excited bounce. "We'll have people falling over themselves pretending to have been there! And no one will want to admit otherwise!" She turned and caught both of Miles's hands in hers. "Brilliant!"

Miles squeezed Henrietta's hands and tried to look as though that was what he had meant all along.

Lord Uppington chuckled. "By the time your mother is through, half the *ton* will have attended your wedding."

"At least three royal dukes," agreed Lady Uppington smugly. Her smug expression faded. "But I do wish one of my children would let themselves be married off normally!"

"There was Charles," pointed out Henrietta.

Lady Uppington waved a dismissive hand. "That doesn't count."

"I won't tell Charles you said that," said Lord Uppington.

Lady Uppington batted her eyelashes at him. "Thank you, darling."

Henrietta and Miles shared a look of pure relief. If her mother was flirting with her father, it meant that good humor had been restored. Of course, it didn't mean that they would hear the end of their precipitate match any time within the next fifty years, Lady Uppington being quite accomplished at the fine art of exhuming past peccadilloes at inconvenient occasions, but the worst was over.

And once her parents left . . . The look between them turned far more meaningful. Miles cocked an eye suggestively at the staircase. Henrietta blushed and broke their gaze, and not a moment too soon. Lady Uppington turned back to them, crooking a finger at Henrietta.

"Come along home, darling. There's much to be done. We'll have you fitted for wedding clothes tomorrow, and there are rumors to plant. . . ."

Lady Uppington started for the door, still talking, but Henrietta remained stubbornly still.

"I would be happy to be fitted tomorrow," Henrietta said, holding on to Miles's hand. "But I live here now."

Lady Uppington's green eyes narrowed. "I'm not sure I like this."

"You knew I would marry sooner or later," said Henrietta.

"I had thought," said Lady Uppington repressively, "that I would be given some warning first."

Henrietta bit her lip. Since that was unanswerable, she didn't even attempt to frame an answer; she simply scrunched her face into an expression of exaggerated remorse. "Sorry?" she tried again. If she repeated it often enough, perhaps it would eventually work.

Lord Uppington came to the rescue, appropriating his wife's arm. "Come along, my dear. You can come back tomorrow and bully Henrietta's staff."

"I don't bully anyone!" protested Lady Uppington. "Although goodness knows, your staff clearly needs a firm hand. I've never seen anything quite so dingy."

Lord Uppington shared a resigned look with his daughter.

Thank you, mouthed Henrietta.

Lord Uppington gave a slight nod, lifting his eyebrows in a way that clearly said, more clearly than words, Just don't let me catch you doing anything this stupid ever again.

Henrietta resolved to be a model of married rectitude. At least, when her parents were nearby.

Lord Uppington turned to Miles. "I'll be by tomorrow to discuss Henrietta's dowry."

Miles nodded stiffly. "Yes, sir."

"And, Miles?" Lord Uppington paused on the threshold, Lady Uppington on his arm. "Welcome to the family."

The door closed firmly behind him.

Miles and Henrietta just looked at each other, in their suddenly very empty foyer. Hands on her shoulders, Miles let his head sag until his forehead touched Henrietta's.

"Phew," he said heavily.

"Phew," agreed Henrietta, enjoying just leaning against him after the tumultuous emotions of the past several hours—of the past several days, in fact.

Miles lifted his head just enough so that he could look at her. "Now that your parents are gone . . . ," he began, eyes narrowing in on Henrietta's mouth in a way that made her lips tingle and her knees wobble and the foyer suddenly seem much, much warmer.

"Oh, they're gone," said Henrietta breathlessly, linking her arms around his neck. "They're very, very gone."

"In that case . . ." Miles leaned purposefully forward.

Crack! The door crashed open

"Oww . . ." Miles staggered back, clutching his nose, which had connected firmly with Henrietta's forehead.

"I came as fast as I could," announced Geoff, striding purposefully across the room.

"Huh?" said Miles irritably, looking at Geoff through watering eyes. "Has anyone ever told you that you have the devil's own timing?"

Geoff skittered to a halt, eyes moving from Miles to Henrietta and back again in some confusion. "Your note?" he said. "The urgent crisis that demanded my attention at once?"

"Oh, that."

"Yes, that," agreed Geoff, with some asperity.

"You're a bit late," said Miles equably. "*We* captured the Black Tulip. Where in the hell were you?"

Geoff's lips tightened. "Nowhere important."

"Composing a sonnet to Mary Alsworthy's eyebrows, no doubt," commented Miles, ostensibly to Henrietta.

Instead of responding in kind, Geoff clapped his hat back on his head, saying tonelessly, "If you don't need me, I'll be off, then. Wickham has an assignment for me. With any luck, it should prove fatal."

Miles looped an arm around Henrietta's waist. "Feel free to see yourself out."

Henrietta caught Geoff's quizzical look and twisted out of Miles's grasp. "It's not what it looks like," she said hastily, automatically reaching up to smooth her hair. "We're married."

She and Miles exchanged the sort of look designed to send bachelors straight to the bottle.

Geoff's lip curled. "Married," he said darkly.

"Thanks, old chap," said Miles.

Geoff pressed his eyes tightly closed. "Oh, hell," he said.

Henrietta looked at him sharply. She had never heard Geoff utter a word of profanity in her presence before, even in the case of extreme provocation, such as Richard being hauled off by the French Ministry of Police.

Geoff shook his head apologetically. "I didn't mean it that way. It was just—never mind. I wish you both very happy. Truly."

"Is something wrong?" asked Henrietta. There were dark circles under Geoff's eyes, and his face had a haggard cast to it.

"Nothing that time and a little hemlock won't cure," said Geoff with forced jollity, hand on the doorknob.

"Who's the hemlock for?" asked Miles.

"Me," said Geoff.

"Well, enjoy," Miles said vaguely. Planting his arm firmly back around Henrietta's waist, he started steering her towards the stairs.

Henrietta swung them back around. "Remember," she said, holding out a hand to Geoff, "we're here if you need us."

"Just not tonight," added Miles.

"Understood. Congratulations, both of you. Although"—Geoff smiled a crooked smile—"I can't say I'm the least bit surprised."

The door opened, closed, and was still.

Henrietta looked at Miles. "Charlotte, Geoff, my parents . . . How did everyone know we were going to get married but us?"

"And Richard," corrected Miles ruefully.

Henrietta sobered. She looked anxiously up at Miles. "Do you mind terribly? About Richard, I mean."

All was silent in the marble foyer. Miles looked Henrietta full in the face, and slowly shook his head. "Not nearly as much as I would have minded losing you."

"So that bit about my being nearly as important to you as Richard . . ."

Miles groaned. "I said a lot of stupid things."

Taking pity on him, Henrietta slid her arms around his waist. "I can think of at least one sensible thing you said."

Miles dropped a kiss on the top of her head. "Pass the ginger biscuits?"

"No."

"Albatross?"

Henrietta poked him. "Not even close."

"Or how about"—Miles's breath feathered the hair next to Henrietta's ear—"I love you?"

Downstairs, in the servants' hall, the word passed around that the master had been seen carrying his wife up the stairs—again.

Chapter Thirty-Eight

———— ❦ ————

"Eloise?"

Grayish yellow sunlight slanted in long rectangles across the library carpet, but I scarcely noticed. Somehow, over the course of the past few hours, I had slid from the overstuffed chair on which I had been sitting to the floor beneath. My shoulders were propped against the red-and-blue upholstered seat, and a Queen Anne ball-and-claw foot made convenient handrests next to each hip. My back was emitting the sort of warning twinges that betokened pain later, but I didn't care at the moment. On my bent knees, which served as an impromptu writing desk, perched a red leather folio. The folio itself was Victorian in date, with marbled endpapers and the sort of intricate embossing beloved of nineteenth-century leatherworkers, swirls and curlicues painstakingly traced in gold. Inside, however, was something else entirely. Onto the crumbling yellow pages had been pasted older material, which the Victorian compiler had chosen to title "Some Memorials of a Lady of the House of Selwick." There was a much longer subtitle, but since it had no relevance to anyone but the enthusiastic amateur archivist, I'll forbear to transcribe it.

The late-nineteenth-century compiler had made a valiant effort to squelch the juicier bits, striking whole paragraphs out with outraged strokes of the pen. Fortunately for me, Henrietta's ink had proved sturdier stuff. It was a bit like reading a medieval palimpsest, those close-written documents where the author wrote literally between the lines to save precious parchment, but with some squinting and cursing, and a bit of turning the pages this way and that, I could still make out the original text under the fading brown ink of the censor's blots.

In their own way, the annotations were hilarious, and I'm sure a cultural historian working on the late nineteenth century could get at least one paper out of them, maybe two. The anonymous archivist— who coyly identified herself as a fellow scion of the house of Selwick and left it at that—seemed to have very little idea of what to do with her adventurous ancestress and kept desperately trying to explain away Henrietta's more outrageous actions. Impromptu marriage? Certainly it couldn't have been that impromptu, anxiously rationalized the editor, if the bishop of London presided over the ceremony. Eavesdropping on a potential spy? It most certainly must have been by accident, since she would never voluntarily lend herself to an activity that must be sure to offend the conscience of any properly bred young lady. Slipping into someone's house disguised as a servant? Of course not. Lady Henrietta was just having her little joke on posterity.

I milked all the amusement I could out of those annotations.

I still had no idea what had happened last night. Zero. Zip. *Nada*. I'm not referring to those momentary lapses in memory that may attend overindulgence in the bottle (after Thursday's fiasco, I had quite scrupulously limited myself to two glasses of wine), but my utter inability to come up with any clear explanation for what had happened in the cloister. I knew how I would have liked to explain it, but there was an absolute lack of corroborating evidence, at least corroborating evidence that would convince any unbiased third party. And I don't mean Pammy.

I had basked in my own virtue at not giving in to the overwhelming desire to ask Sally whether her sarcastic comment arose from Colin's behavior towards me or mine towards him. From there it would only be the merest step to "But do you think he likes me? Like, LIKES likes me?" Instead, I had, with all the subtlety of a wrecking ball, rerouted the subject to monastic ruins.

After Sally showed me around the cloister, I returned to the party with all my antennae on high Colin alert, that sort of superawareness that signals a crush with the same deadly accuracy as pointlessly dropping that person's name in conversation or surreptitious excursions into his past on Google. Instead, I was cornered by the vicar, who had conceived the ambition to impart to me several lesser-known verses of Gilbert and Sullivan, without which my life would be immeasurably the poorer (or so he most solemnly swore). Colin reappeared halfway through *The Gondoliers* and immediately joined a group on the other side of the room. Whether he was avoiding me or the vicar's piercing tenor, I had no idea. I could fill up an entire diary with "Looks, the interpretation of." Old looks, new looks, lost looks. All half-imagined, none probative of anything at all. Other than wishful thinking.

The ride back to Selwick Hall had been . . . cordial. There was no other word for it. Colin asked if I had enjoyed myself; I said I had; he expressed his pleasure at that fact. If there was an undertone to those words that suggested more than bland social conventions . . . well, nothing had occurred to give them substance. In the front hall, as Colin extracted his key and I dithered with my coat, Colin's phone had rung, and he bid me a distracted good night, leaving me to seek my virtuous bed and wonder if Pammy had perhaps been right about that bustier.

Had I imagined it all? I took myself off to bed, but couldn't sleep, mind moving in an endless hamster wheel of *Did he? Or didn't he?* I contemplated venturing down to the kitchen for a midnight cocoa, in the hopes of a "chance" meeting. But there was only so low one could sink. Besides, I was afraid I would get lost on the way to the kitchen. How pathetic to stumble around a strange house in the dark in the hopes of being compromised!

Compromised—I had been spending too much time in the early nineteenth century. Envisioning Colin in knee breeches didn't help matters, either.

Sleep was clearly an impossibility. Wrapping Serena's pashmina over my tank top as a makeshift shawl, I shuffled barefoot down the hallway to the library. After an hour with Henrietta, the Cloister Incident was only a vague murmur at the back of my mind. After two, I couldn't remember my own name, much less his.

Oh, this was going to make a juicy chapter! France's deadliest counterspy, a woman! The women's history crowd were going to go wild. I envisioned conference panels, grant money raining down like ticker tape, job talks, and articles in *Past and Present*, the English historian's answer to the *New York Times*. It was like watching the little windows on a slot machine clink one by one into jackpot.

Forget a mere chapter; this might contain the germ of a second book. I toyed with titles. *A Sampler of Sedition: Female Spies in the Napoleonic Wars*. I discarded that as too much like a reprise of my dissertation, with a gender slant to make it trendy. I could attempt a microhistory, using the marquise as a case study. *The Marquise de Montval: The Making of a Revolutionary*. Now, there was an idea. How did a gently bred young Englishwoman become a fervent adherent of revolutionary principles and a hired killer for Bonaparte? Even better, I could do a companion study of the Pink Carnation and the Black Tulip, comparing their backgrounds, their allegiances, their methods.

There was one slight snag.

"Eloise!" The voice was more insistent now, and, as if from a long way away, I remembered that that was my name, and that it was generally considered a matter of social convention to respond to it.

So I blurted out what was on my mind. "The Black Tulip *escaped*!" I looked up wildly from the pile of papers on my lap, shoving my tousled hair out of my eyes. "I can't believe they let her escape!"

"Eloise!" There was a snap to Colin's voice that jarred me out of my preoccupations. He hadn't even bothered to come all the way into the library; his disembodied head stuck out around the frame of the door like a French nobleman after a jaunt to the guillotine, sans wig or ruffled cravat.

"Yes?" I sat to attention, suddenly very conscious that I was wearing nothing but an ancient white tank top, washed to invisibility, and a pair of fuzzy pajama bottoms printed with French poodles frolicking next to the Eiffel Tower. Yes, I had packed in a hurry Friday afternoon.

I tried to tuck my legs up under me, but Colin wasn't paying any more attention to Fifi the Playful Poodle than he was to the transparency of my tank top.

"Listen," he said tersely. "Something's come up. Can you be ready to leave in fifteen minutes?"

"Fifteen minutes," I repeated blankly. Leave. Fifteen minutes. Leave?

Information did not compute.

"There's a train that leaves at seven thirty-two," Colin continued in that same harried tone. I got the sense that he was already someplace else entirely, the apparition in front of me simply a machine detailed to relay the message. All that was lacking was *Thank-you-for-calling-Selwick-Hall-and-have-a-nice-day*. "I'm terribly sorry, but it can't be helped."

"Of course," I stammered, staggering to my feet with the aid of the chair. "I'll just—"

"Thanks."

"—get myself together," I finished to the inside of the library door. Colin had already gone. Fifteen minutes. He had said fifteen minutes, hadn't he?

I gathered together the welter of papers and folios I had been looking at and sorted them back into their proper places with a numb efficiency born of confusion. I glanced at the big grandfather clock on the far wall. Four minutes gone already. I grabbed for my notebooks, tucking them under my arm. I could read through my notes on the train.

The train. I would have dwelled on that, but I didn't have time now to figure out why I was being tossed from the house like a Victorian housemaid found to be in the family way. *Get ye gone, ye creature of loose morals, and never darken the Squire's door again!* Only, I hadn't had a chance to display any loose morals, more's the pity. So why was he throwing me out?

Oh, God. I paused with one hand on the doorknob of the library door. Was he regretting his impulses of last night, and trying to dispose of the evidence (i.e., me) before I could fling myself at him again? "I didn't mean to lead her on," I could hear him saying to a mate over a pint at the pub. "It was just . . . she was *there*. Female, y'-know." The friend would nod sagely in return, saying, "Don't know where they get these ideas." And they'd both take a long pull of their beers, shaking their head over desperate women. Then they'd proba-bly top it off with a long belch.

It made me cringe just thinking about it.

Five minutes gone. I tabled that thought for later and sprinted to my borrowed room, flinging clothes haphazardly back into my overnight bag, yanking on the same tweed pants I had worn yesterday with an unworn beige sweater. Cursing, I tore the sweater back off over my head, accidentally sending my glasses flying in the process, added bra, replaced sweater, and fumbled around for my glasses, which had scooted all the way under the bed in that way inanimate objects have when you're in a hurry. Had I put on deodorant? I couldn't remember. I yanked up my sweater and lavishly slathered white goo anywhere but where it was supposed to go, most of it onto dry-clean-only cashmere.

Twelve minutes gone. There was no time to put in my contacts. Wiping my glasses clean on a corner of my much-abused sweater, I made sure the lids on my contact lens case were screwed tight and shoved them, my glasses case, and my bottle of contact lens solution into my bag. Tearing a piece of paper out of the back of my notebook, I fished a pen out of my bag, and scribbled a quick note. "Serena, Thanks for the loan of the clothes! Hope you don't mind. Will be glad to return the favor sometime. Yrs, Eloise."

That was the last of my allotted time. I ran a quick scan over dresser, night tables, bed; rescued my almost-forgotten watch from the dresser top; wriggled into my coat, slung my bag over my shoul-der, and bolted for the stairs.

Colin was already in the car, the engine running, drumming his fingers against the steering wheel in an anxious tattoo.

"That was speedy," he said approvingly. The car lurched into ac-tion before I heard the comforting click that told me my door had latched.

"Well, you know," I gasped, flinging my satchel into the backseat of the car, and turning around again to yank down my seat belt. "I didn't have much with me."

"Right," said Colin, leaning over the wheel in that strange way men have when they're intent on emulating the Grand Prix, the automotive equivalent of air guitar. As though sensing that might not have been adequate as a response, he added, "Good."

All the tension that had fizzed between us last night had gone as flat as champagne left out overnight.

I subsided back against my seat. It belatedly occurred to me that I'd never brushed my hair, but I couldn't muster up the energy to care. Outside the window, the countryside jounced past, clothed in morning mist. Had I been in a different sort of mood, I might have waxed rapturous about the mysterious quality of the early-morning light. As it was, it just looked grim and faded, as if the tired landscape couldn't muster the energy to clothe itself in its usual colors, but had let itself dim into an indifferent blur.

I glanced at Colin, but he was far away—away with the fairies, as the local idiom goes, only, judging from the worried line between his eyes, these were hobgoblins he was hobnobbing with. No kinder to him than the trees, the gray morning light transformed him into a sepia photo of himself. His healthy tan had gone the sallow taupe of old parchment, and his skin seemed too tightly drawn over his cheekbones. The pouches that bagged beneath his eyes reminded me of old photographs of the Duke of Windsor, who always looked as though he were perpetually recovering from a hangover.

With all my hyperawareness, I had seen how much Colin had consumed last night. It wasn't a hangover.

As I watched, he rubbed two fingers over his temple as though to scrub away a headache. The homely gesture hit me like a kick in the stomach—no, not any other organ. Obviously, Colin had things on his mind other than aborted smooches and unwanted houseguests.

I remembered that phone call last night, as we returned from the party, and wondered if it had been bad news of some sort. The part of my imagination bequeathed to me by my mother instantly set about producing grisly disaster scenarios. A friend might have been in a car accident: a sudden flash of lights, a twist of the wheel, a car careening out of control on a dark road. His aunt might have had a heart attack. Mrs. Selwick-Alderly looked fairly hale, but one never knew what might lurk in someone's arteries after a lifetime of roast beef and sticky toffee pudding. Of course, these days, it was more likely free-range eggs and doner kebabs, but Mrs. Selwick-Alderly had been raised in an age when meat was brought to your plate still mooing, accompanied by a side of vegetables stewed in butter. And then there was Colin's sister, Serena. She had been suffering from a minor case of food poisoning on Thursday night. What if it hadn't been food poisoning at all, but something far more serious? Cholera, perhaps. Could one even get cholera in England? Even if one couldn't, I was sure that there were plenty of other grisly diseases ripe for the catching. Not to mention all the perils involved in crossing the street, operating a hair dryer, and drinking very hot beverages.

Envisioning Serena strapped to a complicated system of wires and tubes, an oxygen mask covering her mouth, one limp hand protruding from beneath the threadbare hospital coverlet, I felt like a worm. A selfish worm, at that.

"Is everything okay?" I asked.

"Hmm? What?" Colin dragged himself back from the dark lagoons of Never-Never Land with a visible effort. "Yes."

I had never heard such an unconvincing affirmative in my life.

Before I could decide whether or not to press further—to pry, or not to pry?—Colin spoke again. "I'm sorry to toss you out like this."

"That's all right," I lied. "I don't mind the train."

I waited. Patiently. Of course, what I really wanted to do was grab his arm and howl, "WHY?" Now, I thought, would be an excellent time for an explanation as to why I was in his car, heading for a train station unknown, at an ungodly hour of the morning. Wasn't virtue supposed to be rewarded?

Colin's eyes snaked towards mine in the rearview mirror. I schooled my face into an expression that was supposed to be bland yet encouraging, welcoming without displaying unwarranted levity. It came out as a lopsided grimace.

Colin frowned again.

Not exactly the reaction I had hoped to elicit.

"I'll pay your train fare, of course," he said abruptly.

Urgh. So much for an explanation. "That won't be necessary."

"It's the least I can do."

"I'm quite capable of paying for myself."

"That's not the point," said Colin tiredly.

"Give it to charity," I suggested. Feeling slightly guilty over my snippiness, I added, "There must be a fund for indigent phantom monks somewhere."

Colin half-raised an eyebrow, as though he couldn't even be moved to sarcasm. With an efficient movement of his hands on the steering wheel, the car swung around a turn and skidded to a stop in front of Hove Station.

Leaving the engine on idle, Colin turned and snagged my bag for me from the backseat. It took a bit of snagging, since, in the infuriating way of inanimate objects, it had chosen to wedge itself in the cavity beneath the seats. Naturally, it had fallen upside down. Just envisioning what might have fallen out—next time, I'm buying a bag with a zipper—I lurched over the seat to help.

Naturally, I dove over the gearshift just as Colin straightened, bag in hand. If you think this is one of those scenes where the heroine manages to fetch up pressed against the hero, his lips a breath away from hers as she rests stunned—but unhurt—against his manly chest, think again. My elbow whapped painfully into Colin's chest. Dropping my bag, he let out a pained grunt, like a quarterback being hit in the stomach with the ball. I reeled back, clutching my elbow and making incoherent mewing noises. Those blows to the funny bone *hurt*. But not, I imagine, quite as much as a direct whack to the solar plexus with an object just slightly less pointy than Miss Gwen's parasol.

Great. If he wasn't glad to get rid of me before, I'm sure he was now.

"Sorry," I babbled, snatching my bag up off his lap and haphazardly scooping clothes and toiletries back into it. "Sorry, sorry, sorry."

Colin reached down, and produced yesterday's bra from the floor of the car.

"Yours?" he asked with a crooked smile.

"Thanks." Redder than my hair, I snatched it out of his hand and shoved it into the bag. "I'll just be going now. Before I injure you again."

"Anytime," said Colin, as I scrambled ungracefully out of the car, my bag bumping along behind me. I couldn't tell whether he meant I should be leaving anytime now, or to keep the injuries coming. The former sounded far more plausible.

"It's been nice," I said lamely, rocking from one foot to the other just outside the open door of the car as I hauled my bag onto my shoulder. "Thanks for having me. It was really, um, nice of you."

When I would have swung the door closed, Colin stretched out across the empty passenger's seat, one hand resting on the handle of the open door. "I am sorry about this."

I shoved my hair out of my eyes, sending my overnight bag plummeting from my shoulder to a painful halt in the crook of my elbow. "Not as sorry as I am," I said, glancing ruefully at his chest.

"We should have drinks sometime."

"That would be lovely," I said, trying to hoist my bag up again and fervently hoping nothing else embarrassing was sticking out. All I needed was for him to get a good look at those poodle pajamas.

He nodded. "I'm not sure how long I'll be away, but . . . I'll call you when I get back to London."

"Great!" I exclaimed, but my show of enthusiasm was, mercifully, cut off, as Colin slammed the door shut. The car swung away, leaving me standing there, repeating, "Drinks . . . I'll call you . . ." over and over in my head, just to make sure they'd really been said, until the impact of my bag hitting my foot shook me out of my bemused reverie.

Fumbling with the buttons on my coat, I staggered towards the train station, hitching my bag up as it began to slip slyly down my shoulder. It promptly fell again. I didn't care. Drinks. I had assaulted the man, and yet he was still willing to have drinks with me. Who said true heroes were a thing of the past? Shoving some money through the window of the ticket booth and wishing the nonplussed ticket agent an exceptionally good day, I shambled towards the platform, trying to filter pound coins into my change purse and shove the purse back into the depths of my bag without dropping my ticket or tumbling onto the tracks like an absentminded Anna Karenina.

I had no desire to fling myself upon the train tracks of thwarted love. On the contrary, I joyously concluded that the offer of drinks must mean he hadn't been trying to get rid of me! Something must have genuinely come up, something urgent and dreadful. Hey nonny nonny and tra la la! Belatedly, I remembered that taking joy in someone else's misfortune was a Bad Thing, and clamped down on the caroling, even if my heart was secretly singing "tirra lirra" like Sir Lancelot in the poem.

Visions of intimate dinners à deux danced through my head. I imagined a cozy little restaurant somewhere away from the bustle that surrounded my flat in Bayswater. South Kensington would fit the bill, or the less-traveled bits of Notting Hill. I pictured a little box of a place with brick walls and those tiny tables where you couldn't fit more than two, and that only with knees brushing. The music would be as low as the lights, and the waiters would be the sort who didn't barge by every two seconds asking if you were enjoying your meal. There would be no Sally, no Pammy, no Phantom Monk. Just two large-bowled glasses filled with dark red wine, me, and, of course, Colin.

And I would make double sure to turn off my damned cell phone.

While I was at it, why not just add some violins as well? I made a hideous face at myself, and then glanced guiltily around the platform to make sure no one had noticed. No one had, largely because there was no one else there. Thank goodness. I hate it when my inner monologue escapes into my face.

At seven-thirty on a Sunday morning, there were no commuters waiting to go into London. There was just me, alone on the open platform. It was so early that even the ubiquitous AMT coffee stand hadn't yet opened its doors—or whatever you call the opening in an outdoor kiosk. I would have killed for a cup of coffee, as much for the warmth as for the caffeine. The wind scraped at my cheeks, as sharp as memory, wearing down through skin all the way to the raw nerves beneath.

I shoved my bloodless hands into the sleeves of my jacket, and rubbed them against my forearms, but it was about as much use as trying to warm up next to an unplugged space heater. The cold came as much from within as without, that bone-deep chill that comes of lack of sleep and food, and can only be driven off by several dreamless hours under a pile of quilts, with the alarm conveniently turned to off.

For a wonder, the train was actually running on time. The seven-thirty-two chugged its leisurely way into the station, as if preening itself on not having broken down along the way. It was the sort of train you never see in the States, door after door after door, each set of seats with its own personal portal. I suppose it does make for efficiency in getting in and out, but there was something slightly dizzying about that endless line of identical doors, one after the other. You know you're overtired when you start viewing commuter train construction as an allegory for Life. The train compartment less chosen?

With no one else at the station, it was impossible to discern which doors were less traveled. Picking a compartment at random, I opened the yellow door and scrabbled across the seats, dumping my bag on one, and myself onto another. I settled gratefully into the battered seat, and leaned my head back against the headrest, trying not to think of the heads that might have rested there before. Outside, the countryside began moving slowly by, like the backdrop in an old movie, a checkered landscape of fallow winter fields, interspersed at intervals with clusters of grimy brown semidetached houses, huddling together close by the train tracks. Watching the muted scenery chug past, I let myself drift on a pleasant wave of fatigue and idle thought, mulling over what I had read in the library that night.

Especially that last letter. Blotted and blotched, as though Henrietta had leaned too heavily on her pen, she wasted no time in getting to the crux of the problem. The marquise had escaped.

My first thought was that Vaughn had turned traitor. According to Henrietta, however, Vaughn had discharged his duty and delivered the marquise safely into custody. Once there, she had persuaded the guard that there was clearly some mistake; she, after all, was a gently bred lady from a fine old English family and couldn't possibly have anything to do with international espionage. Her? A wilting flower of womanhood? A spy! The very idea—flutter, flutter, simper, simper— was absurd. Henrietta waxed exceedingly bitter and blotty over the effect of the marquise's wiles on the unenlightened. The tactic had worked. The guard informed Wickham (who told Miles, who told Henrietta) that the marquise had been most gracious in accepting his apologies. Henrietta had hit the dot on that *i* in "gracious" so hard that the nib of the pen had pierced the paper. A woman of the marquise's description had last been sighted taking ship for Ireland.

Ireland. An exceedingly popular place all of a sudden. I didn't think it could possibly be a coincidence that both the Pink Carnation and the Black Tulip were converging upon the same place. The Black Tulip might, perhaps, as she vamped her way through the staff of the War Office, have gotten wind of the presence of the Pink Carnation in Ireland (though I had my doubts), but why was Wickham sending Jane there in the first place? Why not leave her in France, where she was well entrenched in Bonaparte's court, well placed to receive information and commit cunning acts of sabotage? A logical cause might be to remove her from suspicion—but, as far as I had read, no one suspected Edouard de Balcourt's cousin of anything other than, perhaps, the odd amour. Being French, they weren't about to condemn that.

Besides, there were other reasons that excuse didn't wash. One other reason, to be precise. Geoffrey Pinchingdale-Snipe. If it were a matter of removing Jane from France, why send Pinchingdale to meet her in Ireland? Because that, according to Henrietta's last letter, was just what William Wickham had ordered. Pinchingdale had been detailed to meet Jane in Ireland, assignment to be relayed en route.

But why Ireland?

It's a complaint among British historians that, the way the field is parceled out, people who call themselves British historians seldom do more than study England. From time to time, someone will call for a new "British" history, and there'll be a spate of papers, perhaps a conference or two, emphasizing the interrelations between the three kingdoms, itemizing the numbers of Scots and Irish in the British army, or assessing the impact of Ireland upon Britain's colonial enterprises, but then most of us merrily subside into just doing England again. The word "insular" applies in more ways than one.

I bore out the stereotype beautifully. I didn't for the life of me know what was going on in Ireland in 1803. I did know—this comes among those basic dates of which no self-respecting English historian can remain in ignorance, or risk extreme embarrassment in the tearoom of the Institute of Historical Research—that Ireland's government had officially been merged with that of Britain with the Act of Union in 1801, its Parliament dissolved and its legislative independence ended. Scotland had gone that way in 1707. I realized that fact had nothing to do with the state of Ireland in 1803, but it did reassure me that all that studying I had done for my General Exams had not been in vain.

I also knew, and far more usefully, that William Wickham had been, at some point, Chief Secretary to the Lord Lieutenant in Ireland. Or, rather, it would be useful if I could remember exactly when Wickham had been in Ireland. If it had been 1803 . . . Was that too much to hope for?

Probably. But it certainly didn't hurt to check. *After* a long nap, followed by a shower, a snack, and a Grande Toffee Nut Latte, I hastily specified to myself.

And there were also Jane, Geoff, and the marquise to follow up on. If only it weren't a Sunday! The British Library would be closed, as would the Institute of Historical Research. Somehow, I doubted that much would appear if I plugged any of their names into the British Library database, but it was certainly worth a try. I wondered if Colin knew where the Pinchingdale family papers were kept—if there were any Pinchingdale family papers. Even if there weren't, it would make a good pretense for calling Colin. . . .

Or would have, if I had had his number.

With that lowering thought came another, even more distressing one. I shot up in my seat so precipitately that my forehead grazed the seat in front of me.

Forget having his number; I had never given him mine. Any of my numbers. He didn't even have my e-mail address. Which meant that his confident "I'll call you" was worth just about as much as the currency of a small former Soviet republic.

It could have been just an oversight on his part.

It could have been. And I heard there were some shares in the Brooklyn Bridge going cheap.

I should have remembered that *We should do drinks sometime* is bloke-speak for *Have a nice life*. I couldn't believe what an idiot I had been.

Or, rather, I could believe it; I just didn't like it.

Whoa. I yanked my rampaging imagination to a halt before I could plunge into full-blown woman-scorned mode, like a team of spooked horses careening towards a cliff. Just because the last man I'd dated had been a cheating slime didn't mean the whole lot of them were accomplished deceivers who would as soon lie to a girl as have a drink with her. After all, Colin had clearly been distracted by something. Whatever that something might be.

Feigning distress, whispered my inner demon (who was clearly a friend of Colin's hobgoblins), could be a good way of getting rid of an unwanted houseguest who has begun evincing signs of a crush. But he had seemed genuinely miserable, my better self argued back. Those circles under his eyes hadn't been makeup. And why suggest drinks if he didn't mean it?

That latter, I was forced to concede to myself, lacked force as an argument. If I had a dime for every time one of my friends complained a guy had promised to call and didn't . . . well, I could finance that research trip to Ireland. I was guilty of it myself, casually tossing off, "We should do coffee," to acquaintances at the Institute of Historical Research, well knowing that I was no more likely to follow up on it than they were to contact me.

The lack of my phone number wasn't fatal. If he were serious about meeting up for drinks, there were half a dozen ways he could acquire my number. Well, maybe not half a dozen, but I could think of at least two. His aunt Arabella, who had foisted me off on him this weekend in the first place, or his sister, Serena, who could, in a pinch, wrest the information from Pammy. If I could think of it, so could he.

If he did manage to acquire my number, it would at least prove that he had been serious about that drink. In old fairy tales, the heroes were frequently put to some sort of test: toting the head of a dragon home to the princess; pinching the feathers off the tail of a mythical bird; defeating an ogre with a halitosis problem in hand-to-hand combat. I didn't delude myself that I was the stuff of which heroines were made. I didn't even have half a kingdom to offer as reward, unless half a kingdom meant half a very small rented flat in a basement in Bayswater. But if the prize was less, so was the task. Braving the dread telephone in exchange for a drink with yours truly. Compared with hacking down a thicket of thorns, acquiring a phone number seemed negligible.

I would give him until . . . was Wednesday too soon? If there was a real crisis, I didn't want to rush out and buy a voodoo doll for no good reason. Thursday, I decided generously. If he hadn't called me by Thursday, I would know that *I'll call you* had simply been short-hand for *not interested*.

In the meantime, I had a spy to track down.

I couldn't follow the Black Tulip and the Pink Carnation to Ireland, but I could seek them out in the manuscript room of the British Library. If that failed . . . Well, Mrs. Selwick-Alderly had told me to keep her abreast of developments in the dissertation. It would only be polite to give her a call.

Leaning one cheek against the windowpane, I wondered who would resurface first. Colin? Or the Black Tulip?

Historical Note

Once again, the time has come to separate fact from fiction, and make my apologies to the altar of historical accuracy. The flower-themed spies do, in fact, have their place in the historical record. Although the Scarlet Pimpernel, the Purple Gentian, and the Pink Carnation are all fictitious, there were flower-named spies romping across the Channel. *La Rose* was the more prominent, but one agent did go under the pseudonym *Le Mouron* (the Pimpernel)—and they identified themselves by means of small cards marked with a scarlet flower. Nor is the notion of a female flower figure, like the Pink Carnation, pure invention. Mlle. Nymphe Roussel de Preville confounded the revolutionary government under the code name *Prime-rose*. Reputed to be stunningly beautiful, like Jane, *La Prime-rose* was a mistress of disguise, equally comfortable gracing a drawing room or masquerading as a man. The ring of spies posing as cravat merchants dispersed by Miles early in the book also have their historical counterparts in the French agents scattered through London posing as tailors, servants, merchants, and milliners.

Back at headquarters in London, there was some shuffling of places and personnel for the purposes of the novel. During the Napoleonic Wars, espionage was largely conducted through a subdepartment of the Home Office called the Alien Office. To avoid confusion, and distressing images of extraterrestrials wandering around London, I followed the fictional tradition that ascribes stealthy deeds of daring to the War Office. As a sop to the shades of those men who labored in the Alien Office, I borrowed their building and staff for the use of my fictitious War Office. Number 20 Crown Street, where Miles receives his instructions from William Wickham, had been the headquarters of the Alien Office since its inception in 1793.

As for William Wickham . . . I have very poor luck with spymasters, who seem to have a habit of resigning just before I need them. In 1802, Wickham left the Alien Office and sailed for Dublin in his new capacity as Chief Secretary to the Lord Lieutenant of Ireland. However, Wickham is to the English secret service what Fouché was to the French. Using the Alien Office as a base, he built a network of spies— or, as Wickham himself euphemistically termed it, a "preventive police"—that spanned the Continent and terrified the enemies of England. Wickham's new title changed little; he continued to hold sway over England's efforts at espionage, first from the Irish Office and later from the Treasury. Despite his Irish appointment, Wickham was, in fact, physically present in London in early summer of 1803, and would have been on hand to give Miles his marching orders.

My final mea culpa is for those avid students of the Regency era who will have noticed some importations from slightly later in the century. Almack's, "the Marriage Mart," where Miles hid from matchmaking mothers behind convenient outcroppings of masonry, had been in operation since 1765. The tepid lemonade, knee breeches for the gentlemen (the Duke of Wellington was once refused admittance for committing the unpardonable gaffe of appearing in trousers), and the firm closing of the door upon any unfortunates who desired entry after the magical hour of eleven would all have been familiar to Henrietta and Miles. They would have blinked in confusion, however, at the mention of the quadrille, which was not introduced into England until 1808, although it had already attained popularity across the Channel. Likewise, Sarah, Lady Jersey, was only seventeen in 1803, and would not marry the future Earl of Jersey for another year, nor become Lady Jersey until 1805 (not to be confused with the other

Lady Jersey, her mother-in-law, chiefly famed for extraconjugal cavorting with Prinny). Nonetheless, both the quadrille and Lady Jersey are such commonplaces of the period that the ballroom felt incomplete without them.

As always, for the bulk of the details relating to espionage during the Napoleonic Wars, I am deeply indebted to Elizabeth Sparrow's minutely researched work on the subject, *Secret Service: British Agents in France, 1792–1815.* For pretty much everything else, heartfelt thanks go to Dee Hendrickson and her brilliant *Regency Reference Book* (aka *Everything You Wanted to Know About the Regency but Were Afraid to Ask*), and the ever-resourceful ladies of the Beau Monde and Writing Regency, whose encyclopedic knowledge of the early nineteenth century saved Henrietta—and her author—from any number of shocking gaffes.

Acknowledgments

I had hoped that a year's passage would render me the blasé sort of second-time author who could pass by the acknowledgments page with a mere flick of a pen. Instead, I've accumulated yet more people to whom thanks are due.

First, to the marvelous people at Dutton, who have entered into the spirit of the Pink Carnation with a zeal that would alarm Napoleon; to my miracle-working agent, whose resourcefulness and patience are equaled only by his ability to leap tall buildings in a single bound; and to the wonderful women of Romance Writers of America (with special love to the New England Chapter), who generously received me into their ranks.

To my parents, who now own the largest collection of pink books in the Western hemisphere and who continue to welcome me home and feed me despite my technically having an apartment of my own; to my brother, Spencer, without whose timely care package of truffles and cheese, Henrietta and Miles would still be stuck in the middle of Westminster Bridge; and to my little sister, Brooke, who more than earned the dedication of this book—even if she did filch all my Julia Quinns.

To the usual suspects, aka Nancy, Abby, and Claudia, pillars of my existence; to Liz, who puzzled over plots till our coffee went cold; to

Jenny, who was never too busy to listen to the Crisis of the Day (and to Jenny's mother, whose Pink Carnation purchases rival those of my parents); to Lila, who throws the best party this side of the Atlantic; to Kimberly, who hasn't yet learned that "How is the new book going?" is a very dangerous question to ask; to Chris and Aaron, who were each man enough to read a book with a pink cover—in public; to Weatherly and Elina, who make even medieval jurisprudence fun; and to the 2005 Cravath summers, who livened up legal practice (you know who you are—and if you don't, you were drinking way too much at the Zoo Party).

And, last but not least, to the caffeine-creating wizards at the Broadway Market Starbucks, who not only allowed me to occupy the little table in the back for whole days at a time, but supplied me with gingerbread lattes while I did so.

Thank you all!

Lauren Willig is a Ph.D. candidate in history at Harvard University, where she recently graduated from law school. Originally from New York, she lives in Cambridge, Massachusetts. Visit her Web site at www.LaurenWillig.com.

THE MASQUE OF THE
Black Tulip

Lauren Willig

A CONVERSATION WITH LAUREN WILLIG

(through questions posed by her characters)

Q. **Eloisa Kelly:** *Not that I'm not grateful for everything you've done—I mean, the dissertation has never gone better—but can you give me just a hint about Colin? Have I made a complete idiot of myself for nothing?*

A. Silly Eloise! It's only in books that the heroine gets to peek at the blurb on the back and figure out how it's all going to turn out. Oh, wait. You are in a book. Never mind that. As the first-person viewpoint character, you're going to have to labor under the same disadvantages shared by the real-world dating population—you can't know for sure just how it's going to turn out until it does. In the meantime, you're stuck overanalyzing Colin's behavior—and probably getting it wrong—like the rest of us. Even so, I would say there is a good chance that Colin is interested. Not madly in love, not tormented with desire, but definitely interested. Just hang in there!

Q. **Eloisa Kelly:** *Hi, it's me again! Eloise, I mean. I just wanted to ask, why does the name Donwell Abbey sound so familiar? Thanks.*

A. It sounds familiar because it is. I think it of it as the Curse of the Liberal Arts Education (a phrase with an appropriately Gothic ring to it, in this instance). My brain is crammed full of free-floating facts and phrases that surge to the fore with no particular rhyme or reason. As I was fishing about for a name for the haunted abbey next door to Selwick Hall, the name Donwell popped up, like one of those little cards in a Magic 8-ball. Donwell just sounded right with Abbey. The two names went together like purple and gentian. Of course, they did. Four days later, I remembered why. Donwell Abbey was the name of Knightly's home in Jane Austen's *Emma*. By that time, the neighboring estate was firmly fixed in my imagination as Donwell Abbey, so I decided to leave it in the hope that those who recognized the reference would appreciate it as a form of inside joke.

The Phantom Monk emerged from a different Austen novel. There isn't—at least, not that I recall—any actual Phantom Monk in *Northanger Abbey*, but I was inspired by the general Gothic overtones. *Northanger Abbey* was a great deal on my mind as I wrote the modern portions of *Black Tulip*, largely since, like someone else I know, Catherine Morland is a master at jumping to incorrect conclusions. Sorry, Eloise, but it *is* true.

*Q. **Lady Henrietta Selwick** (in considerable perturbation): A girl named Brooke, who claims to be your close relation, keeps telling me that I am really she. We do look rather alike, but given her odd speech and dress, I really don't see how this can be. Is it true?*

P.S. What are "low-rise jeans"?

A. I was afraid you were going to ask that sooner or later. I certainly didn't set out to create an exact replica of my little sister. In fact, I don't think I could produce a proper reproduction of a living character if I tried. No matter how well we think we know someone, we can never map all the hidden recesses of their soul well enough to faithfully preserve them in ink. It's far more interesting (and less conducive to libel charges) to take little bits and pieces and meld them into entirely new entities.

All that being said, while I was working on Richard and Amy's story, it became a running joke that any little sister character naturally had to be based on Brooke. Egged on by Brooke and various others, I began including the more obvious sorts of Brooke characteristics, such as her hair color, her glorious singing voice, and her dilapidated stuffed animal, Doggie-the-doggy. (Fearing embarrassing publicity, Doggie asked to be granted an alias for the purposes of the book, appearing under his screen name of Bunny-the-bunny.) But don't fret, Lady Henrietta— Brooke already informed me that Miles isn't her type, so you don't have to worry about the competition.

As for the jeans, you don't want to know. Trust me. Just stick with your sprig muslin.

*Q. **The Hon. Miles Charles Edward Arthur Dorrington:** Why does Richard always get to be the dashing one?*

A. Oh, Miles. Not everyone can be relentlessly suave. Don't worry. It's all part of your charm. In fact, the driving idea behind *Black Tulip* (aside from "Hey! Miles and Henrietta are clearly meant for each other!") was the following: What happens when you take a pair of fundamentally ordinary people and place them in an extraordinary situation? What I had in mind, to a large extent, was Racine's *Andromache*. In a long-ago French lit class at Yale, we had an extensive conversation about the psychology of the "second generation," those characters who have grown up and lived their lives in the shadow of heroism, but are not themselves heroic—in that case, Hector's widow and Achilles' son; in this case, the Purple Gentian's little sister and best friend. Of course, the one is tragic and the other is decidedly not, nor are there any Greeks running around firing Trojan cities in *Black Tulip*, so there any comparison necessarily ends. But that was the conceit behind it all.

In the end, what I hoped my main characters would realize (hint, hint, Miles) was that while they might not be the world's most adept stalkers of French spies, they didn't have to be the Purple Gentian in order to be lovable, loved, and happy. After all, the world would be a far less interesting place if all heroes and heroines were cut from the same mold. There is, in its own way, a great charm to the ordinary—or else why would we have all those movies about girls next door? If Henrietta is the girl next door, Miles is the consummate boy next door, a guy's guy to his very fingertips, and all the more lovable for it.

Isn't that much better than being able to swing flawlessly through a window on a rope?

Q. **Gaston Delaroche** *(former assistant to the minister of police and eleventh-most-feared man in France): First you mock me and zen you scorn me by removing zee one* chapître *in wheech I appear en* Black Tuleep. *Eeet eez a slight against France. Why do you 'ate zee French? And why do you make me to speak in zees accent ridiculeuse?*

A. **Reginald "Turnip" Fitzhugh:** I love many things French. Brie. Champagne. Voltaire. Oh, yes, and Mom. Mom left France when she was quite young, but her former nationality worked in my favor in a number of ways as I was growing up, the two primary ones being Mom's belief that wine was an essential ingredient in almost any culinary endeavor (whether in the recipe or in the glass) and the fact that, as soon as I trotted out *"ma mère est née en Paris,"* my elementary school French teachers automatically added an extra five points onto my grade, whether I deserved it or not. But in every swashbuckler, there must be good guys and bad guys. Clearly, the guys with the guillotine are the bad guys. If they wanted to be the good guys, they should have thought about that before they started lopping off heads and marching across large chunks of Europe. As to the ridiculous accent, I greatly fear, M. Delaroche, that you fell victim to a long-running family joke. Growing up, we were all addicted to a British comedy (yes, it would be British) set in occupied France during World War II, which worked on the happy premise that any time the characters spoke in an exaggerated French accent, they were "speaking French," and could not be understood by stranded British airmen and the like, leading to lots of linguistic confusion and much amusement for the rest of us, especially with the addition of an undercover English agent who "spoke French" very badly. When together, my little sister and I quite frequently lapse into "French" under the guise of our alter egos, Gigi and Fifi (for those who care, I am Gigi, she is Fifi, and occasionally both of us are Dominique de Villepin, which takes far too much explaining to go into between parentheses). I say, thanks awfully for including me in this papery thingy, and all that. But must a chap be a turnip? Carnations are much more the thing, y'know.

A. Sorry, Turnip, old bean, but you really couldn't be anything else. Just as sheep are to the animal kingdom, turnips are inherently amusing vegetables, especially after years of watching *Blackadder*. And I'm afraid the name Carnation was already reserved for someone else.

Q. **Miss Gwendolyn Meadows:** *Having taken the trouble to review the manuscript, I was appalled to find that I was nowhere within it. The feelings of discerning readers everywhere cannot help but revolt* *at this singular want of judgment on the part of the author. This I take to be a sign of shoddy construction, and trust it will be remedied in the next chronicle.*

A. Well, you should have thought of that before you went back to France at the end of *Pink Carnation*. Since the action of *Black Tulip* was largely in London, it would have been very distracting to keep popping the story back over to France. I have taken your complaint into consideration, however, and can assure you that *The Deception of the Emerald Ring* offers considerable scope for your unique talents. Don't forget to bring your parasol.

Q. **Geoffrey, Viscount Pinchingdale:** *I find myself in a slightly embarrassing quandary. Could you perhaps aid me in finding a suitable word to rhyme with* delight? *Any assistance would be much appreciated—as would the loan of a gag for use on a certain Mr. Miles Dorrington.*

A. My dear Lord Pinchingdale, I would be more than happy to be of assistance (I've written a few lovelorn sonnet sequences in my time), but I am afraid you are not going to need that poem in the next book. In fact, you might want to divest yourself of any poetry, correspondence, or portrait miniatures having to do with Mary Alsworthy since you're about to be married to someone else. Mary's sister, Letty, in fact. It's all right there in *The Deception of the Emerald Ring*. Before you get annoyed with me, I would like to point out that if you hadn't tried to elope with Mary (really, Lord Pinchindgale, what were you thinking?), Letty wouldn't have been carried off by accident, and you would never have been forced to marry her.

I'll just fetch that gag for Miles for you, shall I? I think you're going to need it....

QUESTIONS
FOR DISCUSSION

1. Do you find Miles and Henrietta's transition from friendship to love convincing?

2. Miles's estrangement from his parents is mentioned in passing several times over the course of the novel. How do you think that Miles's family situation has shaped his character? How does it impact his relationship with Henrietta?

3. Why is it so important to the emotional development of the plot that Miles be forced to repudiate his relationship with Richard?

4. Is Lord Vaughn good or evil? How does the snake imagery and his recitation of *Paradise Lost* affect your perception of him?

5. Who did you think the Black Tulip might be? Why?

6. At the end of the book, Henrietta tells Lord Vaughn that what

he needs is not a Beatrice but a Boadicea. What does Henrietta mean by this? And do you agree with her?

7. How do the codebook excerpts at the start of each chapter color your perception of the action?

8. How would you explain Colin's behavior to Eloise? Is there subtext there for her to read in to, or is she constructing a relationship in her own head?

9. How do Eloise's interactions with Colin contrast with Henrietta and Miles's story? Do the modern and historical characters play off one another?

Read on for a sneak peak of Lauren Willig's next exciting novel continuing the adventures of Eloise Kelly and her search for the identity of the Black Tulip. . . .

THE DECEPTION OF THE EMERALD RING

Available in Hardcover from Dutton

It's 1803 and England and France remain at odds. Hoping to break the English once and for all, Napoleon is backing a ring of Irish rebels in uprisings against the English. To help the Irish in their efforts, the Black Tulip, France's most deadly spy, has arrived on the emerald continent. Also, in Ireland, the Pink Carnation, England's top spy, is working to shut down the rebels.

Meanwhile back in England: Letty Alsworthy intercepts a note indicating that her sister, Mary, is about to make the very grave mistake of eloping with Geoffrey Pinchingdale-Snipe (second in command of the League of the Purple Gentian). In an attempt to save the family name, Letty tries to stop the elopement, but instead finds herself swept away in the midnight carriage meant for her sister. To each other's horror, Letty and Geoff find themselves forced into matrimony. Called to Ireland on business on their wedding day, Geoff leaves Letty in the middle of the night convinced Letty manipulated their marriage. Determined to clear her name, Letty books her own passage to Ireland, never expecting that when she arrives, she'll be brought into a circle of dangerous spies and swept on the grandest adventure of her life. . . .

I scurried through the massive iron gates that front the courtyard of the British Library. The pigeons, bloated with the lunchtime leavings of scholars and tourists, cast me baleful glances from their beady black eyes as I weaved around them, making for the automatic doors at the entrance. It was early enough that there was a mere straggle of tourists lined up in front of the coat check in the basement.

Feeling superior, I made straight for the table on the other side of the room, transferring the day's essentials from my computer bag into one of the sturdy bags of clear plastic provided for researchers: laptop for transcribing documents; notebook in case the laptop broke down; pencils, ditto; mobile, for compulsive checking during lunch and bathroom breaks; wallet, for the buying of lunch; and a novel, carefully hidden between laptop and notebook, for propping up at the edge of my tray during lunchtime. The bag began to sag ominously.

I could see the point of the plastic bags as a means of preventing hardened document thieves from slipping out with a scrap of Dickens's correspondence, but it had a decidedly dampening effect on my choice of lunchtime reading material. And it was sheer hell smuggling in tampons.

Toting my bulging load, I made my way up in the elevator, past the brightly colored chairs in the mezzanine café, past the dispirited beige of the lunchroom, up to the third floor, where the ceilings were lower and tourists feared to tread. Perhaps fear was the wrong word; I couldn't imagine that they would want to.

Flashing my ID at the guard on duty at the desk in the manuscripts room, I dumped my loot on my favorite desk, earning a glare from a person studying an illuminated medieval manuscript three desks down. I smiled apologetically and insincerely, and began systematically unpacking my computer, computer cord, adapter, notebook, arraying them around the raised foam manuscript stand in the center of the desk with the ease of long practice. I'd done this so many times that I had the routine down. Computer to the right, angled in so the person next to me couldn't peek; notebook to the left, pencil neatly resting on top; bag with phone, wallet, and incriminating leisure fiction shoved as far beneath the desk as it could go, but not so far that I couldn't occasionally make the plastic crinkle with my foot to make sure it was still there and some intrepid purse snatcher disguised as a researcher hadn't crawled underneath and made off with my lunch money.

Having staked out my desk, I made for the computer station at the front of the room. I might know who the Pink Carnation was, but I stood a better chance of making my case to a skeptical academic audience if I could definitively link many, if not all, of the Pink Carnation's recorded exploits to Miss Jane Wooliston. After all, just because Jane had started out as the Pink Carnation didn't mean she had remained in possession of the title. What if, like the Dread Pirate Roberts, she had handed the name off to someone else? I didn't think so—having worked with several of Jane's letters, I couldn't imagine anyone else being able to muster quite the same combination of rigorous logic and reckless daring—but it was the sort of objection someone was sure to propound. At great length. With lots of footnotes.

I needed footnotes of my own to counteract that. It was the usual sort of academic battle: footnotes at ten paces, bolstered by snide articles in academic journals, and lots of sniping about methodology, a thrust and parry of source and countersource. My sources had to be better.

From my little dip into Colin's library that past weekend, I had learned that Jane had been sent to Ireland to deal with the threat of an uprising against British rule egged on by France in the hopes that, with Ireland in disarray, England would prove an easy target. Ten points to me, since one of the daring exploits with which the Pink Carnation was credited was quelling the Irish rebellion of 1803. But I didn't know anything beyond that. I didn't have any proof that Jane was actually there. In the official histories, the failure of the rebellion tended to be attributed to a more mundane series of mistakes and misfortunes, rather than the agency of any one person.

According to the Selwick documents, Jane wasn't the only one to be dispatched to Ireland. Geoffrey Pinchingdale-Snipe, who had served as second in command of the League of the Purple Gentian, had also received his marching orders from the War Office. A search for Jane's name in the records of the British Library was sure to yield nothing, but what if I looked for Lord Pinchingdale? Ever since reading the papers at Mrs. Selwick-Alderly's flat, I'd been meaning to look into Geoffrey Pinchingdale-Snipe, anyway, if only to add more footnotes to my dissertation chapter on the internal workings of the League of the Purple Gentian.

I hadn't had a chance to pursue that angle because I had gone straight off to Sussex.

With Colin.

The agitated bleep of the computer as I accidentally leaned on one of the keys didn't do anything to make me popular with any of the other researchers, but it did bring me back from the remoter realms of daydream.

Right. I straightened up and purposefully punched in "Pinching-dale-Snipe." Nothing. Ah, déjà vu. Futile archive searches had been my way of life for a very long time before having the good fortune to stumble across the Selwicks. Clearly, I hadn't lost the knack of it. Getting back into gear, I tried just plain "Pinchingdale." Four hits! Unfortunately, three of them were treatises on botany by an eighteenth-century Pinchingdale with a horticultural bent, and one the correspondence of a Sir Marmaduke Pinchingdale, who was two hundred years too early for me, in addition to being decidedly not a Geoffrey. There was no way anyone could confuse those two names, not even with very bad spelling and even worse handwriting.

The logical thing to do would have been to call Mrs. Selwick-Alderly, Colin's aunt. Even if the materials I was looking for weren't in her private collection, she would likely have a good notion of where I should start. But to call Mrs. Selwick-Alderly veered dangerously close to calling Colin. Really, could there be anything more pathetic than looking for excuses to call his relations and fish for information about his whereabouts? I refused to be That Girl.

Of course, that begged the question of whether it was any less pathetic to check my phone for messages every five minutes.

Preferring not to pursue that line of thought, I stared blankly at the computer screen. It stared equally blankly back at me. Behind me, I could hear the subtle brush of fabric that meant someone was shuffling his feet against the carpet in a passive-aggressive attempt to communicate that he was waiting to use the terminal. Damn.

On a whim, I tapped out the name "Alsworthy," just to show that I was still doing something, and not uselessly frittering away valuable computer time. From what I had read in the Selwick collection, Geoffrey Pinchingdale-Snipe had been ridiculously besotted with a woman named Mary Alsworthy—although none of his friends seemed to think terribly much of her. The words "shallow flirt" had come up more than once. Geoffrey Pinchingdale-Snipe's indiscretion might be my good fortune. In the throes of infatuation, wasn't it only logical that a man might reveal a little more than he ought? Especially over the course of a separation? If the War Office was sending Lord Pinchingdale off to Ireland, it made sense that he would continue to correspond with his beloved. And in the course of that correspondence . . .

Buoyed by my own theory, I scrolled down through a long list of Victorian Alsworthys, World War I Alsworthys, Alsworthys from every conceivable time period. For crying out loud, you'd think their name was Smith. The foot-shuffling man behind me gave up on shuffling and upped the level of unspoken aggression by conspicuously flipping through the ancient volumes of paper catalogues next to me.

I was too busy scanning dates to feel guilty. Alsworthys, Alsworthys everywhere, and not a one of any use to me.

Or maybe not. My hand stilled on the scroll button as the dates 1784–1863 flashed by. I quickly scrolled back up, clumsily engaging in mental math. Take 1784 away from 1803 . . . and you got eighteen. Um, I meant nineteen. This is why my checkbook never balances. Either way, it was an eminently appropriate age for an English debutante in London for the Season.

There was only one slight hitch. The name beside the dates wasn't Mary. It was Laetitia.

That, I assured myself rapidly, scribbling down the call number, didn't necessarily mean anything. After all, my friend Pammy's real first name was Alexandra, but she had gone by her middle name, Pamela, ever since we were in kindergarten, largely because her mother was an Alexandra, too, and it created all sorts of confusion. Forget all that rose by another name rubbish. Pammy had been Pammy for so long that it was impossible to imagine her as anything else.

Behind me, the foot-shuffling man claimed my vacant seat with an air of barely restrained triumph. Prolonged exposure to the Manuscript Room does sad, sad things to some people.

I handed in my call slip to the man behind the desk and retreated to my own square of territory, nudging my plastic bag with my foot to make sure everything was still there. Between Mary and Laetitia . . . well, I would have chosen to be called Laetitia, but there was no accounting for taste. Maybe she got sick of dealing with variant spellings.

Except . . . I scowled at my empty manuscript stand. There *was* a Laetitia Alsworthy. Just to make sure, I scooted my computer to a more comfortable angle, and opened up the file into which I had transcribed my notes from Sussex. Sure enough, there it was. One Letty Alsworthy, who appeared to be friends with Lady Henrietta Selwick. Not close friends, I clarified for myself, squinting at my transcription of Lady Henrietta's account of her ballroom activities in the summer of 1803, but the sort of second- or third-tier friend you're always pleased to run into, have good chats with, and keep meaning to get to know better if only you had the time. I had a bunch of those in college. And, in its own way, the London Season wasn't all that different from college, minus the classes. You had a set group of people, all revolving between the same events, with a smattering of culture masking more primal purposes, i.e., men trying to get women into bed, and women trying to get men to commit. Yep, I decided, just like college.

Pleased as I was with my little insight, that didn't solve the problem that Letty was a real, live human being with an independent existence from her sister, Mary. Her sister, Mary, who might have corresponded with Geoffrey Pinchingdale-Snipe.

I should have known that Mary wouldn't be the writing type.

Behind me, the little trolley used to transport books from the bowels of the British Library to the wraiths who haunted the Reading Room rolled to a stop. Checking the number on the slip against the number on my desk, the library attendant handed me a thick folio volume, bound in fading cardboard that had seen its heyday sometime before Edward VIII ran off with Mrs. Simpson.

Propping the heavy volume on the foam stand, I listlessly flipped open the cover. I had ordered it, so I might as well look at it. Besides, the computer in the back was now occupied, and I doubted its present occupant would show me any more mercy than I had shown him. A salutary lesson on "do unto others," and one that I was sure I would forget by lunchtime.

The documents at the front of the volume were far too late, Mitfordesque accounts of nightclub peccadilloes during the Roaring Twenties. I'd come across this kind of volume before, letters pasted onto the leaves of the folio with glorious unconcern for chronology, medieval manuscript pages sandwiched between Edwardian recipes and Stuart sermon literature. Otherwise known as someone cleaning out the family attic and shipping the lot off to the British Library. Checking the number I had scribbled down from the computer, I saw that it had marked the Laetitia Alsworthy material as running from f. 48 to f. 63, and then again from f. 152 on.

After lunch, I was really going to have to give in and call Mrs. Selwick-Alderly.

After I turned by rote to page forty-eight, my hand stilled on the crackly paper. The letter pressed into the center of the page was short, only three lines. Despite having been pasted into the folio quite some time ago, I could still make out the phantom impressions of two deep lines incised into the paper, one vertically, one horizontally, as though it had been folded into a very small square, the better for passing unseen from hand to hand. There was also a series of crinkles that prevented the paper from lying completely flat against the page, as though someone had crumpled it up with great force, and then smoothed it out again.

But it was the signature that caught my attention. One word. One name.

Pinchingdale.

As in Geoffrey, Lord Pinchingdale. The signature was unmistakable. It most certainly wasn't Marmaduke. What on earth was he doing writing to Mary's sister? Forgetting about computer hogs and lunch plans and the way the wool of my pants rasped against my waist, I settled the folio more firmly on its stand and hunched over to read Lord Pinchingdale's short and peculiar note.

"All is in readiness. An unmarked carriage will be waiting for you behind the house at midnight. . . ."